big
NATE
GOES BANANAS!

Complete Your *Big Nate* Collection

big NATE
FROM THE TOP
by LINCOLN PEIRCE

big NATE
OUT LOUD
by LINCOLN PEIRCE

big NATE
AND FRIENDS
by LINCOLN PEIRCE

big NATE
MAKES THE GRADE
by LINCOLN PEIRCE

big NATE
GAME ON!
by LINCOLN PEIRCE

big NATE
I CAN'T TAKE IT!

big NATE
GREAT MINDS THINK ALIKE
by LINCOLN PEIRCE

big NATE
THE CROWD GOES WILD!
by LINCOLN PEIRCE

big NATE
SAY GOOD-BYE TO DORK CITY
by LINCOLN PEIRCE

big NATE
WELCOME TO MY WORLD
by LINCOLN PEIRCE

big NATE
THUNKA THUNKA THUNKA
by LINCOLN PEIRCE

big NATE
REVENGE OF THE CREAM PUFFS
by LINCOLN PEIRCE

big NATE
WHAT'S A LITTLE NOOGIE BETWEEN FRIENDS?
by LINCOLN PEIRCE

big NATE
A GOOD OLD-FASHIONED WEDGIE
by LINCOLN PEIRCE

big NATE
SILENT BUT DEADLY
by LINCOLN PEIRCE

SPECIAL COLLECTIONS

big NATE'S
GREATEST HITS
by LINCOLN PEIRCE

NATE
el Grande
¡HOLA!
por LINCOLN PEIRCE
BIG NATE IN SPANISH!

big NATE
ALL WORK AND NO PLAY
A Collection of Sundays
by LINCOLN PEIRCE

EPIC big NATE

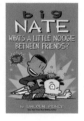

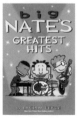

big NATE
GOES BANANAS!

by LINCOLN PEIRCE

Andrews McMeel
PUBLISHING®

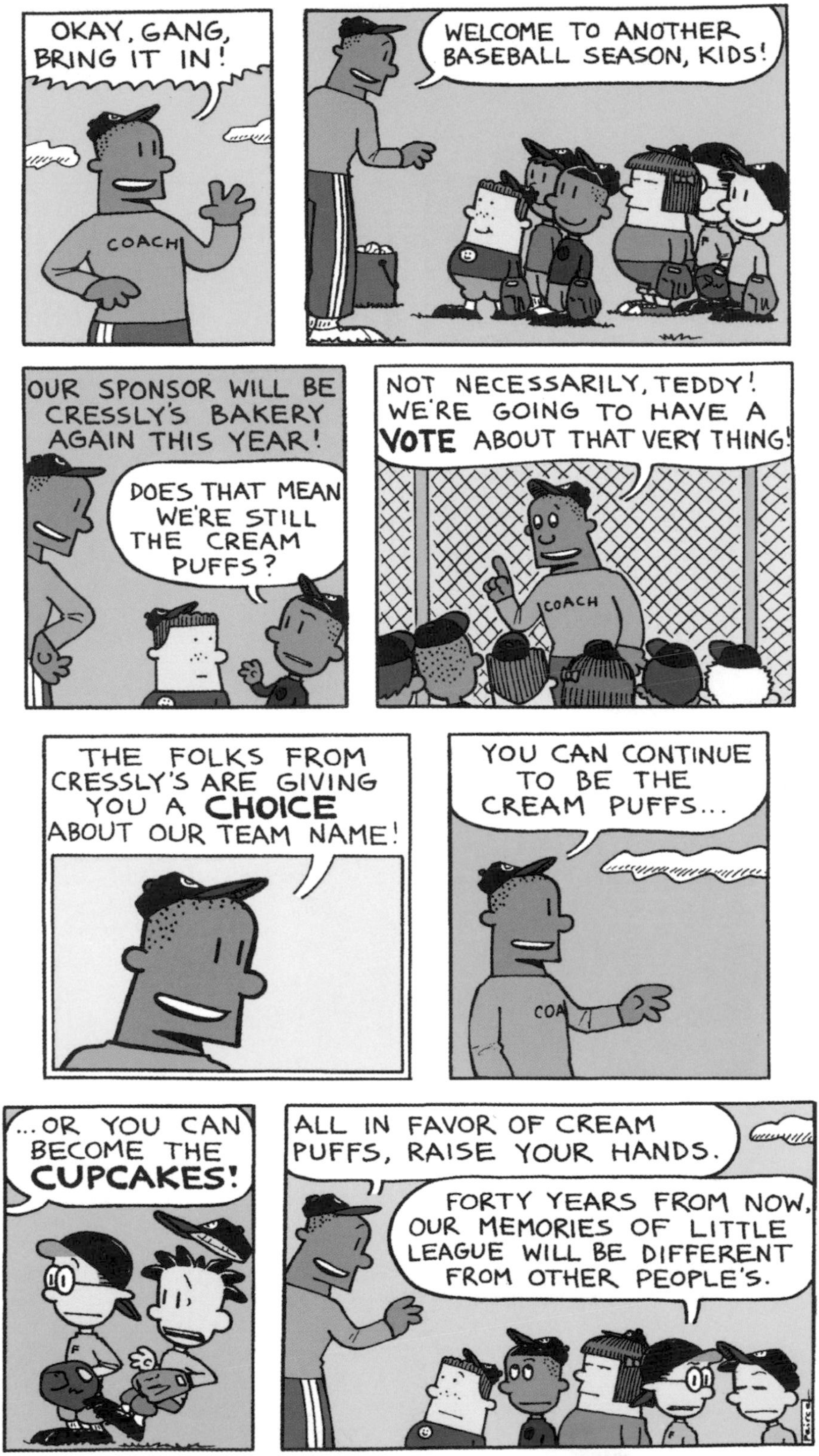
OKAY, GANG, BRING IT IN!
WELCOME TO ANOTHER BASEBALL SEASON, KIDS!
OUR SPONSOR WILL BE CRESSLY'S BAKERY AGAIN THIS YEAR!
DOES THAT MEAN WE'RE STILL THE CREAM PUFFS?
NOT NECESSARILY, TEDDY! WE'RE GOING TO HAVE A VOTE ABOUT THAT VERY THING!
COACH
THE FOLKS FROM CRESSLY'S ARE GIVING YOU A CHOICE ABOUT OUR TEAM NAME!
YOU CAN CONTINUE TO BE THE CREAM PUFFS...
...OR YOU CAN BECOME THE CUPCAKES!
ALL IN FAVOR OF CREAM PUFFS, RAISE YOUR HANDS.
FORTY YEARS FROM NOW, OUR MEMORIES OF LITTLE LEAGUE WILL BE DIFFERENT FROM OTHER PEOPLE'S.

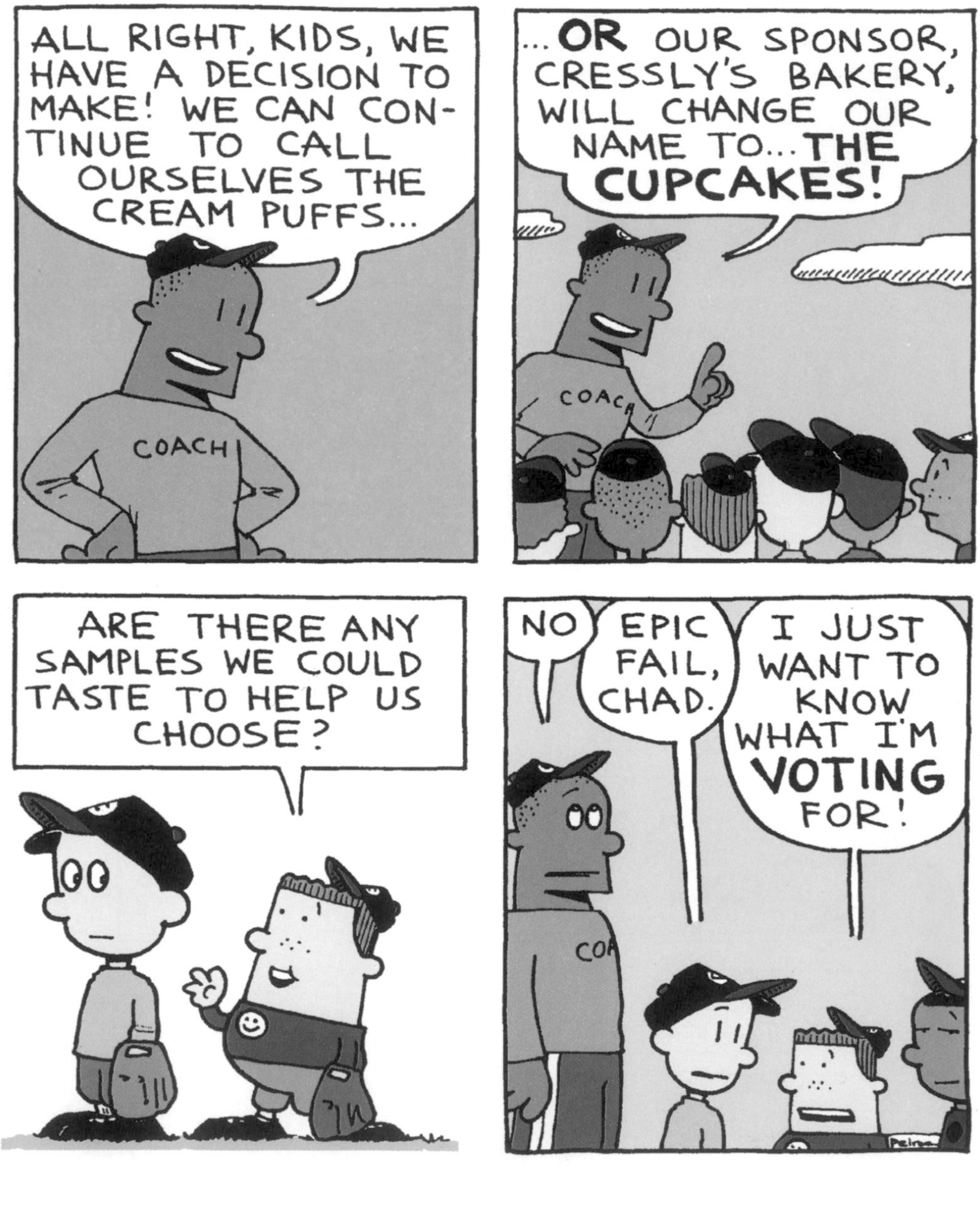

ALL RIGHT, KIDS, WE HAVE A DECISION TO MAKE! WE CAN CONTINUE TO CALL OURSELVES THE CREAM PUFFS...
COACH
...OR OUR SPONSOR, CRESSLY'S BAKERY, WILL CHANGE OUR NAME TO... THE CUPCAKES!
COACH
ARE THERE ANY SAMPLES WE COULD TASTE TO HELP US CHOOSE?
NO
EPIC FAIL, CHAD.
I JUST WANT TO KNOW WHAT I'M VOTING FOR!

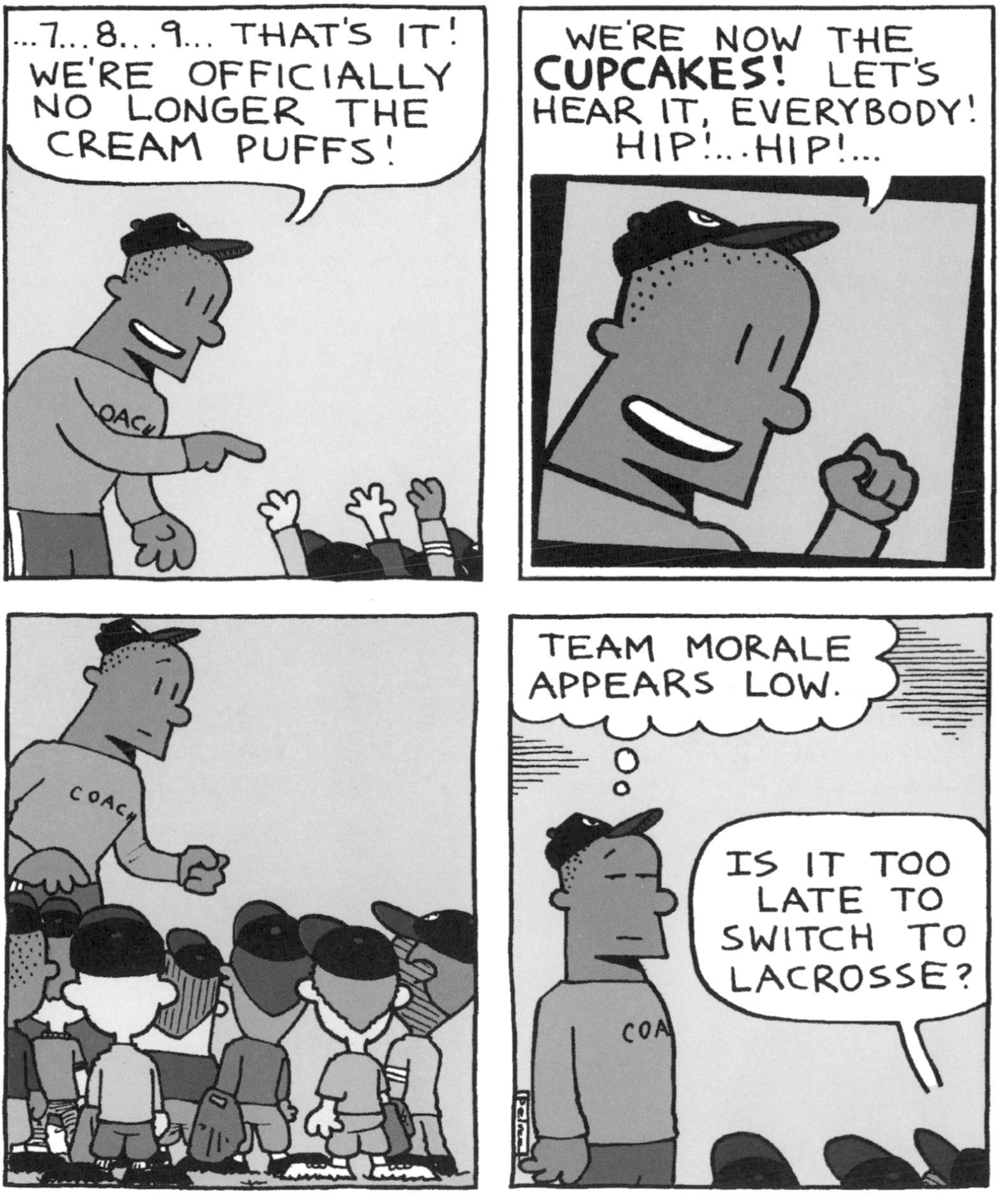
...7...8...9... THAT'S IT! WE'RE OFFICIALLY NO LONGER THE CREAM PUFFS!
COACH
WE'RE NOW THE **CUPCAKES!** LET'S HEAR IT, EVERYBODY! HIP!...HIP!...
COACH
TEAM MORALE APPEARS LOW.
COA
IS IT TOO LATE TO SWITCH TO LACROSSE?

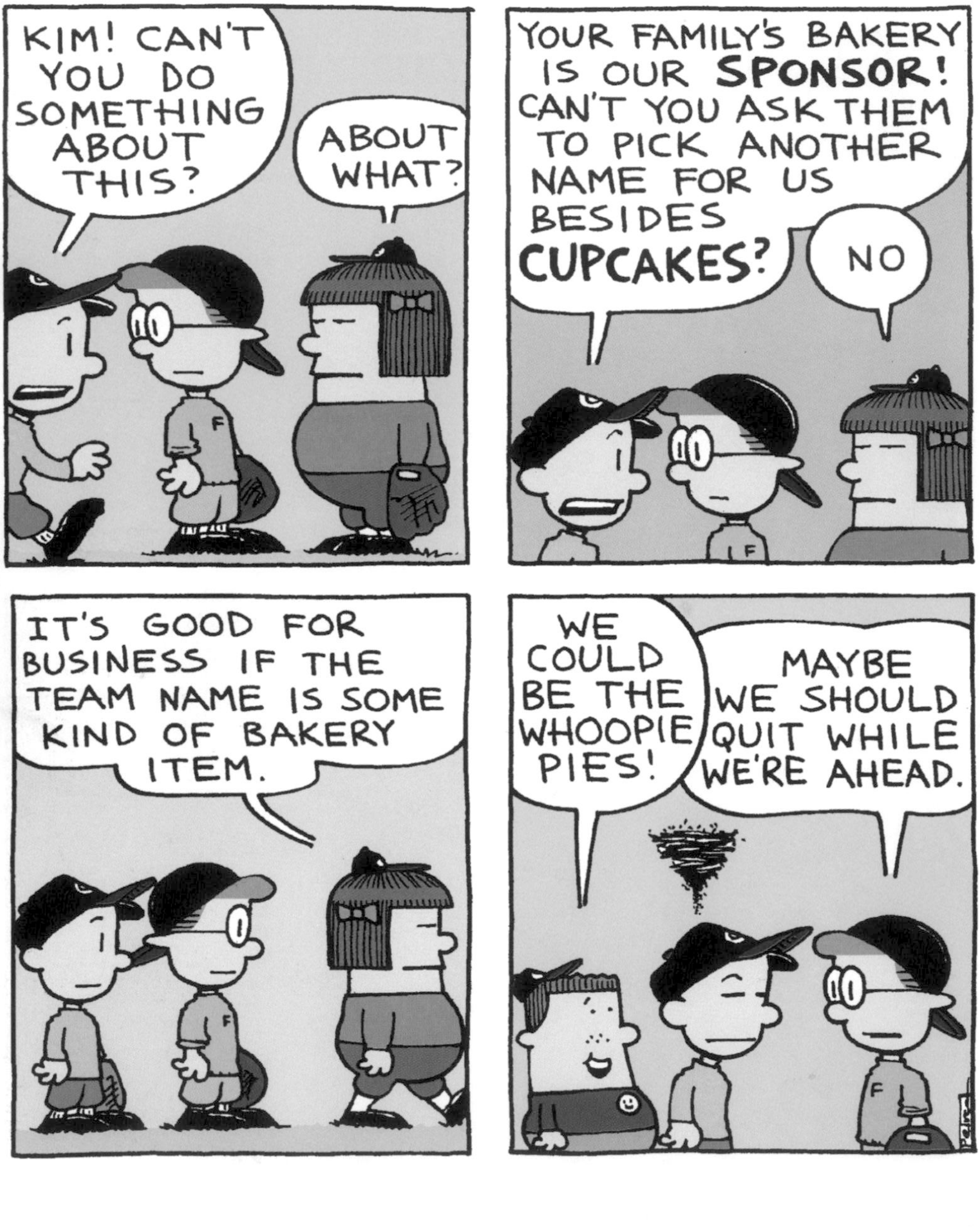
KIM! CAN'T YOU DO SOMETHING ABOUT THIS?
ABOUT WHAT?
YOUR FAMILY'S BAKERY IS OUR **SPONSOR**! CAN'T YOU ASK THEM TO PICK ANOTHER NAME FOR US BESIDES **CUPCAKES**?
NO
IT'S GOOD FOR BUSINESS IF THE TEAM NAME IS SOME KIND OF BAKERY ITEM.
WE COULD BE THE WHOOPIE PIES!
MAYBE WE SHOULD QUIT WHILE WE'RE AHEAD.

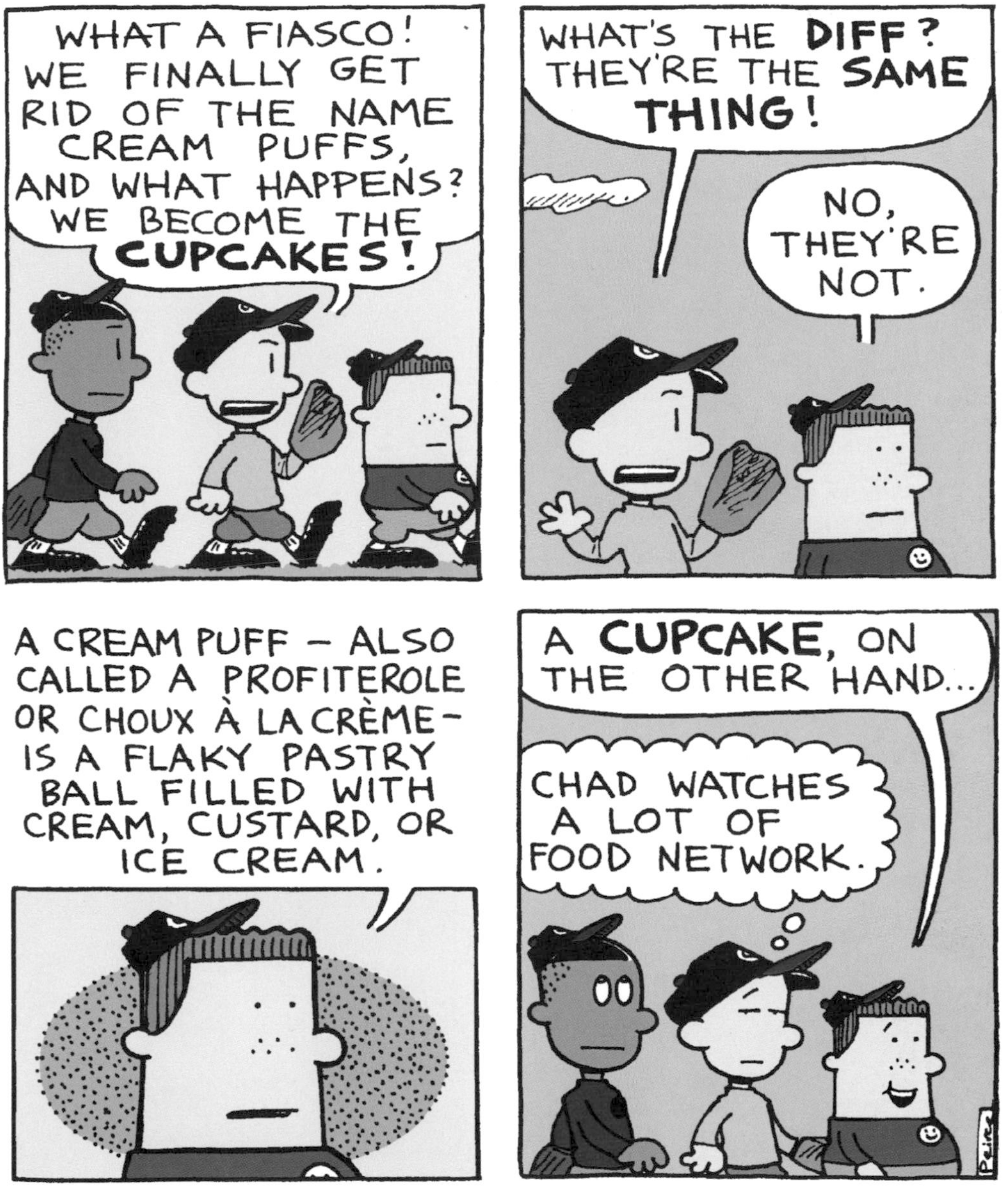
WHAT A FIASCO! WE FINALLY GET RID OF THE NAME CREAM PUFFS, AND WHAT HAPPENS? WE BECOME THE **CUPCAKES**!
WHAT'S THE **DIFF**? THEY'RE THE **SAME THING**!
NO, THEY'RE NOT.
A CREAM PUFF – ALSO CALLED A PROFITEROLE OR CHOUX À LA CRÈME – IS A FLAKY PASTRY BALL FILLED WITH CREAM, CUSTARD, OR ICE CREAM.
A **CUPCAKE**, ON THE OTHER HAND...
CHAD WATCHES A LOT OF FOOD NETWORK.
PEIRCE

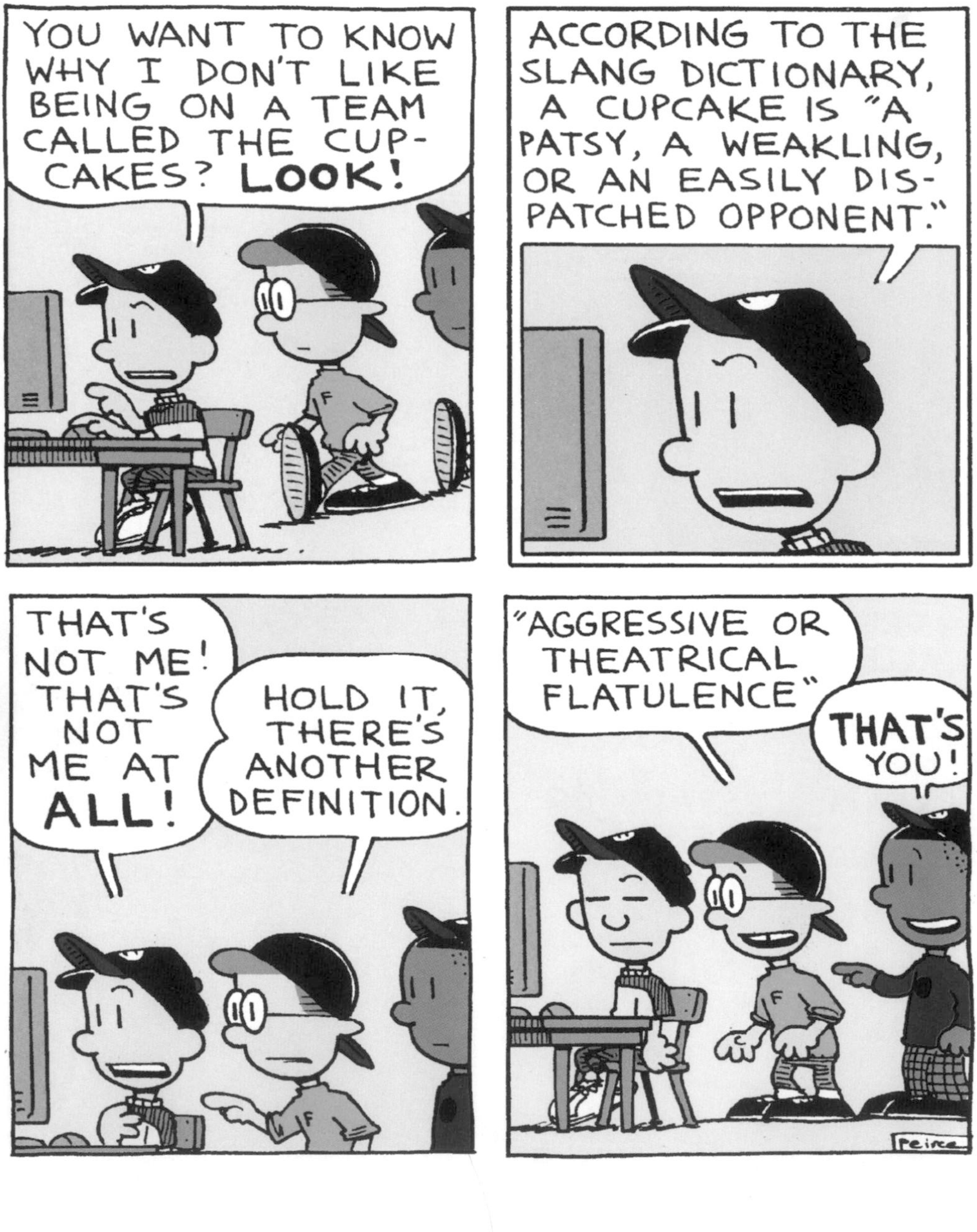
YOU WANT TO KNOW WHY I DON'T LIKE BEING ON A TEAM CALLED THE CUP-CAKES? LOOK!
ACCORDING TO THE SLANG DICTIONARY, A CUPCAKE IS "A PATSY, A WEAKLING, OR AN EASILY DIS-PATCHED OPPONENT."
THAT'S NOT ME! THAT'S NOT ME AT ALL!
HOLD IT, THERE'S ANOTHER DEFINITION.
"AGGRESSIVE OR THEATRICAL FLATULENCE"
THAT'S YOU!
peirce

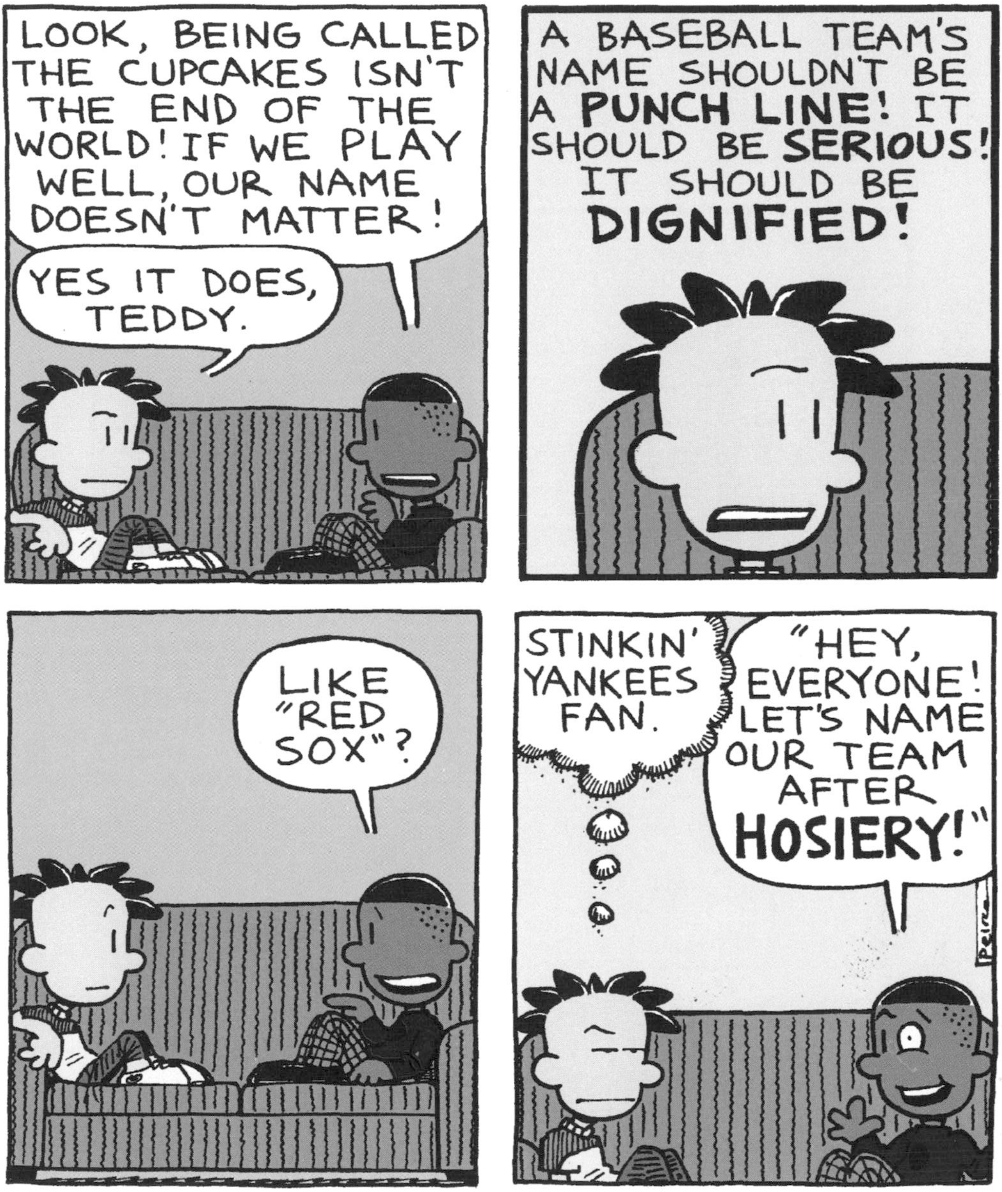
LOOK, BEING CALLED THE CUPCAKES ISN'T THE END OF THE WORLD! IF WE PLAY WELL, OUR NAME DOESN'T MATTER!
YES IT DOES, TEDDY.
A BASEBALL TEAM'S NAME SHOULDN'T BE A PUNCH LINE! IT SHOULD BE SERIOUS! IT SHOULD BE DIGNIFIED!
LIKE "RED SOX"?
STINKIN' YANKEES FAN.
"HEY, EVERYONE! LET'S NAME OUR TEAM AFTER HOSIERY!"
Peirce

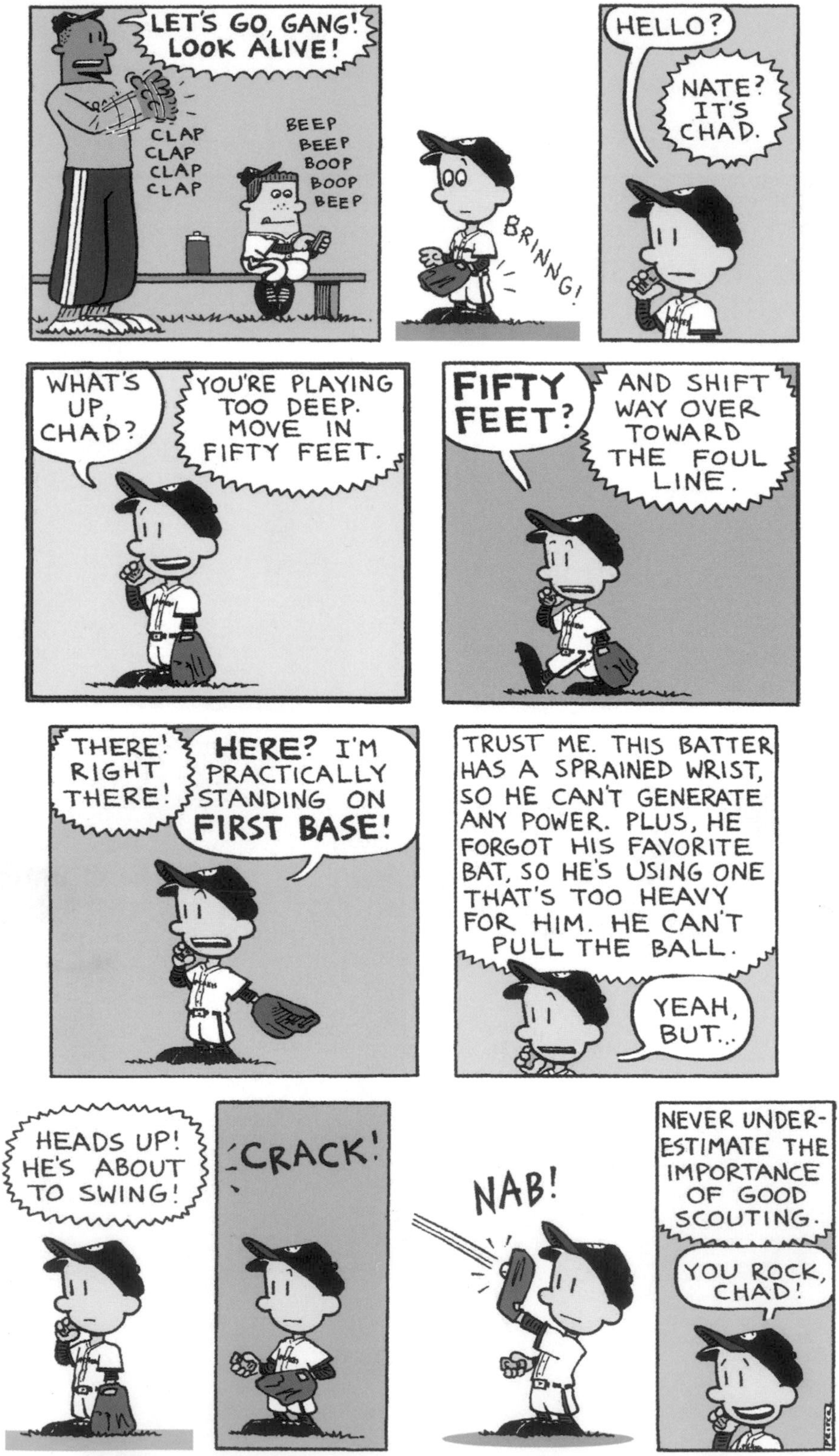

LET'S GO, GANG! LOOK ALIVE!
CLAP CLAP CLAP CLAP
BEEP BEEP BOOP BOOP BEEP
BRINNNG!
HELLO?
NATE? IT'S CHAD.
WHAT'S UP, CHAD?
YOU'RE PLAYING TOO DEEP. MOVE IN FIFTY FEET.
FIFTY FEET?
AND SHIFT WAY OVER TOWARD THE FOUL LINE.
THERE! RIGHT THERE!
HERE? I'M PRACTICALLY STANDING ON FIRST BASE!
TRUST ME. THIS BATTER HAS A SPRAINED WRIST, SO HE CAN'T GENERATE ANY POWER. PLUS, HE FORGOT HIS FAVORITE BAT, SO HE'S USING ONE THAT'S TOO HEAVY FOR HIM. HE CAN'T PULL THE BALL.
YEAH, BUT...
HEADS UP! HE'S ABOUT TO SWING!
CRACK!
NAB!
NEVER UNDER-ESTIMATE THE IMPORTANCE OF GOOD SCOUTING.
YOU ROCK, CHAD!

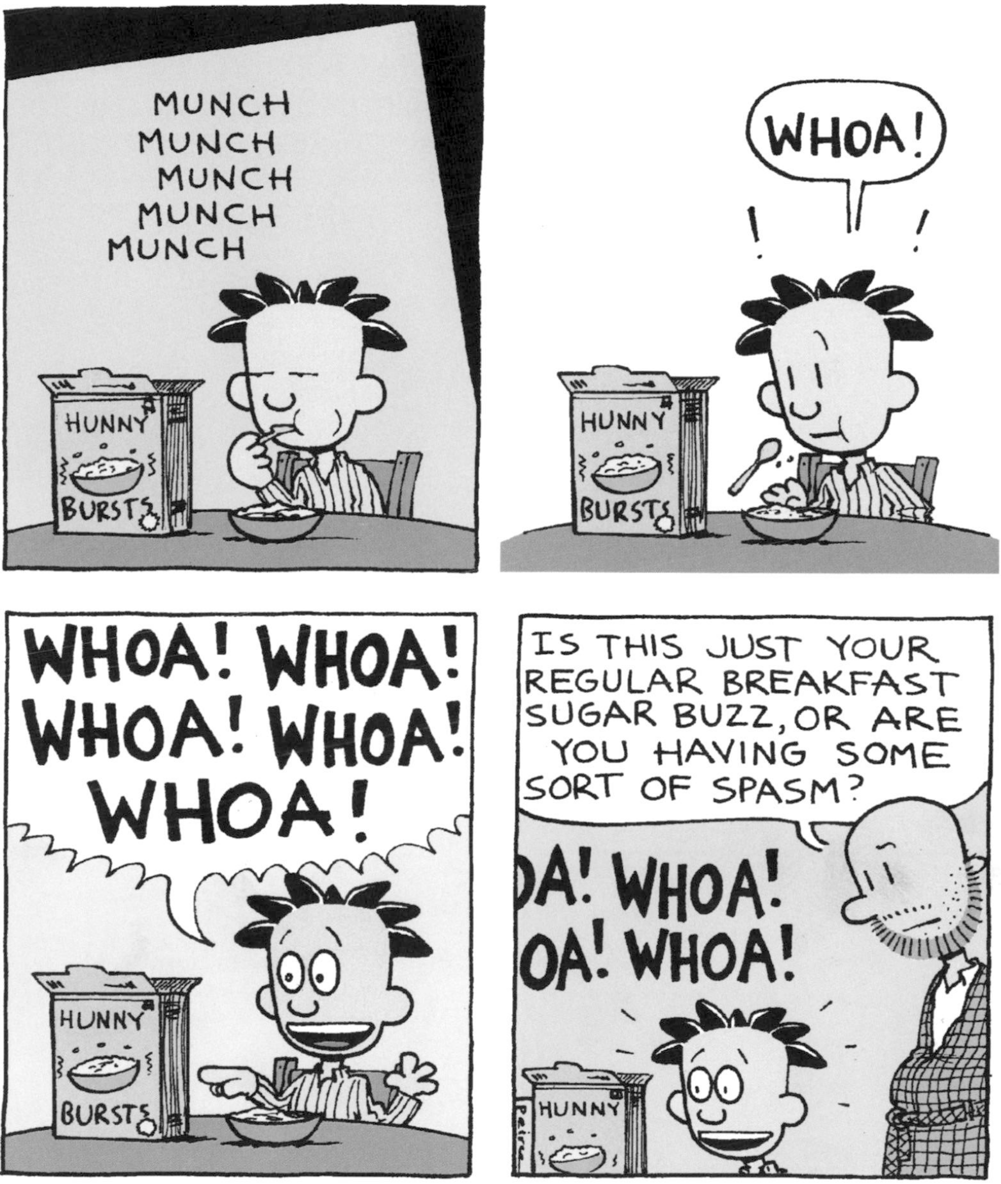
MUNCH
MUNCH
MUNCH
MUNCH
MUNCH
HUNNY
BURSTS
WHOA!
HUNNY
BURSTS
WHOA! WHOA!
WHOA! WHOA!
WHOA!
HUNNY
BURSTS
IS THIS JUST YOUR REGULAR BREAKFAST SUGAR BUZZ, OR ARE YOU HAVING SOME SORT OF SPASM?
OA! WHOA!
OA! WHOA!
HUNNY

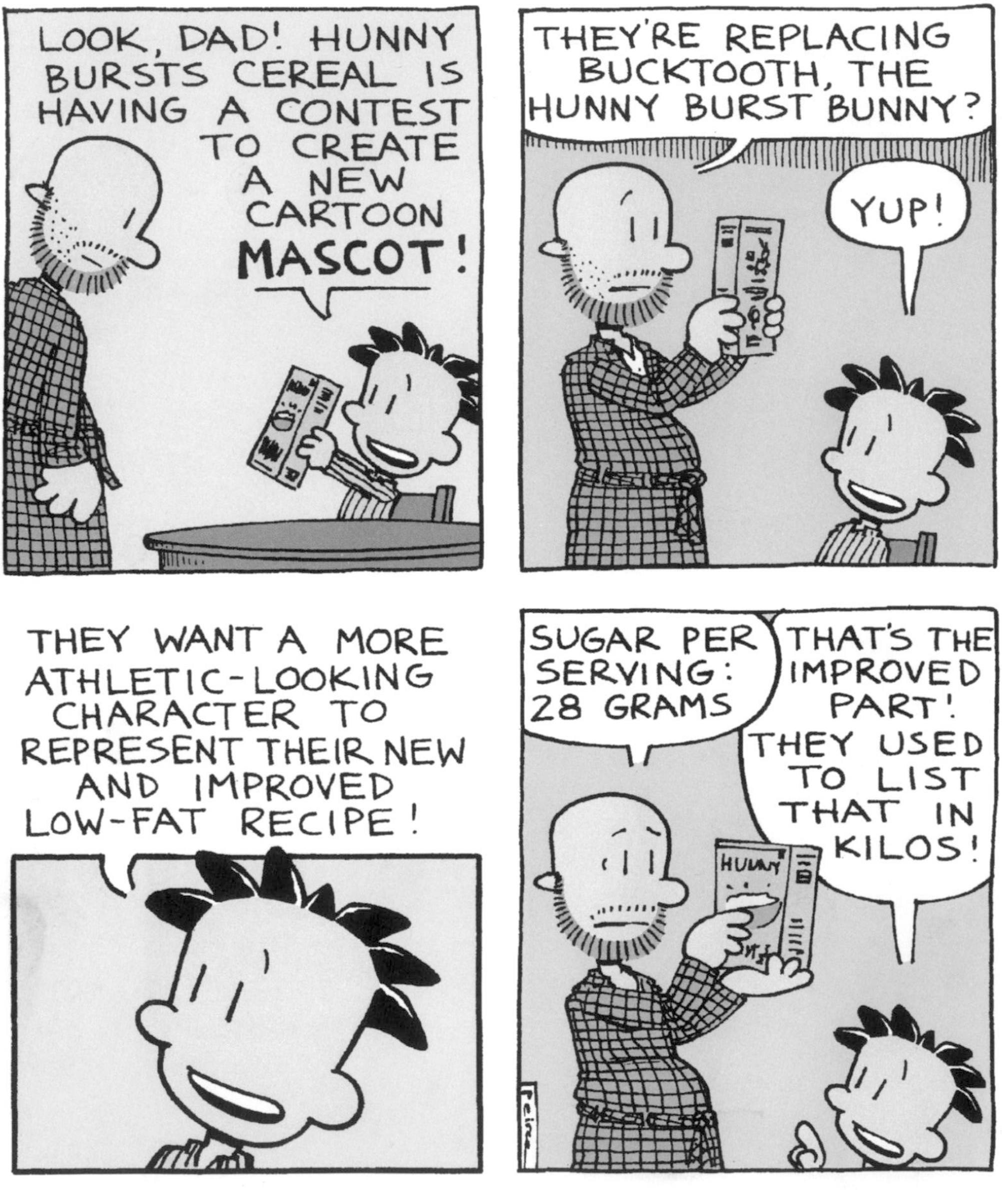
LOOK, DAD! HUNNY BURSTS CEREAL IS HAVING A CONTEST TO CREATE A NEW CARTOON **MASCOT**!
THEY'RE REPLACING BUCKTOOTH, THE HUNNY BURST BUNNY?
YUP!
THEY WANT A MORE ATHLETIC-LOOKING CHARACTER TO REPRESENT THEIR NEW AND IMPROVED LOW-FAT RECIPE!
SUGAR PER SERVING: 28 GRAMS
THAT'S THE IMPROVED PART! THEY USED TO LIST THAT IN KILOS!

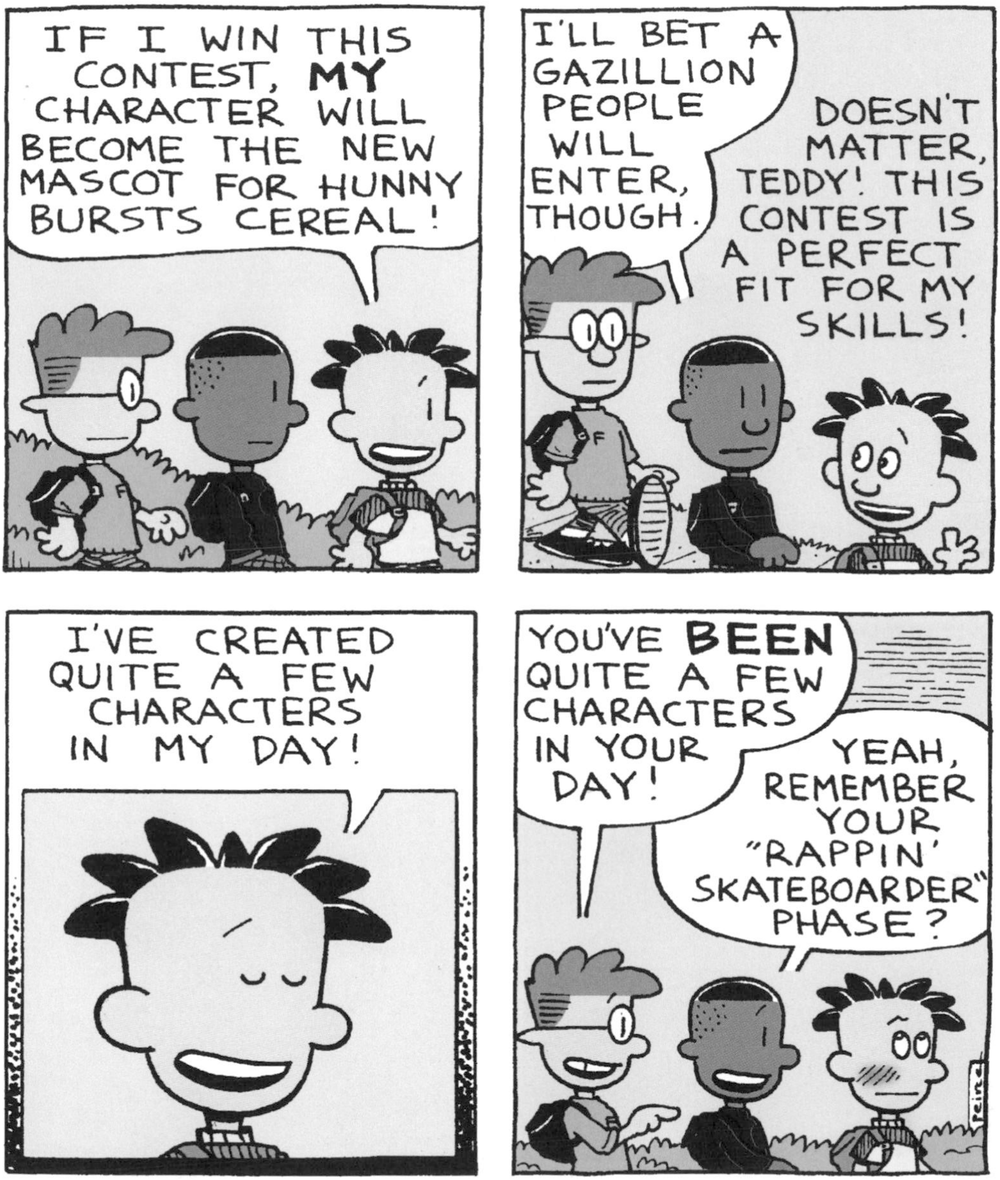
IF I WIN THIS CONTEST, **MY** CHARACTER WILL BECOME THE NEW MASCOT FOR HUNNY BURSTS CEREAL!
I'LL BET A GAZILLION PEOPLE WILL ENTER, THOUGH.
DOESN'T MATTER, TEDDY! THIS CONTEST IS A PERFECT FIT FOR MY SKILLS!
I'VE CREATED QUITE A FEW CHARACTERS IN MY DAY!
YOU'VE **BEEN** QUITE A FEW CHARACTERS IN YOUR DAY!
YEAH, REMEMBER YOUR "RAPPIN' SKATEBOARDER" PHASE?
PEIRCE

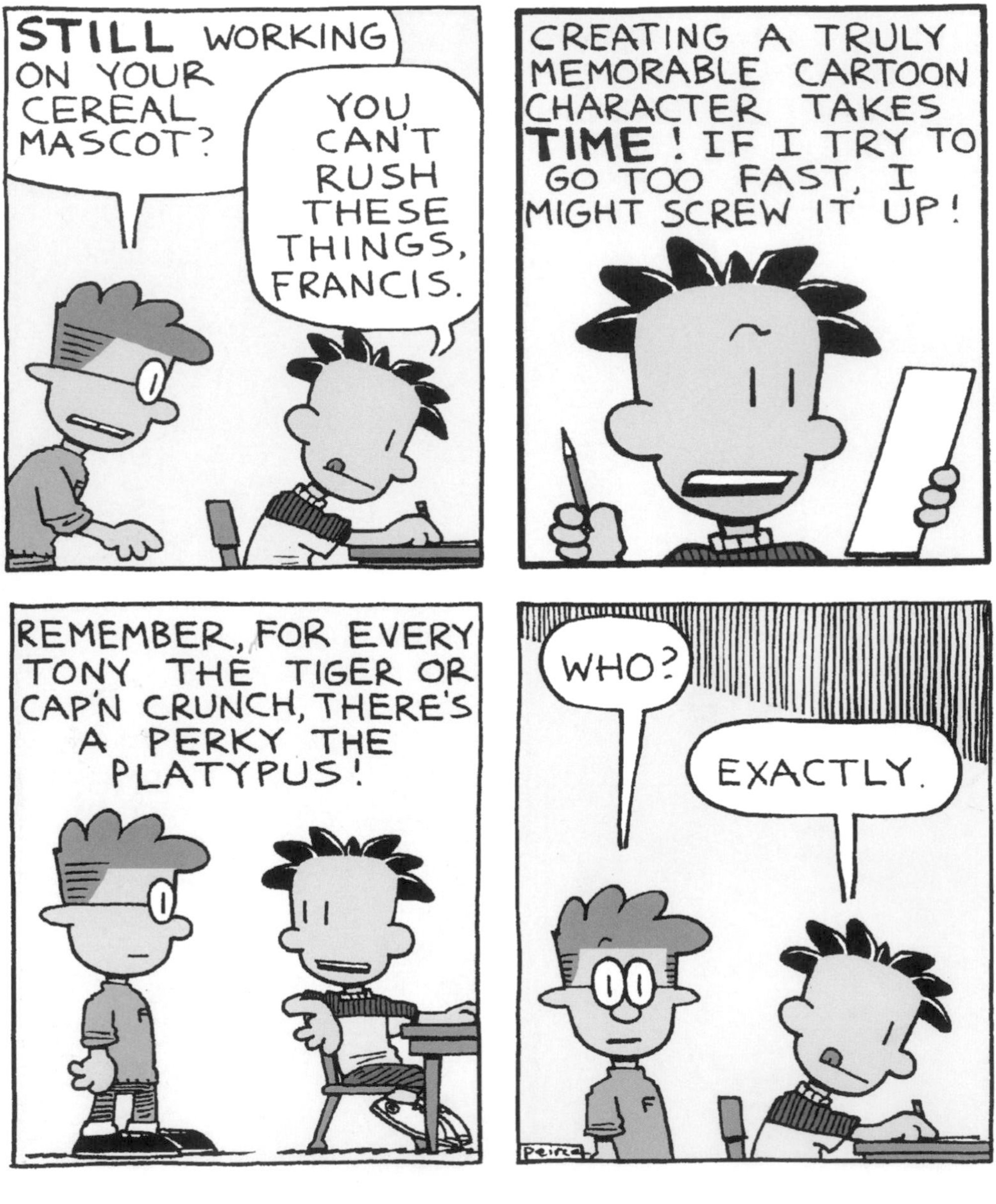
STILL WORKING ON YOUR CEREAL MASCOT?
YOU CAN'T RUSH THESE THINGS, FRANCIS.
CREATING A TRULY MEMORABLE CARTOON CHARACTER TAKES TIME! IF I TRY TO GO TOO FAST, I MIGHT SCREW IT UP!
REMEMBER, FOR EVERY TONY THE TIGER OR CAP'N CRUNCH, THERE'S A PERKY THE PLATYPUS!
WHO?
EXACTLY.
Peirce

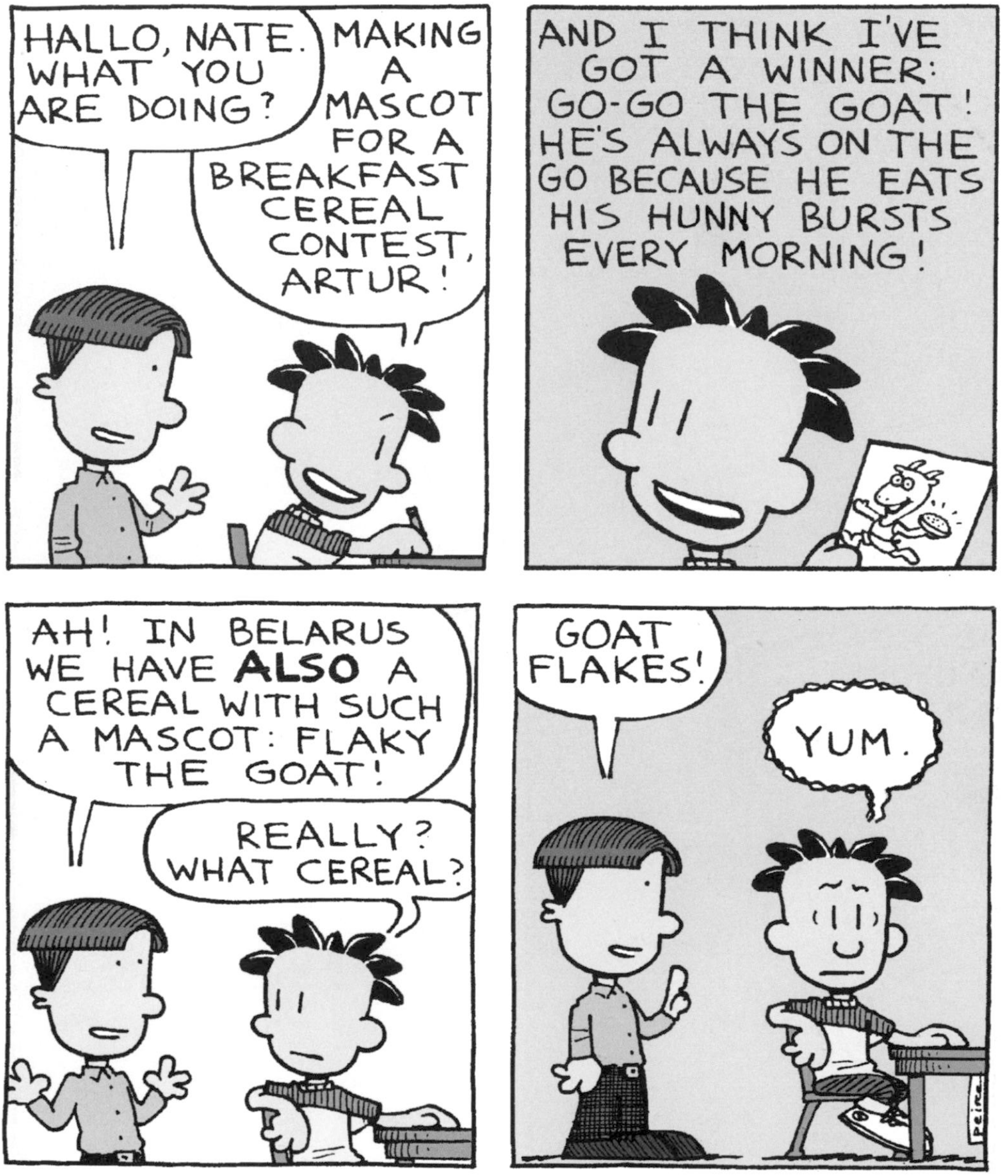
HALLO, NATE. WHAT YOU ARE DOING?
MAKING A MASCOT FOR A BREAKFAST CEREAL CONTEST, ARTUR!
AND I THINK I'VE GOT A WINNER: GO-GO THE GOAT! HE'S ALWAYS ON THE GO BECAUSE HE EATS HIS HUNNY BURSTS EVERY MORNING!
AH! IN BELARUS WE HAVE **ALSO** A CEREAL WITH SUCH A MASCOT: FLAKY THE GOAT!
REALLY? WHAT CEREAL?
GOAT FLAKES!
YUM.
peirce

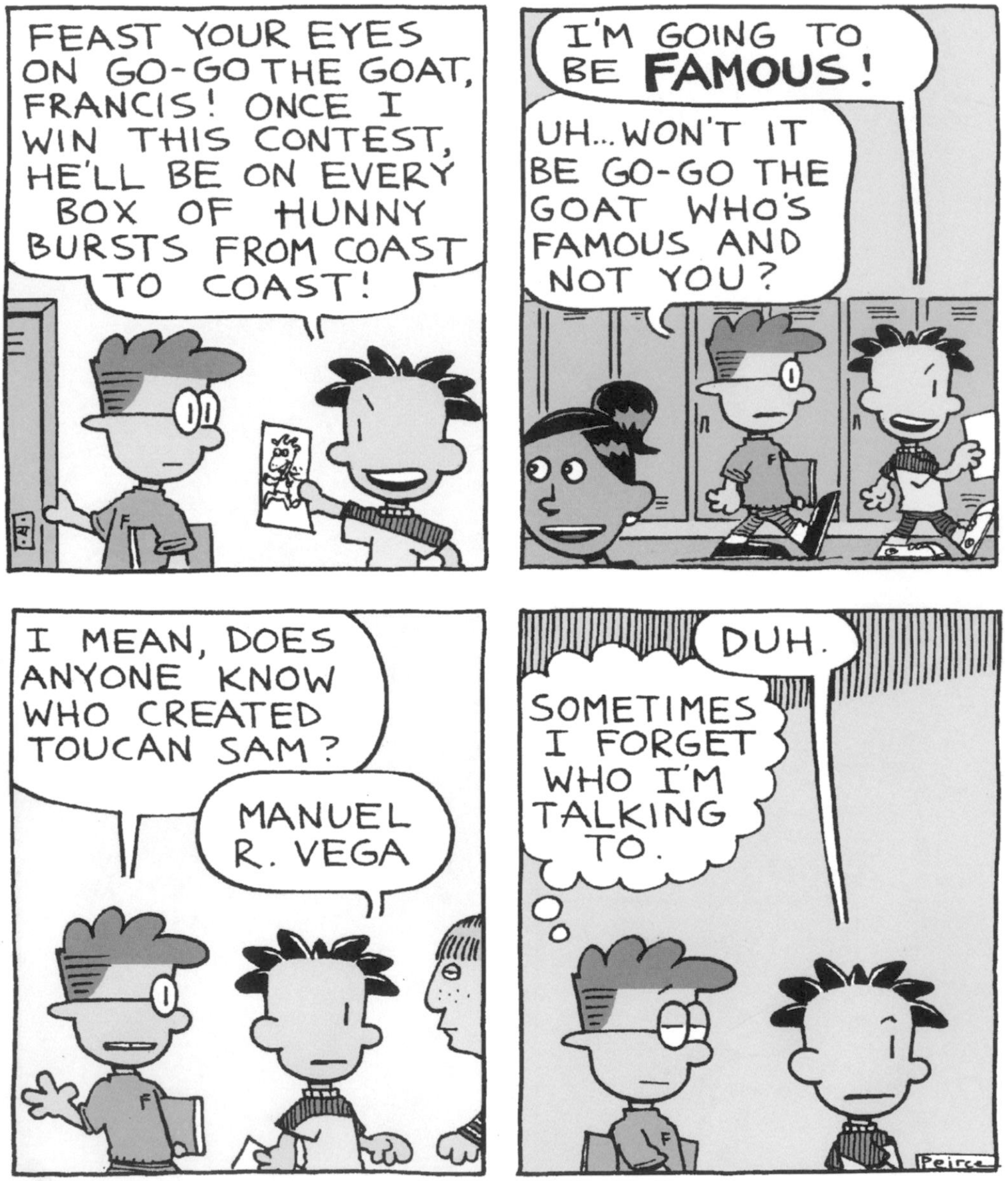
FEAST YOUR EYES ON GO-GO THE GOAT, FRANCIS! ONCE I WIN THIS CONTEST, HE'LL BE ON EVERY BOX OF HUNNY BURSTS FROM COAST TO COAST!
I'M GOING TO BE FAMOUS!
UH... WON'T IT BE GO-GO THE GOAT WHO'S FAMOUS AND NOT YOU?
I MEAN, DOES ANYONE KNOW WHO CREATED TOUCAN SAM?
MANUEL R. VEGA
DUH.
SOMETIMES I FORGET WHO I'M TALKING TO.
Peirce

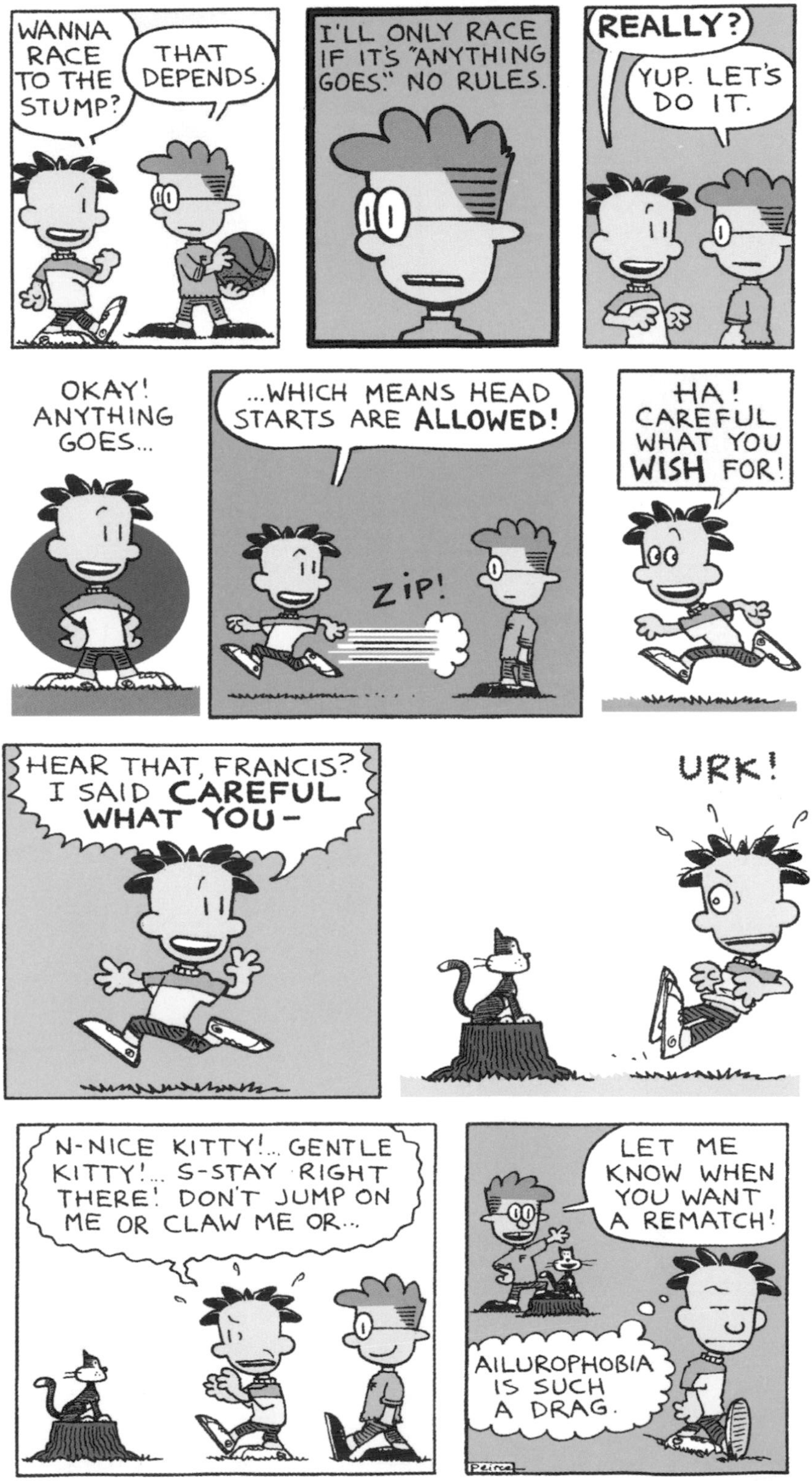
WANNA RACE TO THE STUMP?
THAT DEPENDS.
I'LL ONLY RACE IF IT'S "ANYTHING GOES." NO RULES.
REALLY?
YUP. LET'S DO IT.
OKAY! ANYTHING GOES...
...WHICH MEANS HEAD STARTS ARE ALLOWED!
ZIP!
HA! CAREFUL WHAT YOU WISH FOR!
HEAR THAT, FRANCIS? I SAID CAREFUL WHAT YOU-
URK!
N-NICE KITTY!... GENTLE KITTY!... S-STAY RIGHT THERE! DON'T JUMP ON ME OR CLAW ME OR...
LET ME KNOW WHEN YOU WANT A REMATCH!
AILUROPHOBIA IS SUCH A DRAG.
Peirce

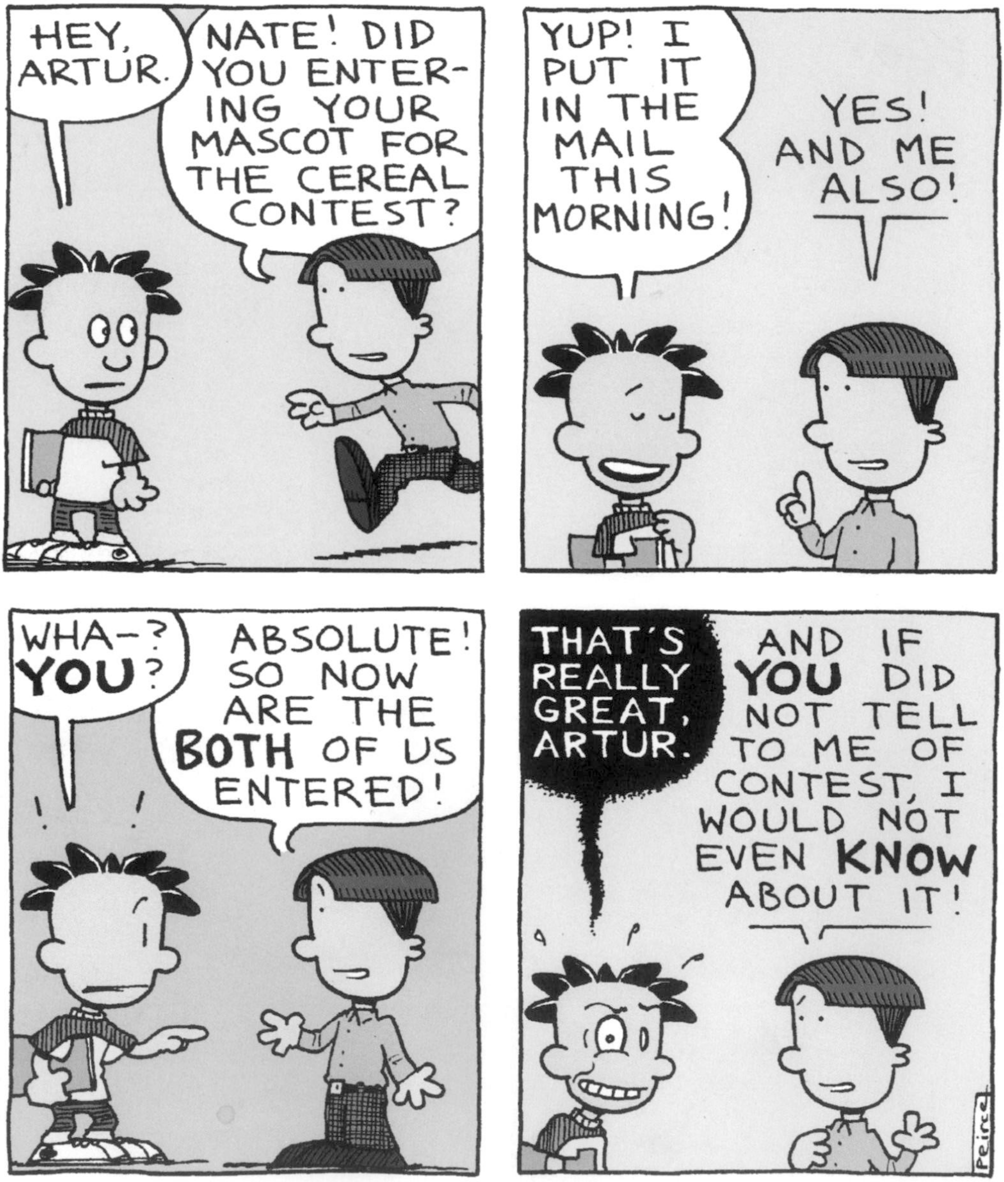
HEY, ARTUR.
NATE! DID YOU ENTER-ING YOUR MASCOT FOR THE CEREAL CONTEST?
YUP! I PUT IT IN THE MAIL THIS MORNING!
YES! AND ME ALSO!
WHA-? YOU?
ABSOLUTE! SO NOW ARE THE BOTH OF US ENTERED!
THAT'S REALLY GREAT, ARTUR.
AND IF YOU DID NOT TELL TO ME OF CONTEST, I WOULD NOT EVEN KNOW ABOUT IT!
Peirce

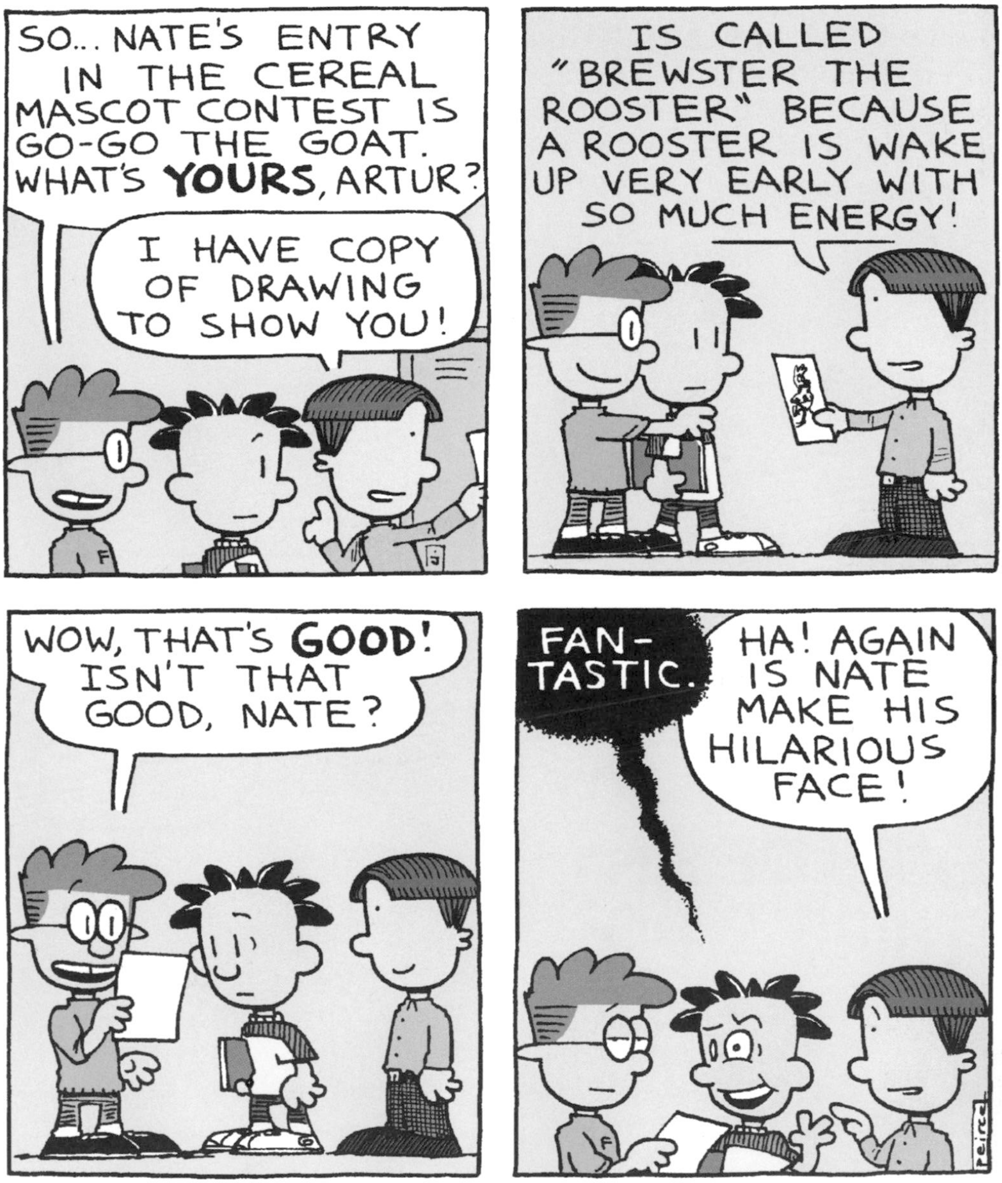
SO... NATE'S ENTRY IN THE CEREAL MASCOT CONTEST IS GO-GO THE GOAT. WHAT'S **YOURS**, ARTUR?
I HAVE COPY OF DRAWING TO SHOW YOU!
IS CALLED "BREWSTER THE ROOSTER" BECAUSE A ROOSTER IS WAKE UP VERY EARLY WITH SO MUCH ENERGY!
WOW, THAT'S **GOOD**! ISN'T THAT GOOD, NATE?
FAN-TASTIC.
HA! AGAIN IS NATE MAKE HIS HILARIOUS FACE!
peirce

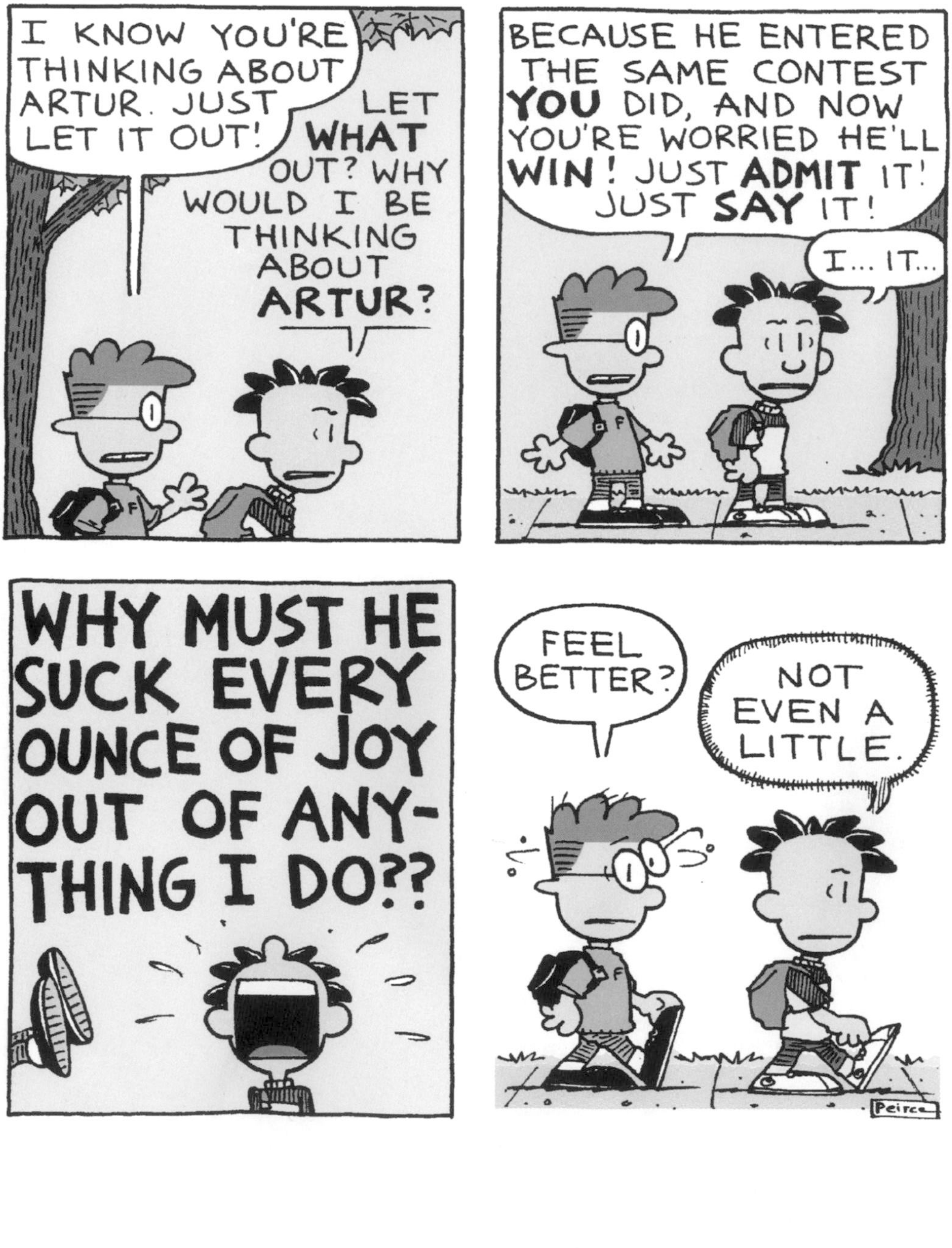
I KNOW YOU'RE THINKING ABOUT ARTUR. JUST LET IT OUT!
LET WHAT OUT? WHY WOULD I BE THINKING ABOUT ARTUR?
BECAUSE HE ENTERED THE SAME CONTEST YOU DID, AND NOW YOU'RE WORRIED HE'LL WIN! JUST ADMIT IT! JUST SAY IT!
I... IT...
WHY MUST HE SUCK EVERY OUNCE OF JOY OUT OF ANY-THING I DO??
FEEL BETTER?
NOT EVEN A LITTLE.
Peirce

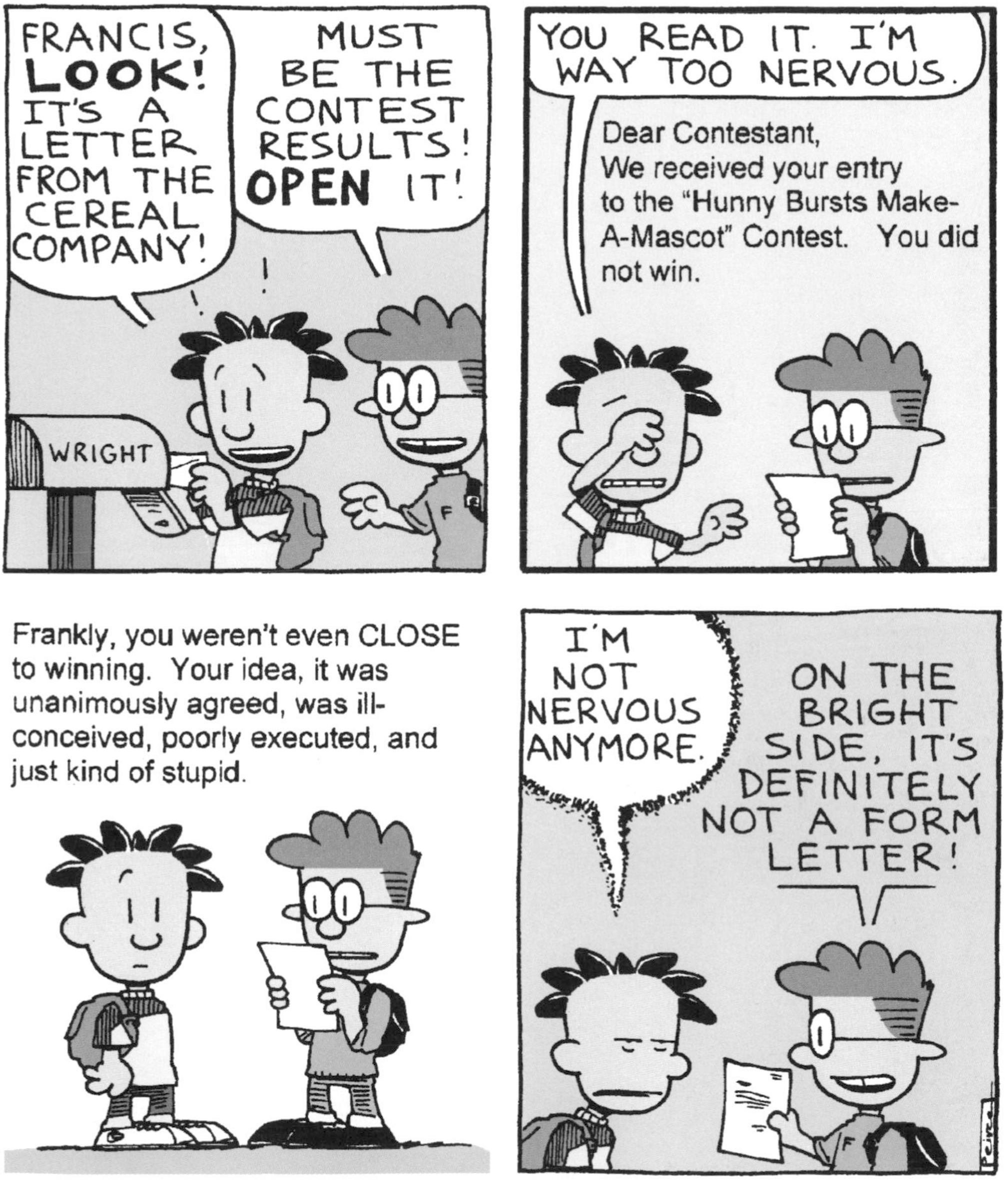
FRANCIS, LOOK! IT'S A LETTER FROM THE CEREAL COMPANY!
MUST BE THE CONTEST RESULTS! OPEN IT!
WRIGHT
YOU READ IT. I'M WAY TOO NERVOUS.
Dear Contestant,
We received your entry to the "Hunny Bursts Make-A-Mascot" Contest. You did not win.
Frankly, you weren't even CLOSE to winning. Your idea, it was unanimously agreed, was ill-conceived, poorly executed, and just kind of stupid.
I'M NOT NERVOUS ANYMORE.
ON THE BRIGHT SIDE, IT'S DEFINITELY NOT A FORM LETTER!
Peirce

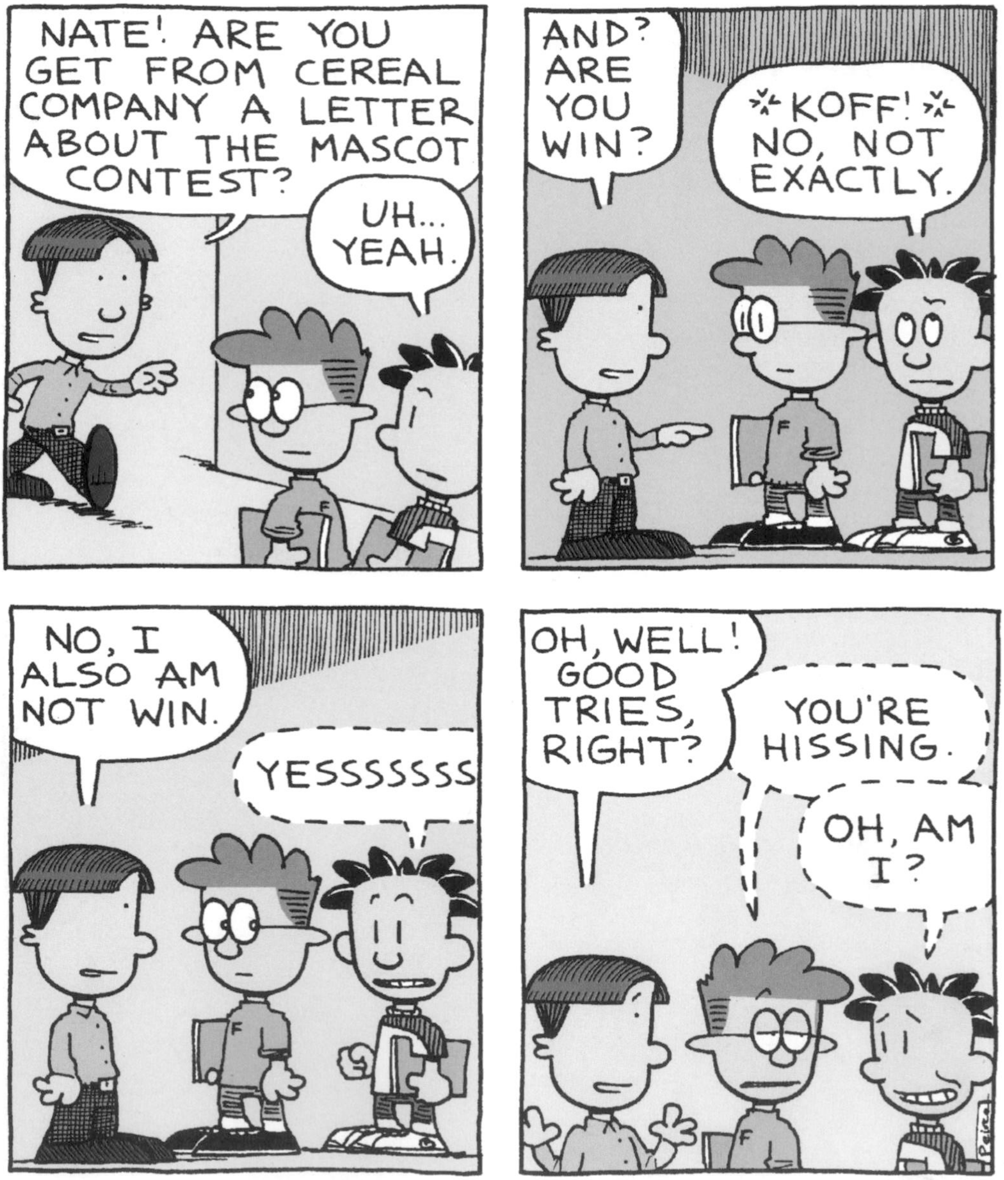
NATE! ARE YOU GET FROM CEREAL COMPANY A LETTER ABOUT THE MASCOT CONTEST?
UH... YEAH.
AND? ARE YOU WIN?
KOFF! NO, NOT EXACTLY.
NO, I ALSO AM NOT WIN.
YESSSSSSS
OH, WELL! GOOD TRIES, RIGHT?
YOU'RE HISSING.
OH, AM I?

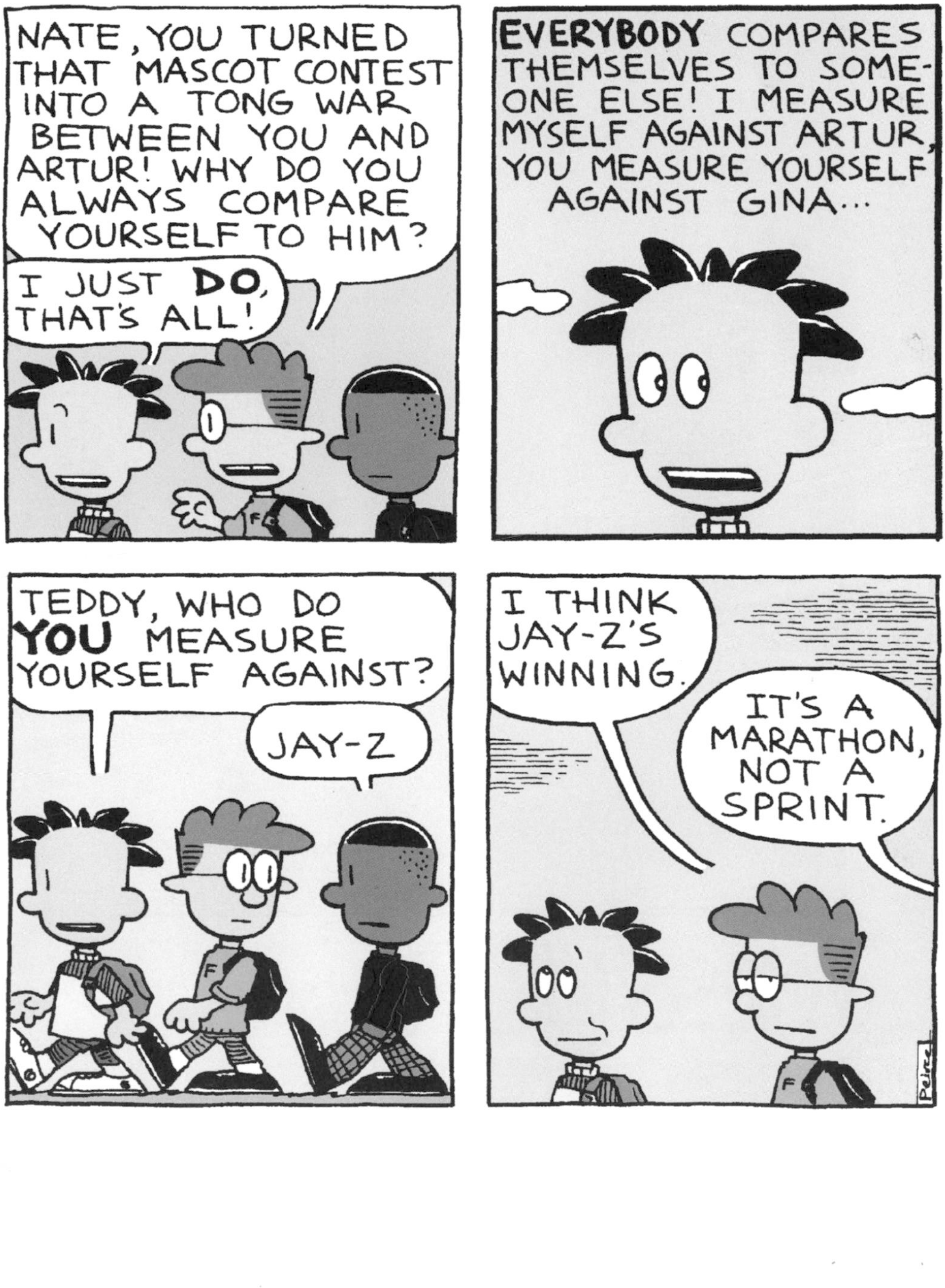
NATE, YOU TURNED THAT MASCOT CONTEST INTO A TONG WAR BETWEEN YOU AND ARTUR! WHY DO YOU ALWAYS COMPARE YOURSELF TO HIM?
I JUST **DO**, THAT'S ALL!
EVERYBODY COMPARES THEMSELVES TO SOMEONE ELSE! I MEASURE MYSELF AGAINST ARTUR, YOU MEASURE YOURSELF AGAINST GINA...
TEDDY, WHO DO **YOU** MEASURE YOURSELF AGAINST?
JAY-Z
I THINK JAY-Z'S WINNING.
IT'S A MARATHON, NOT A SPRINT.
Peirce

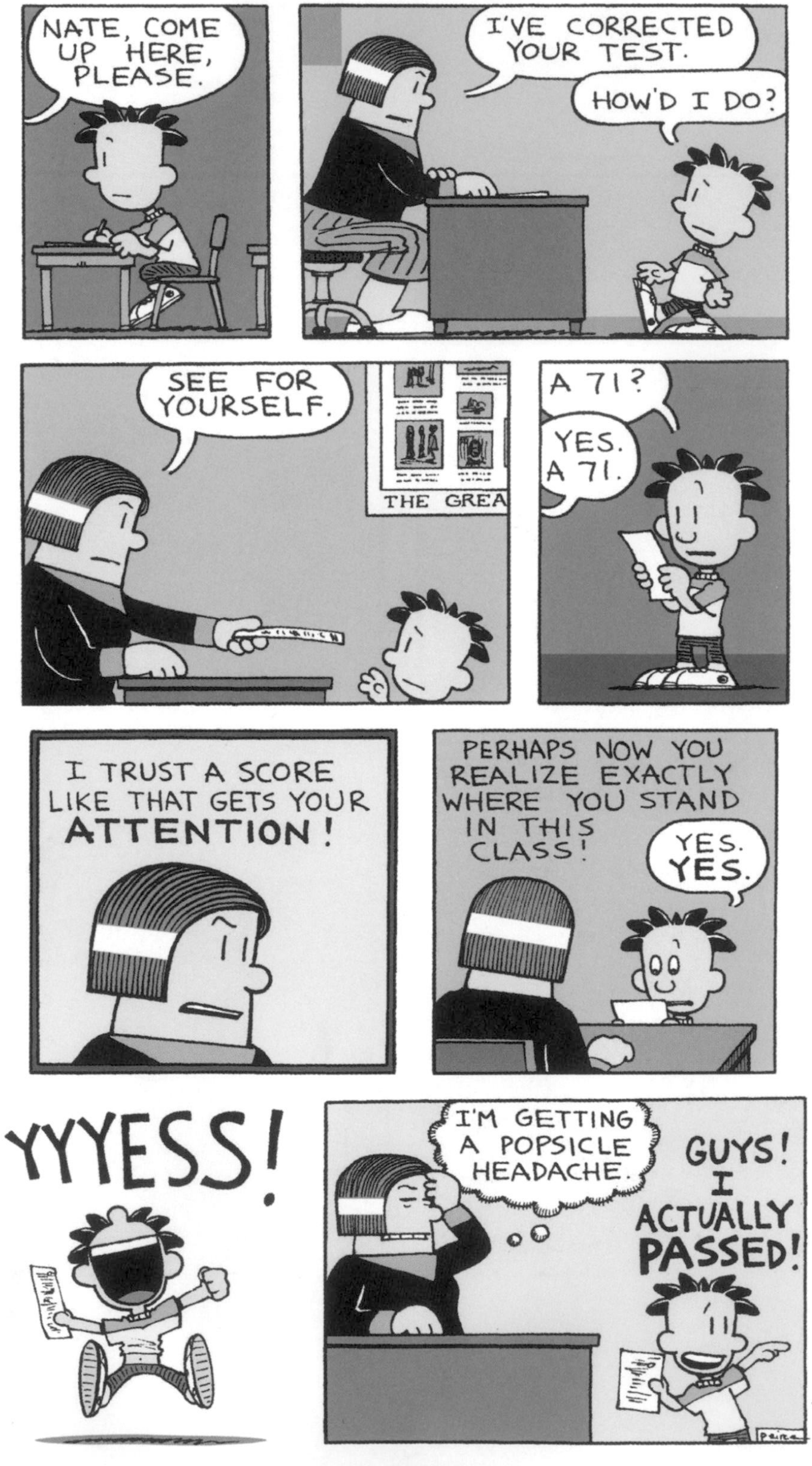
NATE, COME UP HERE, PLEASE.
I'VE CORRECTED YOUR TEST.
HOW'D I DO?
SEE FOR YOURSELF.
THE GREA
A 71?
YES. A 71.
I TRUST A SCORE LIKE THAT GETS YOUR ATTENTION!
PERHAPS NOW YOU REALIZE EXACTLY WHERE YOU STAND IN THIS CLASS!
YES. YES.
YYYESS!
I'M GETTING A POPSICLE HEADACHE.
GUYS! I ACTUALLY PASSED!

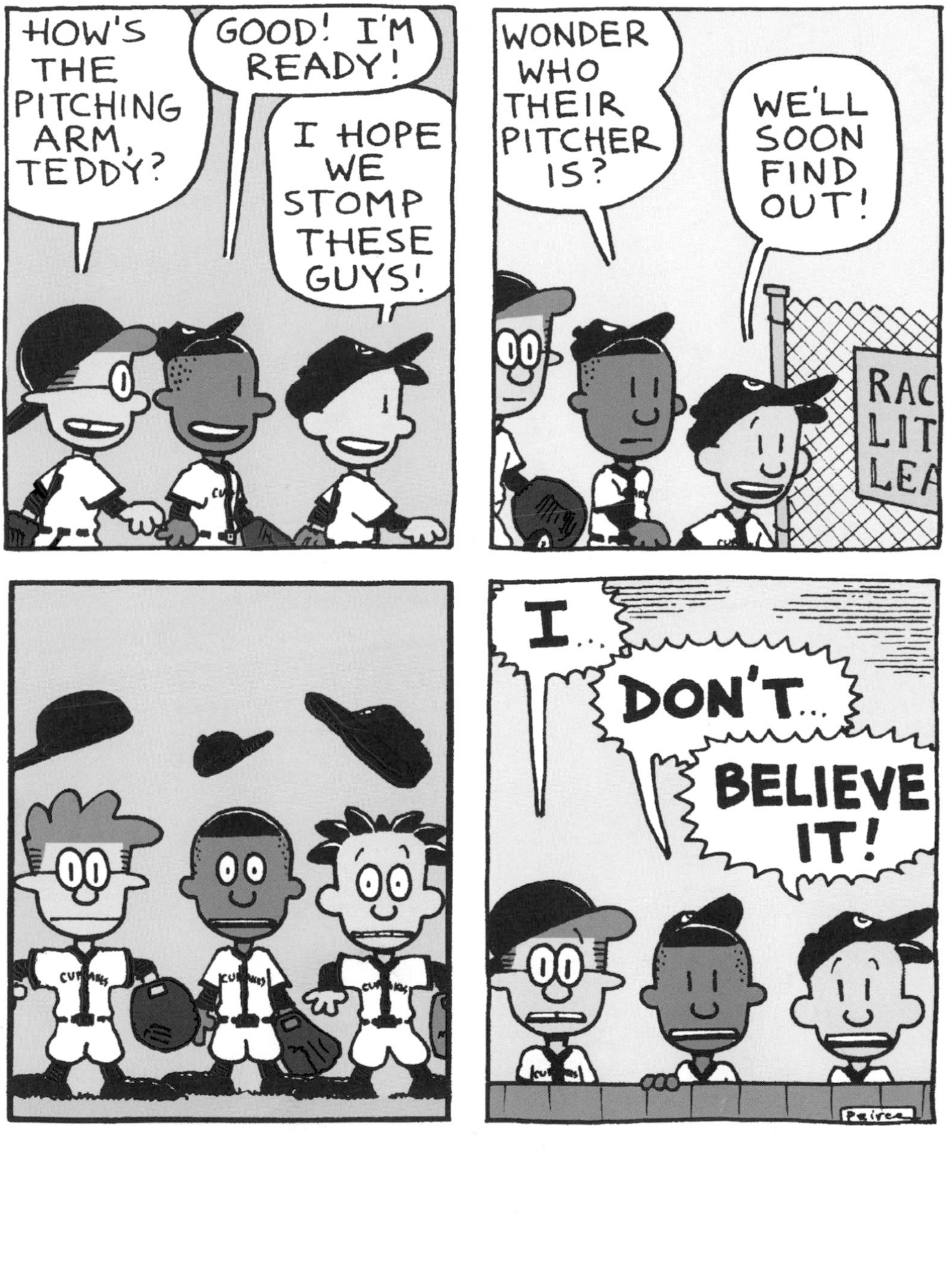
HOW'S THE PITCHING ARM, TEDDY?
GOOD! I'M READY!
I HOPE WE STOMP THESE GUYS!
WONDER WHO THEIR PITCHER IS?
WE'LL SOON FIND OUT!
RAC
LIT
LEA
I...
DON'T...
BELIEVE IT!

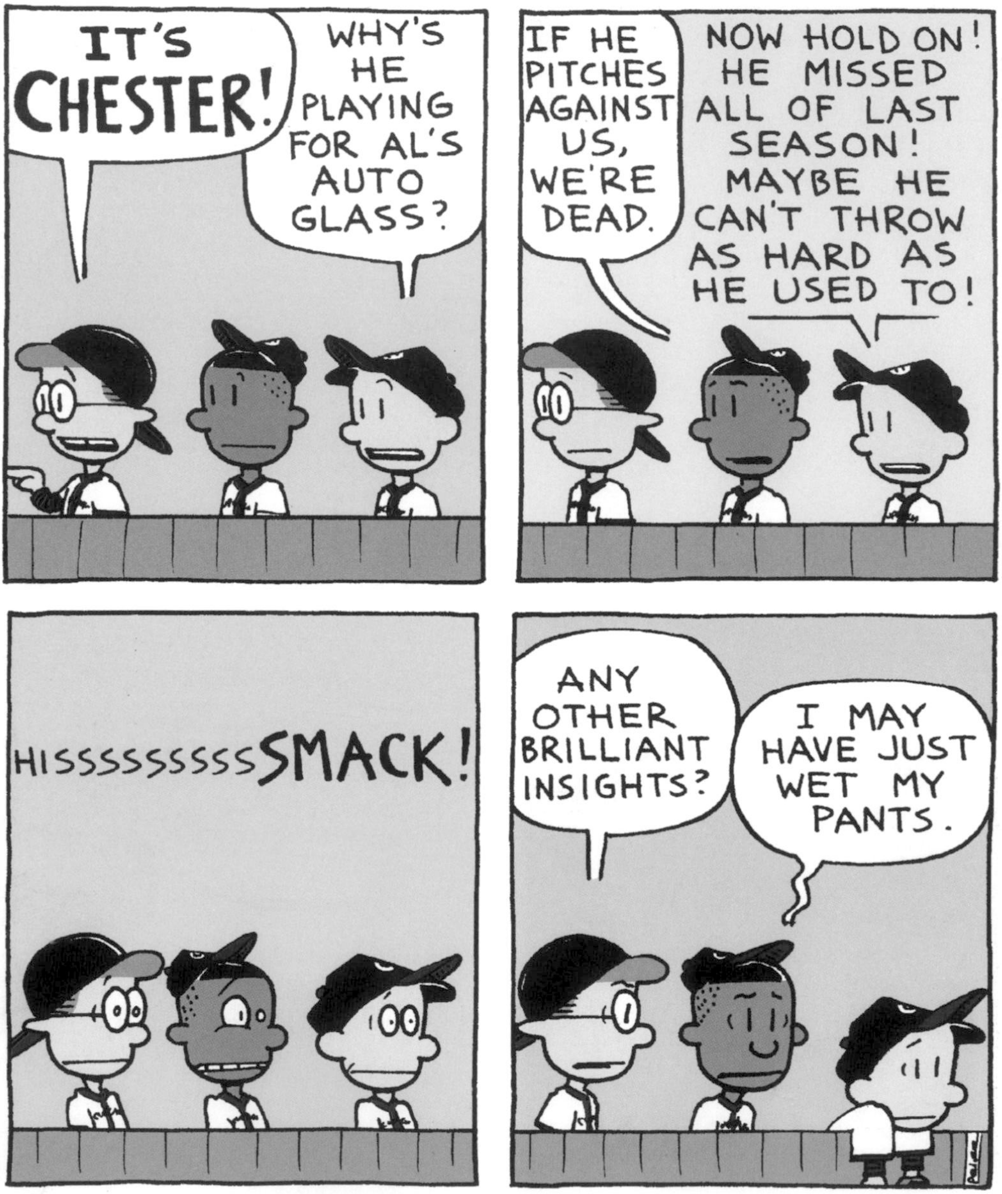
IT'S CHESTER!
WHY'S HE PLAYING FOR AL'S AUTO GLASS?
IF HE PITCHES AGAINST US, WE'RE DEAD.
NOW HOLD ON! HE MISSED ALL OF LAST SEASON! MAYBE HE CAN'T THROW AS HARD AS HE USED TO!
HISSSSSSSSSSMACK!
ANY OTHER BRILLIANT INSIGHTS?
I MAY HAVE JUST WET MY PANTS.

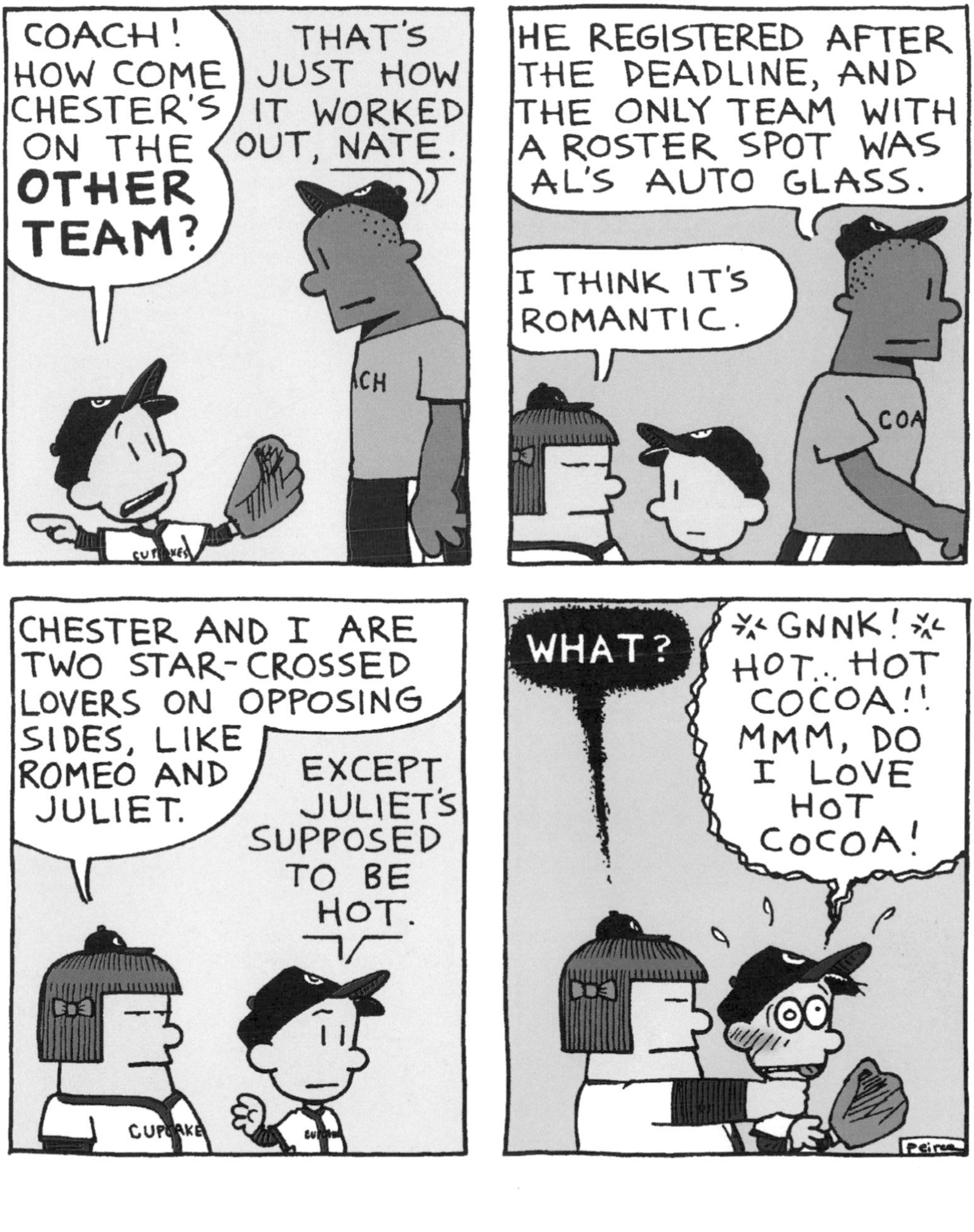
COACH! HOW COME CHESTER'S ON THE OTHER TEAM?
THAT'S JUST HOW IT WORKED OUT, NATE.
HE REGISTERED AFTER THE DEADLINE, AND THE ONLY TEAM WITH A ROSTER SPOT WAS AL'S AUTO GLASS.
I THINK IT'S ROMANTIC.
CHESTER AND I ARE TWO STAR-CROSSED LOVERS ON OPPOSING SIDES, LIKE ROMEO AND JULIET.
EXCEPT JULIET'S SUPPOSED TO BE HOT.
WHAT?
GNNK! HOT... HOT COCOA!! MMM, DO I LOVE HOT COCOA!
Peirce

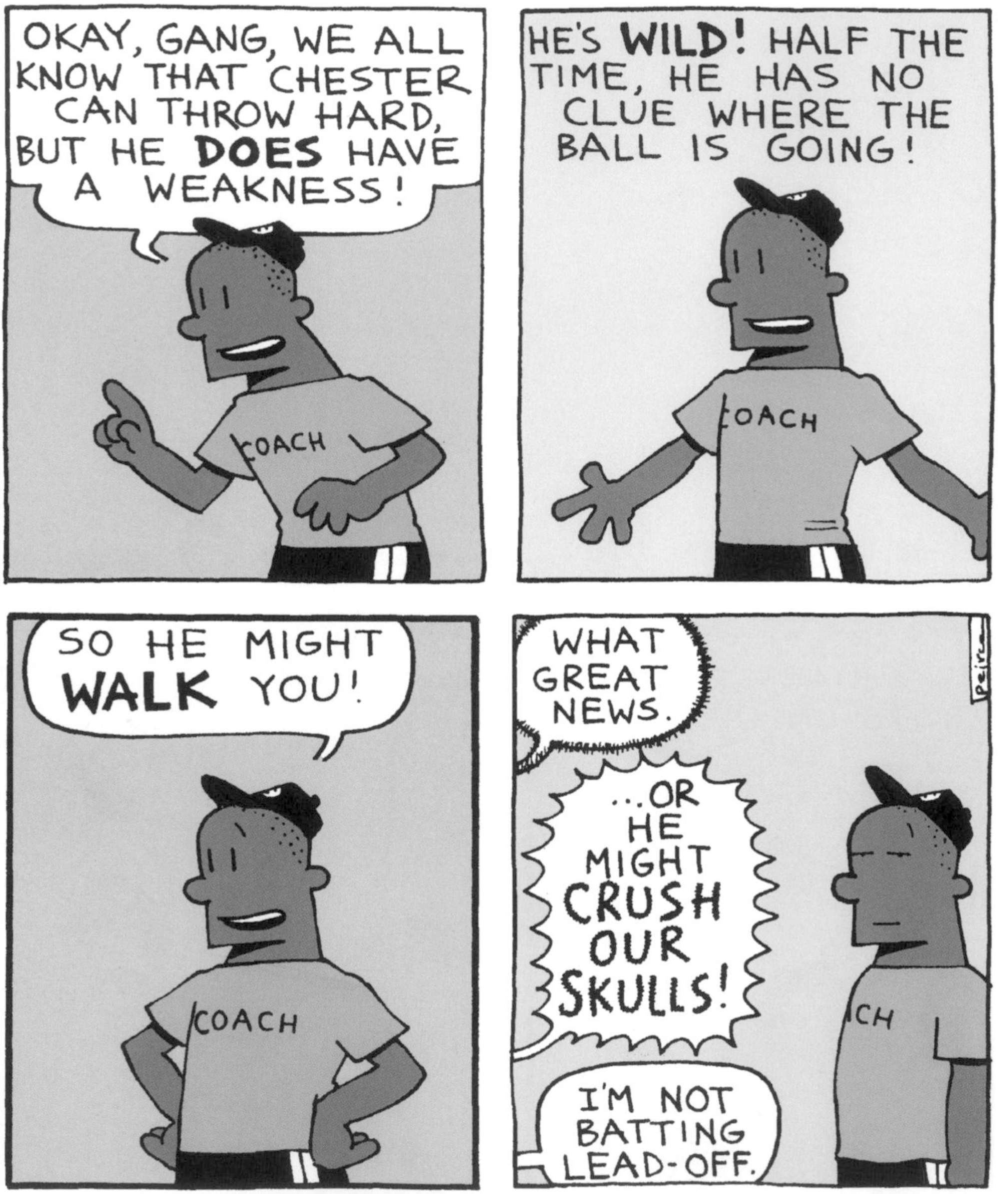
OKAY, GANG, WE ALL KNOW THAT CHESTER CAN THROW HARD, BUT HE DOES HAVE A WEAKNESS!
COACH
HE'S WILD! HALF THE TIME, HE HAS NO CLUE WHERE THE BALL IS GOING!
COACH
SO HE MIGHT WALK YOU!
COACH
WHAT GREAT NEWS.
...OR HE MIGHT CRUSH OUR SKULLS!
I'M NOT BATTING LEAD-OFF.
CH
Peirce

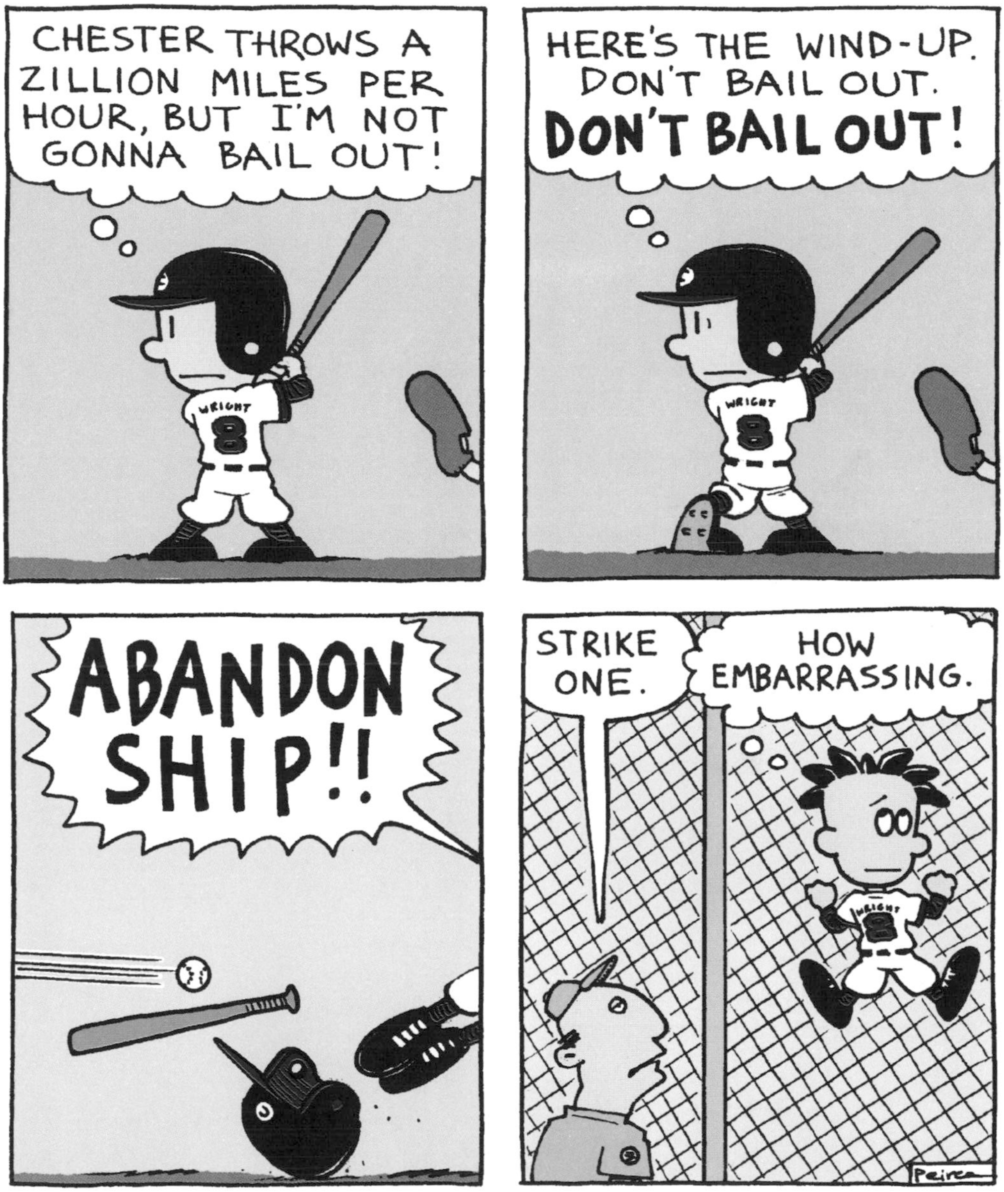
CHESTER THROWS A ZILLION MILES PER HOUR, BUT I'M NOT GONNA BAIL OUT!
WRIGHT
8
HERE'S THE WIND-UP. DON'T BAIL OUT. DON'T BAIL OUT!
WRIGHT
8
ABANDON SHIP!!
STRIKE ONE.
HOW EMBARRASSING.
8
Peirce

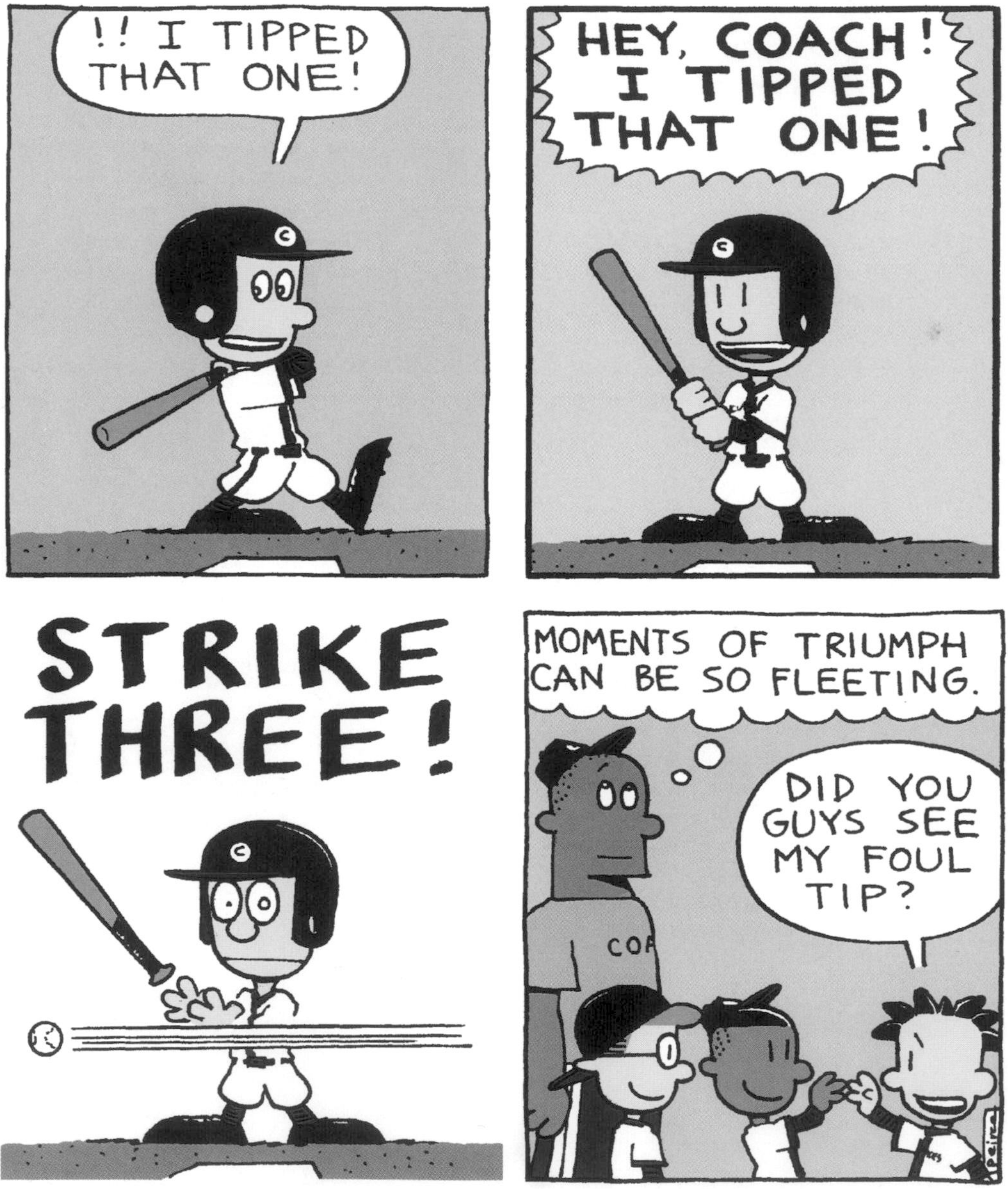
!! I TIPPED THAT ONE!
HEY, COACH! I TIPPED THAT ONE!
STRIKE THREE!
MOMENTS OF TRIUMPH CAN BE SO FLEETING.
DID YOU GUYS SEE MY FOUL TIP?

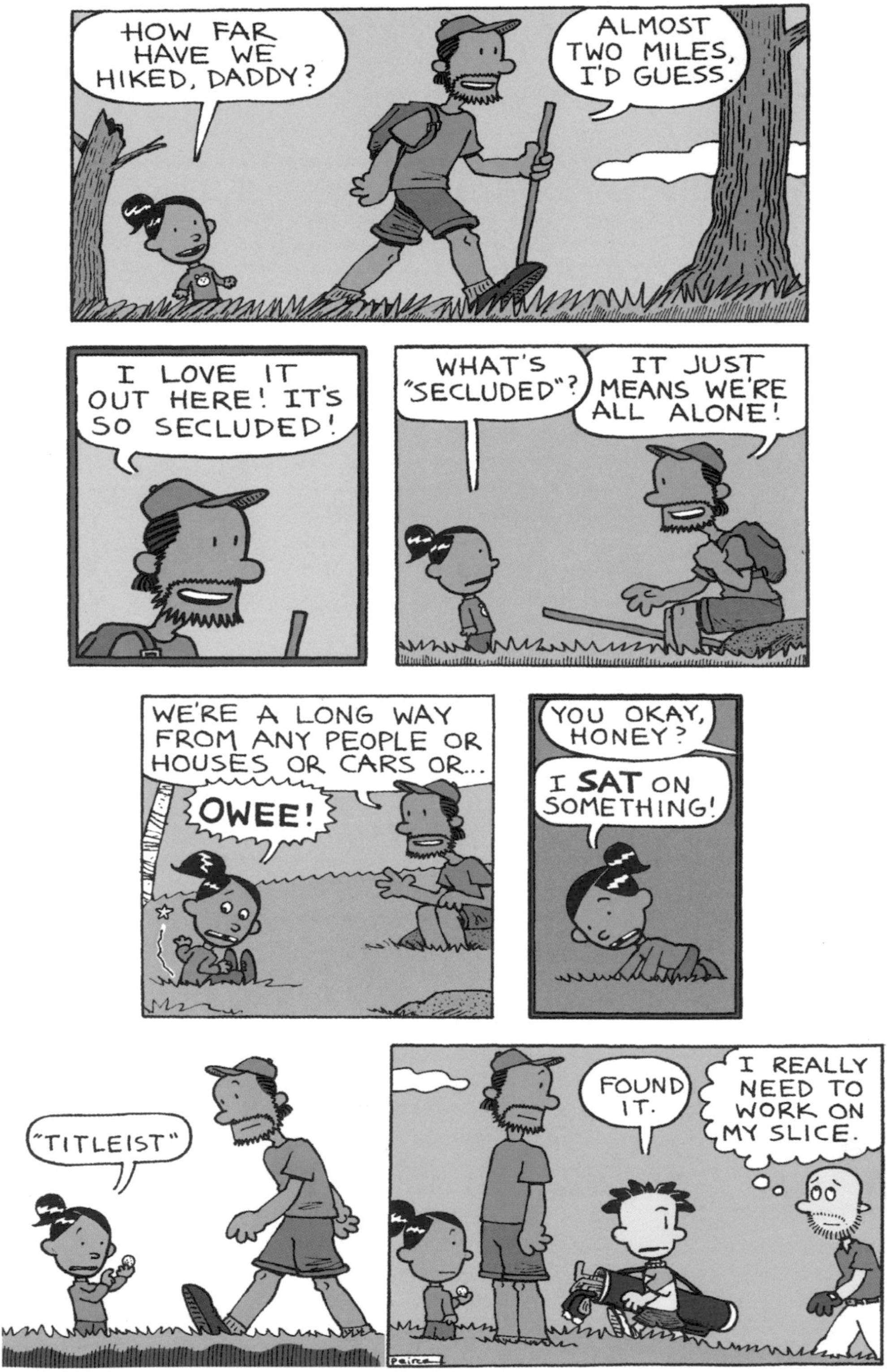
HOW FAR HAVE WE HIKED, DADDY?
ALMOST TWO MILES, I'D GUESS.
I LOVE IT OUT HERE! IT'S SO SECLUDED!
WHAT'S "SECLUDED"?
IT JUST MEANS WE'RE ALL ALONE!
WE'RE A LONG WAY FROM ANY PEOPLE OR HOUSES OR CARS OR...
OWEE!
YOU OKAY, HONEY?
I SAT ON SOMETHING!
"TITLEIST"
FOUND IT.
I REALLY NEED TO WORK ON MY SLICE.
peirce

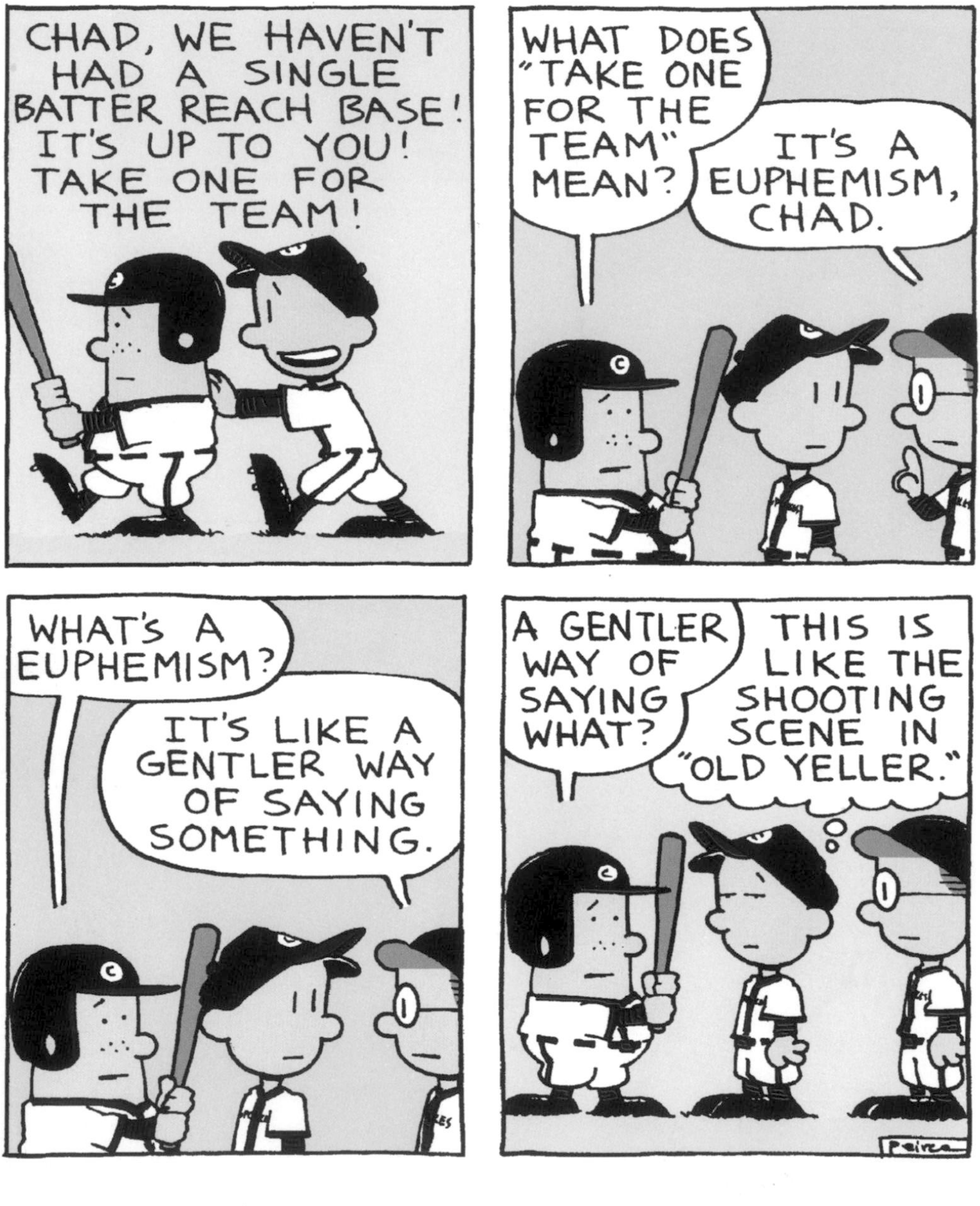
CHAD, WE HAVEN'T HAD A SINGLE BATTER REACH BASE! IT'S UP TO YOU! TAKE ONE FOR THE TEAM!
WHAT DOES "TAKE ONE FOR THE TEAM" MEAN?
IT'S A EUPHEMISM, CHAD.
WHAT'S A EUPHEMISM?
IT'S LIKE A GENTLER WAY OF SAYING SOMETHING.
A GENTLER WAY OF SAYING WHAT?
THIS IS LIKE THE SHOOTING SCENE IN "OLD YELLER."
Peirce

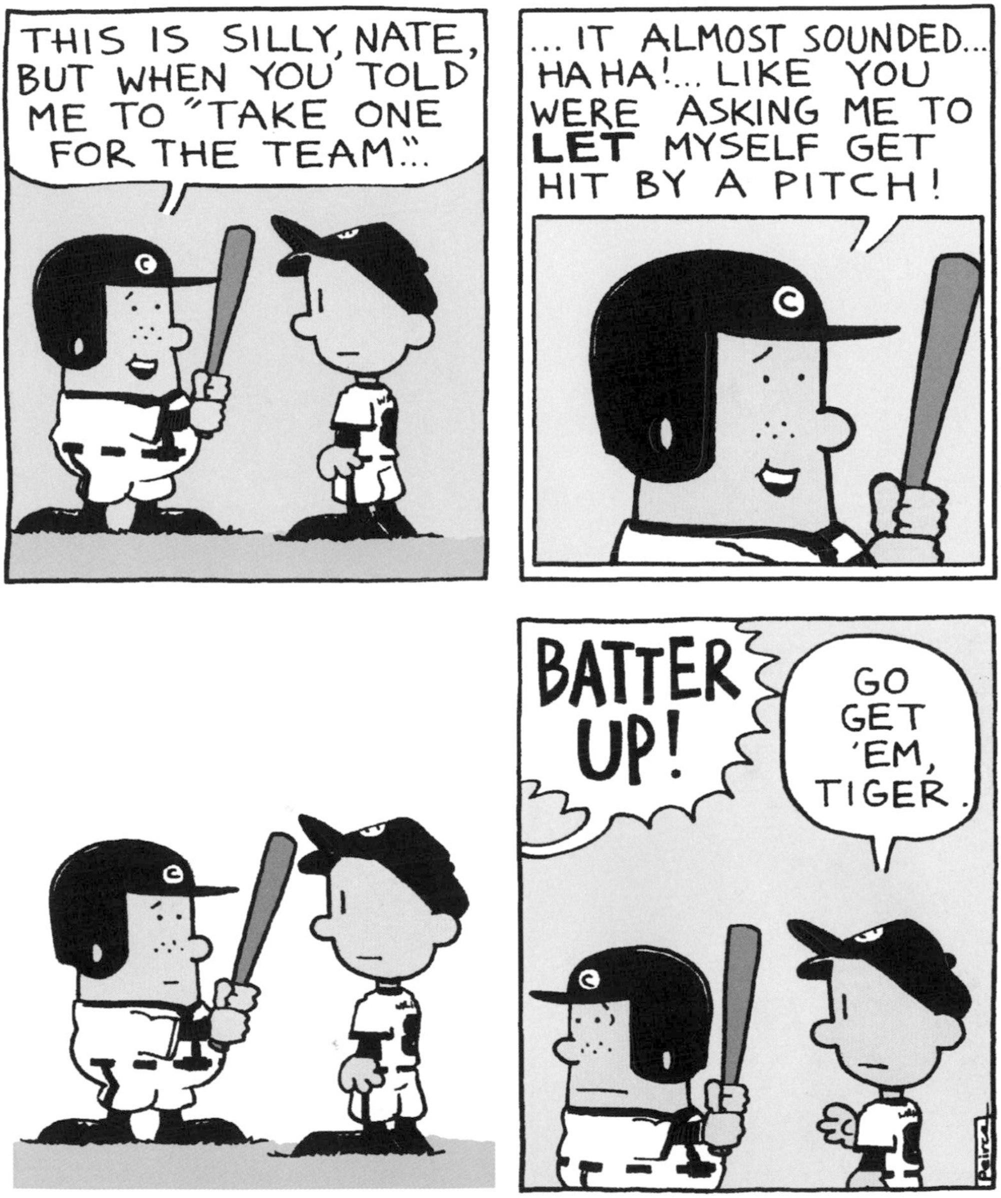
THIS IS SILLY, NATE, BUT WHEN YOU TOLD ME TO "TAKE ONE FOR THE TEAM"...
... IT ALMOST SOUNDED... HA HA!... LIKE YOU WERE ASKING ME TO **LET** MYSELF GET HIT BY A PITCH!
BATTER UP!
GO GET 'EM, TIGER.
Peirce

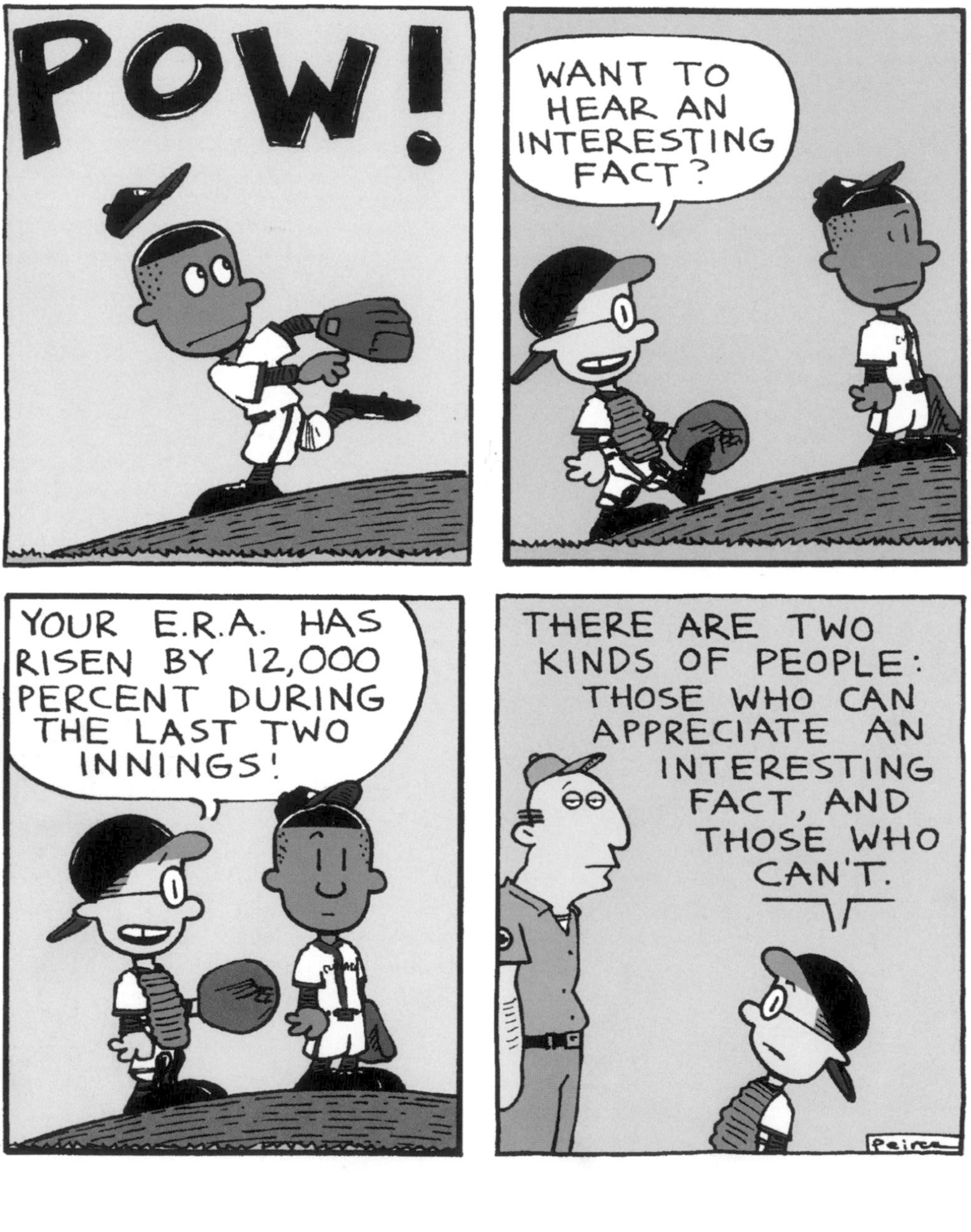
POW!
WANT TO HEAR AN INTERESTING FACT?
YOUR E.R.A. HAS RISEN BY 12,000 PERCENT DURING THE LAST TWO INNINGS!
THERE ARE TWO KINDS OF PEOPLE: THOSE WHO CAN APPRECIATE AN INTERESTING FACT, AND THOSE WHO CAN'T.
Peirce

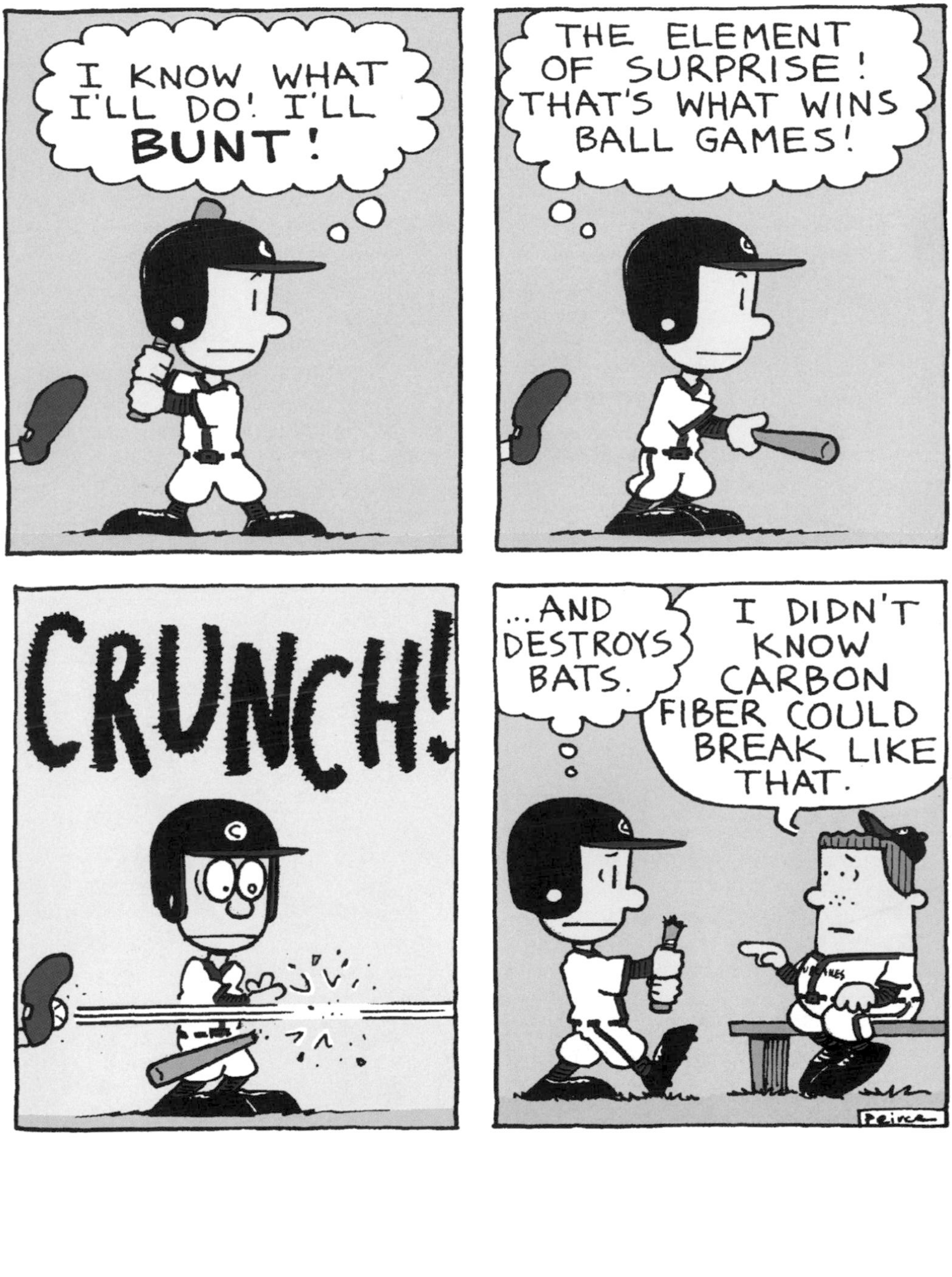
I KNOW WHAT I'LL DO! I'LL **BUNT**!
THE ELEMENT OF SURPRISE! THAT'S WHAT WINS BALL GAMES!
CRUNCH!
...AND DESTROYS BATS.
I DIDN'T KNOW CARBON FIBER COULD BREAK LIKE THAT.
Peirce

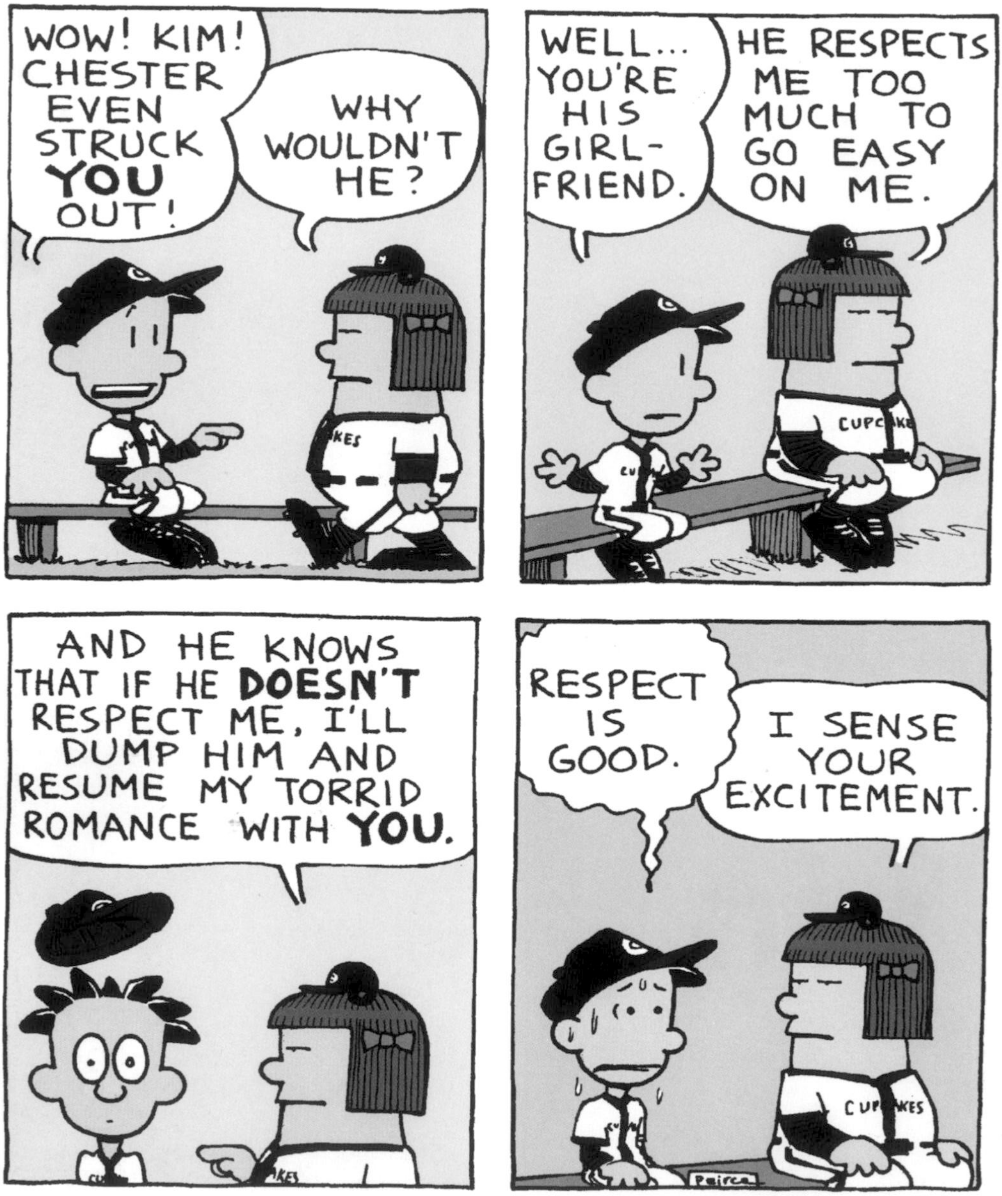

WOW! KIM! CHESTER EVEN STRUCK **YOU** OUT!
WHY WOULDN'T HE?
WELL... YOU'RE HIS GIRL-FRIEND.
HE RESPECTS ME TOO MUCH TO GO EASY ON ME.
AND HE KNOWS THAT IF HE **DOESN'T** RESPECT ME, I'LL DUMP HIM AND RESUME MY TORRID ROMANCE WITH **YOU**.
RESPECT IS GOOD.
I SENSE YOUR EXCITEMENT.
Peirce

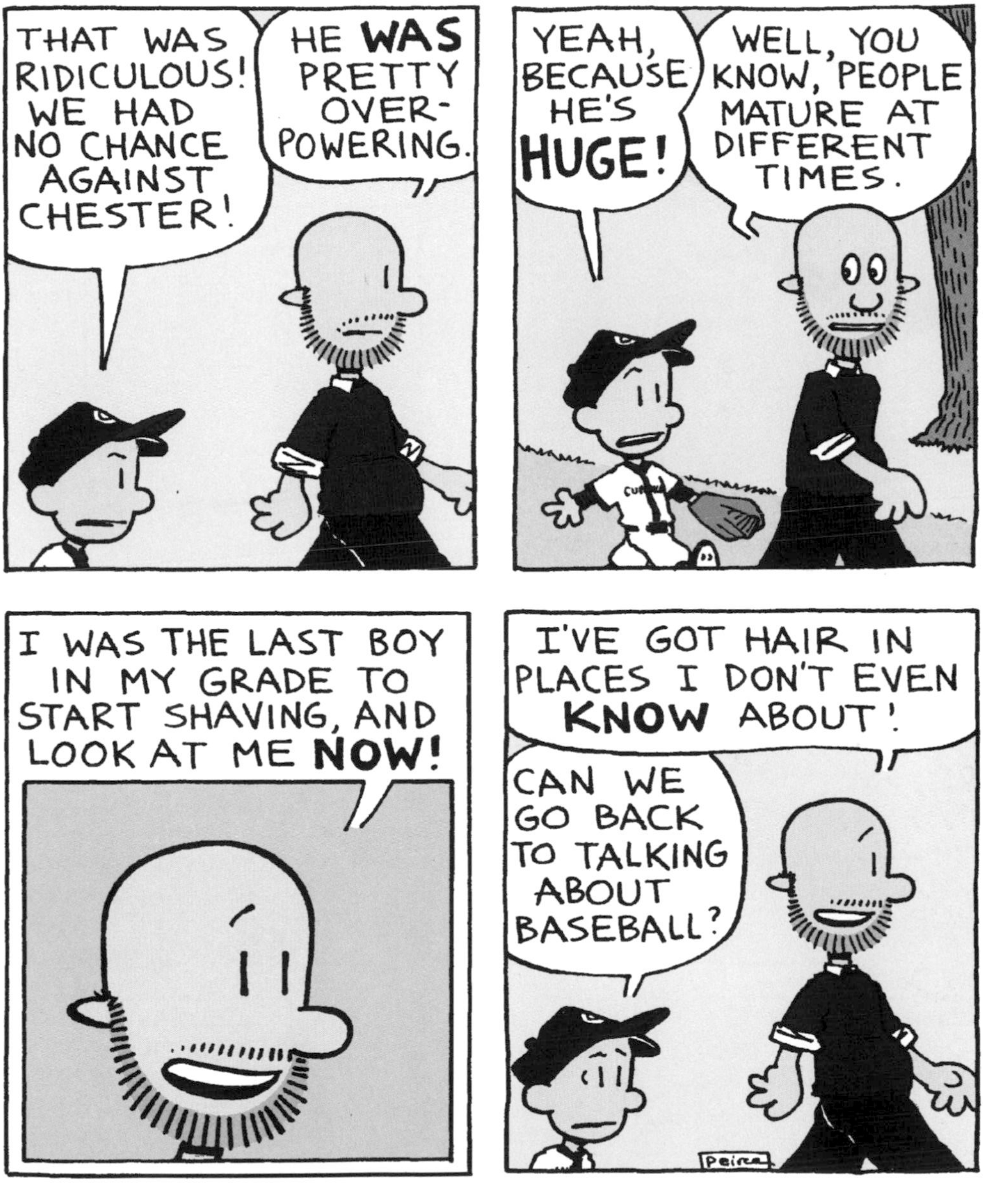
THAT WAS RIDICULOUS! WE HAD NO CHANCE AGAINST CHESTER!
HE **WAS** PRETTY OVER-POWERING.
YEAH, BECAUSE HE'S **HUGE!**
WELL, YOU KNOW, PEOPLE MATURE AT DIFFERENT TIMES.
I WAS THE LAST BOY IN MY GRADE TO START SHAVING, AND LOOK AT ME **NOW!**
I'VE GOT HAIR IN PLACES I DON'T EVEN **KNOW** ABOUT!
CAN WE GO BACK TO TALKING ABOUT BASEBALL?
Peirce

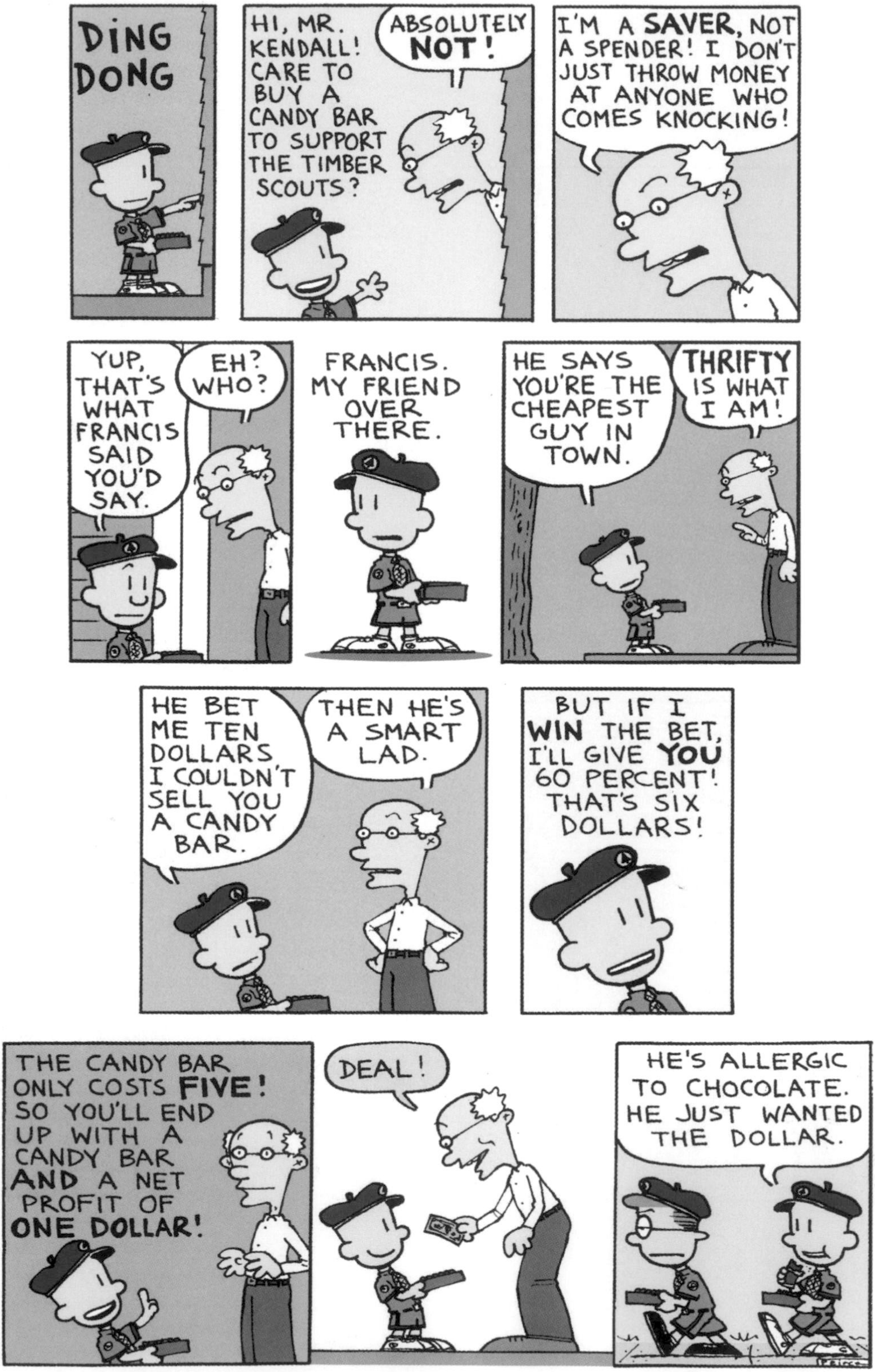
DING DONG
HI, MR. KENDALL! CARE TO BUY A CANDY BAR TO SUPPORT THE TIMBER SCOUTS?
ABSOLUTELY NOT!
I'M A SAVER, NOT A SPENDER! I DON'T JUST THROW MONEY AT ANYONE WHO COMES KNOCKING!
YUP, THAT'S WHAT FRANCIS SAID YOU'D SAY.
EH? WHO?
FRANCIS. MY FRIEND OVER THERE.
HE SAYS YOU'RE THE CHEAPEST GUY IN TOWN.
THRIFTY IS WHAT I AM!
HE BET ME TEN DOLLARS I COULDN'T SELL YOU A CANDY BAR.
THEN HE'S A SMART LAD.
BUT IF I WIN THE BET, I'LL GIVE YOU 60 PERCENT! THAT'S SIX DOLLARS!
THE CANDY BAR ONLY COSTS FIVE! SO YOU'LL END UP WITH A CANDY BAR AND A NET PROFIT OF ONE DOLLAR!
DEAL!
HE'S ALLERGIC TO CHOCOLATE. HE JUST WANTED THE DOLLAR.

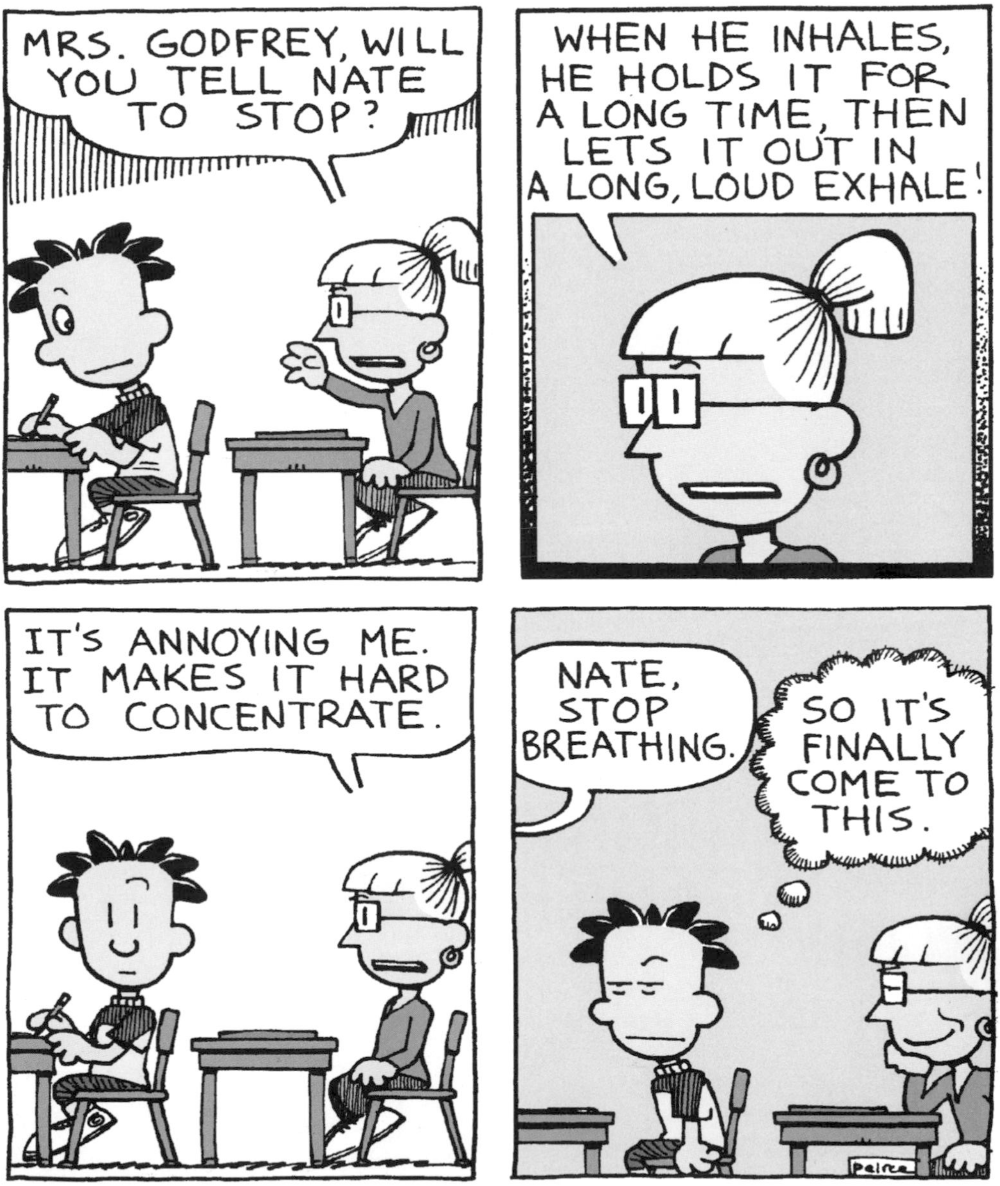
MRS. GODFREY, WILL YOU TELL NATE TO STOP?
WHEN HE INHALES, HE HOLDS IT FOR A LONG TIME, THEN LETS IT OUT IN A LONG, LOUD EXHALE!
IT'S ANNOYING ME. IT MAKES IT HARD TO CONCENTRATE.
NATE, STOP BREATHING.
SO IT'S FINALLY COME TO THIS.
Peirce

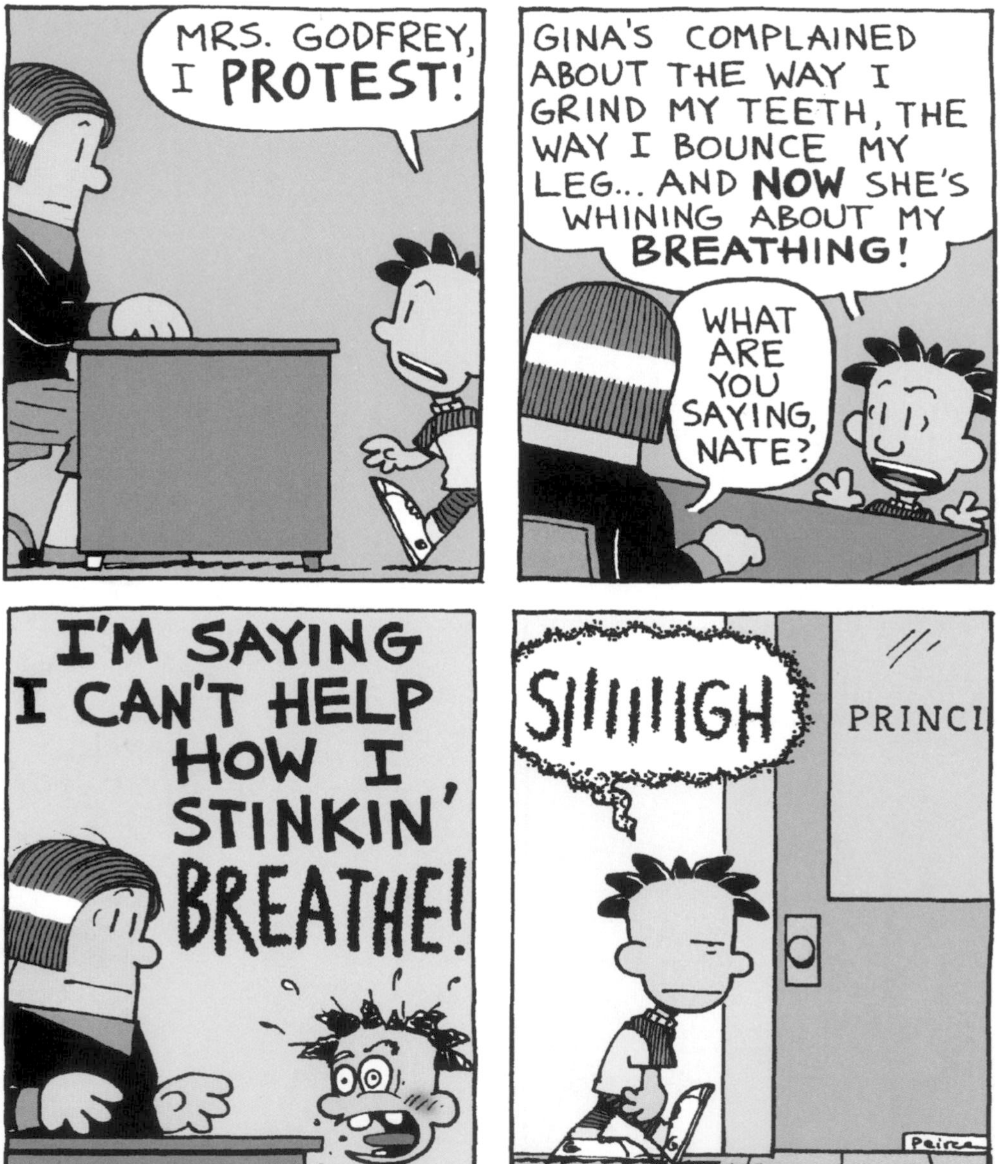

MRS. GODFREY, I **PROTEST!**
GINA'S COMPLAINED ABOUT THE WAY I GRIND MY TEETH, THE WAY I BOUNCE MY LEG... AND **NOW** SHE'S WHINING ABOUT MY **BREATHING!**
WHAT ARE YOU SAYING, NATE?
I'M SAYING I CAN'T HELP HOW I STINKIN' BREATHE!
SIIIIIGH
PRINCI
Peirce

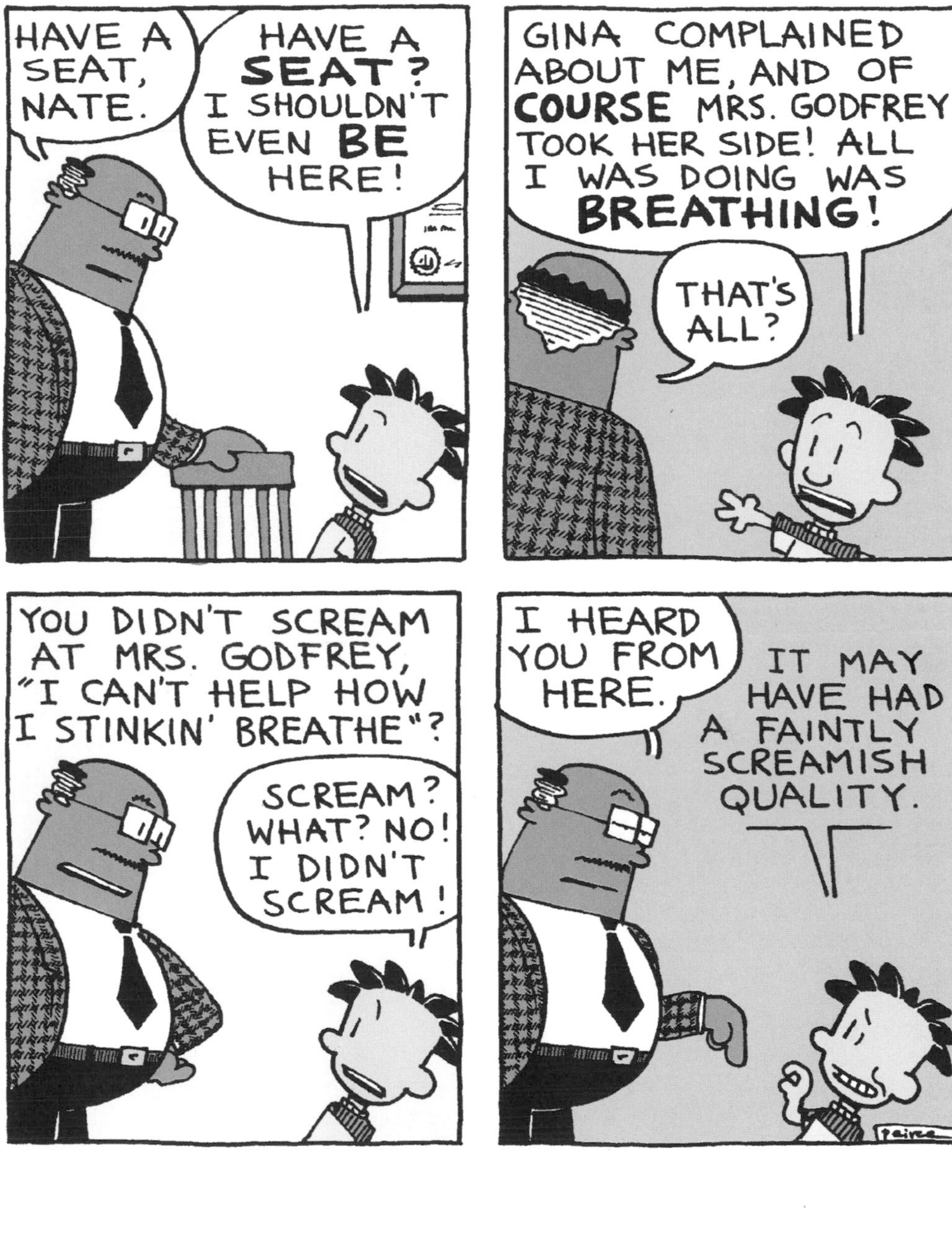
HAVE A SEAT, NATE.
HAVE A **SEAT**? I SHOULDN'T EVEN **BE** HERE!
GINA COMPLAINED ABOUT ME, AND OF **COURSE** MRS. GODFREY TOOK HER SIDE! ALL I WAS DOING WAS **BREATHING**!
THAT'S ALL?
YOU DIDN'T SCREAM AT MRS. GODFREY, "I CAN'T HELP HOW I STINKIN' BREATHE"?
SCREAM? WHAT? NO! I DIDN'T SCREAM!
I HEARD YOU FROM HERE.
IT MAY HAVE HAD A FAINTLY SCREAMISH QUALITY.

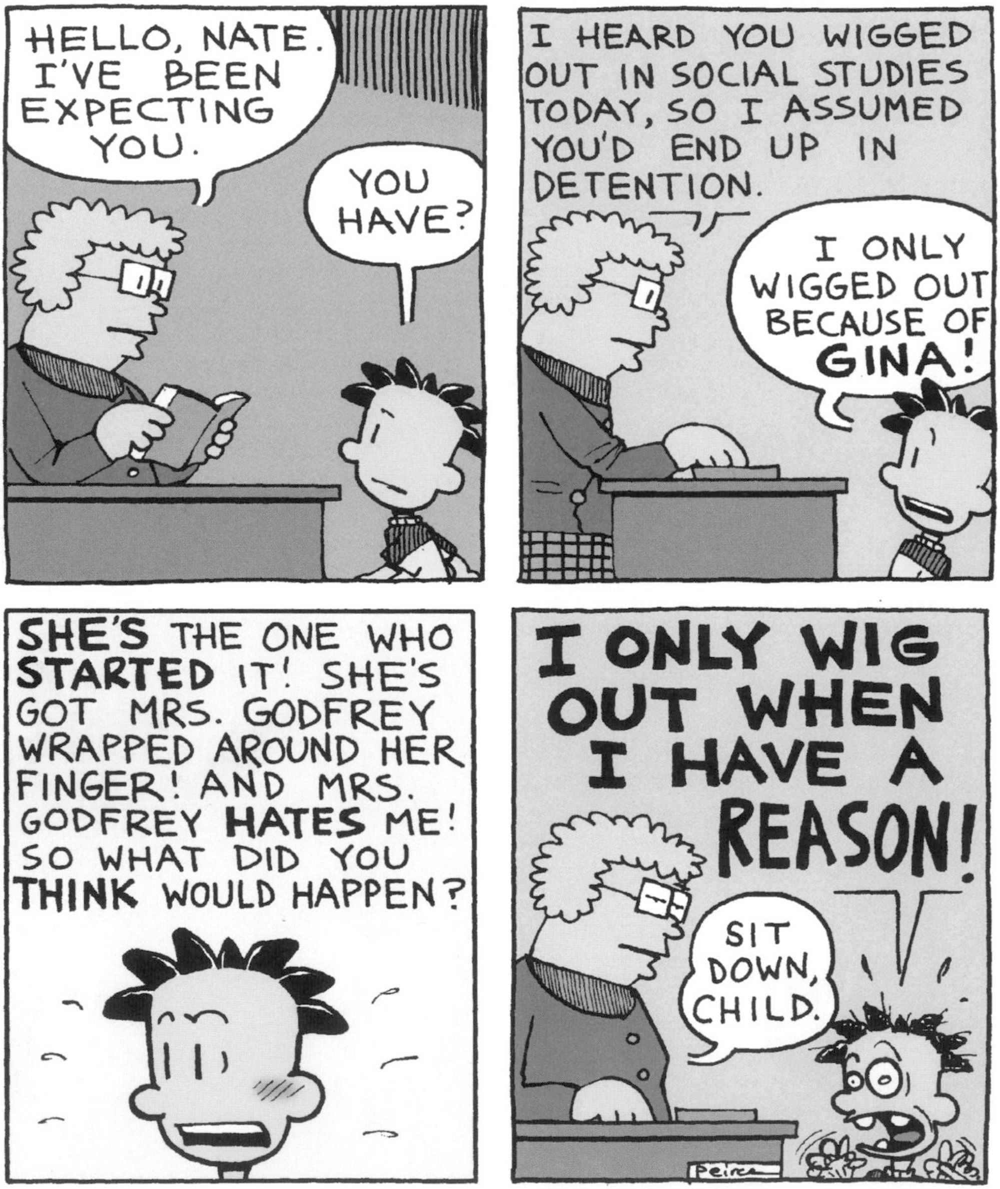
HELLO, NATE. I'VE BEEN EXPECTING YOU.
YOU HAVE?
I HEARD YOU WIGGED OUT IN SOCIAL STUDIES TODAY, SO I ASSUMED YOU'D END UP IN DETENTION.
I ONLY WIGGED OUT BECAUSE OF GINA!
SHE'S THE ONE WHO STARTED IT! SHE'S GOT MRS. GODFREY WRAPPED AROUND HER FINGER! AND MRS. GODFREY HATES ME! SO WHAT DID YOU THINK WOULD HAPPEN?
I ONLY WIG OUT WHEN I HAVE A REASON!
SIT DOWN, CHILD.
Peirce

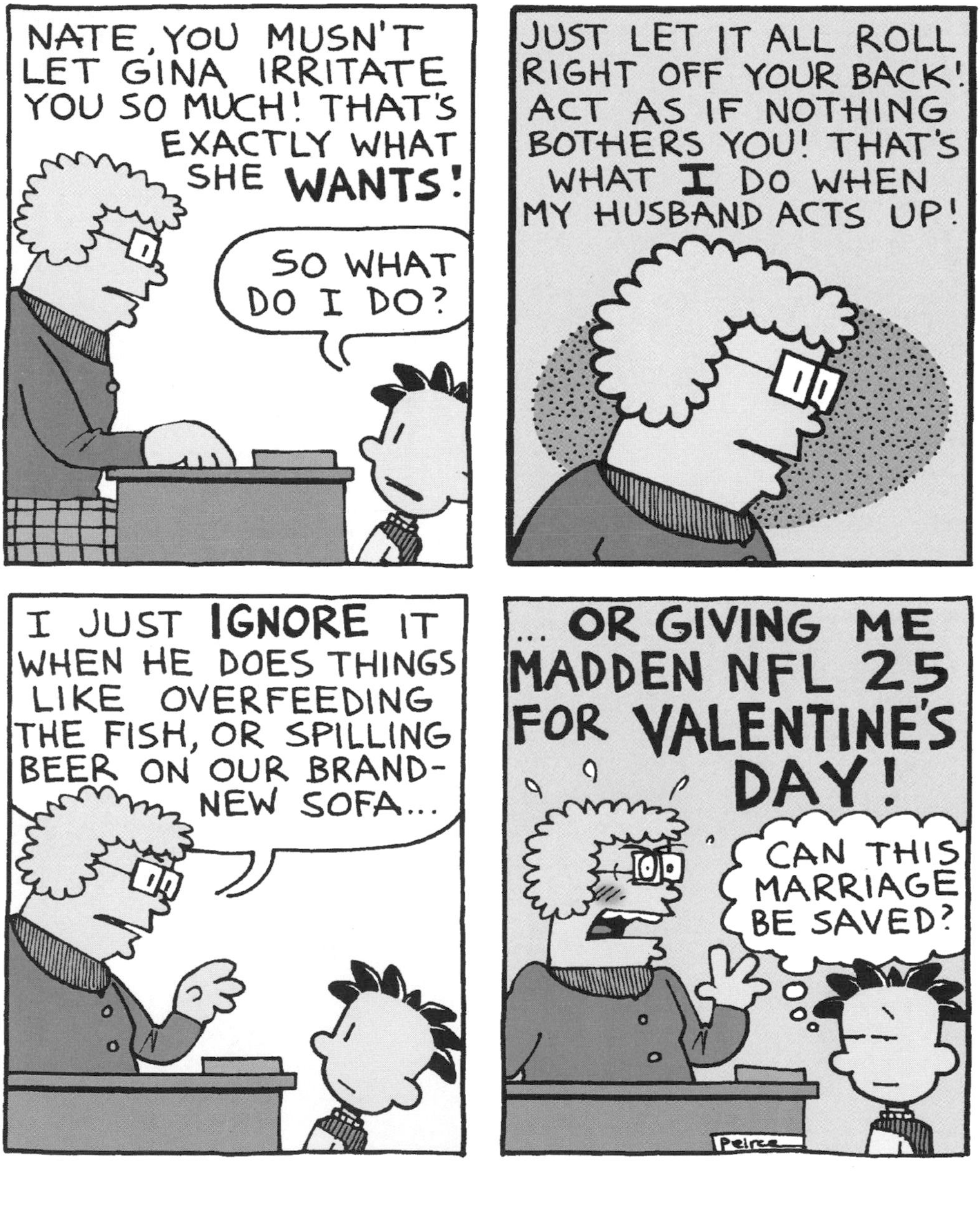
NATE, YOU MUSN'T LET GINA IRRITATE YOU SO MUCH! THAT'S EXACTLY WHAT SHE WANTS!
SO WHAT DO I DO?
JUST LET IT ALL ROLL RIGHT OFF YOUR BACK! ACT AS IF NOTHING BOTHERS YOU! THAT'S WHAT I DO WHEN MY HUSBAND ACTS UP!
I JUST IGNORE IT WHEN HE DOES THINGS LIKE OVERFEEDING THE FISH, OR SPILLING BEER ON OUR BRAND-NEW SOFA...
... OR GIVING ME MADDEN NFL 25 FOR VALENTINE'S DAY!
CAN THIS MARRIAGE BE SAVED?
Peirce

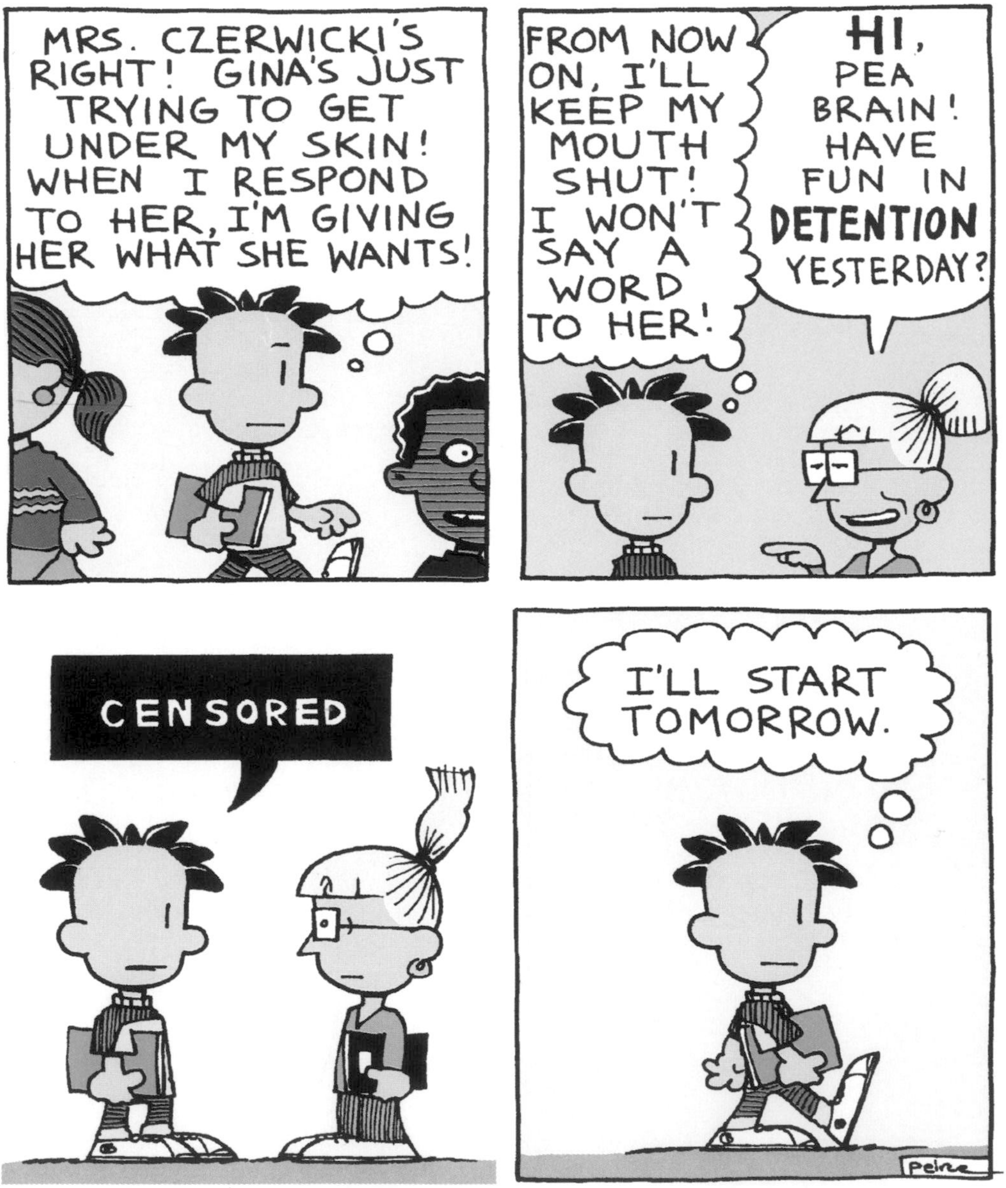
MRS. CZERWICKI'S RIGHT! GINA'S JUST TRYING TO GET UNDER MY SKIN! WHEN I RESPOND TO HER, I'M GIVING HER WHAT SHE WANTS!
FROM NOW ON, I'LL KEEP MY MOUTH SHUT! I WON'T SAY A WORD TO HER!
HI, PEA BRAIN! HAVE FUN IN DETENTION YESTERDAY?
CENSORED
I'LL START TOMORROW.
Peirce

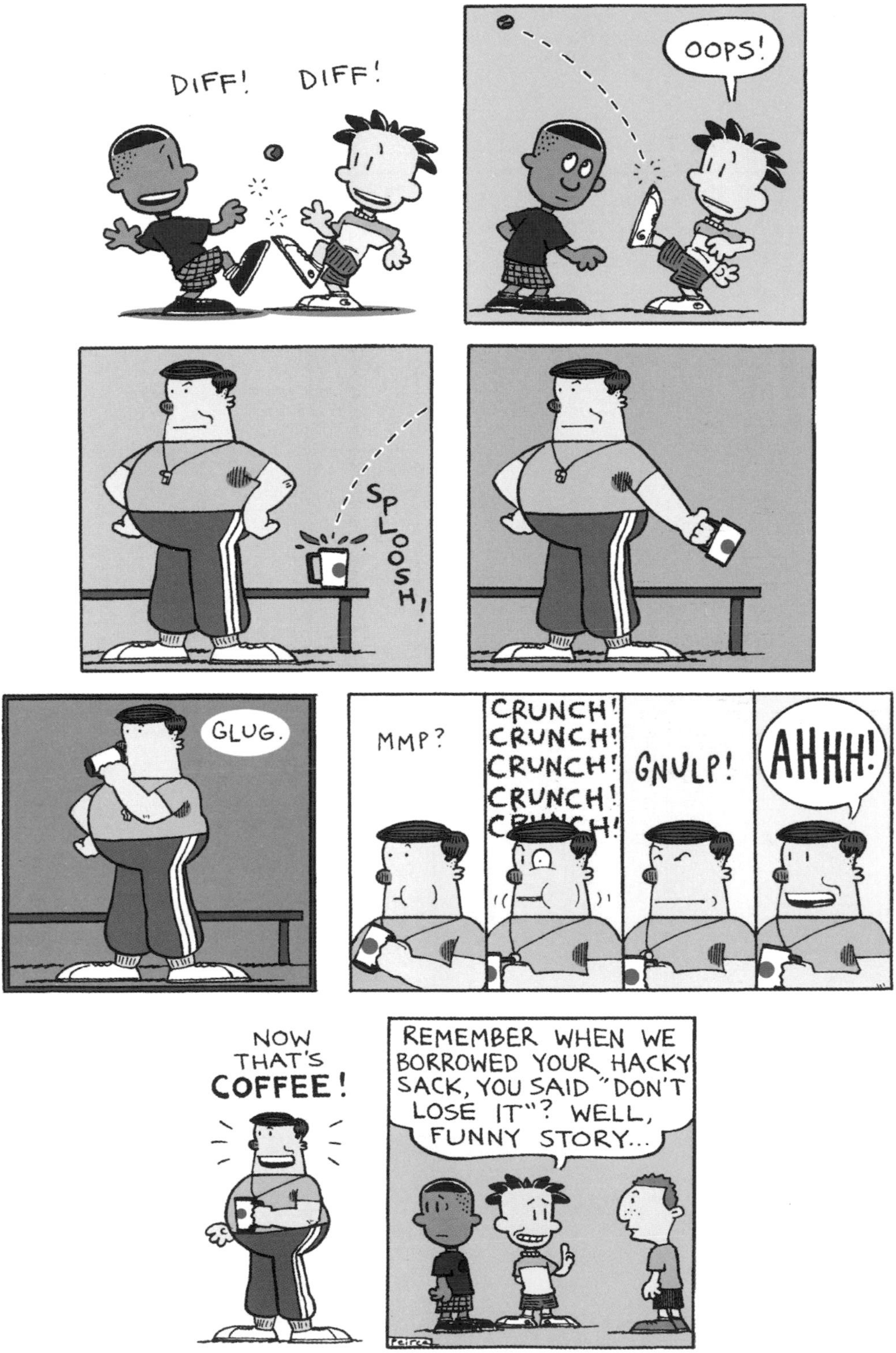
DIFF! DIFF!
OOPS!
SPLOOSH!
GLUG.
MMP?
CRUNCH! CRUNCH! CRUNCH! CRUNCH! CRUNCH!
GNULP!
AHHH!
NOW THAT'S **COFFEE**!
REMEMBER WHEN WE BORROWED YOUR HACKY SACK, YOU SAID "DON'T LOSE IT"? WELL, FUNNY STORY...
Peirce

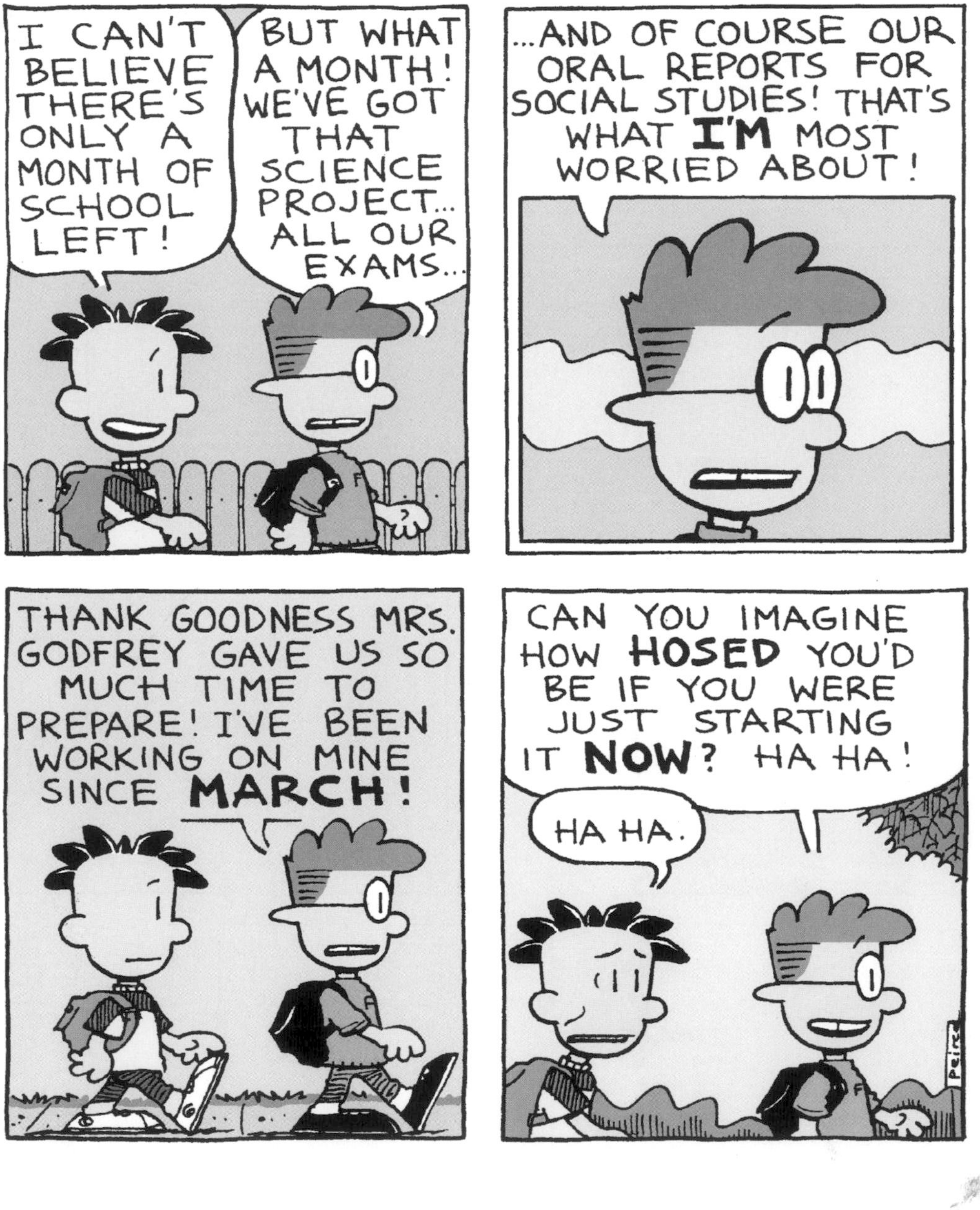
I CAN'T BELIEVE THERE'S ONLY A MONTH OF SCHOOL LEFT!
BUT WHAT A MONTH! WE'VE GOT THAT SCIENCE PROJECT... ALL OUR EXAMS...
...AND OF COURSE OUR ORAL REPORTS FOR SOCIAL STUDIES! THAT'S WHAT I'M MOST WORRIED ABOUT!
THANK GOODNESS MRS. GODFREY GAVE US SO MUCH TIME TO PREPARE! I'VE BEEN WORKING ON MINE SINCE MARCH!
CAN YOU IMAGINE HOW HOSED YOU'D BE IF YOU WERE JUST STARTING IT NOW? HA HA!
HA HA.
Peirce

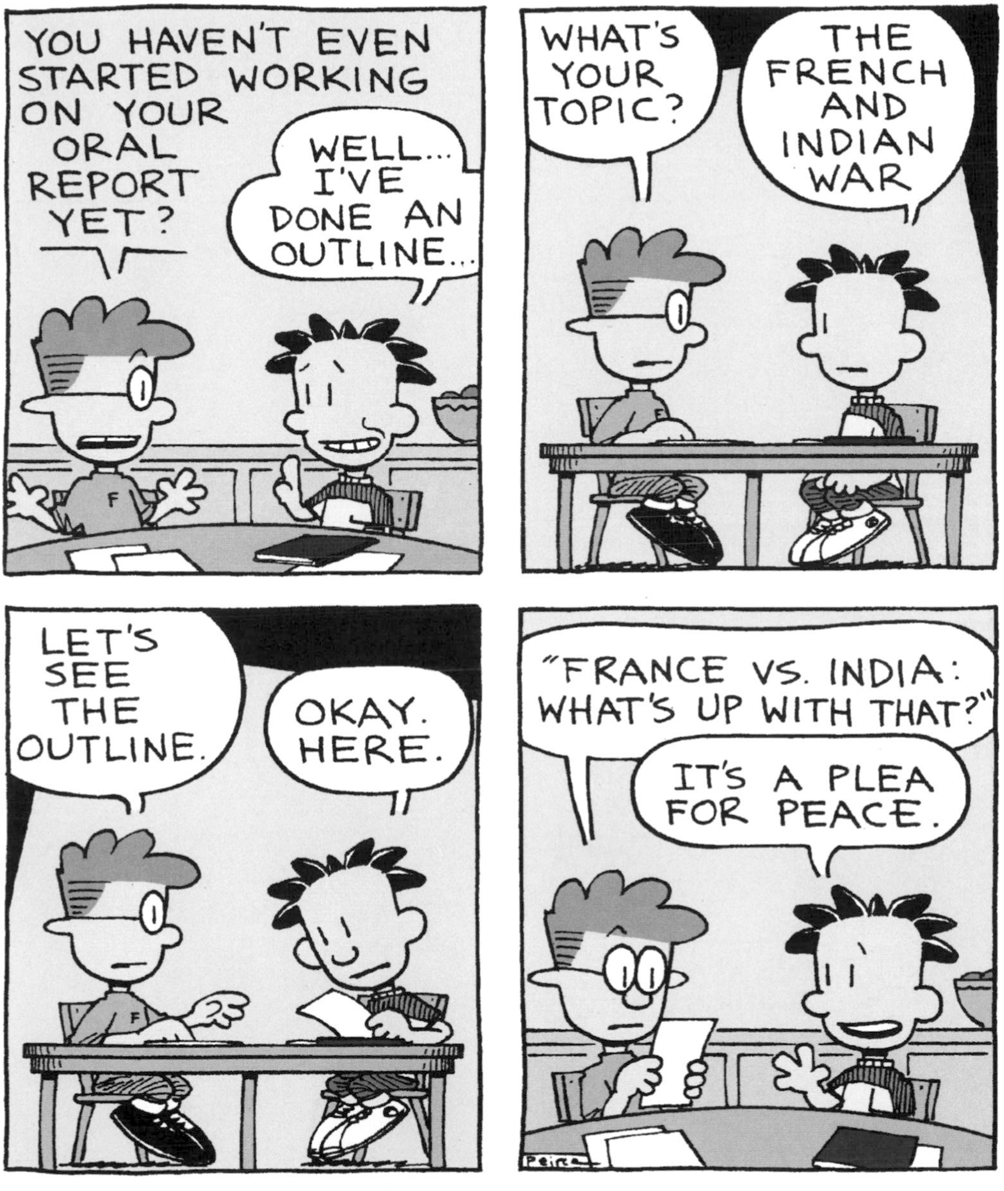

YOU HAVEN'T EVEN STARTED WORKING ON YOUR ORAL REPORT YET?
WELL... I'VE DONE AN OUTLINE...
WHAT'S YOUR TOPIC?
THE FRENCH AND INDIAN WAR
LET'S SEE THE OUTLINE.
OKAY. HERE.
"FRANCE VS. INDIA: WHAT'S UP WITH THAT?"
IT'S A PLEA FOR PEACE.
PEIRCE

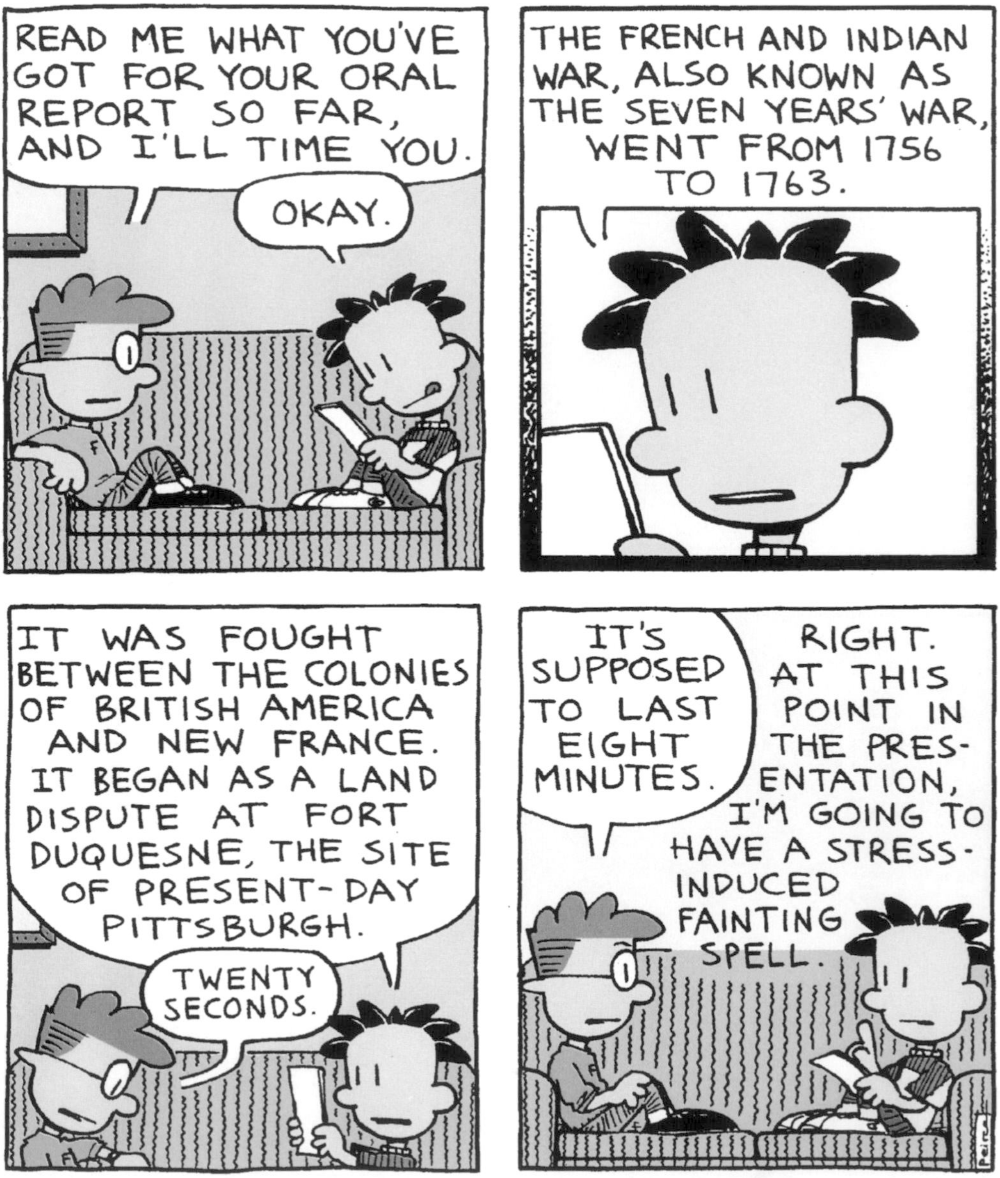
READ ME WHAT YOU'VE GOT FOR YOUR ORAL REPORT SO FAR, AND I'LL TIME YOU.
OKAY.
THE FRENCH AND INDIAN WAR, ALSO KNOWN AS THE SEVEN YEARS' WAR, WENT FROM 1756 TO 1763.
IT WAS FOUGHT BETWEEN THE COLONIES OF BRITISH AMERICA AND NEW FRANCE. IT BEGAN AS A LAND DISPUTE AT FORT DUQUESNE, THE SITE OF PRESENT-DAY PITTSBURGH.
TWENTY SECONDS.
IT'S SUPPOSED TO LAST EIGHT MINUTES.
RIGHT. AT THIS POINT IN THE PRESENTATION, I'M GOING TO HAVE A STRESS-INDUCED FAINTING SPELL.
Peirce

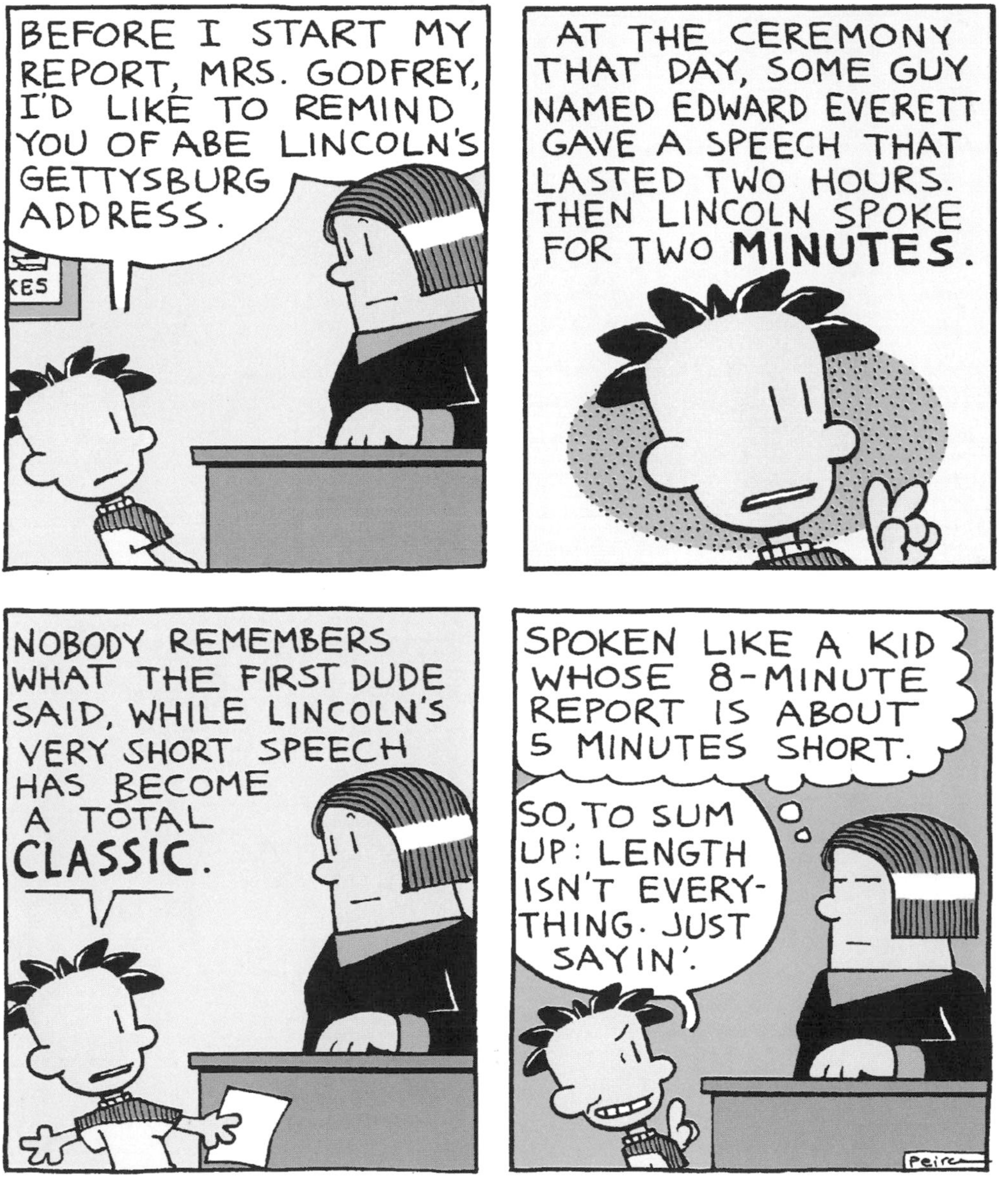
BEFORE I START MY REPORT, MRS. GODFREY, I'D LIKE TO REMIND YOU OF ABE LINCOLN'S GETTYSBURG ADDRESS.
KES
AT THE CEREMONY THAT DAY, SOME GUY NAMED EDWARD EVERETT GAVE A SPEECH THAT LASTED TWO HOURS. THEN LINCOLN SPOKE FOR TWO MINUTES.
NOBODY REMEMBERS WHAT THE FIRST DUDE SAID, WHILE LINCOLN'S VERY SHORT SPEECH HAS BECOME A TOTAL CLASSIC.
SPOKEN LIKE A KID WHOSE 8-MINUTE REPORT IS ABOUT 5 MINUTES SHORT.
SO, TO SUM UP: LENGTH ISN'T EVERYTHING. JUST SAYIN'.
Peirce

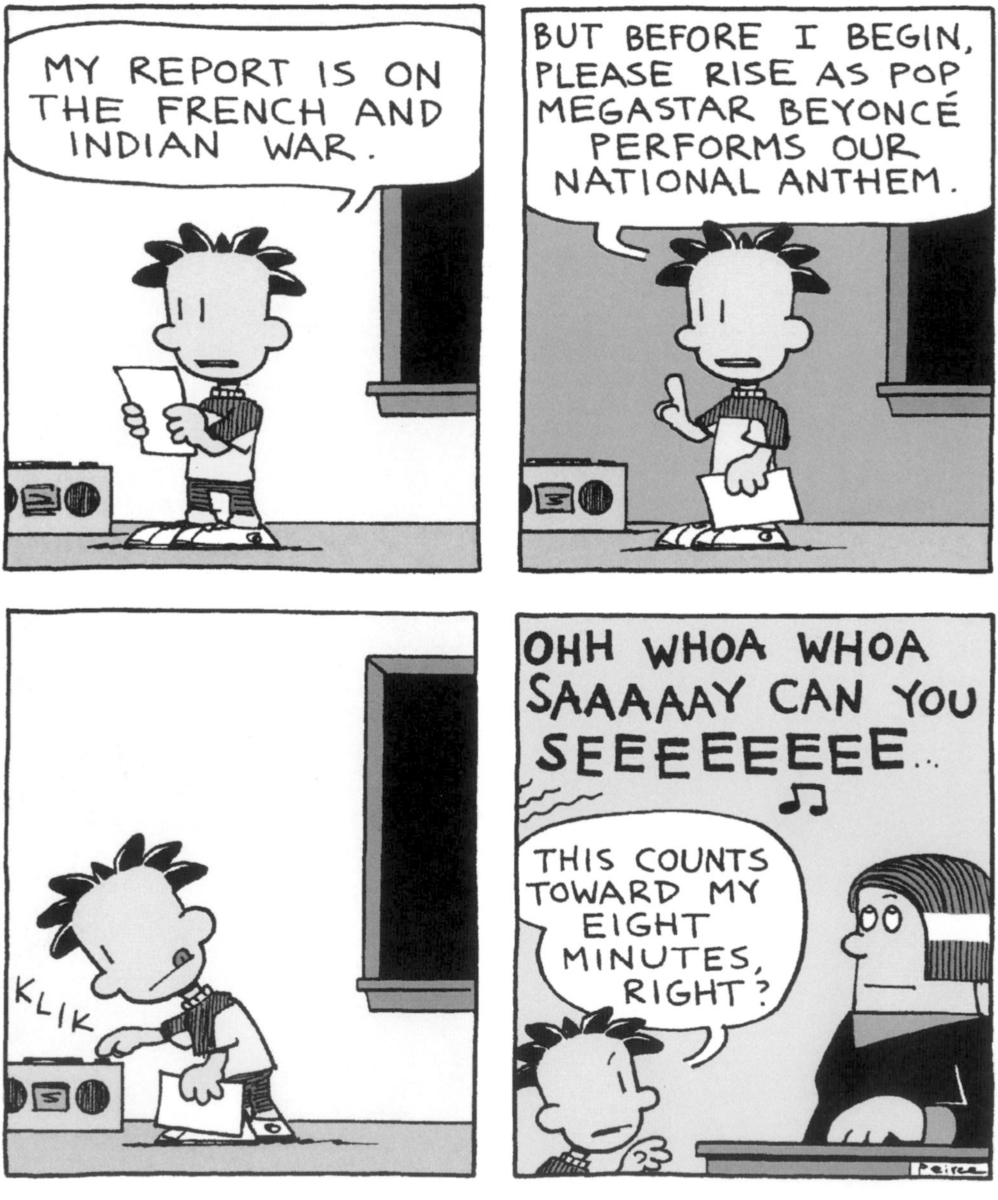
MY REPORT IS ON THE FRENCH AND INDIAN WAR.
BUT BEFORE I BEGIN, PLEASE RISE AS POP MEGASTAR BEYONCÉ PERFORMS OUR NATIONAL ANTHEM.
KLIK
OHH WHOA WHOA SAAAAAY CAN YOU SEEEEEEEE...
THIS COUNTS TOWARD MY EIGHT MINUTES, RIGHT?
Peirce

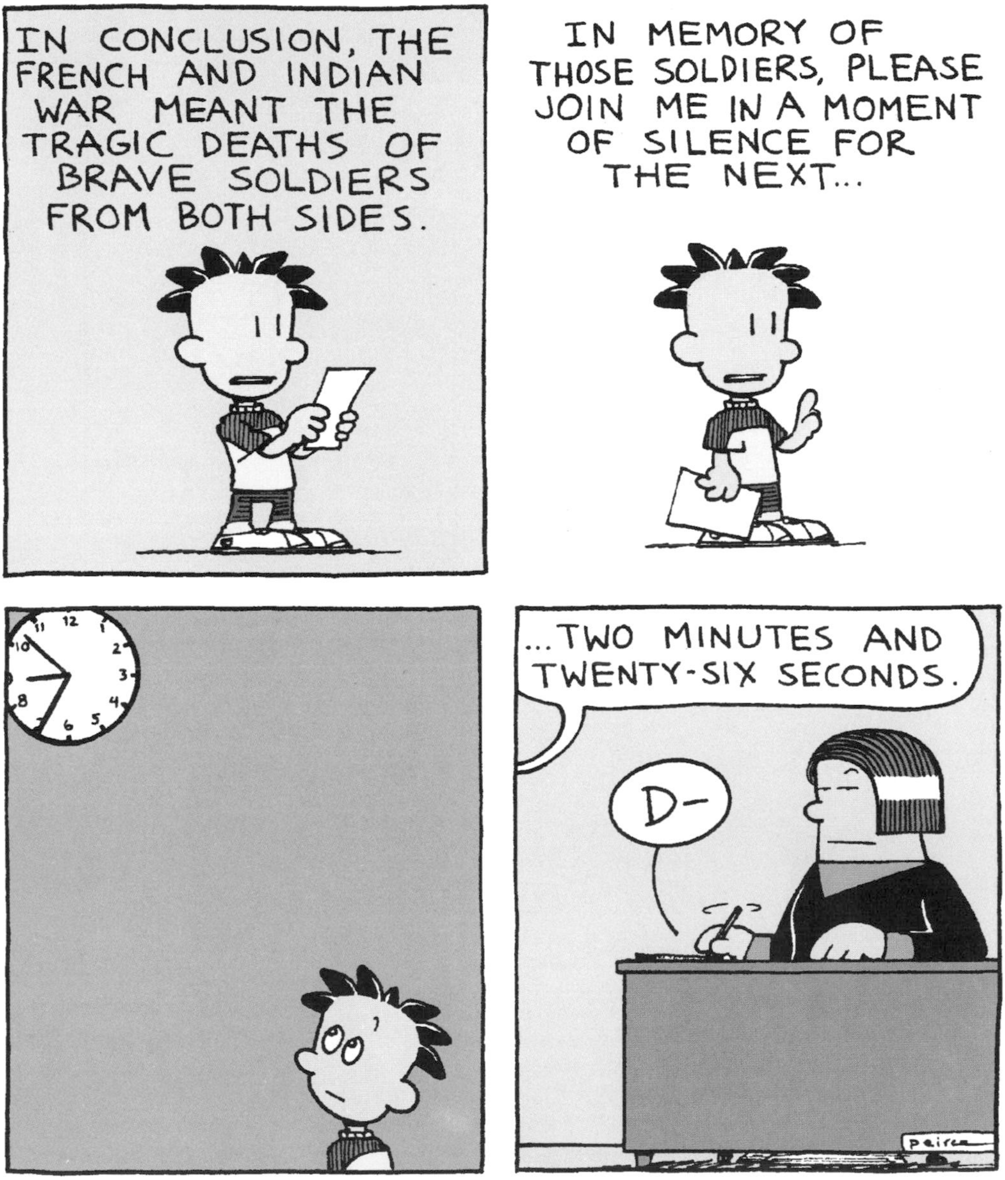

IN CONCLUSION, THE FRENCH AND INDIAN WAR MEANT THE TRAGIC DEATHS OF BRAVE SOLDIERS FROM BOTH SIDES.
IN MEMORY OF THOSE SOLDIERS, PLEASE JOIN ME IN A MOMENT OF SILENCE FOR THE NEXT...
...TWO MINUTES AND TWENTY-SIX SECONDS.
D-
peirce

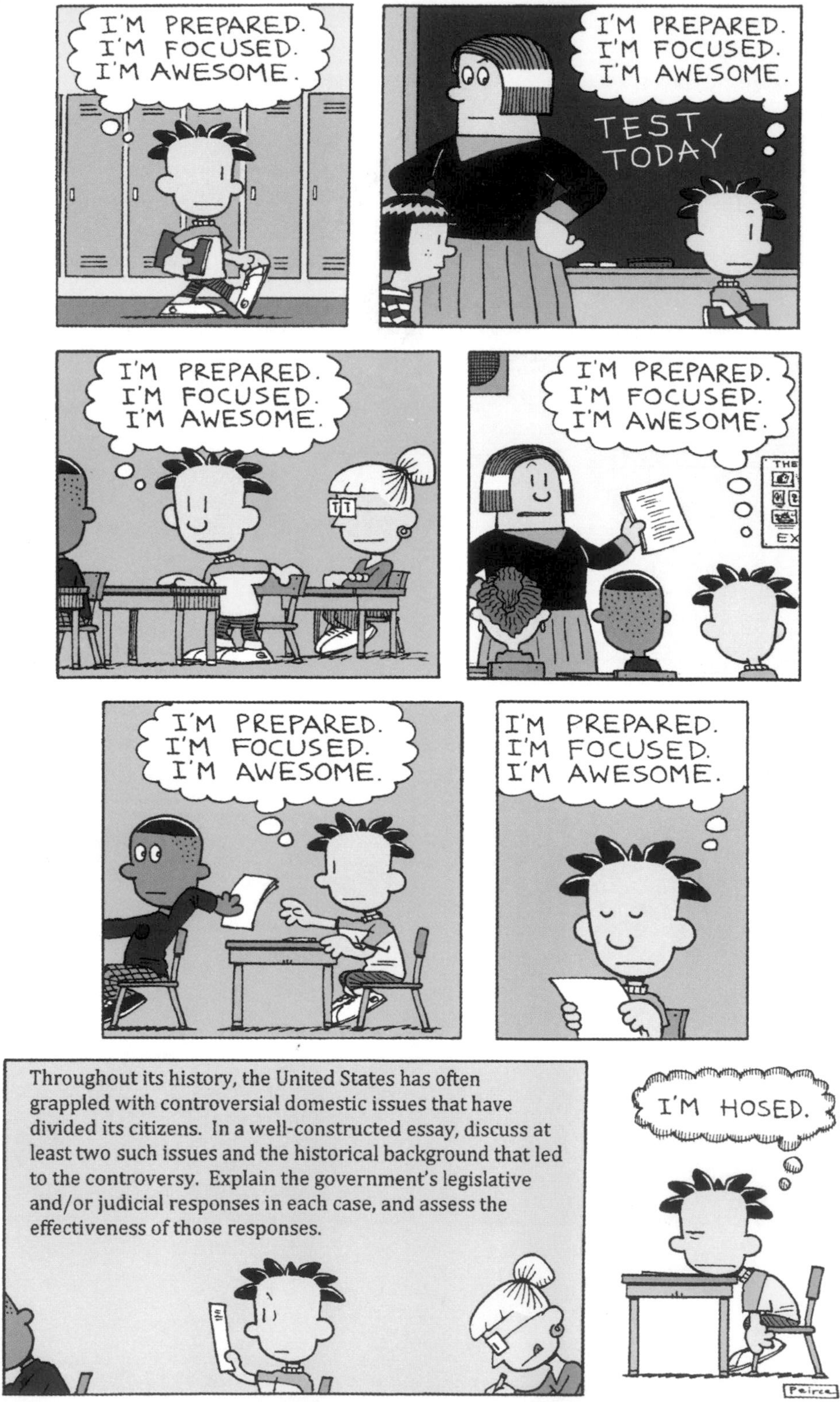
I'M PREPARED. I'M FOCUSED. I'M AWESOME.
I'M PREPARED. I'M FOCUSED. I'M AWESOME.
TEST TODAY
I'M PREPARED. I'M FOCUSED. I'M AWESOME.
I'M PREPARED. I'M FOCUSED. I'M AWESOME.
I'M PREPARED. I'M FOCUSED. I'M AWESOME.
I'M PREPARED. I'M FOCUSED. I'M AWESOME.
Throughout its history, the United States has often grappled with controversial domestic issues that have divided its citizens. In a well-constructed essay, discuss at least two such issues and the historical background that led to the controversy. Explain the government's legislative and/or judicial responses in each case, and assess the effectiveness of those responses.
I'M HOSED.
Peirce

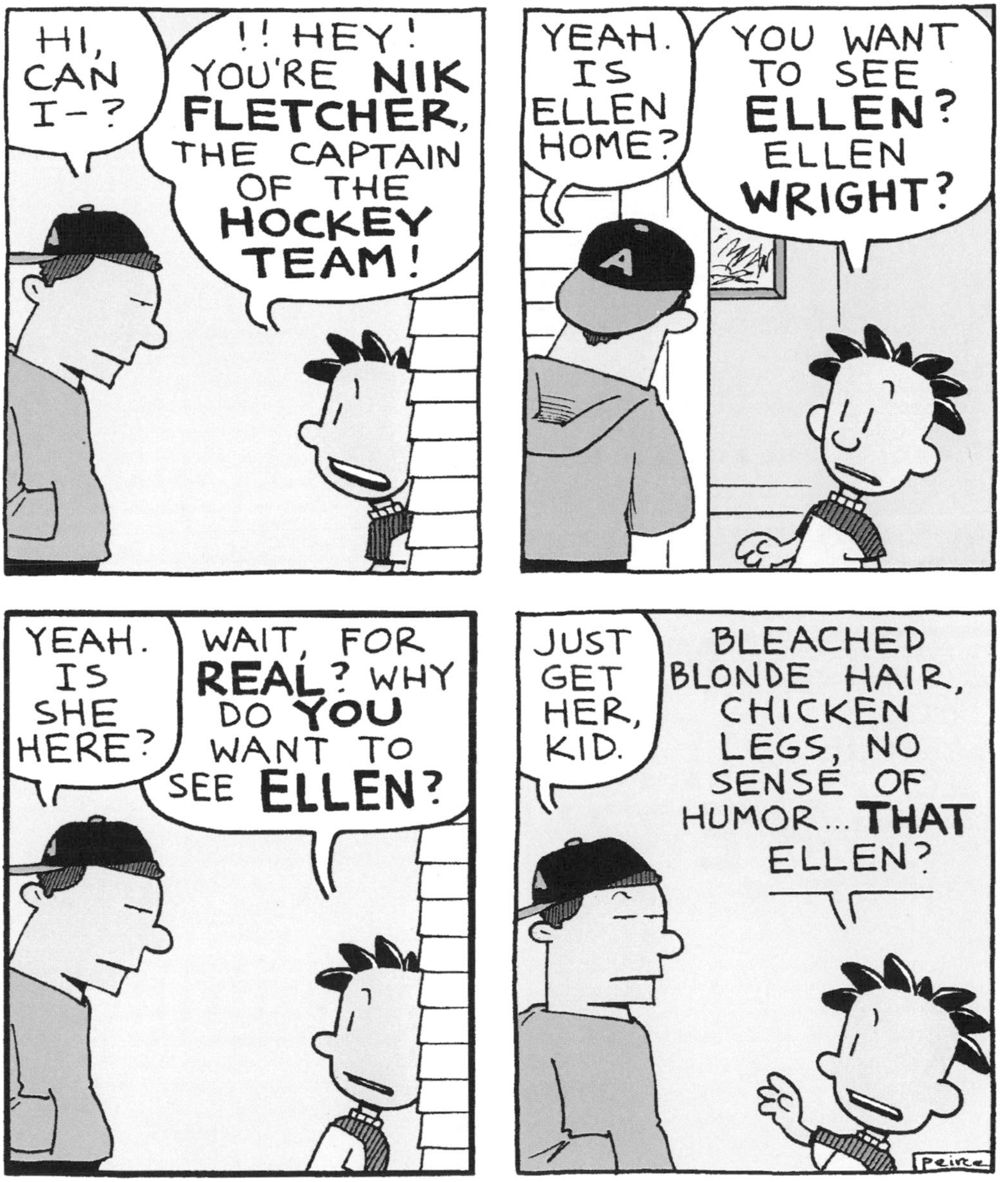
HI, CAN I-?
!! HEY! YOU'RE NIK FLETCHER, THE CAPTAIN OF THE HOCKEY TEAM!
YEAH. IS ELLEN HOME?
YOU WANT TO SEE ELLEN? ELLEN WRIGHT?
YEAH. IS SHE HERE?
WAIT, FOR REAL? WHY DO YOU WANT TO SEE ELLEN?
JUST GET HER, KID.
BLEACHED BLONDE HAIR, CHICKEN LEGS, NO SENSE OF HUMOR... THAT ELLEN?
Peirce

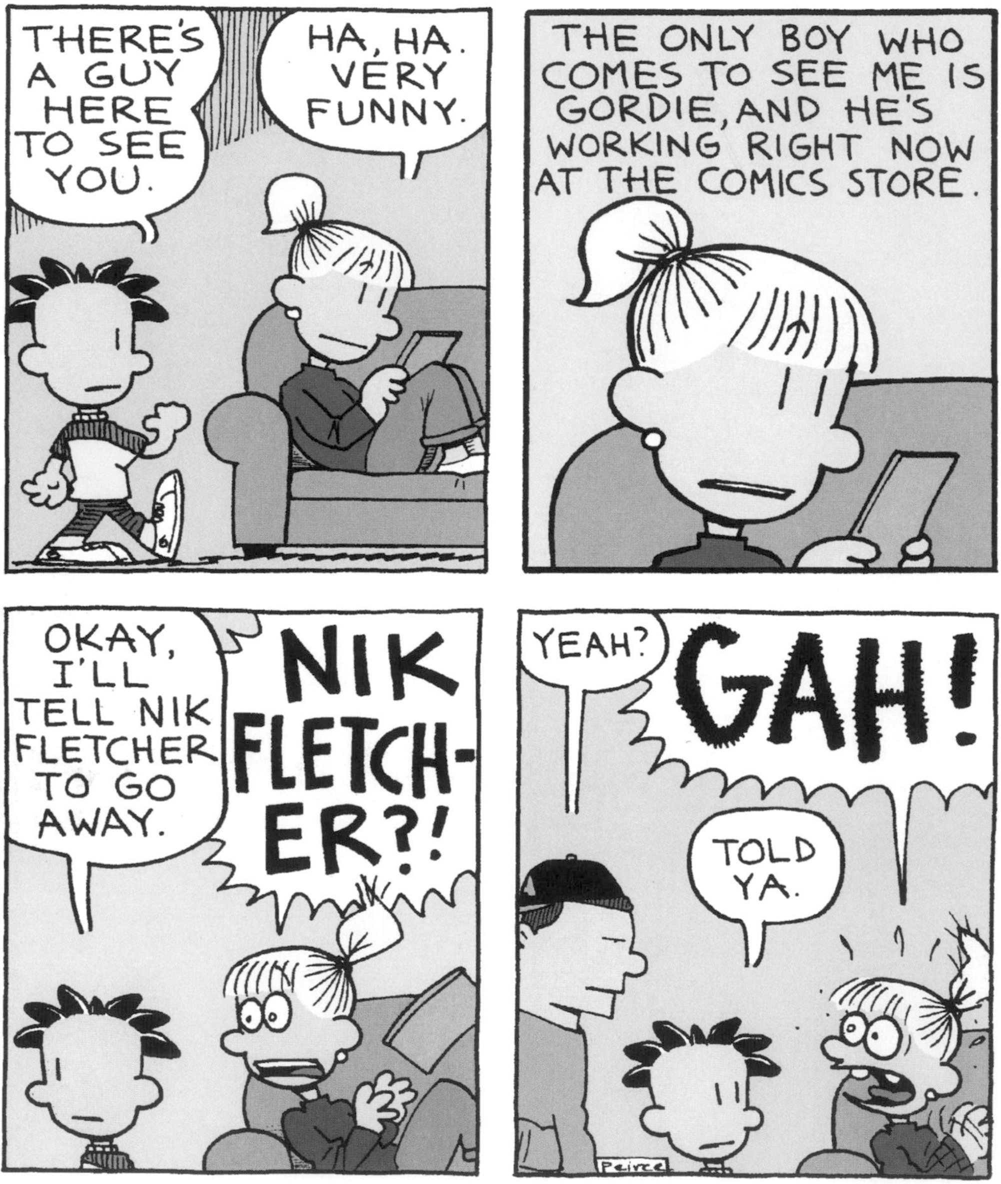
THERE'S A GUY HERE TO SEE YOU.
HA, HA. VERY FUNNY.
THE ONLY BOY WHO COMES TO SEE ME IS GORDIE, AND HE'S WORKING RIGHT NOW AT THE COMICS STORE.
OKAY, I'LL TELL NIK FLETCHER TO GO AWAY.
NIK FLETCH-ER?!
YEAH?
GAH!
TOLD YA.
Peirce

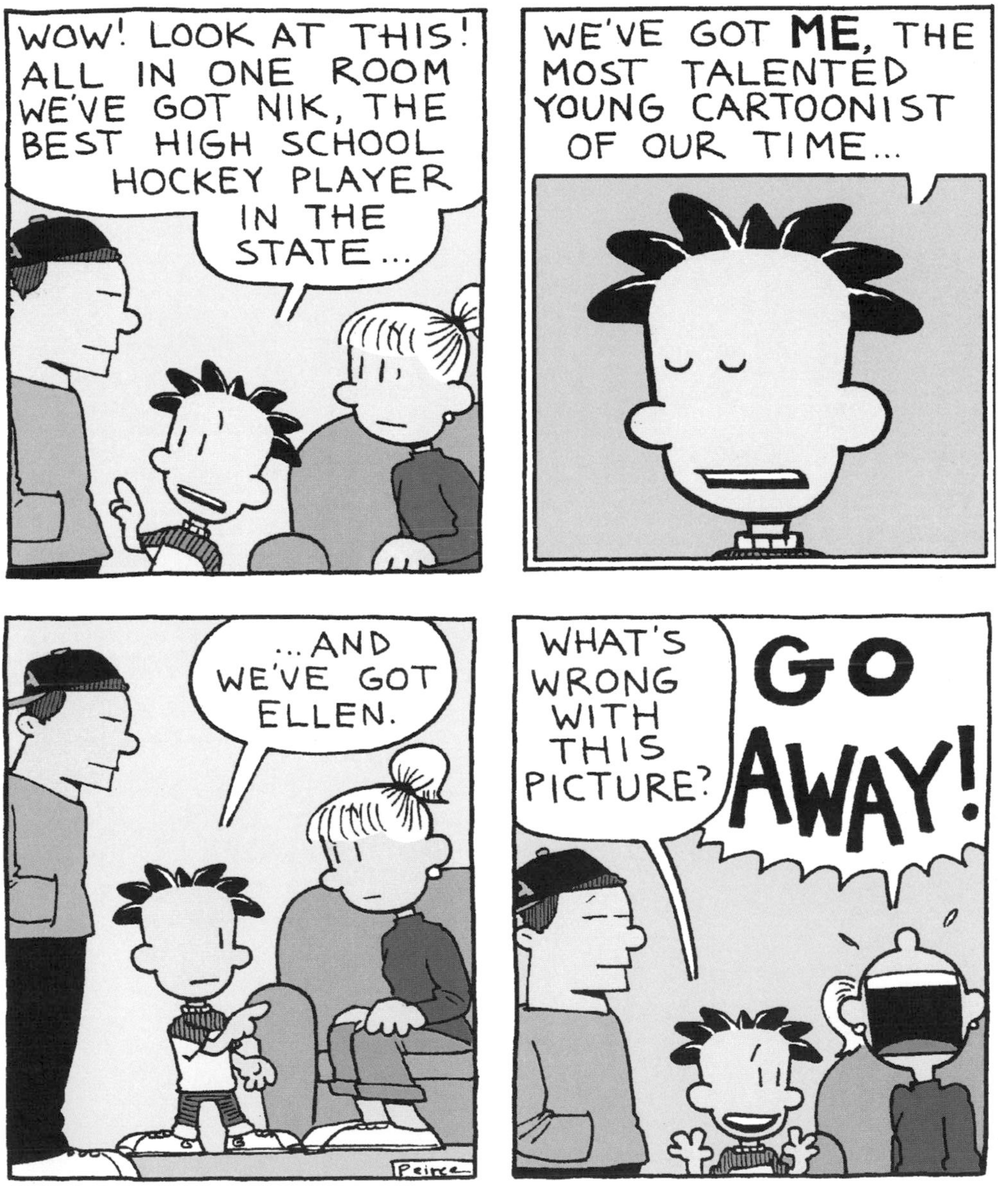
WOW! LOOK AT THIS! ALL IN ONE ROOM WE'VE GOT NIK, THE BEST HIGH SCHOOL HOCKEY PLAYER IN THE STATE...
WE'VE GOT **ME**, THE MOST TALENTED YOUNG CARTOONIST OF OUR TIME...
...AND WE'VE GOT ELLEN.
Peirce
WHAT'S WRONG WITH THIS PICTURE?
GO AWAY!

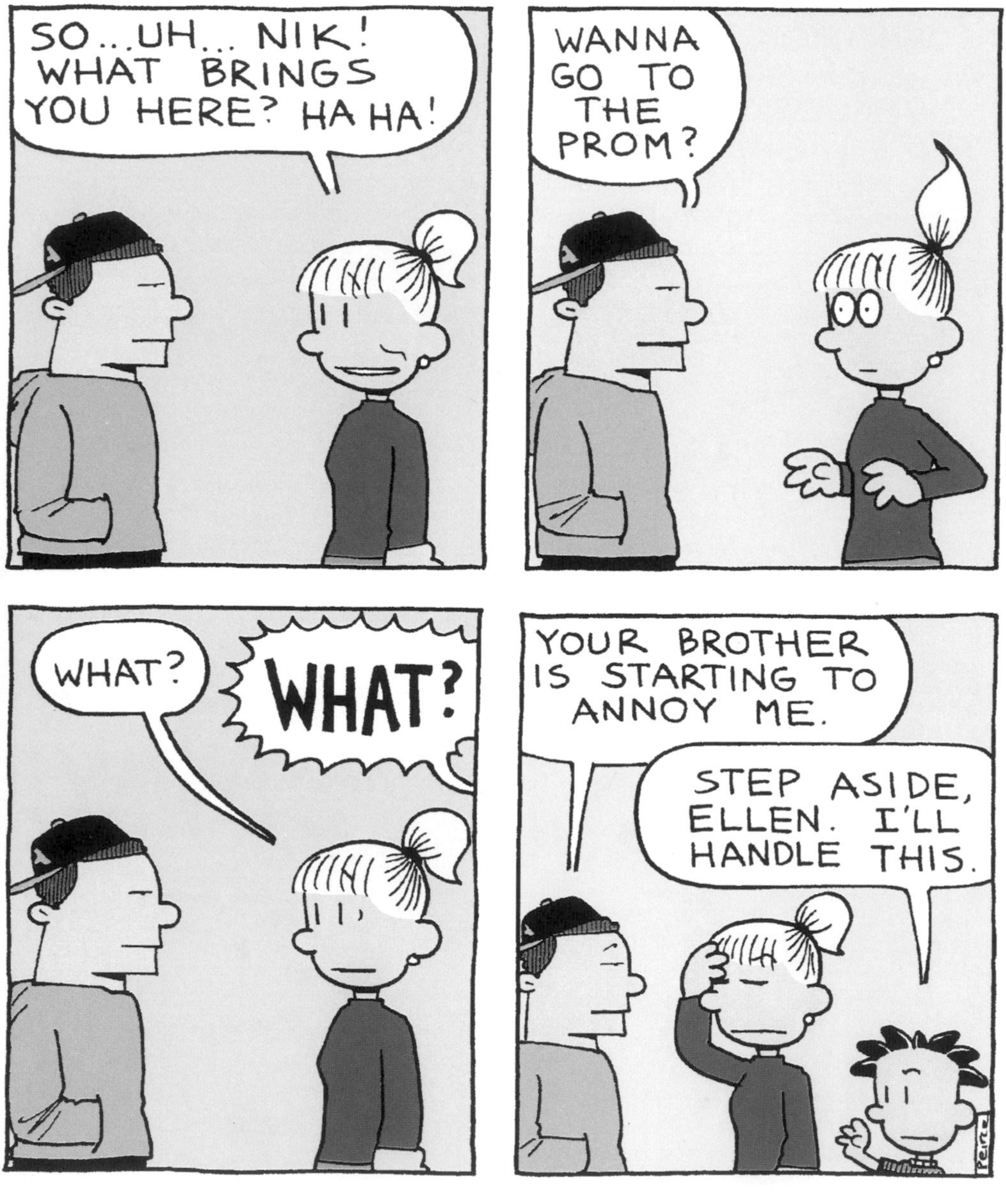
SO...UH... NIK! WHAT BRINGS YOU HERE? HA HA!
WANNA GO TO THE PROM?
WHAT?
WHAT?
YOUR BROTHER IS STARTING TO ANNOY ME.
STEP ASIDE, ELLEN. I'LL HANDLE THIS.
PEIRCE

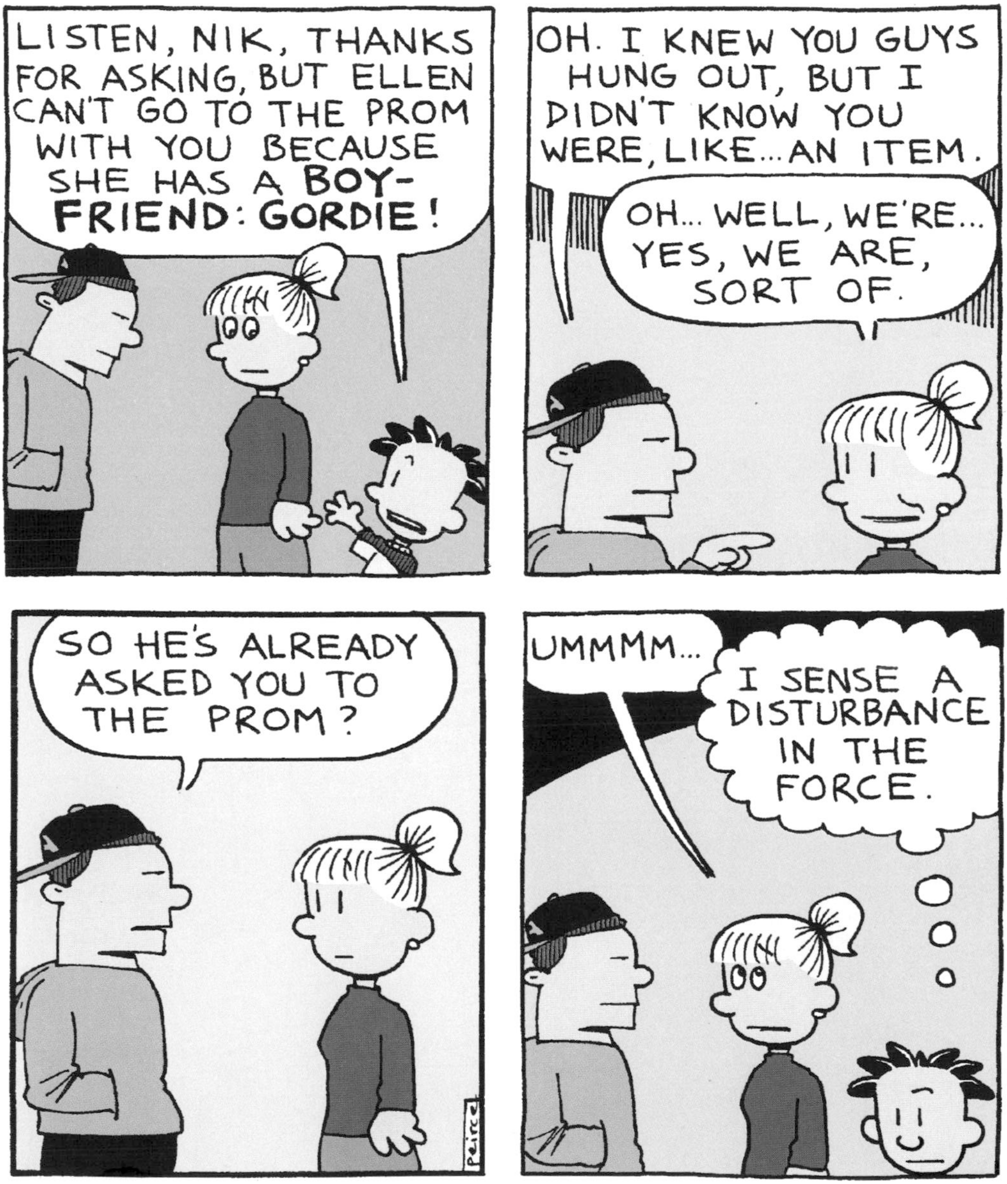
LISTEN, NIK, THANKS FOR ASKING, BUT ELLEN CAN'T GO TO THE PROM WITH YOU BECAUSE SHE HAS A **BOY-FRIEND: GORDIE**!
OH. I KNEW YOU GUYS HUNG OUT, BUT I DIDN'T KNOW YOU WERE, LIKE... AN ITEM.
OH... WELL, WE'RE... YES, WE ARE, SORT OF.
SO HE'S ALREADY ASKED YOU TO THE PROM?
peirce
UMMMM...
I SENSE A DISTURBANCE IN THE FORCE.

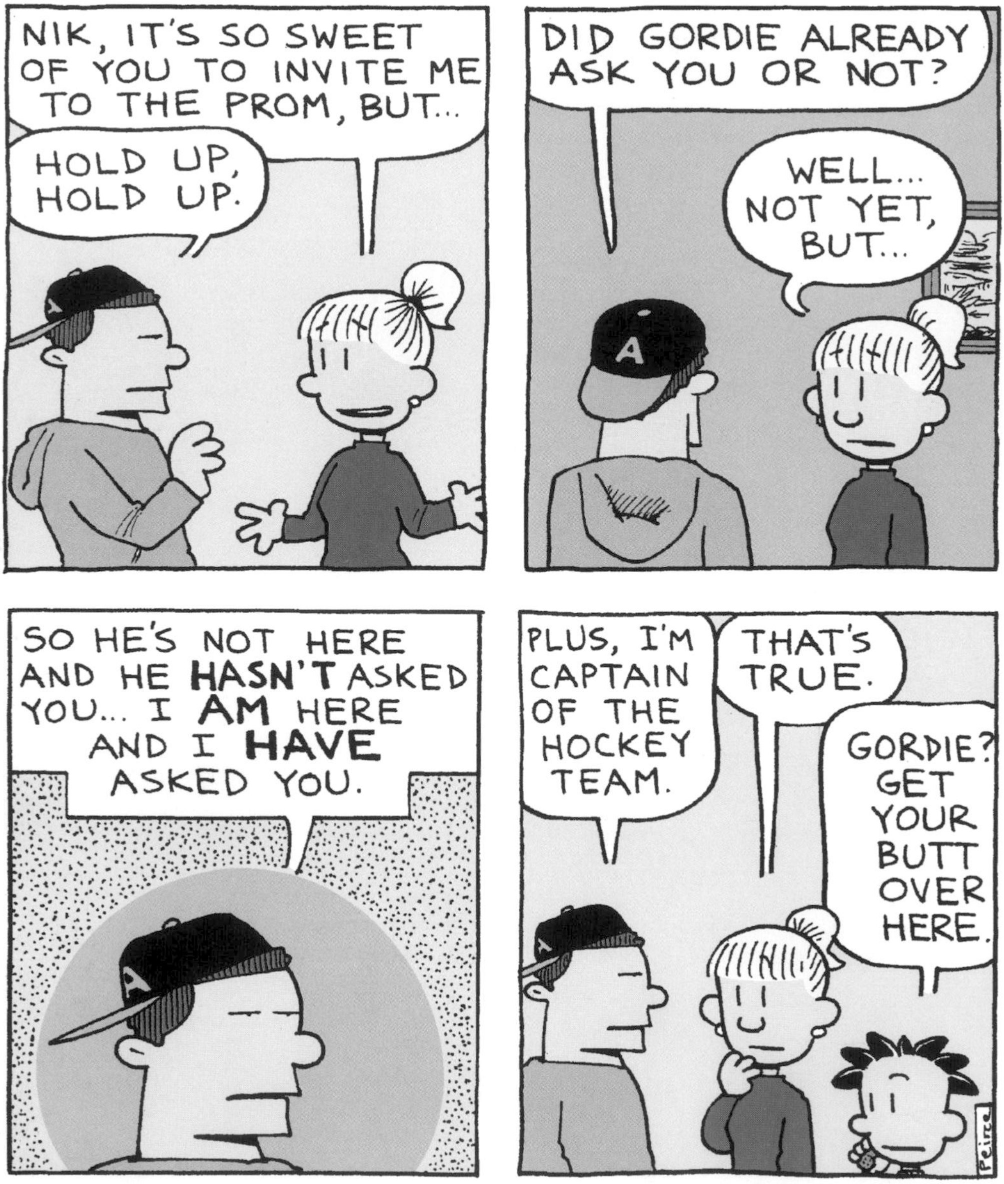
NIK, IT'S SO SWEET OF YOU TO INVITE ME TO THE PROM, BUT...
HOLD UP, HOLD UP.
DID GORDIE ALREADY ASK YOU OR NOT?
WELL... NOT YET, BUT...
SO HE'S NOT HERE AND HE **HASN'T** ASKED YOU... I **AM** HERE AND I **HAVE** ASKED YOU.
PLUS, I'M CAPTAIN OF THE HOCKEY TEAM.
THAT'S TRUE.
GORDIE? GET YOUR BUTT OVER HERE.
Peirce

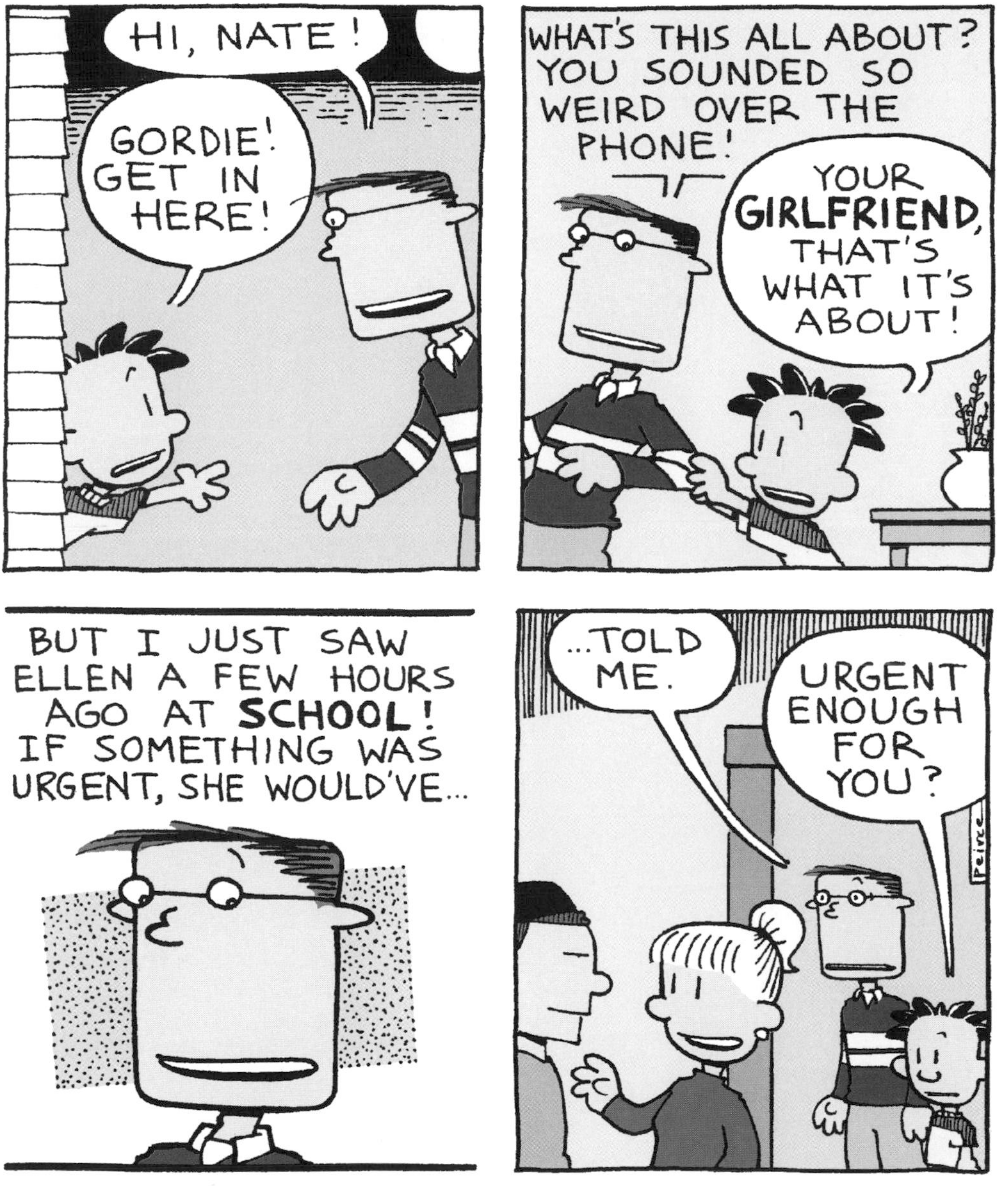
HI, NATE!
GORDIE! GET IN HERE!
WHAT'S THIS ALL ABOUT? YOU SOUNDED SO WEIRD OVER THE PHONE!
YOUR **GIRLFRIEND**, THAT'S WHAT IT'S ABOUT!
BUT I JUST SAW ELLEN A FEW HOURS AGO AT **SCHOOL**! IF SOMETHING WAS URGENT, SHE WOULD'VE...
...TOLD ME.
URGENT ENOUGH FOR YOU?
Peirce

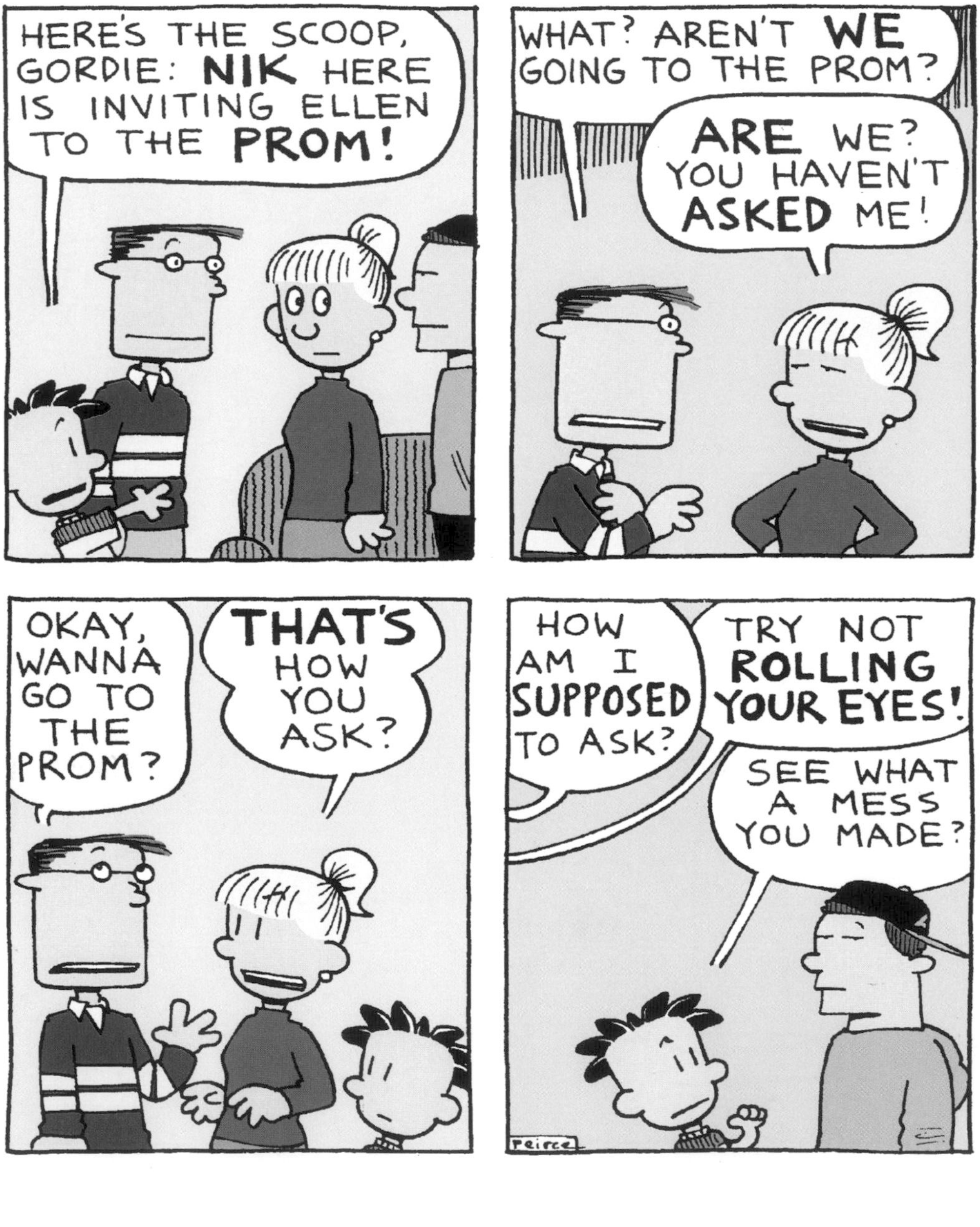
HERE'S THE SCOOP, GORDIE: NIK HERE IS INVITING ELLEN TO THE PROM!
WHAT? AREN'T WE GOING TO THE PROM?
ARE WE? YOU HAVEN'T ASKED ME!
OKAY, WANNA GO TO THE PROM?
THAT'S HOW YOU ASK?
HOW AM I SUPPOSED TO ASK?
TRY NOT ROLLING YOUR EYES!
SEE WHAT A MESS YOU MADE?
Peirce

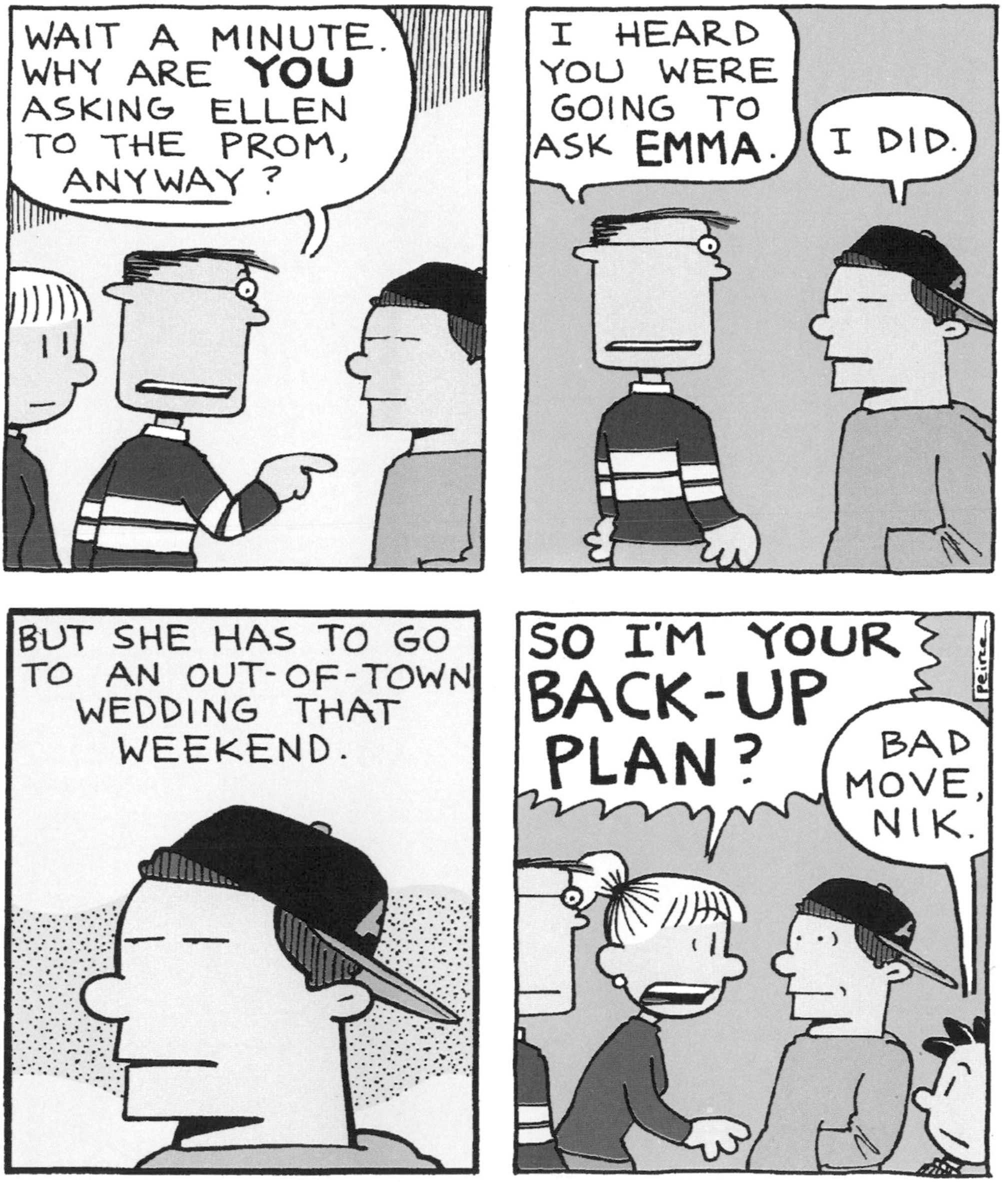
WAIT A MINUTE. WHY ARE **YOU** ASKING ELLEN TO THE PROM, ANYWAY?
I HEARD YOU WERE GOING TO ASK **EMMA**.
I DID.
BUT SHE HAS TO GO TO AN OUT-OF-TOWN WEDDING THAT WEEKEND.
SO I'M YOUR **BACK-UP PLAN?**
BAD MOVE, NIK.
Peirce

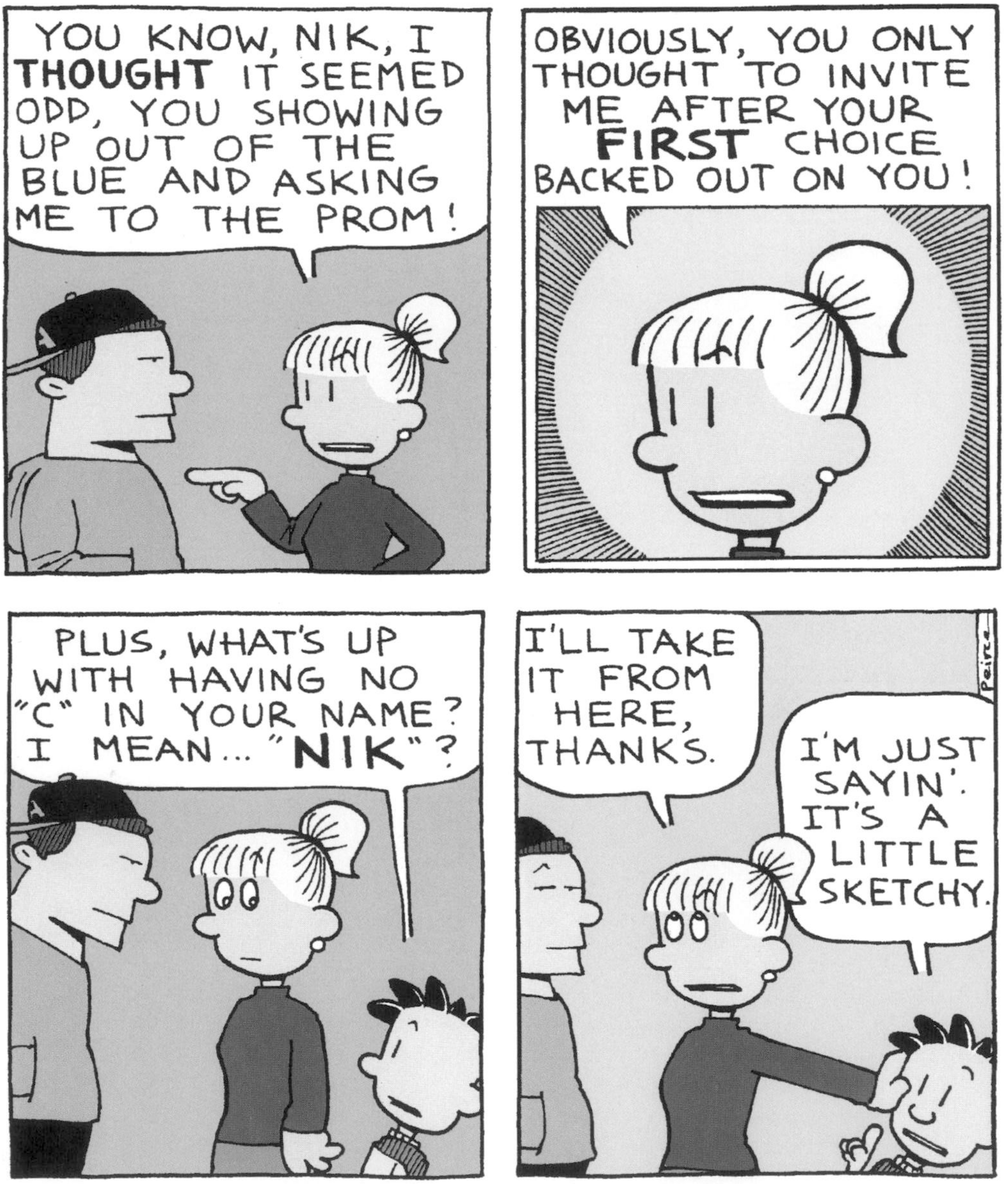
YOU KNOW, NIK, I THOUGHT IT SEEMED ODD, YOU SHOWING UP OUT OF THE BLUE AND ASKING ME TO THE PROM!
OBVIOUSLY, YOU ONLY THOUGHT TO INVITE ME AFTER YOUR FIRST CHOICE BACKED OUT ON YOU!
PLUS, WHAT'S UP WITH HAVING NO "C" IN YOUR NAME? I MEAN... "NIK"?
I'LL TAKE IT FROM HERE, THANKS.
I'M JUST SAYIN'. IT'S A LITTLE SKETCHY.
Peirce

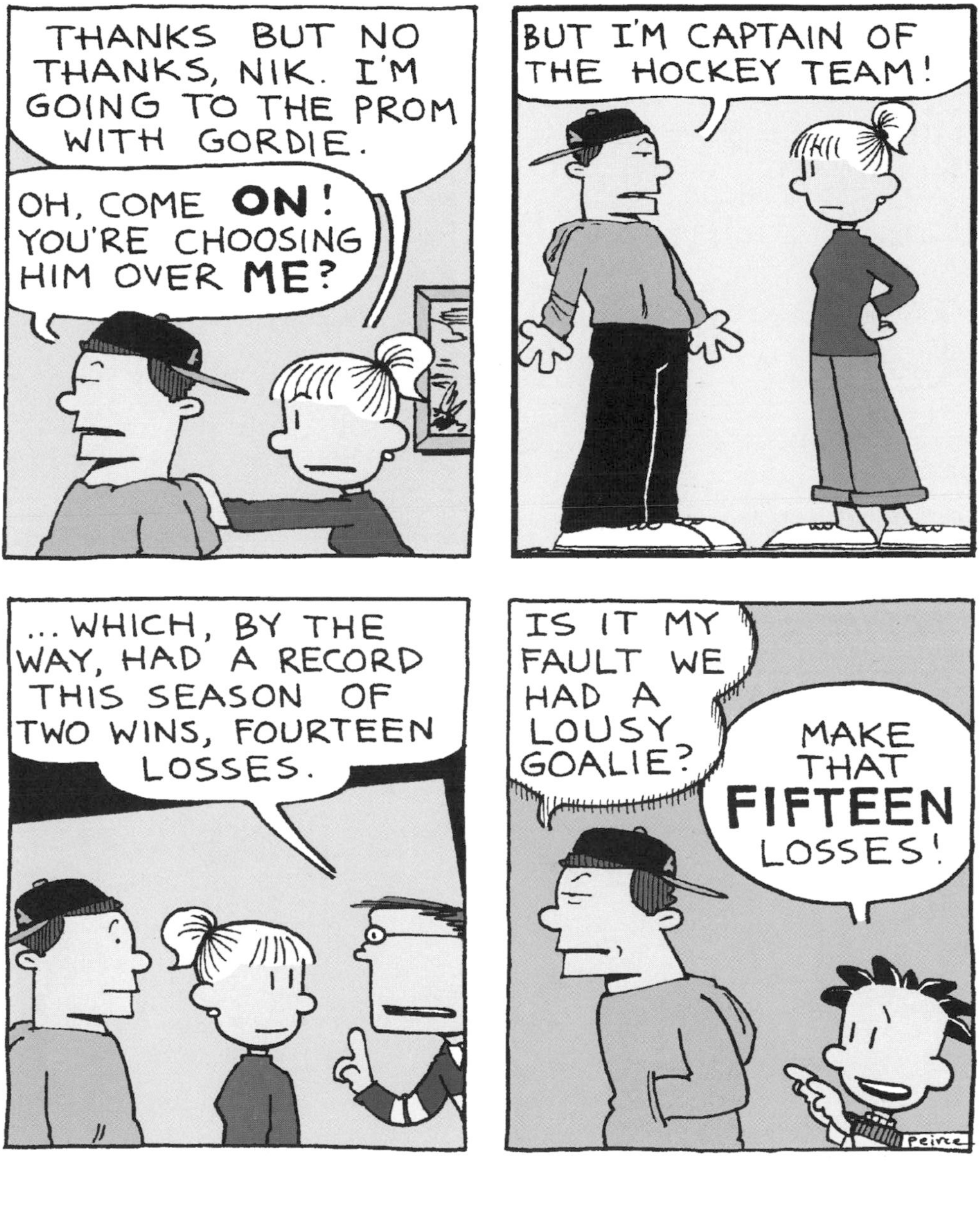
THANKS BUT NO THANKS, NIK. I'M GOING TO THE PROM WITH GORDIE.
OH, COME **ON**! YOU'RE CHOOSING HIM OVER **ME**?
BUT I'M CAPTAIN OF THE HOCKEY TEAM!
...WHICH, BY THE WAY, HAD A RECORD THIS SEASON OF TWO WINS, FOURTEEN LOSSES.
IS IT MY FAULT WE HAD A LOUSY GOALIE?
MAKE THAT **FIFTEEN** LOSSES!
peirce

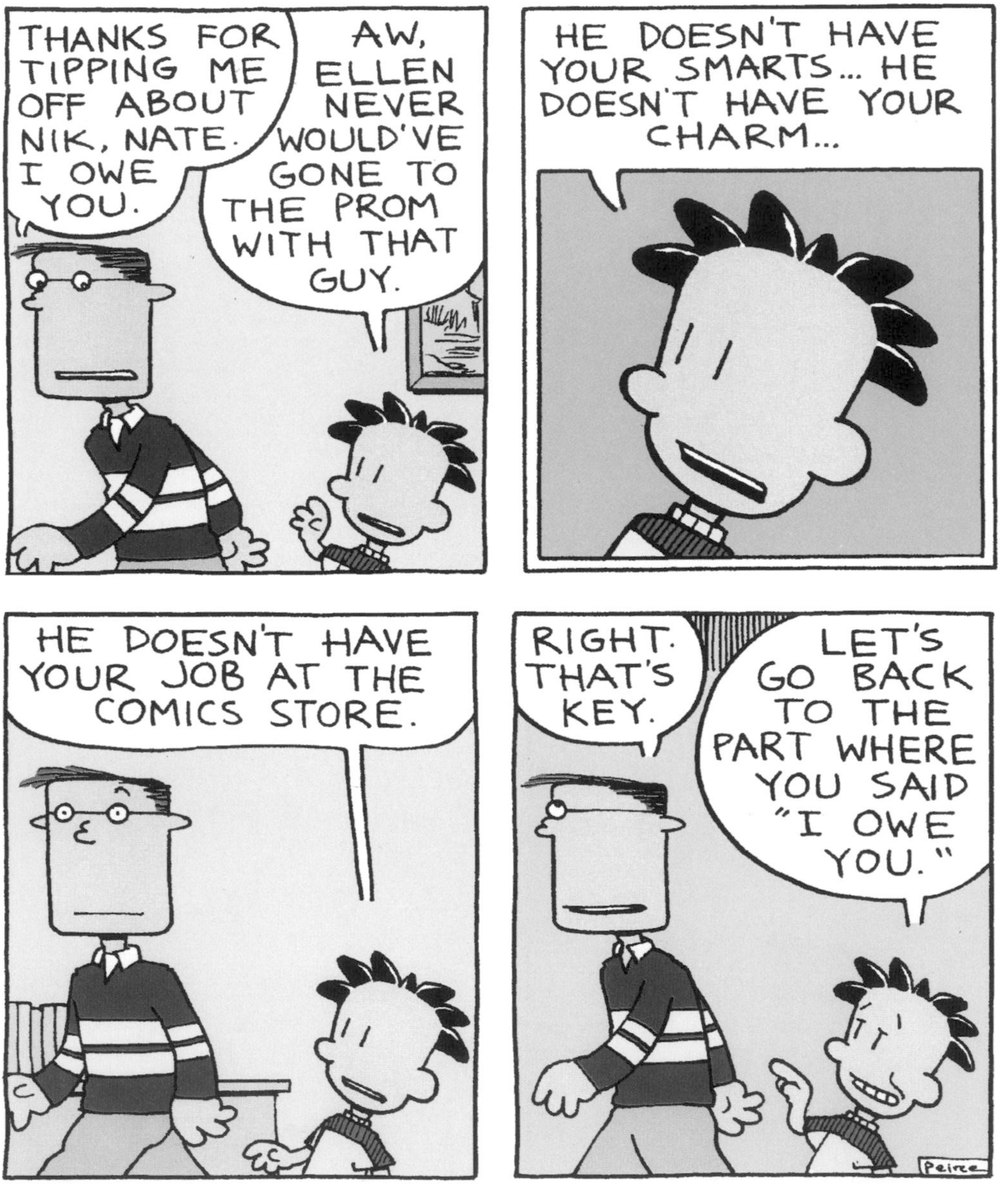
THANKS FOR TIPPING ME OFF ABOUT NIK, NATE. I OWE YOU.
AW, ELLEN NEVER WOULD'VE GONE TO THE PROM WITH THAT GUY.
HE DOESN'T HAVE YOUR SMARTS... HE DOESN'T HAVE YOUR CHARM...
HE DOESN'T HAVE YOUR JOB AT THE COMICS STORE.
RIGHT. THAT'S KEY.
LET'S GO BACK TO THE PART WHERE YOU SAID "I OWE YOU."
Peirce

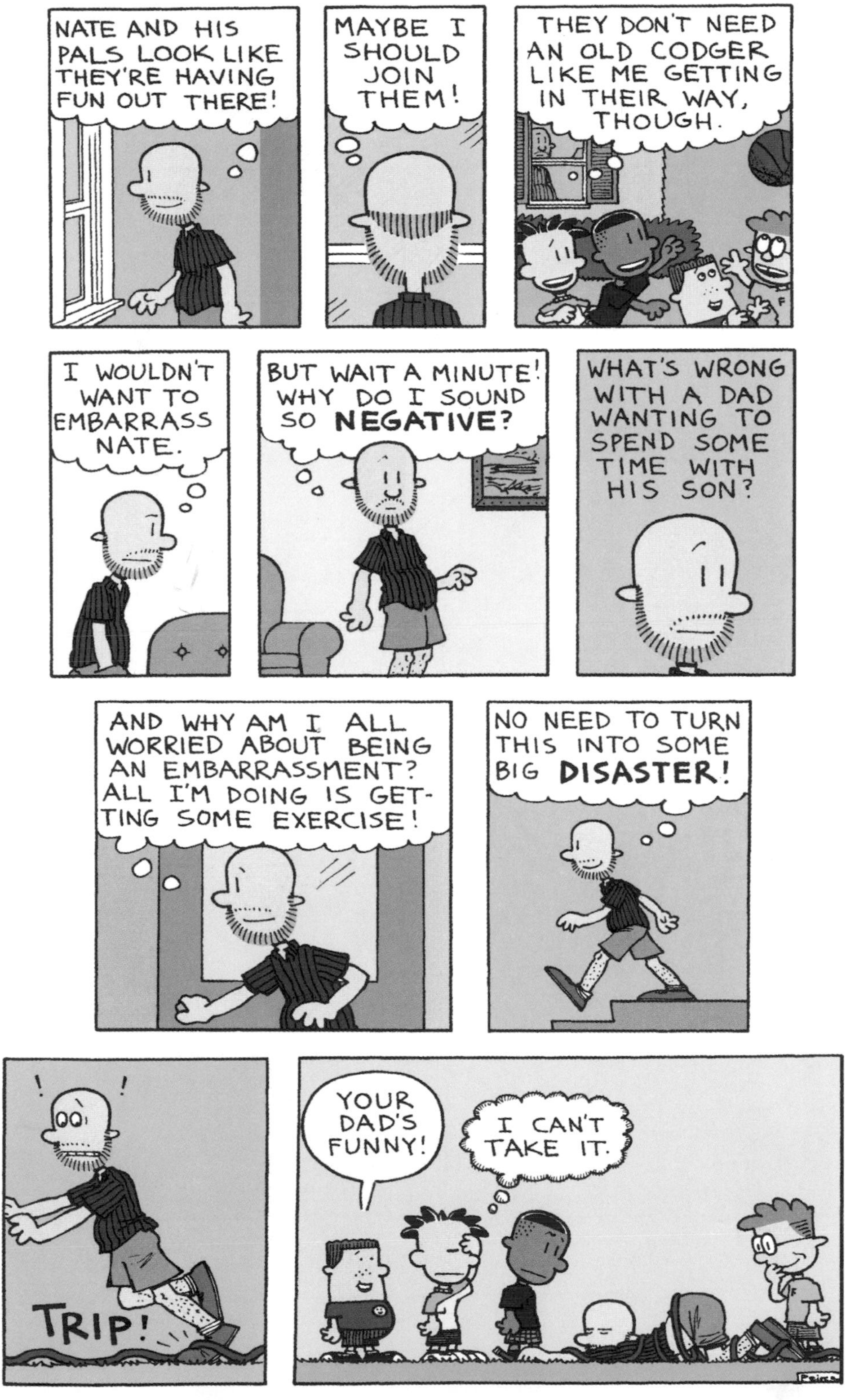
NATE AND HIS PALS LOOK LIKE THEY'RE HAVING FUN OUT THERE!
MAYBE I SHOULD JOIN THEM!
THEY DON'T NEED AN OLD CODGER LIKE ME GETTING IN THEIR WAY, THOUGH.
I WOULDN'T WANT TO EMBARRASS NATE.
BUT WAIT A MINUTE! WHY DO I SOUND SO **NEGATIVE**?
WHAT'S WRONG WITH A DAD WANTING TO SPEND SOME TIME WITH HIS SON?
AND WHY AM I ALL WORRIED ABOUT BEING AN EMBARRASSMENT? ALL I'M DOING IS GETTING SOME EXERCISE!
NO NEED TO TURN THIS INTO SOME BIG **DISASTER**!
! !
TRIP!
YOUR DAD'S FUNNY!
I CAN'T TAKE IT.

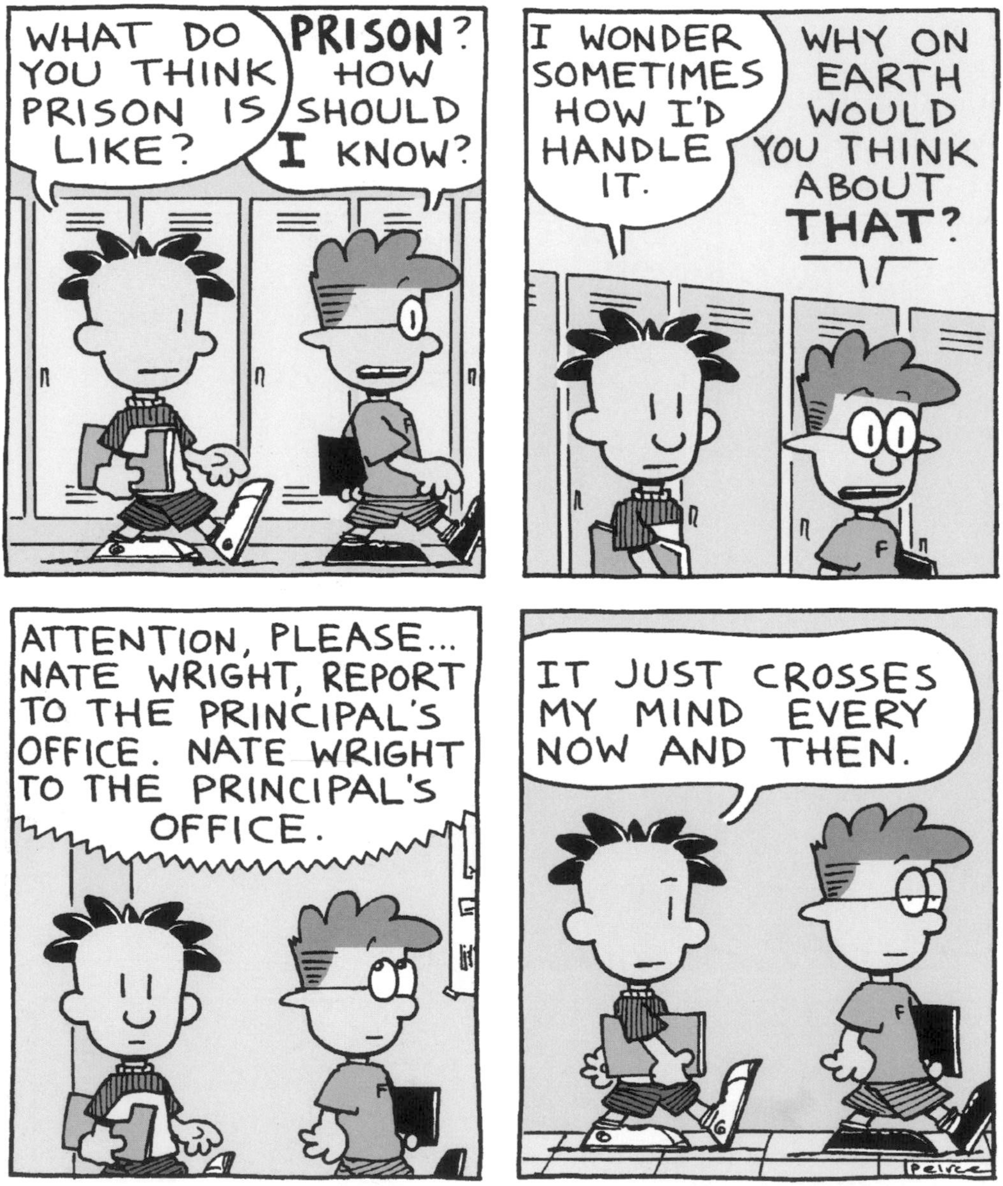
WHAT DO YOU THINK PRISON IS LIKE?
PRISON? HOW SHOULD I KNOW?
I WONDER SOMETIMES HOW I'D HANDLE IT.
WHY ON EARTH WOULD YOU THINK ABOUT THAT?
ATTENTION, PLEASE... NATE WRIGHT, REPORT TO THE PRINCIPAL'S OFFICE. NATE WRIGHT TO THE PRINCIPAL'S OFFICE.
IT JUST CROSSES MY MIND EVERY NOW AND THEN.
Peirce

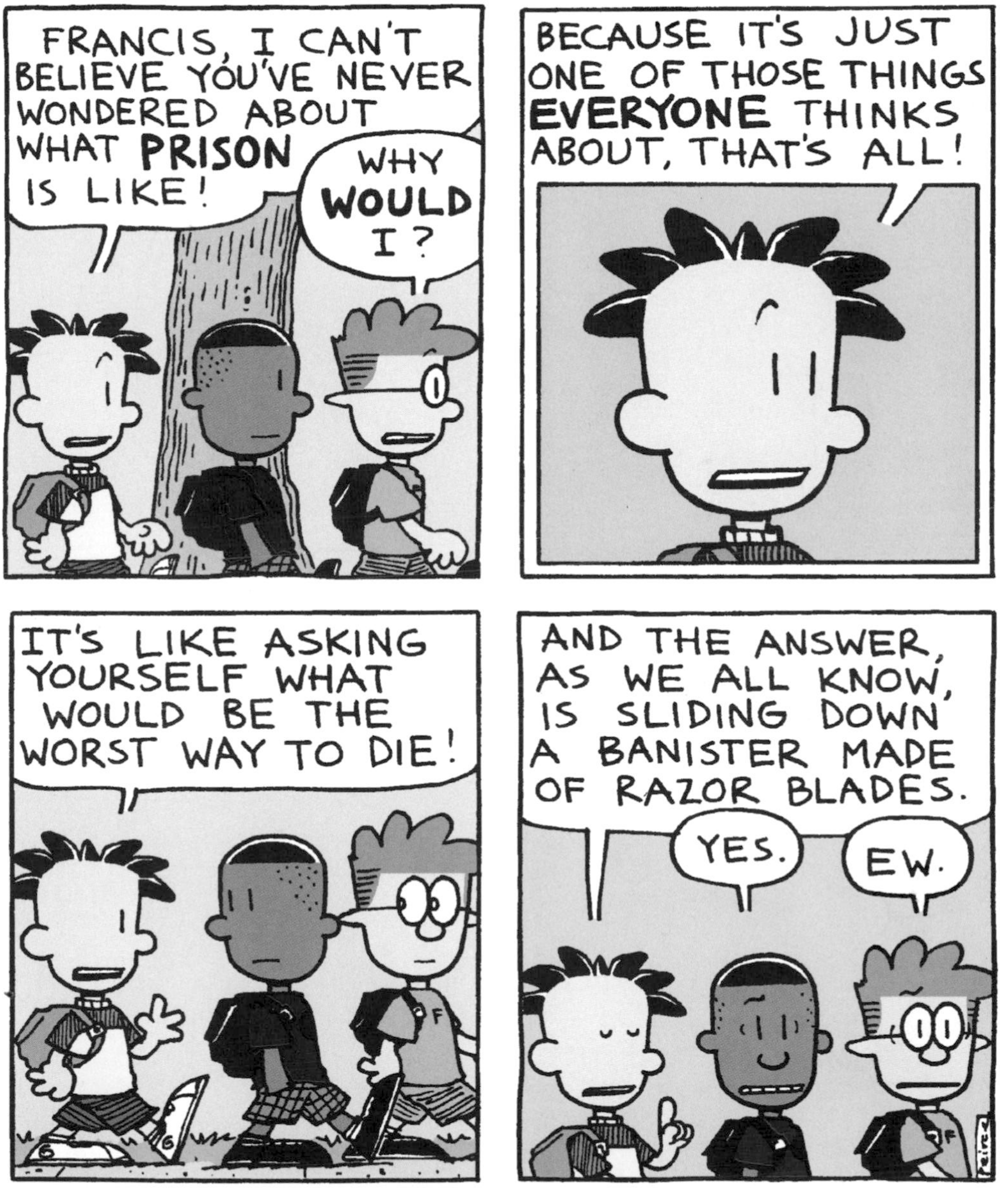
FRANCIS, I CAN'T BELIEVE YOU'VE NEVER WONDERED ABOUT WHAT **PRISON** IS LIKE!
WHY **WOULD** I?
BECAUSE IT'S JUST ONE OF THOSE THINGS **EVERYONE** THINKS ABOUT, THAT'S ALL!
IT'S LIKE ASKING YOURSELF WHAT WOULD BE THE WORST WAY TO DIE!
AND THE ANSWER, AS WE ALL KNOW, IS SLIDING DOWN A BANISTER MADE OF RAZOR BLADES.
YES.
EW.

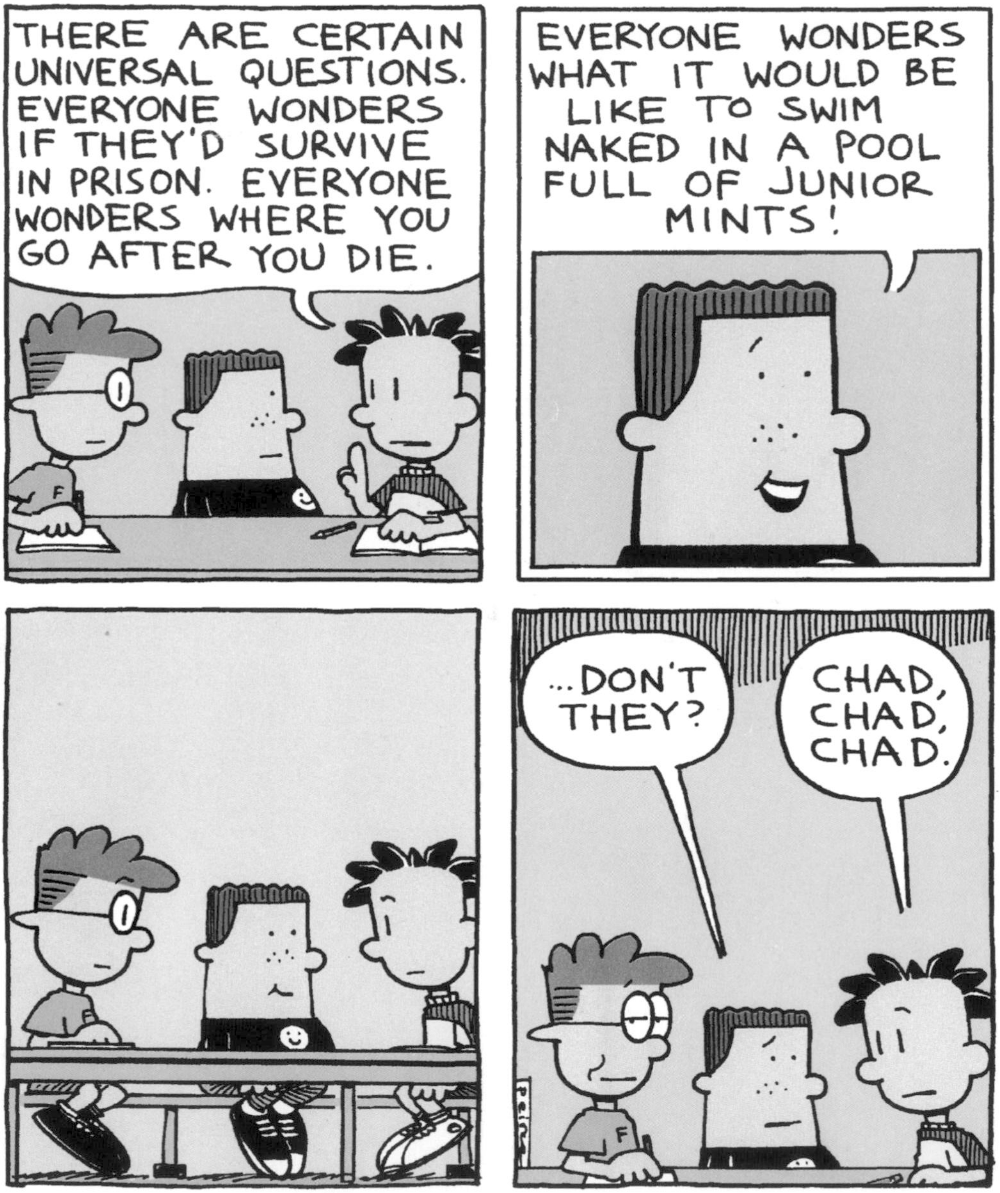
THERE ARE CERTAIN UNIVERSAL QUESTIONS. EVERYONE WONDERS IF THEY'D SURVIVE IN PRISON. EVERYONE WONDERS WHERE YOU GO AFTER YOU DIE.
EVERYONE WONDERS WHAT IT WOULD BE LIKE TO SWIM NAKED IN A POOL FULL OF JUNIOR MINTS!
...DON'T THEY?
CHAD, CHAD, CHAD.

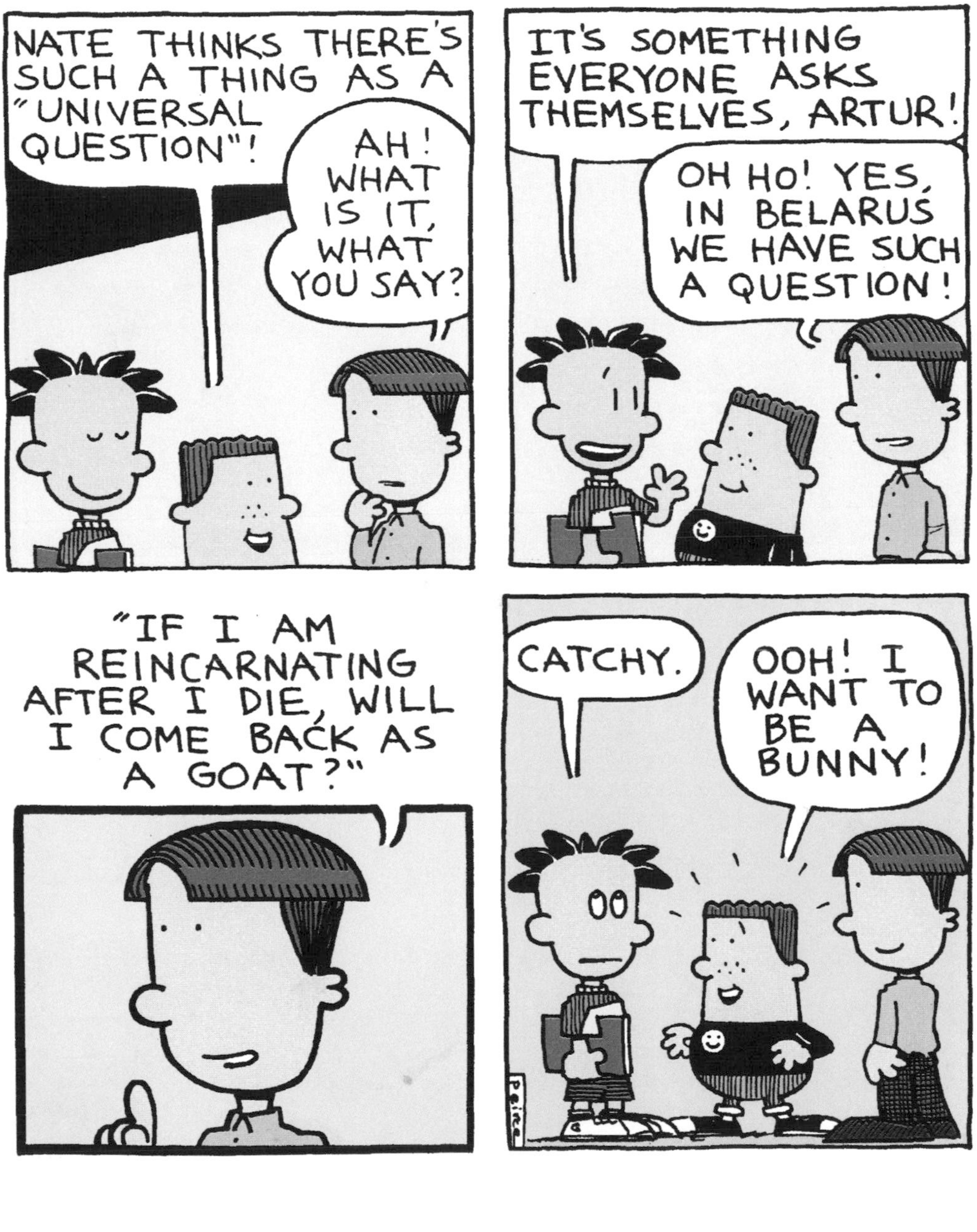
NATE THINKS THERE'S SUCH A THING AS A "UNIVERSAL QUESTION"!
AH! WHAT IS IT, WHAT YOU SAY?
IT'S SOMETHING EVERYONE ASKS THEMSELVES, ARTUR!
OH HO! YES, IN BELARUS WE HAVE SUCH A QUESTION!
"IF I AM REINCARNATING AFTER I DIE, WILL I COME BACK AS A GOAT?"
CATCHY.
OOH! I WANT TO BE A BUNNY!
Peirce

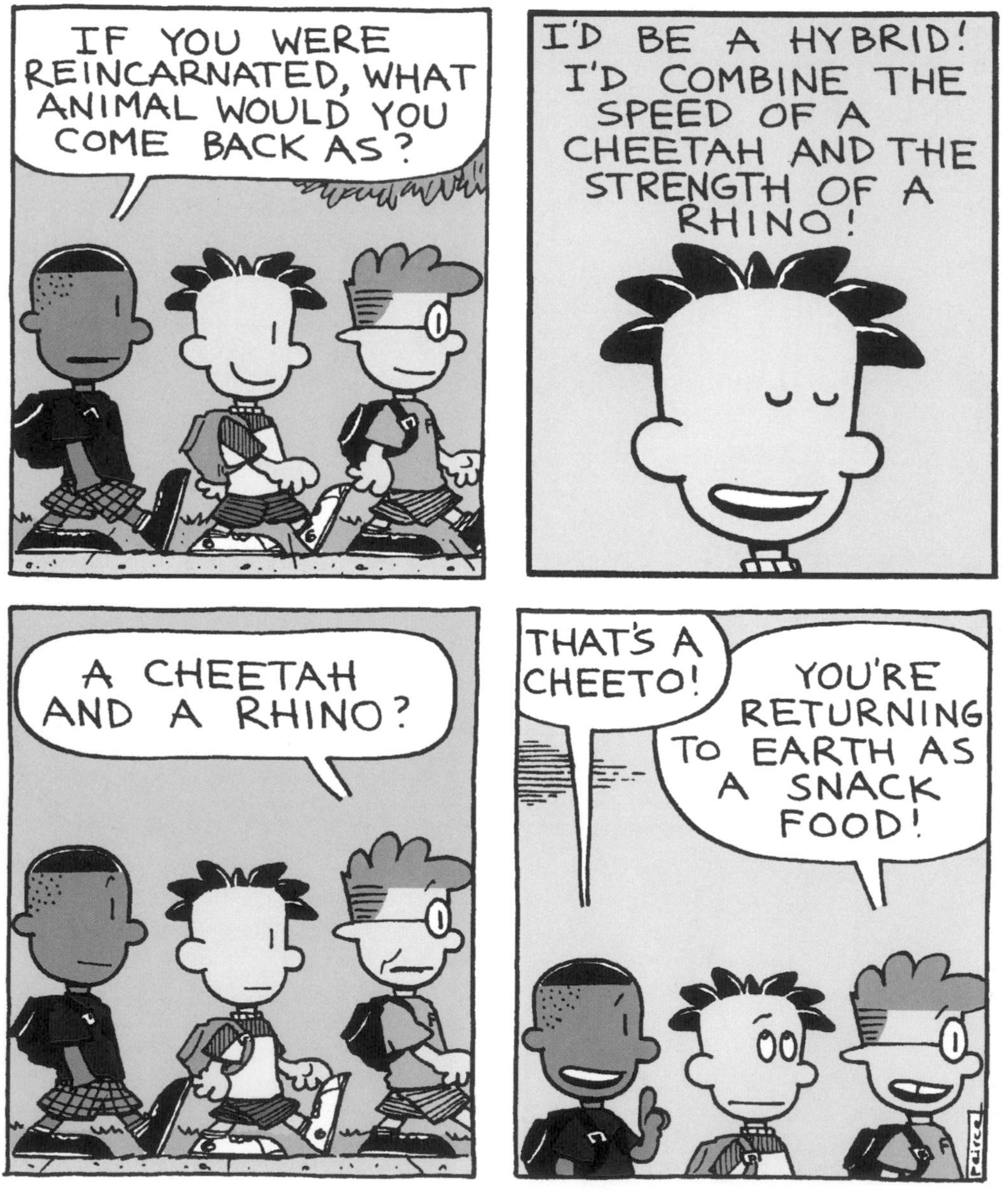
IF YOU WERE REINCARNATED, WHAT ANIMAL WOULD YOU COME BACK AS?
I'D BE A HYBRID! I'D COMBINE THE SPEED OF A CHEETAH AND THE STRENGTH OF A RHINO!
A CHEETAH AND A RHINO?
THAT'S A CHEETO!
YOU'RE RETURNING TO EARTH AS A SNACK FOOD!

MRS. GODFREY, SOME OF US HAVE BEEN TALKING ABOUT REINCARNATION!

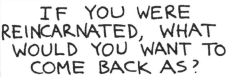

IF YOU WERE REINCARNATED, WHAT WOULD YOU WANT TO COME BACK AS?

I'D COME BACK AS **MYSELF**, SO I COULD LIVE MY LIFE OVER AND OVER AGAIN. FOREVER.

I HAD HER PEGGED AS A WATER BUFFALO.

F-F-F-F-FOREVER.

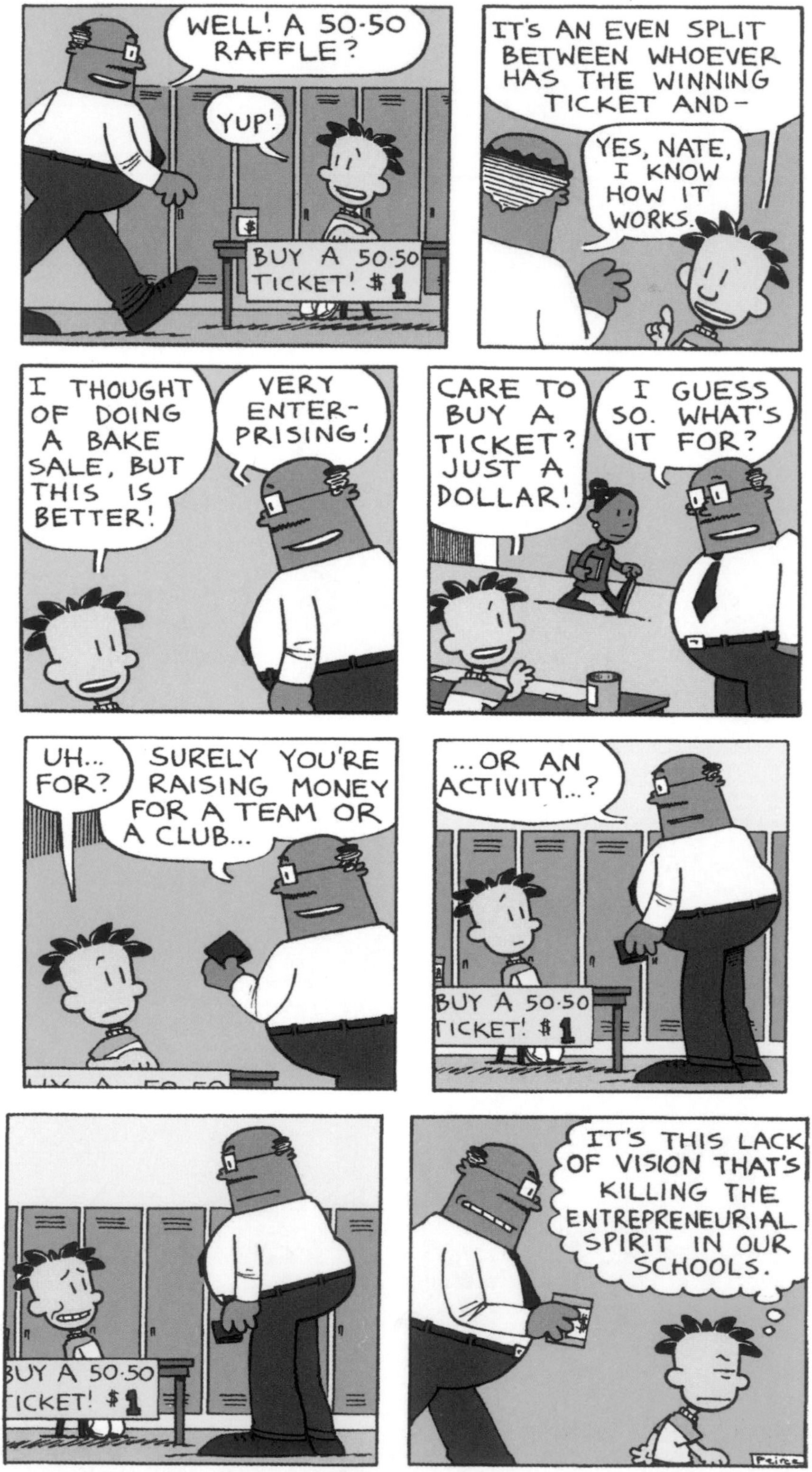
WELL! A 50-50 RAFFLE?
YUP!
BUY A 50-50 TICKET! $1
IT'S AN EVEN SPLIT BETWEEN WHOEVER HAS THE WINNING TICKET AND–
YES, NATE, I KNOW HOW IT WORKS.
I THOUGHT OF DOING A BAKE SALE, BUT THIS IS BETTER!
VERY ENTER-PRISING!
CARE TO BUY A TICKET? JUST A DOLLAR!
I GUESS SO. WHAT'S IT FOR?
UH... FOR?
SURELY YOU'RE RAISING MONEY FOR A TEAM OR A CLUB...
...OR AN ACTIVITY...?
BUY A 50-50 TICKET! $1
BUY A 50-50 TICKET! $1
IT'S THIS LACK OF VISION THAT'S KILLING THE ENTREPRENEURIAL SPIRIT IN OUR SCHOOLS.

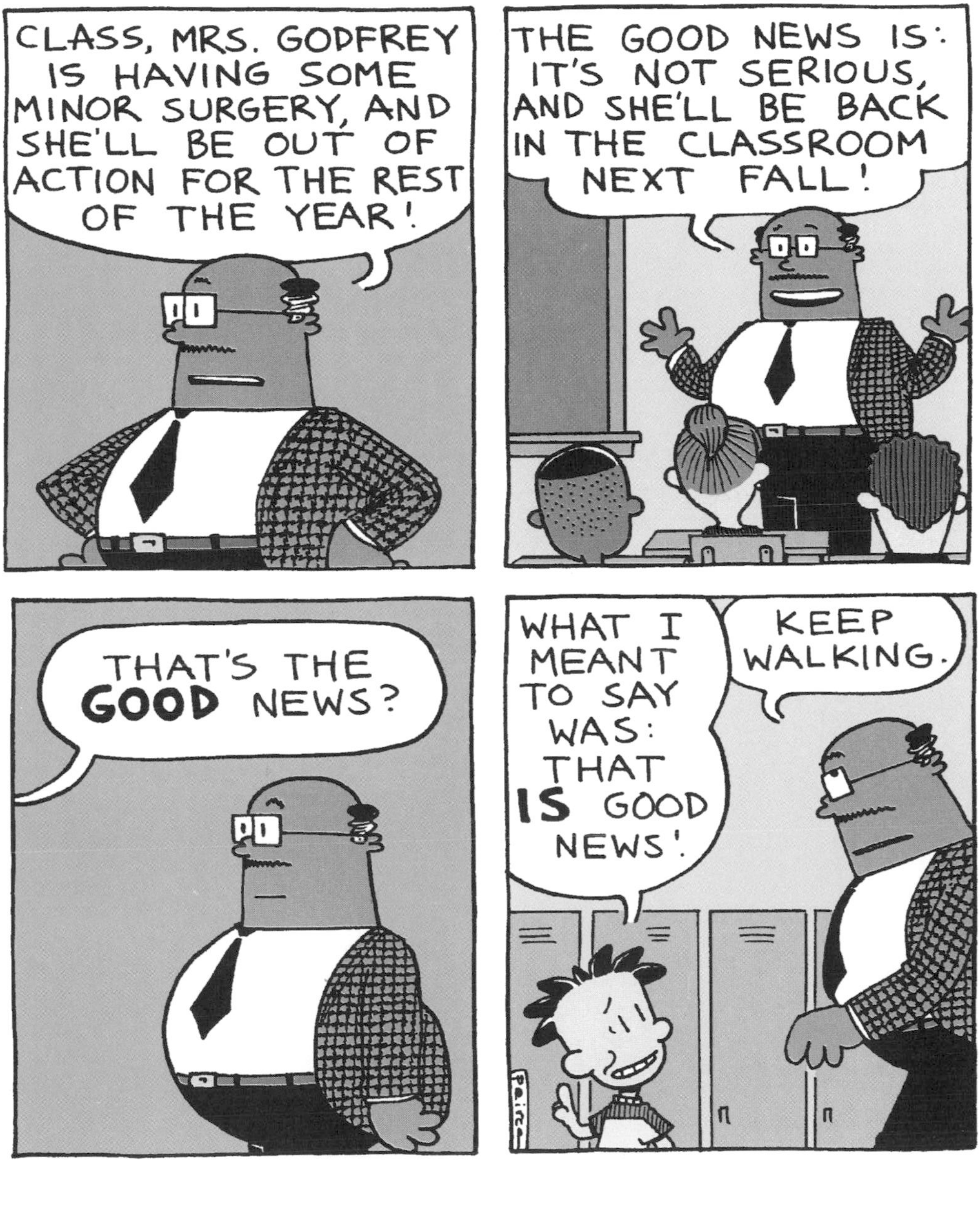
CLASS, MRS. GODFREY IS HAVING SOME MINOR SURGERY, AND SHE'LL BE OUT OF ACTION FOR THE REST OF THE YEAR!
THE GOOD NEWS IS: IT'S NOT SERIOUS, AND SHE'LL BE BACK IN THE CLASSROOM NEXT FALL!
THAT'S THE **GOOD** NEWS?
WHAT I MEANT TO SAY WAS: THAT **IS** GOOD NEWS!
KEEP WALKING.
peirce

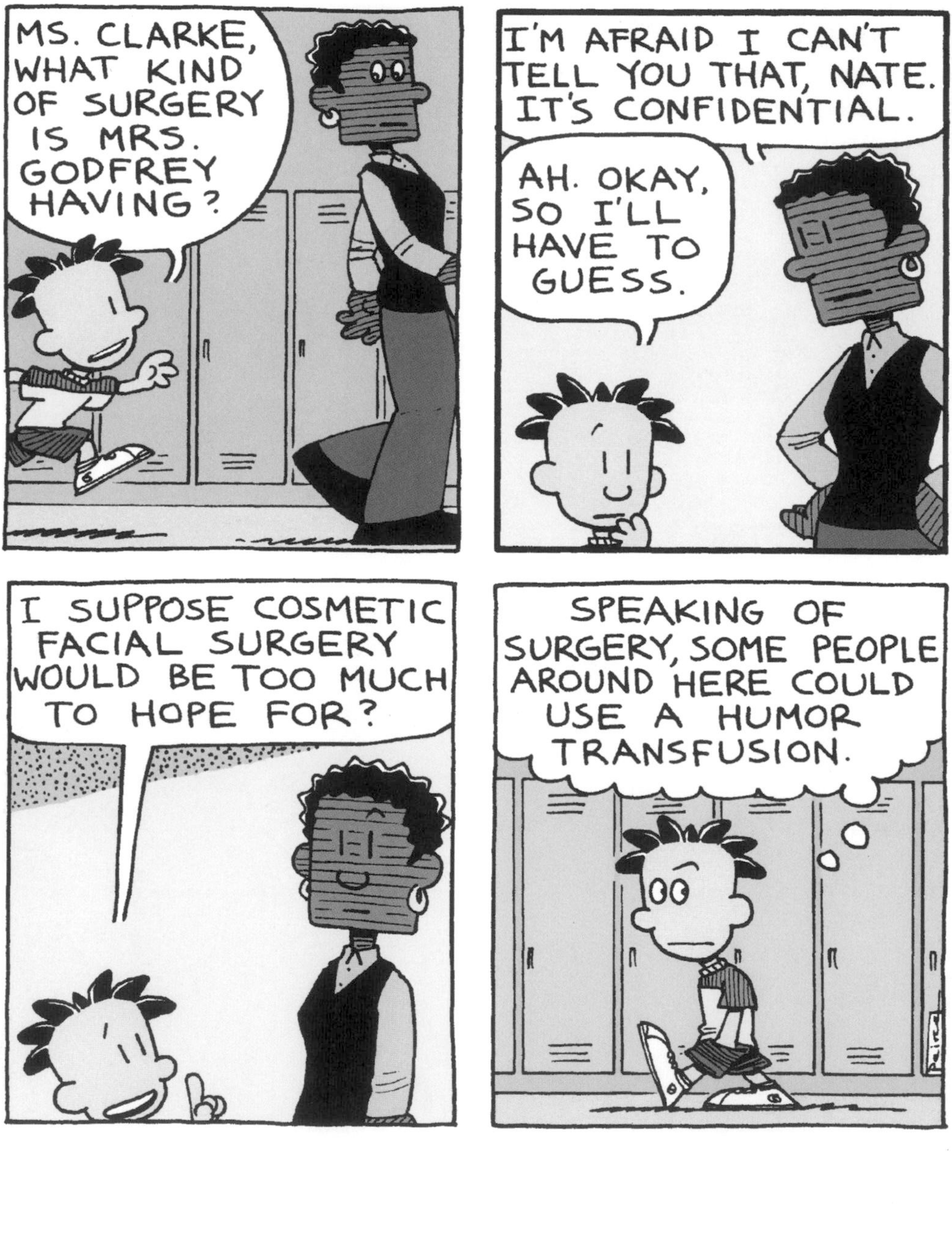
MS. CLARKE, WHAT KIND OF SURGERY IS MRS. GODFREY HAVING?
I'M AFRAID I CAN'T TELL YOU THAT, NATE. IT'S CONFIDENTIAL.
AH. OKAY, SO I'LL HAVE TO GUESS.
I SUPPOSE COSMETIC FACIAL SURGERY WOULD BE TOO MUCH TO HOPE FOR?
SPEAKING OF SURGERY, SOME PEOPLE AROUND HERE COULD USE A HUMOR TRANSFUSION.

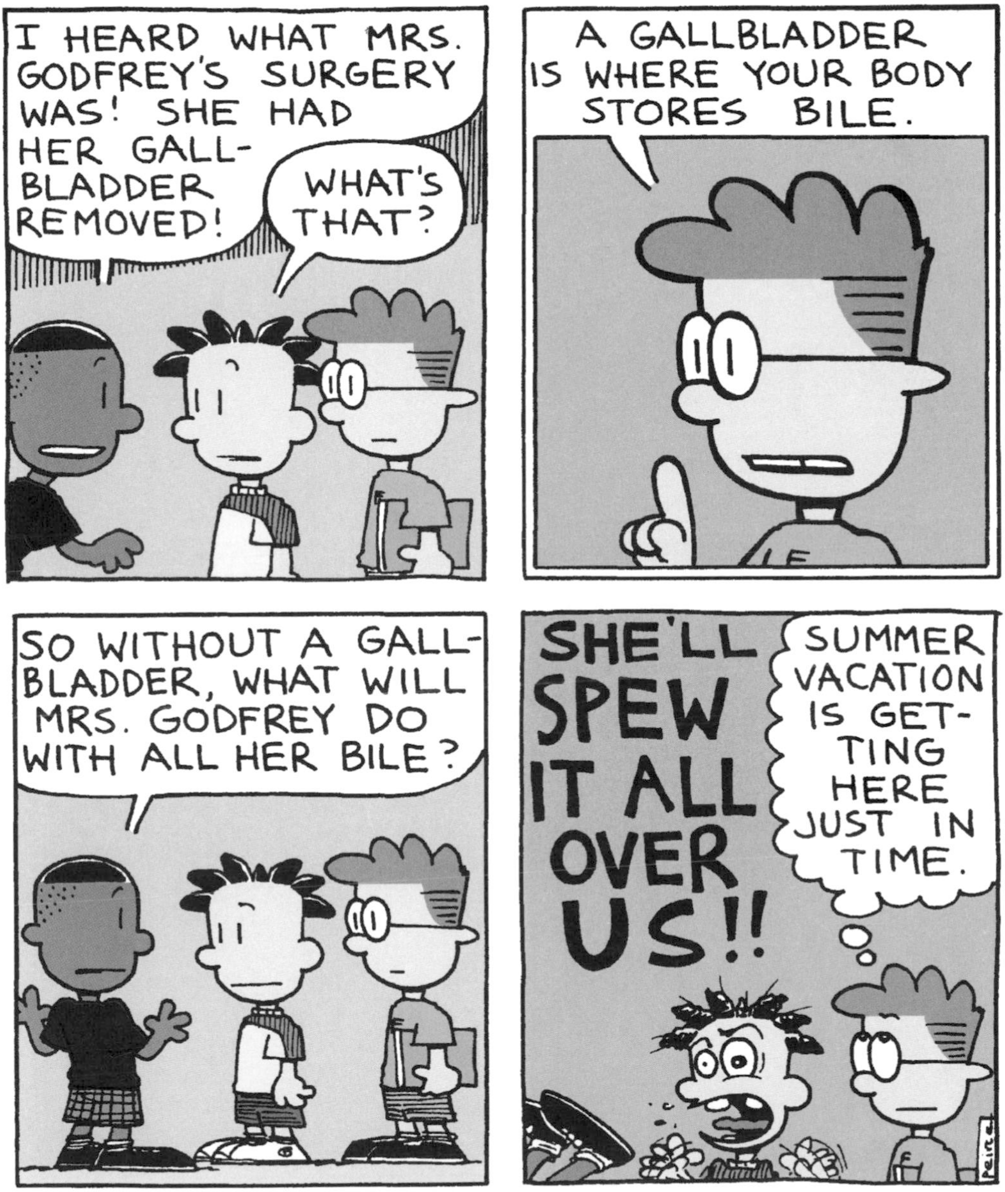
I HEARD WHAT MRS. GODFREY'S SURGERY WAS! SHE HAD HER GALL-BLADDER REMOVED!
WHAT'S THAT?
A GALLBLADDER IS WHERE YOUR BODY STORES BILE.
SO WITHOUT A GALL-BLADDER, WHAT WILL MRS. GODFREY DO WITH ALL HER BILE?
SHE'LL SPEW IT ALL OVER US!!
SUMMER VACATION IS GET-TING HERE JUST IN TIME.
PEIRCE

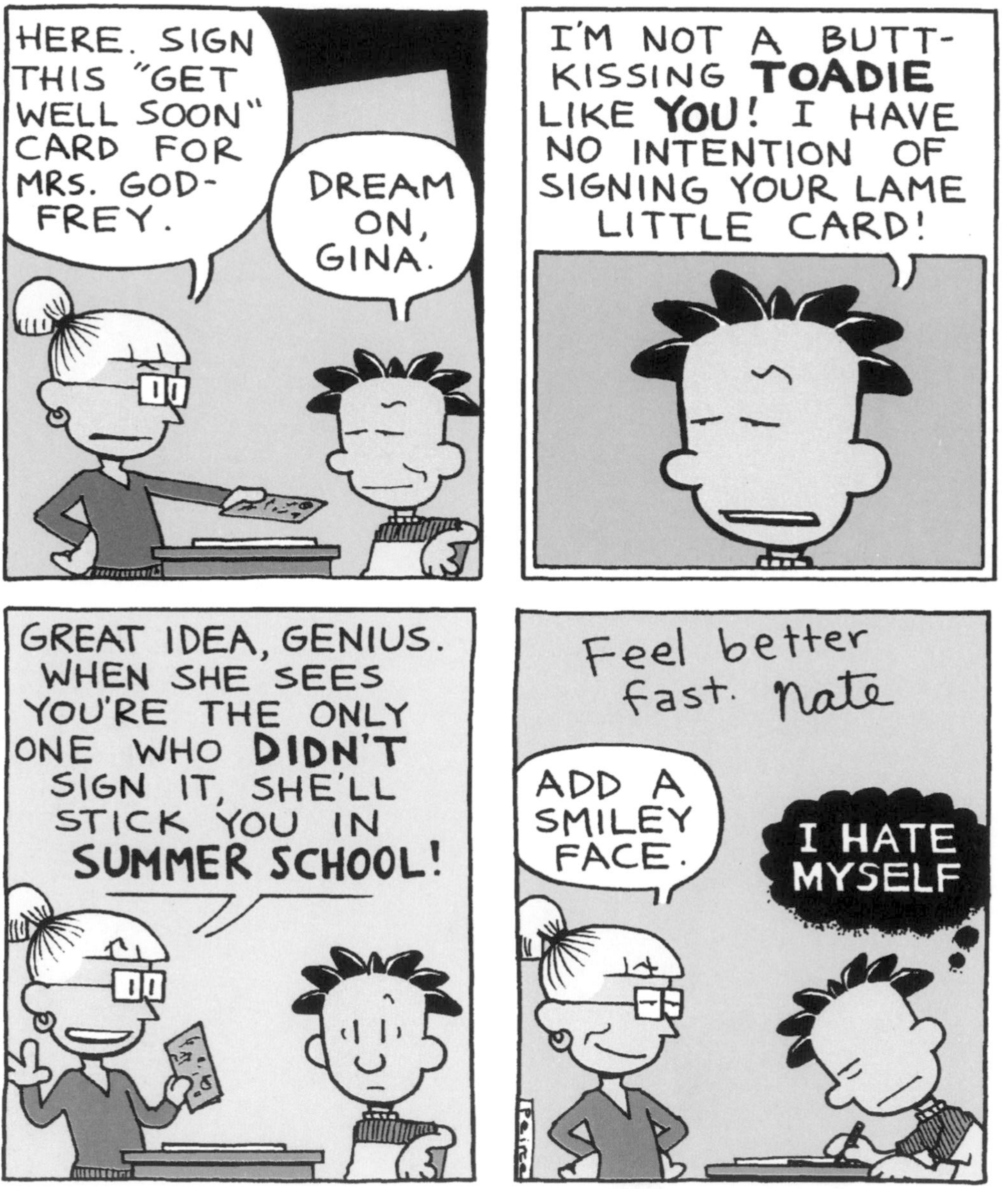
HERE. SIGN THIS "GET WELL SOON" CARD FOR MRS. GODFREY.
DREAM ON, GINA.
I'M NOT A BUTT-KISSING TOADIE LIKE YOU! I HAVE NO INTENTION OF SIGNING YOUR LAME LITTLE CARD!
GREAT IDEA, GENIUS. WHEN SHE SEES YOU'RE THE ONLY ONE WHO DIDN'T SIGN IT, SHE'LL STICK YOU IN SUMMER SCHOOL!
Feel better fast. Nate
ADD A SMILEY FACE.
I HATE MYSELF
Peirce

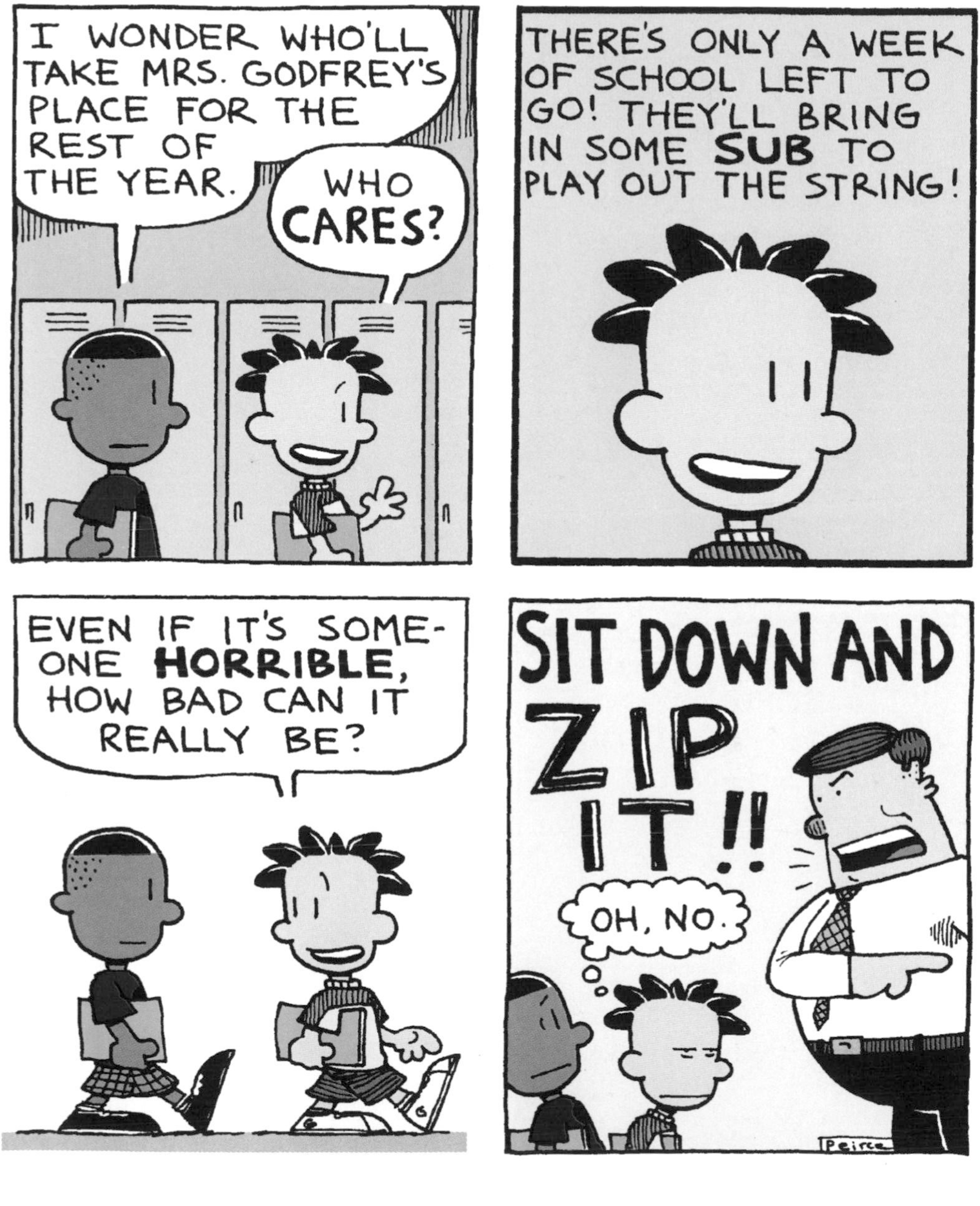
I WONDER WHO'LL TAKE MRS. GODFREY'S PLACE FOR THE REST OF THE YEAR.
WHO CARES?
THERE'S ONLY A WEEK OF SCHOOL LEFT TO GO! THEY'LL BRING IN SOME SUB TO PLAY OUT THE STRING!
EVEN IF IT'S SOMEONE HORRIBLE, HOW BAD CAN IT REALLY BE?
SIT DOWN AND ZIP IT!!
OH, NO.
Peirce

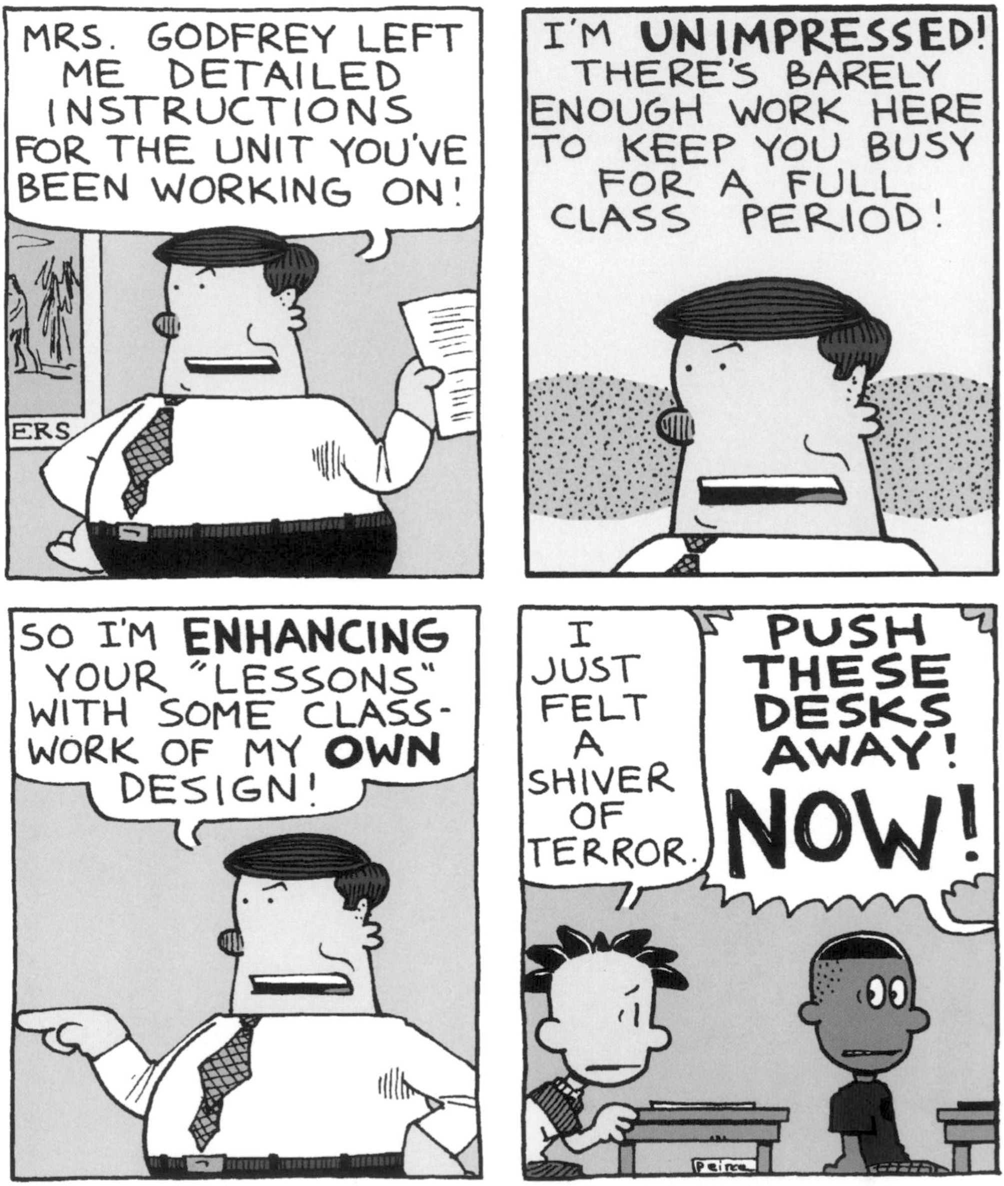
MRS. GODFREY LEFT ME DETAILED INSTRUCTIONS FOR THE UNIT YOU'VE BEEN WORKING ON!
ERS
I'M **UNIMPRESSED**! THERE'S BARELY ENOUGH WORK HERE TO KEEP YOU BUSY FOR A FULL CLASS PERIOD!
SO I'M **ENHANCING** YOUR "LESSONS" WITH SOME CLASS-WORK OF MY **OWN** DESIGN!
I JUST FELT A SHIVER OF TERROR.
PUSH THESE DESKS AWAY! NOW!
Peirce

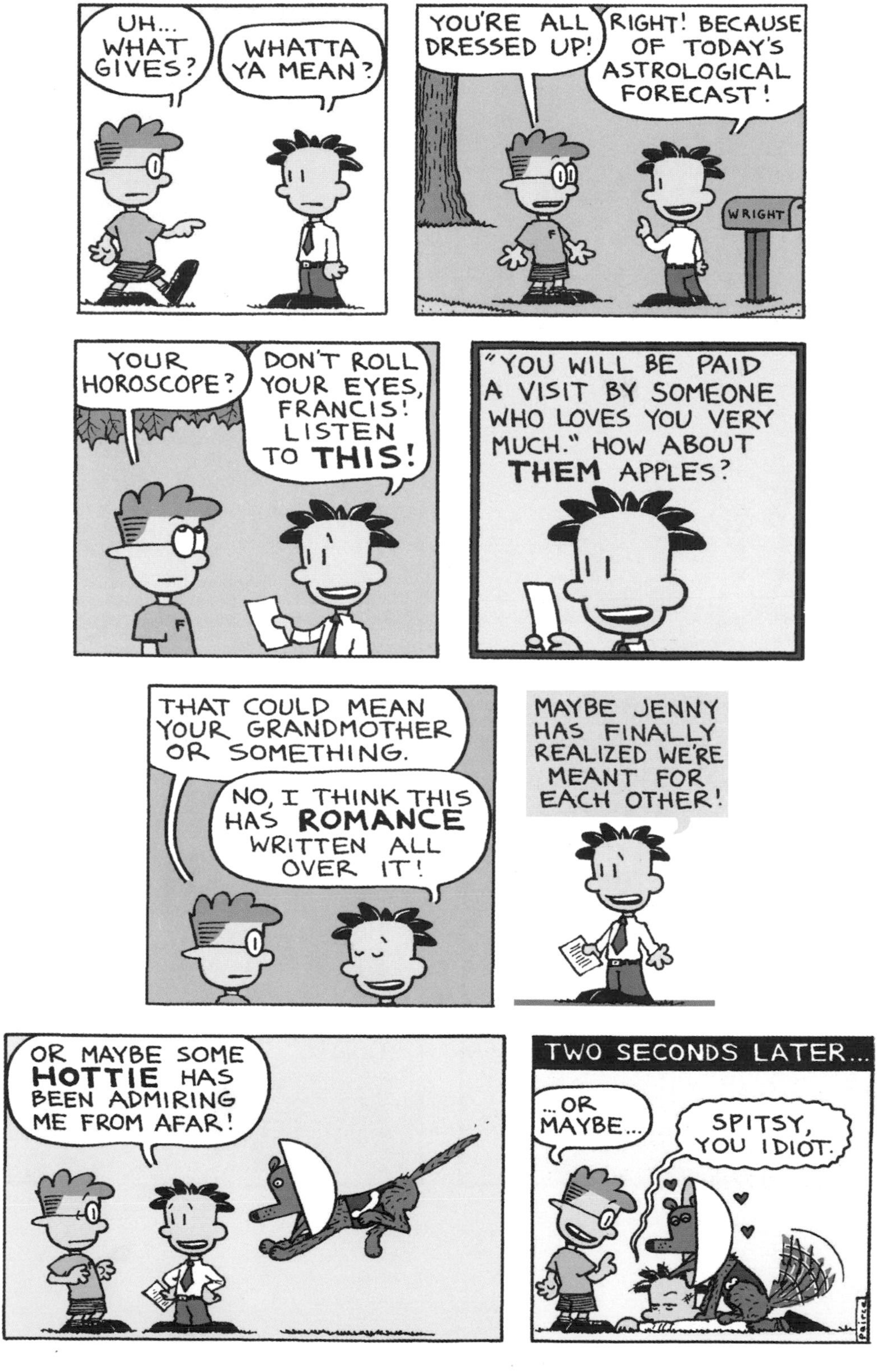
UH... WHAT GIVES?
WHATTA YA MEAN?
YOU'RE ALL DRESSED UP!
RIGHT! BECAUSE OF TODAY'S ASTROLOGICAL FORECAST!
WRIGHT
YOUR HOROSCOPE?
DON'T ROLL YOUR EYES, FRANCIS! LISTEN TO THIS!
"YOU WILL BE PAID A VISIT BY SOMEONE WHO LOVES YOU VERY MUCH." HOW ABOUT THEM APPLES?
THAT COULD MEAN YOUR GRANDMOTHER OR SOMETHING.
NO, I THINK THIS HAS ROMANCE WRITTEN ALL OVER IT!
MAYBE JENNY HAS FINALLY REALIZED WE'RE MEANT FOR EACH OTHER!
OR MAYBE SOME HOTTIE HAS BEEN ADMIRING ME FROM AFAR!
TWO SECONDS LATER...
...OR MAYBE...
SPITSY, YOU IDIOT.
Peirce

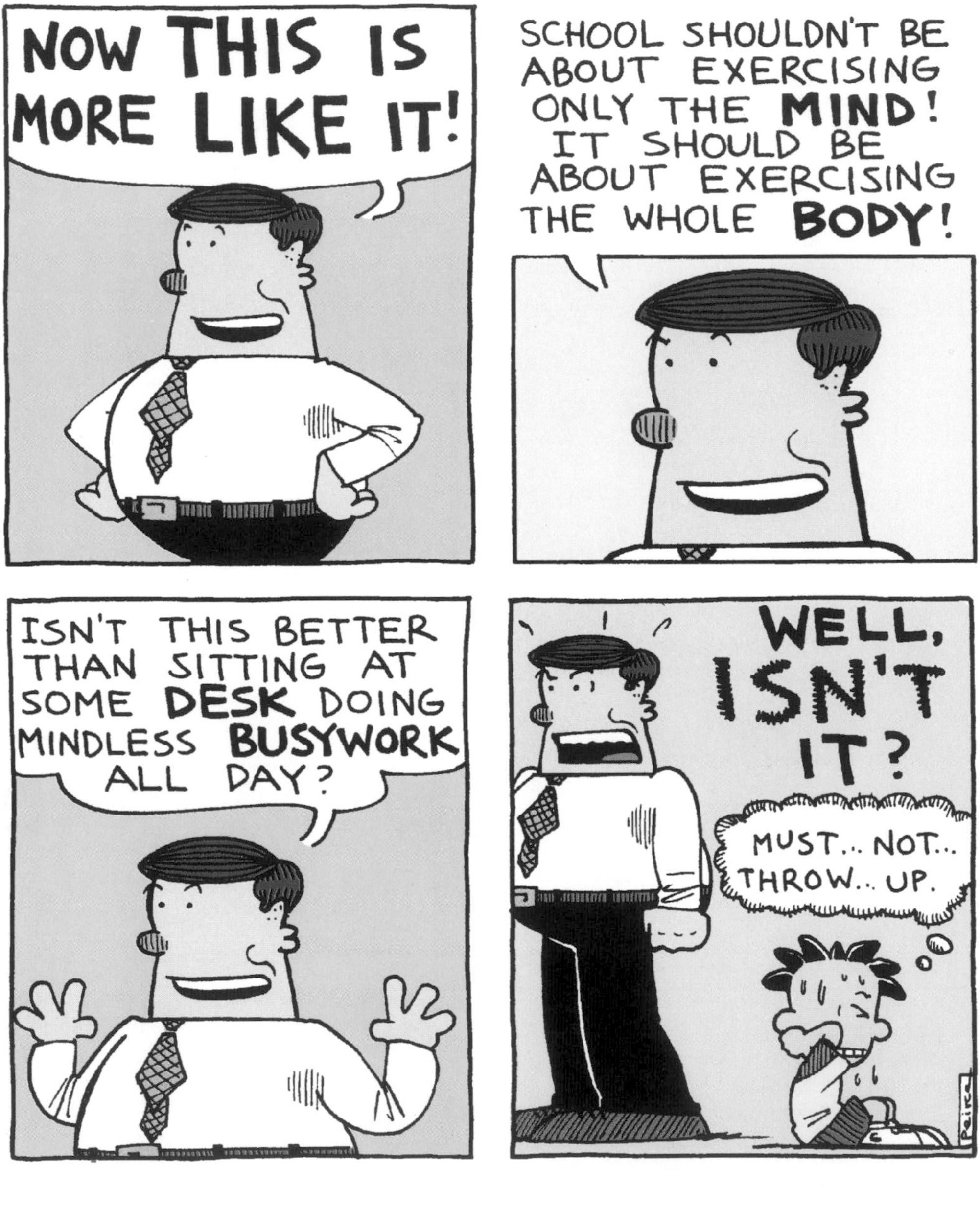
NOW THIS IS MORE LIKE IT!
SCHOOL SHOULDN'T BE ABOUT EXERCISING ONLY THE MIND! IT SHOULD BE ABOUT EXERCISING THE WHOLE BODY!
ISN'T THIS BETTER THAN SITTING AT SOME DESK DOING MINDLESS BUSYWORK ALL DAY?
WELL, ISN'T IT?
MUST... NOT... THROW... UP.
Peirce

I'M SO READY FOR SUMMER VACATION.

COACH JOHN FILLING IN FOR MRS. GODFREY HAS BEEN A **NIGHTMARE!**

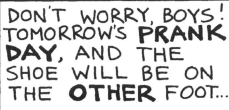

DON'T WORRY, BOYS! TOMORROW'S **PRANK DAY**, AND THE SHOE WILL BE ON THE **OTHER** FOOT...

...❋CHUCKLE!❋...IF YOU KNOW WHAT I MEAN!

OH, I KNOW WHAT YOU MEAN, ALL RIGHT!

NATE'S GOING TO SWITCH COACH JOHN'S SHOES AROUND!

CHAD, CHAD, CHAD.

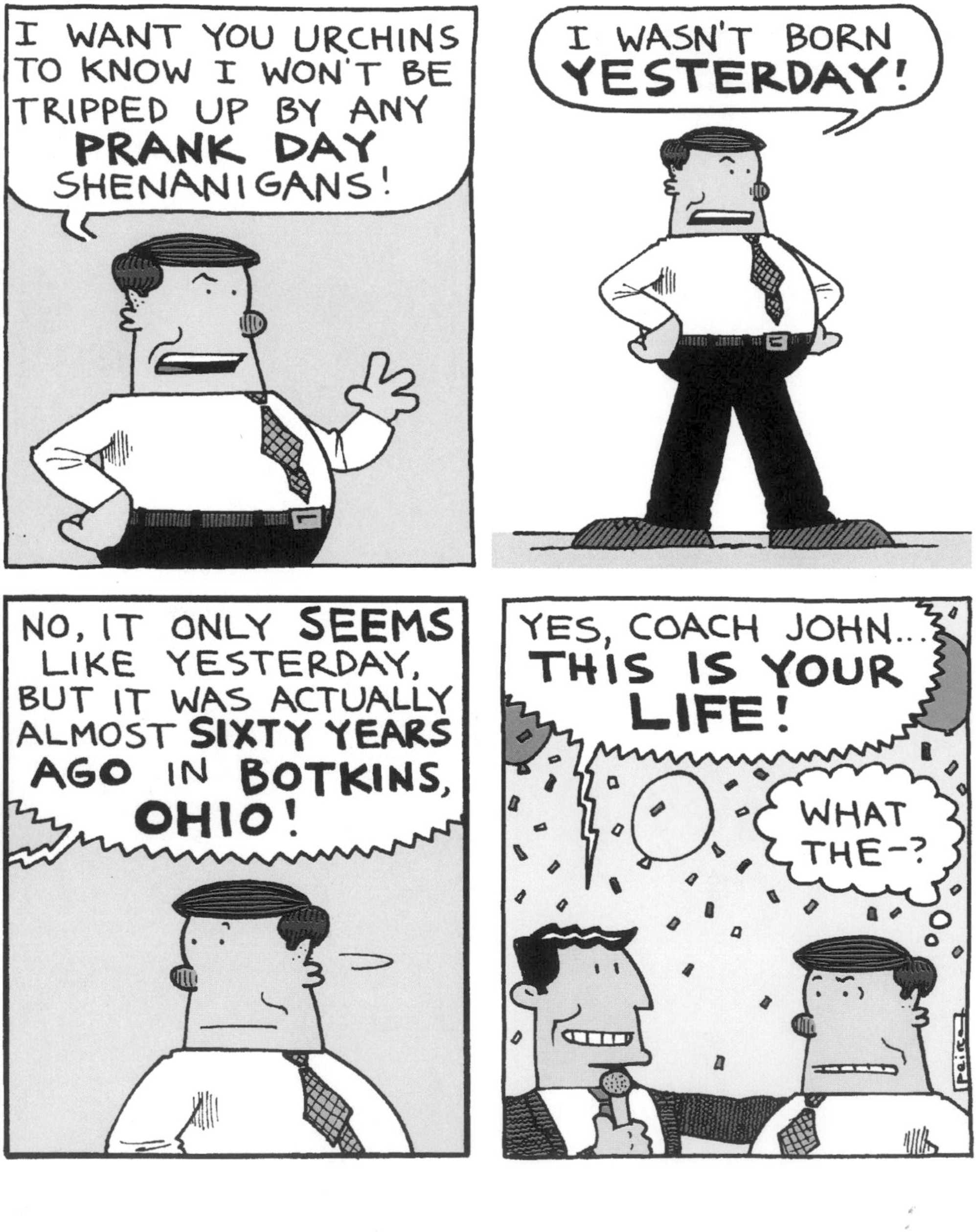
I WANT YOU URCHINS TO KNOW I WON'T BE TRIPPED UP BY ANY PRANK DAY SHENANIGANS!
I WASN'T BORN YESTERDAY!
NO, IT ONLY SEEMS LIKE YESTERDAY, BUT IT WAS ACTUALLY ALMOST SIXTY YEARS AGO IN BOTKINS, OHIO!
YES, COACH JOHN... THIS IS YOUR LIFE!
WHAT THE-?
PEIRCE

THIS IS YOUR LIFE, COACH JOHN! YOU WERE A SHY, SICKLY CHILD IN THE TINY VILLAGE OF BOTKINS, OHIO!...
THIS IS YOUR LI
YOUR ONLY COMPANION WAS YOUR IMAGINARY FRIEND, A KOALA BEAR NAMED RICKY! AND HERE HE IS!
THIS IS YOUR LI
JOHNNY BOY!
GAH!
IS IS YOU LIFE
THIS IS YOUR WORK, ISN'T IT?
I HAVE NO IDEA WHAT YOU'RE TALKING ABOUT.

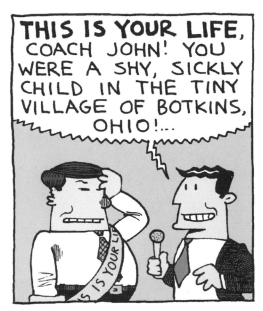

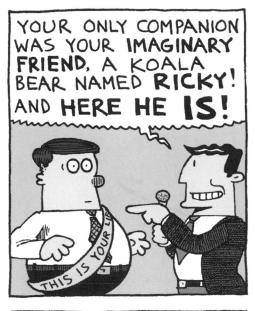

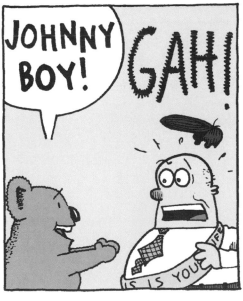

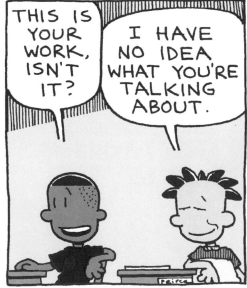

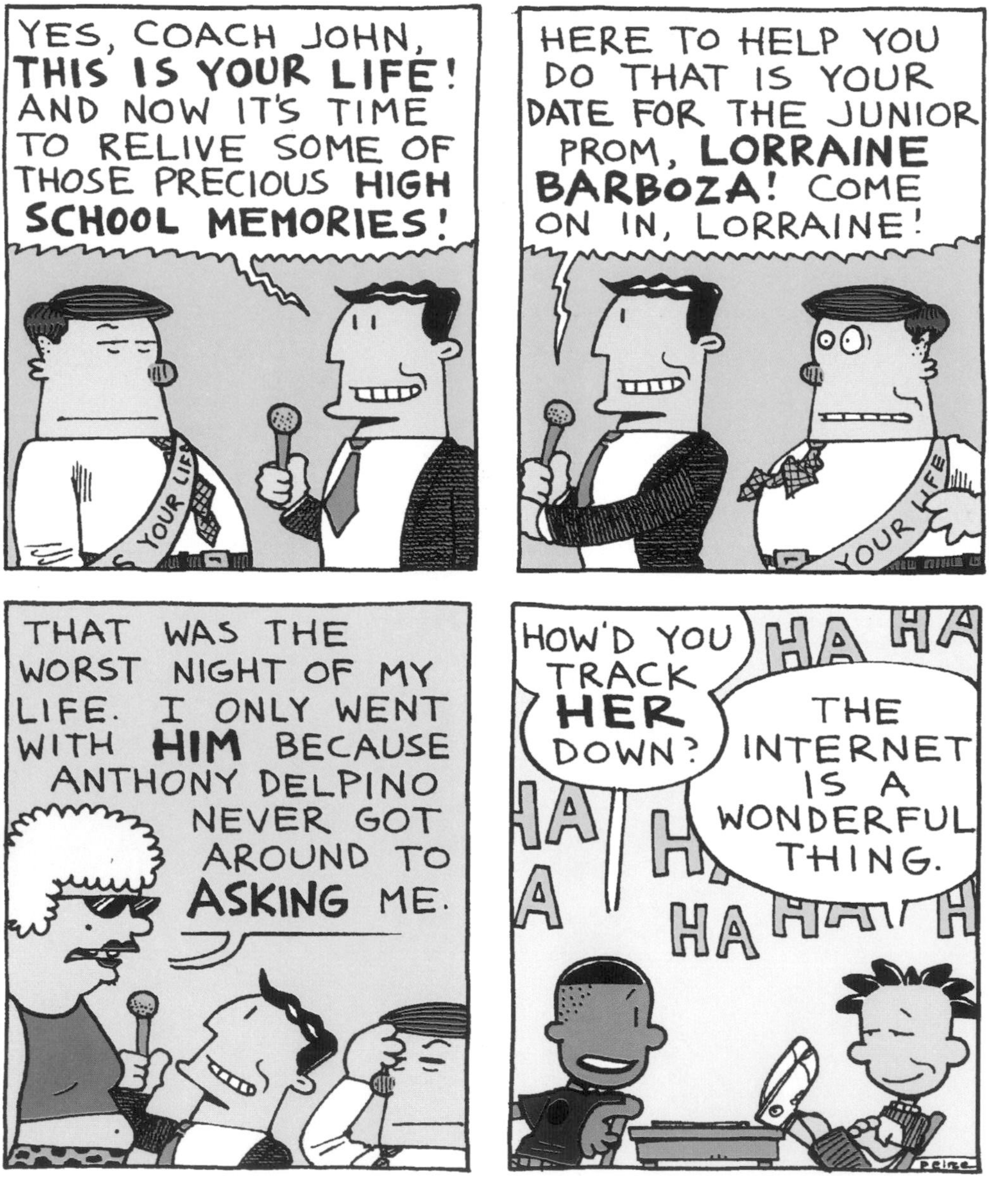
YES, COACH JOHN, **THIS IS YOUR LIFE**! AND NOW IT'S TIME TO RELIVE SOME OF THOSE PRECIOUS **HIGH SCHOOL MEMORIES**!
YOUR LIFE
HERE TO HELP YOU DO THAT IS YOUR DATE FOR THE JUNIOR PROM, **LORRAINE BARBOZA**! COME ON IN, LORRAINE!
YOUR LIFE
THAT WAS THE WORST NIGHT OF MY LIFE. I ONLY WENT WITH **HIM** BECAUSE ANTHONY DELPINO NEVER GOT AROUND TO **ASKING** ME.
HA HA HA HA HA
HOW'D YOU TRACK **HER** DOWN?
THE INTERNET IS A WONDERFUL THING.

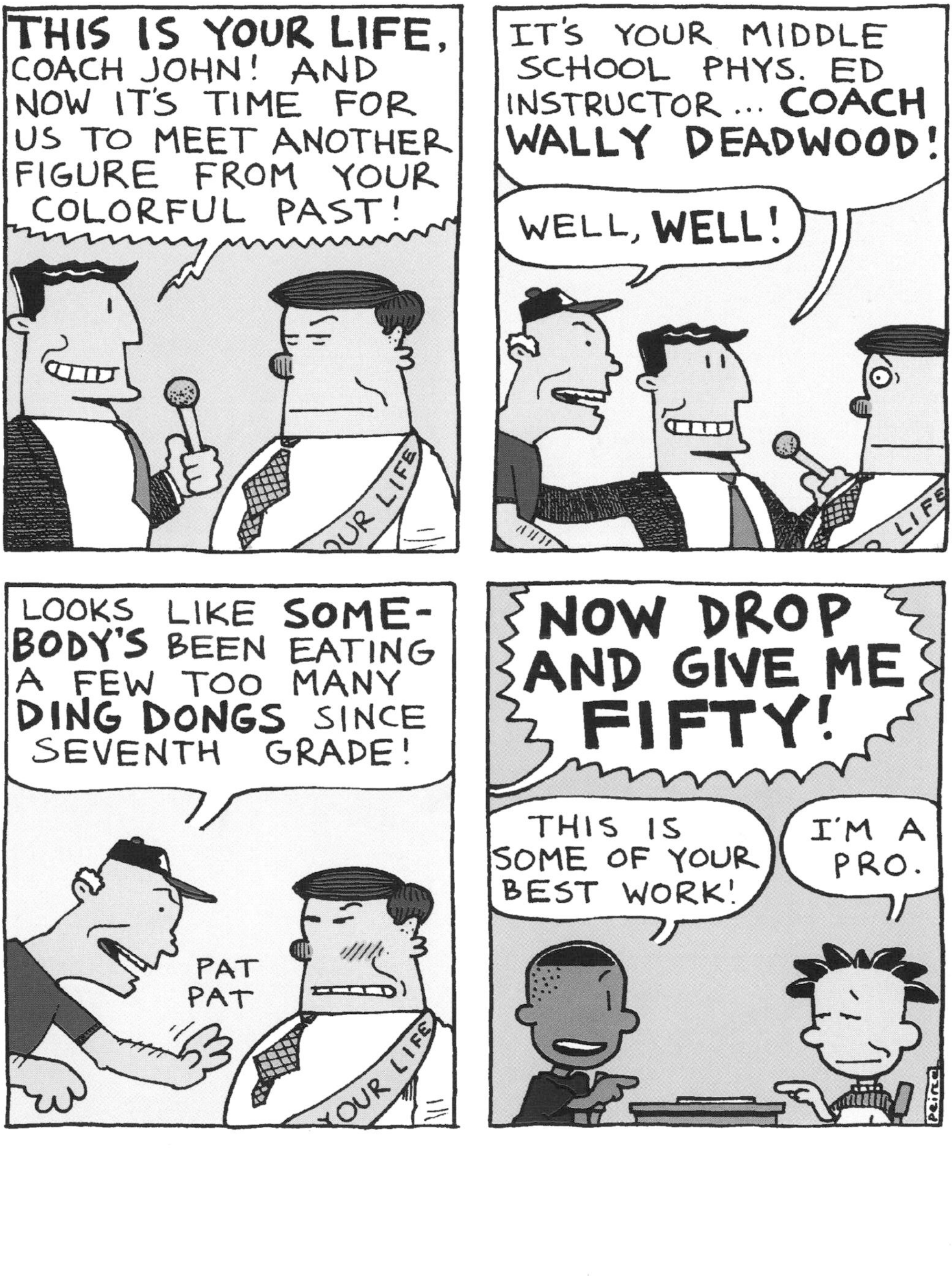
THIS IS YOUR LIFE, COACH JOHN! AND NOW IT'S TIME FOR US TO MEET ANOTHER FIGURE FROM YOUR COLORFUL PAST!
IT'S YOUR MIDDLE SCHOOL PHYS. ED INSTRUCTOR ... COACH WALLY DEADWOOD!
WELL, WELL!
LOOKS LIKE SOMEBODY'S BEEN EATING A FEW TOO MANY DING DONGS SINCE SEVENTH GRADE!
PAT PAT
NOW DROP AND GIVE ME FIFTY!
THIS IS SOME OF YOUR BEST WORK!
I'M A PRO.
Peirce

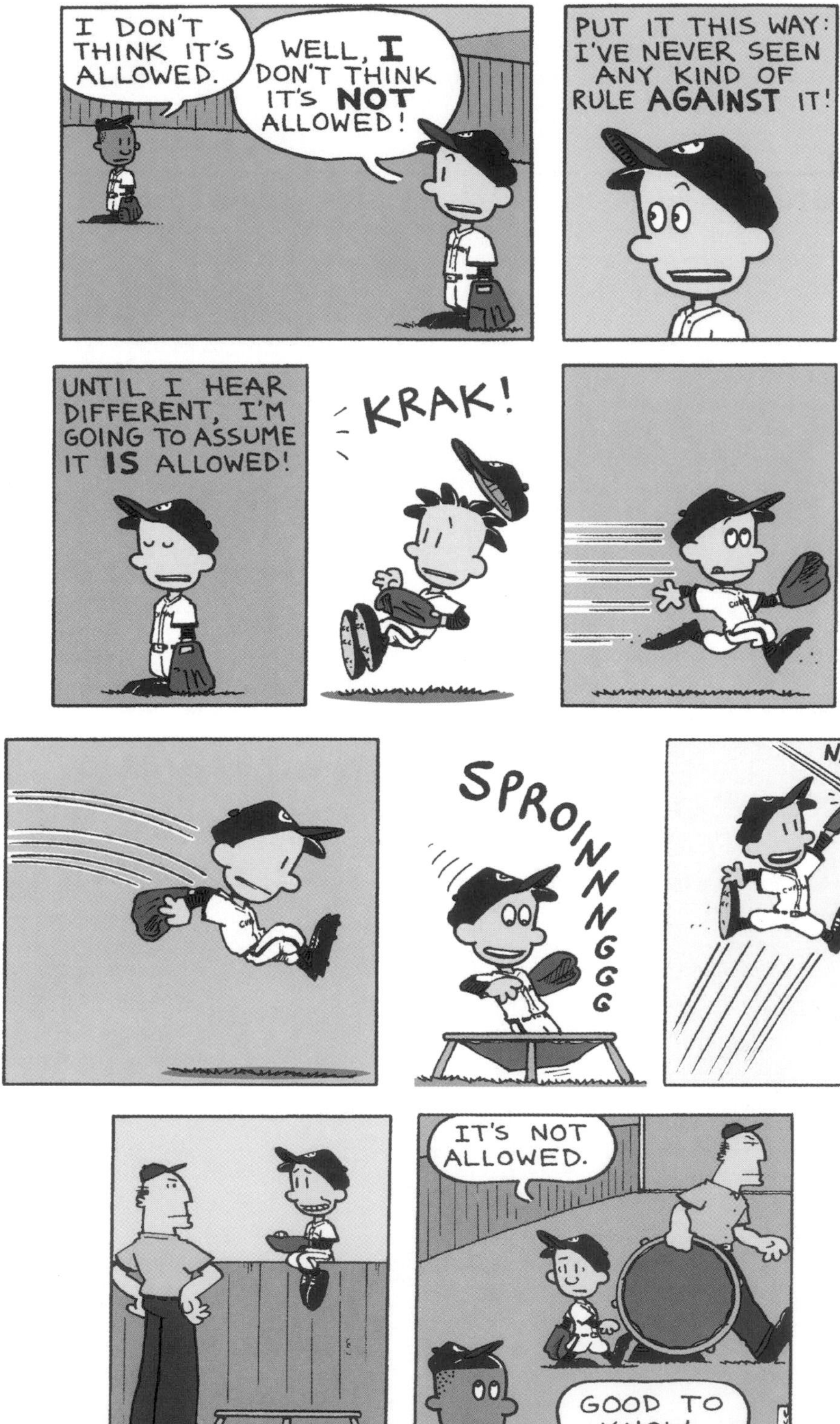
I DON'T THINK IT'S ALLOWED.
WELL, **I** DON'T THINK IT'S **NOT** ALLOWED!
PUT IT THIS WAY: I'VE NEVER SEEN ANY KIND OF RULE **AGAINST** IT!
UNTIL I HEAR DIFFERENT, I'M GOING TO ASSUME IT **IS** ALLOWED!
KRAK!
SPROINNNNGGG
NAB!
IT'S NOT ALLOWED.
GOOD TO KNOW.
Peirce

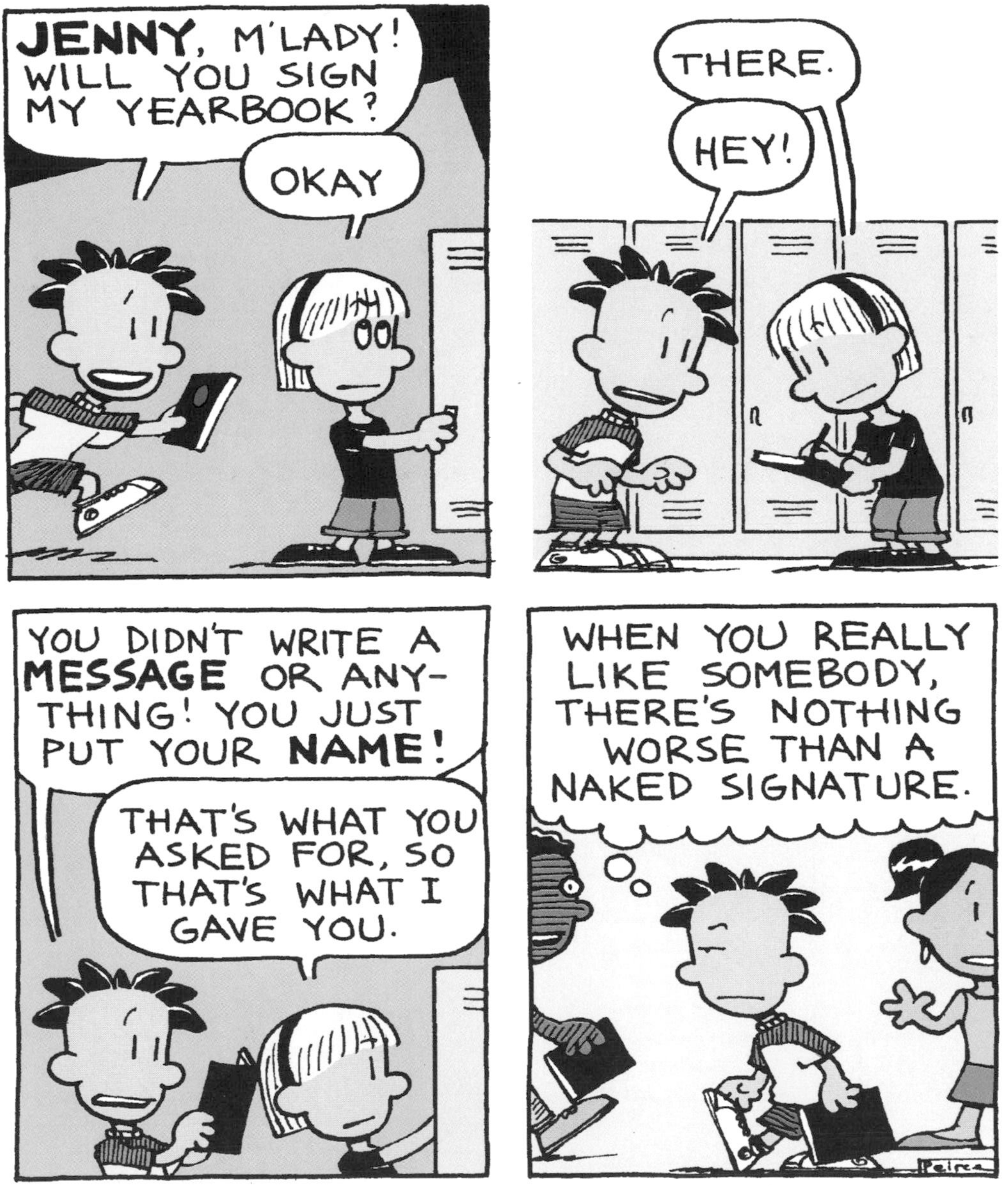
JENNY, M'LADY! WILL YOU SIGN MY YEARBOOK?
OKAY
THERE.
HEY!
YOU DIDN'T WRITE A MESSAGE OR ANY-THING! YOU JUST PUT YOUR NAME!
THAT'S WHAT YOU ASKED FOR, SO THAT'S WHAT I GAVE YOU.
WHEN YOU REALLY LIKE SOMEBODY, THERE'S NOTHING WORSE THAN A NAKED SIGNATURE.
Peirce

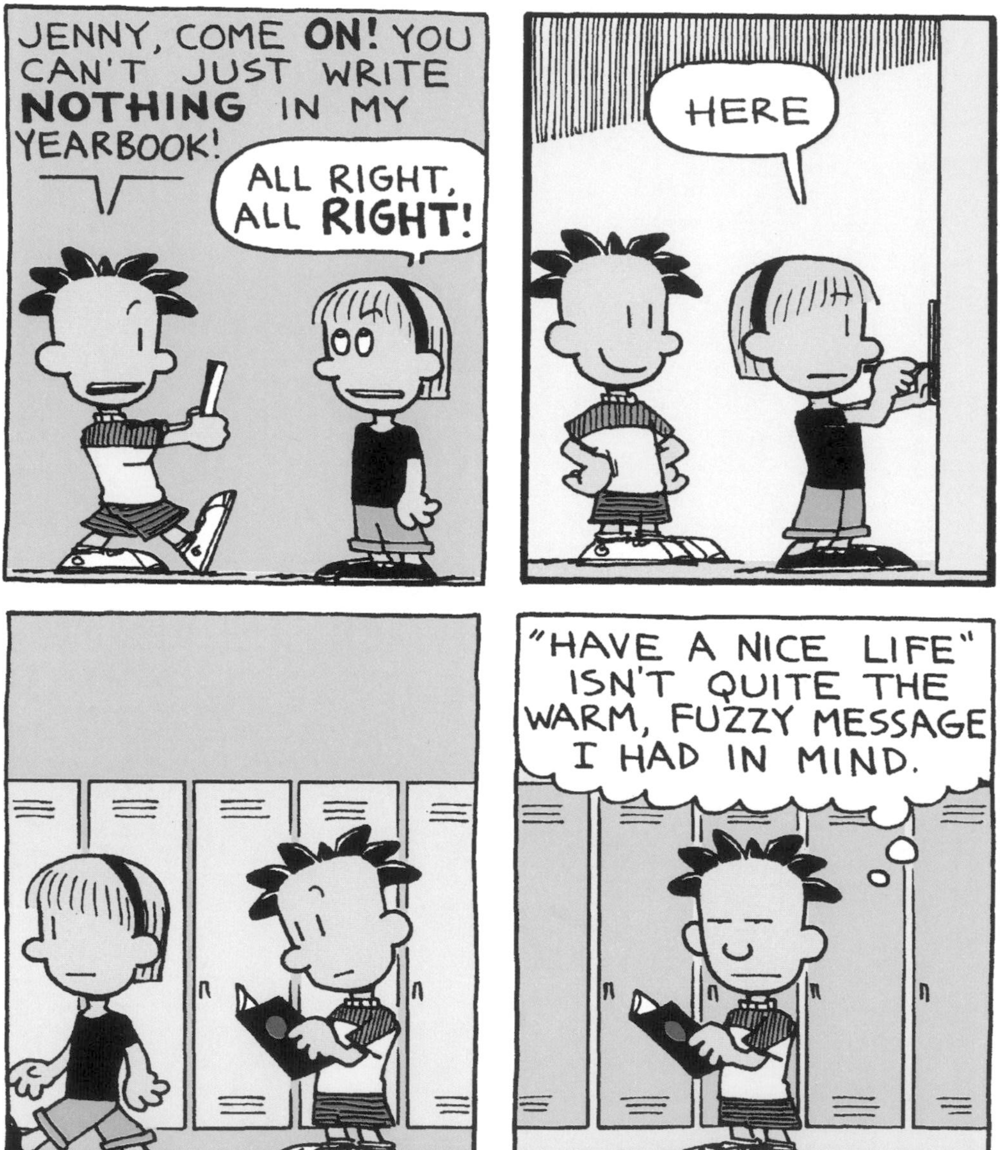
JENNY, COME **ON!** YOU CAN'T JUST WRITE **NOTHING** IN MY YEARBOOK!
ALL RIGHT, ALL **RIGHT!**
HERE
"HAVE A NICE LIFE" ISN'T QUITE THE WARM, FUZZY MESSAGE I HAD IN MIND.
Peirce

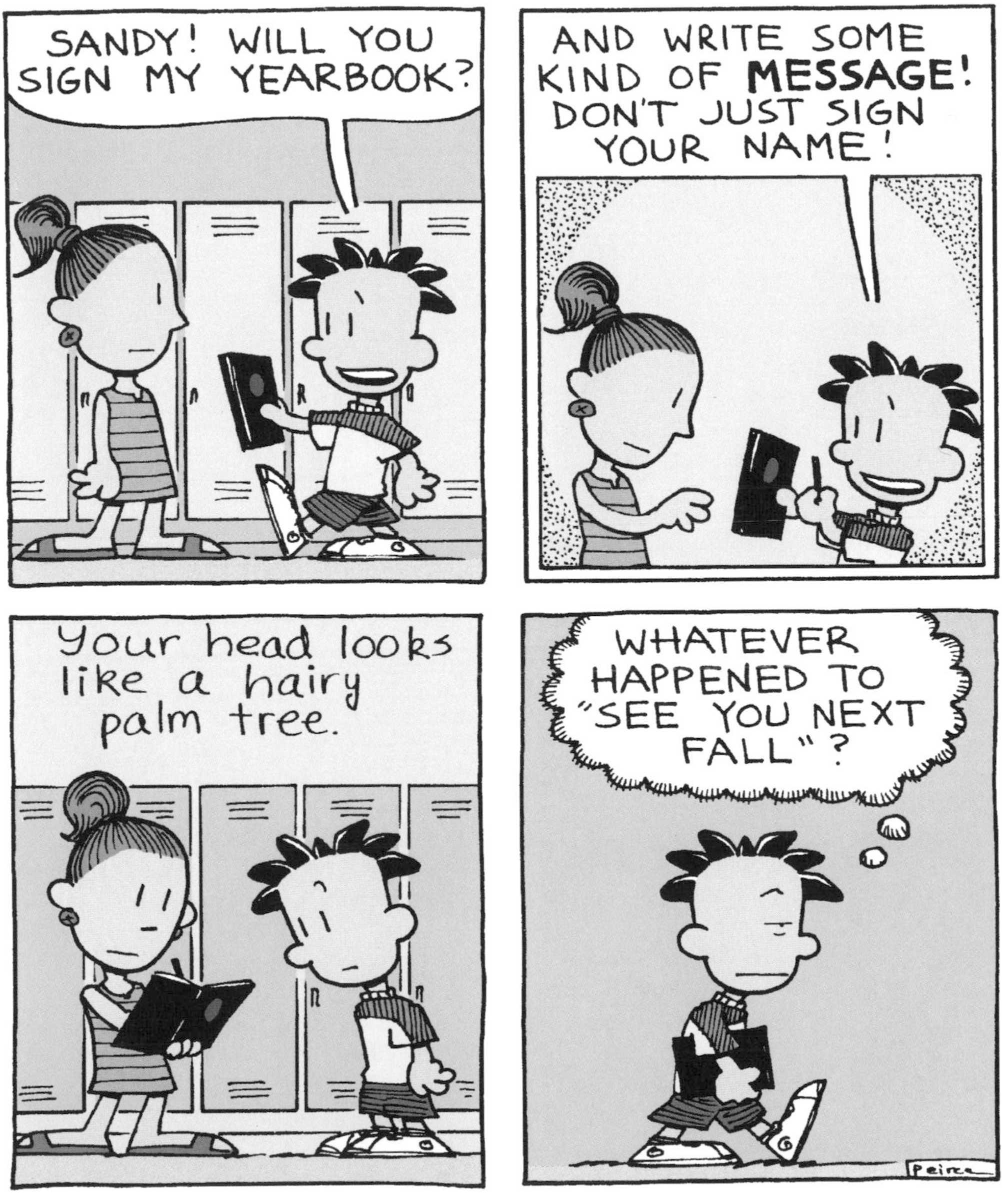
SANDY! WILL YOU SIGN MY YEARBOOK?
AND WRITE SOME KIND OF **MESSAGE**! DON'T JUST SIGN YOUR NAME!
Your head looks like a hairy palm tree.
WHATEVER HAPPENED TO "SEE YOU NEXT FALL"?
Peirce

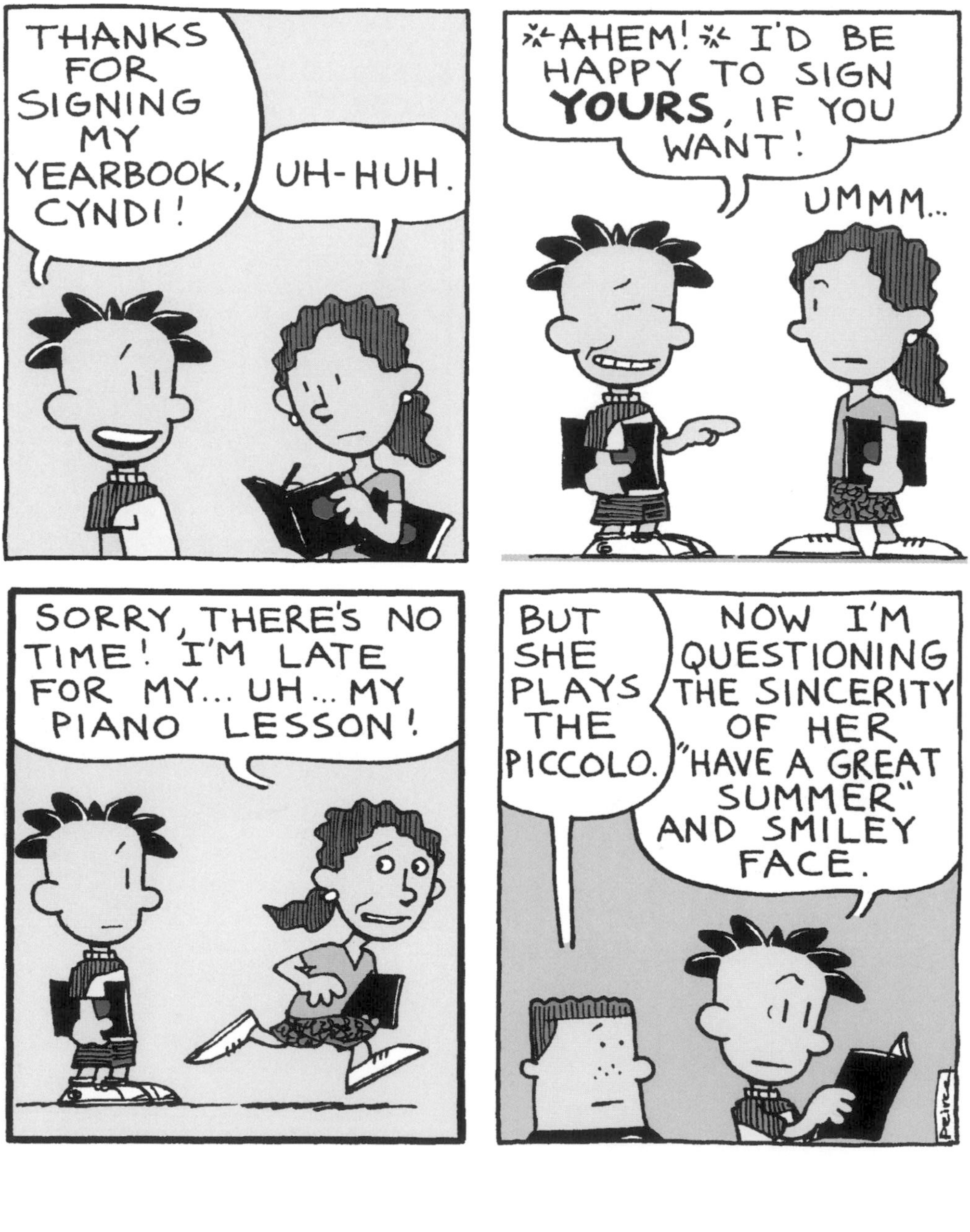
THANKS FOR SIGNING MY YEARBOOK, CYNDI!
UH-HUH.
AHEM! I'D BE HAPPY TO SIGN **YOURS**, IF YOU WANT!
UMMM...
SORRY, THERE'S NO TIME! I'M LATE FOR MY... UH... MY PIANO LESSON!
BUT SHE PLAYS THE PICCOLO.
NOW I'M QUESTIONING THE SINCERITY OF HER "HAVE A GREAT SUMMER" AND SMILEY FACE.
Peirce

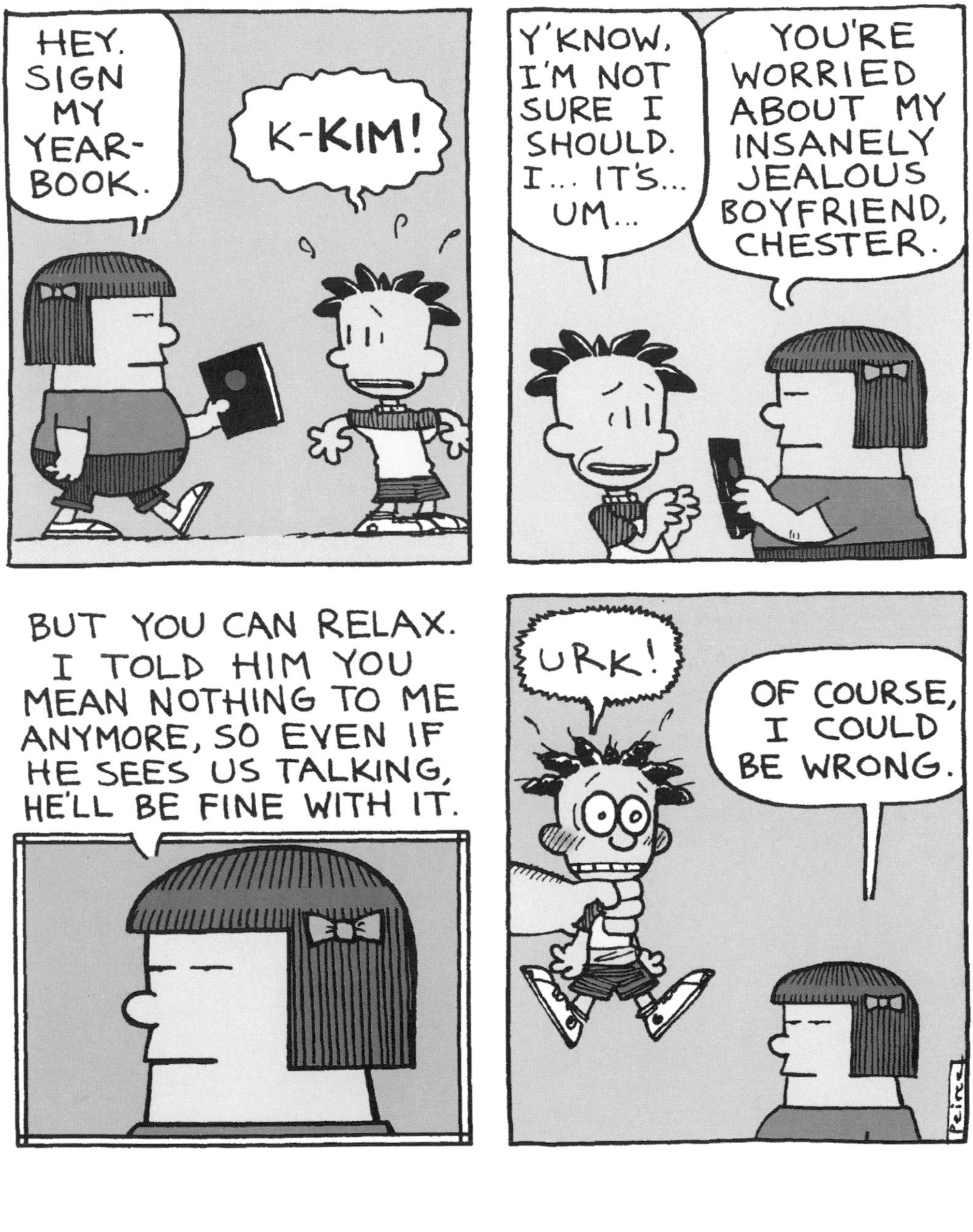
HEY. SIGN MY YEARBOOK.
K-KIM!
Y'KNOW, I'M NOT SURE I SHOULD. I... IT'S... UM...
YOU'RE WORRIED ABOUT MY INSANELY JEALOUS BOYFRIEND, CHESTER.
BUT YOU CAN RELAX. I TOLD HIM YOU MEAN NOTHING TO ME ANYMORE, SO EVEN IF HE SEES US TALKING, HE'LL BE FINE WITH IT.
URK!
OF COURSE, I COULD BE WRONG.
Peirce

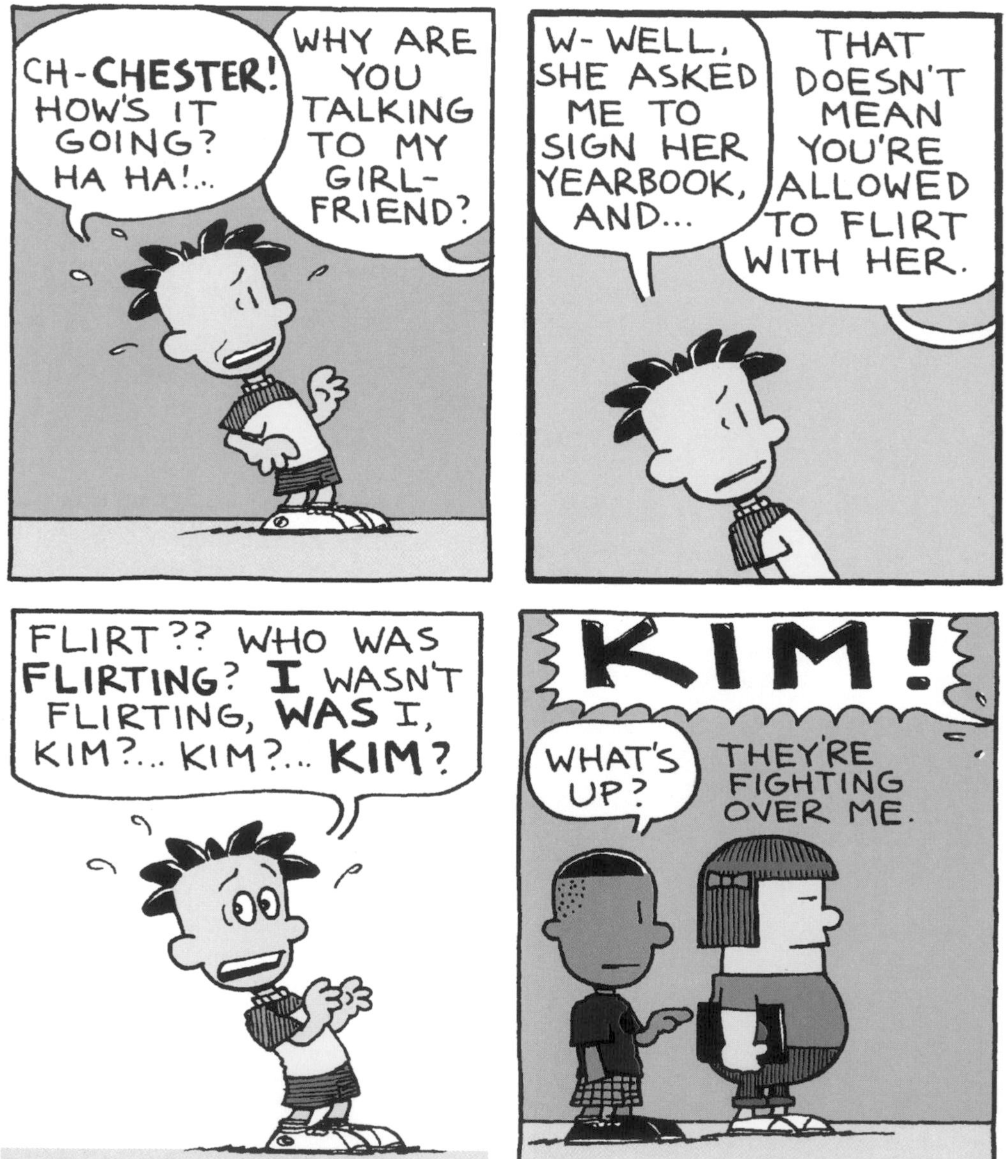
CH-**CHESTER**! HOW'S IT GOING? HA HA!...
WHY ARE YOU TALKING TO MY GIRL-FRIEND?
W-WELL, SHE ASKED ME TO SIGN HER YEARBOOK, AND...
THAT DOESN'T MEAN YOU'RE ALLOWED TO FLIRT WITH HER.
FLIRT?? WHO WAS **FLIRTING**? **I** WASN'T FLIRTING, **WAS** I, KIM?... KIM?... **KIM**?
KIM!
WHAT'S UP?
THEY'RE FIGHTING OVER ME.
Peirce

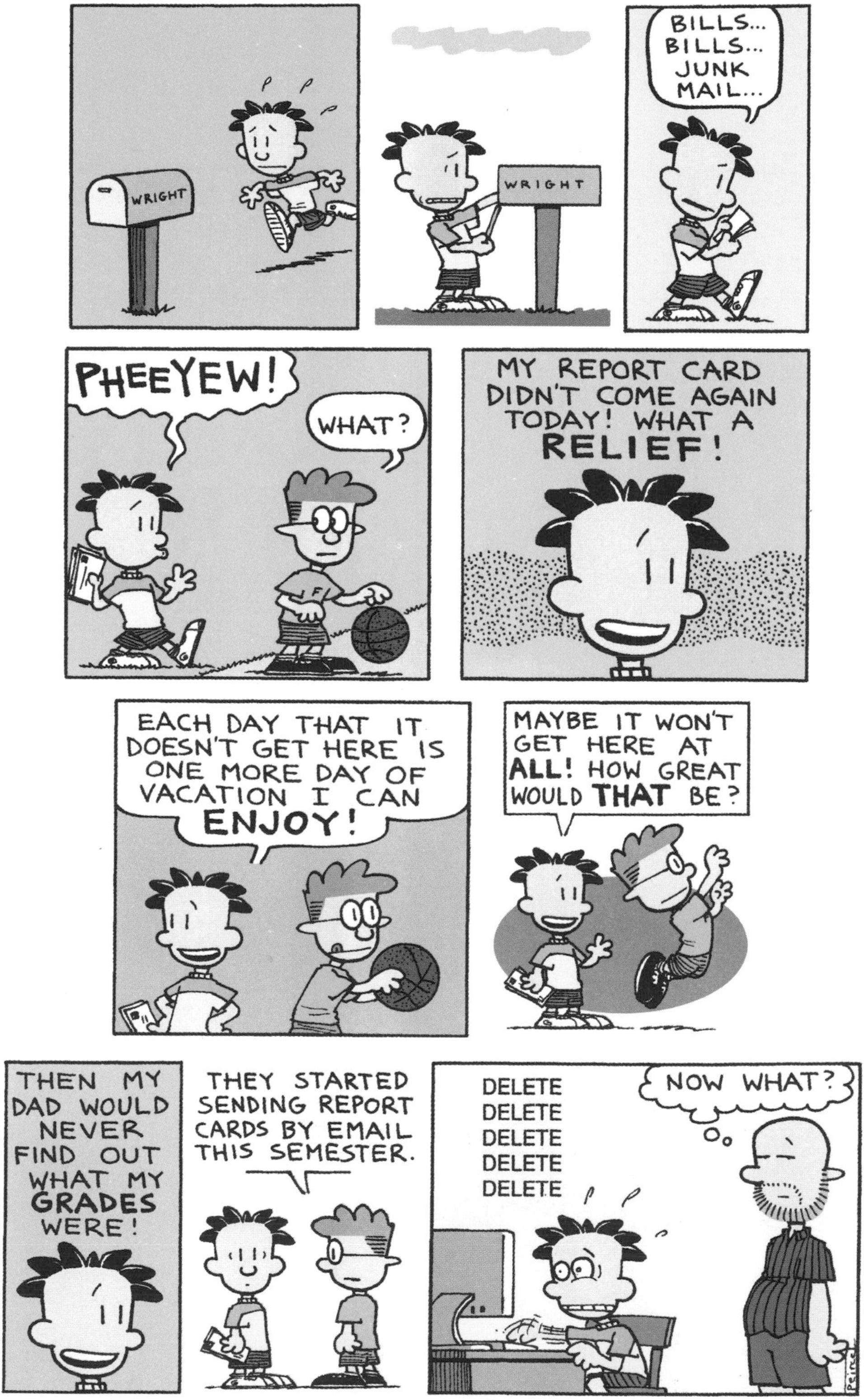
WRIGHT
WRIGHT
BILLS... BILLS... JUNK MAIL...
PHEEYEW!
WHAT?
MY REPORT CARD DIDN'T COME AGAIN TODAY! WHAT A **RELIEF**!
EACH DAY THAT IT DOESN'T GET HERE IS ONE MORE DAY OF VACATION I CAN **ENJOY**!
MAYBE IT WON'T GET HERE AT **ALL**! HOW GREAT WOULD **THAT** BE?
THEN MY DAD WOULD NEVER FIND OUT WHAT MY **GRADES** WERE!
THEY STARTED SENDING REPORT CARDS BY EMAIL THIS SEMESTER.
DELETE
DELETE
DELETE
DELETE
DELETE
NOW WHAT?

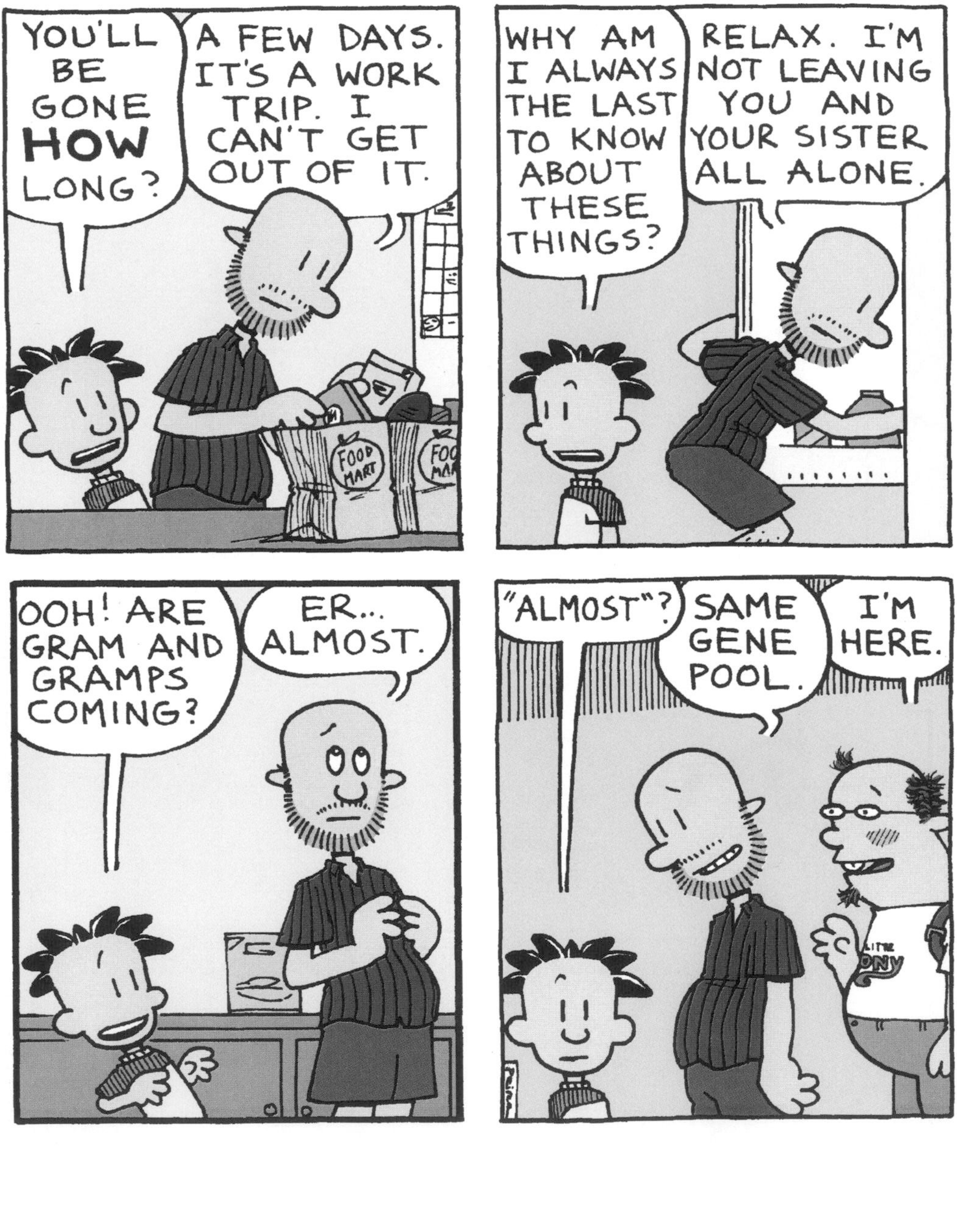
YOU'LL BE GONE **HOW** LONG?
A FEW DAYS. IT'S A WORK TRIP. I CAN'T GET OUT OF IT.
WHY AM I ALWAYS THE LAST TO KNOW ABOUT THESE THINGS?
RELAX. I'M NOT LEAVING YOU AND YOUR SISTER ALL ALONE.
OOH! ARE GRAM AND GRAMPS COMING?
ER... ALMOST.
"ALMOST"?
SAME GENE POOL.
I'M HERE.

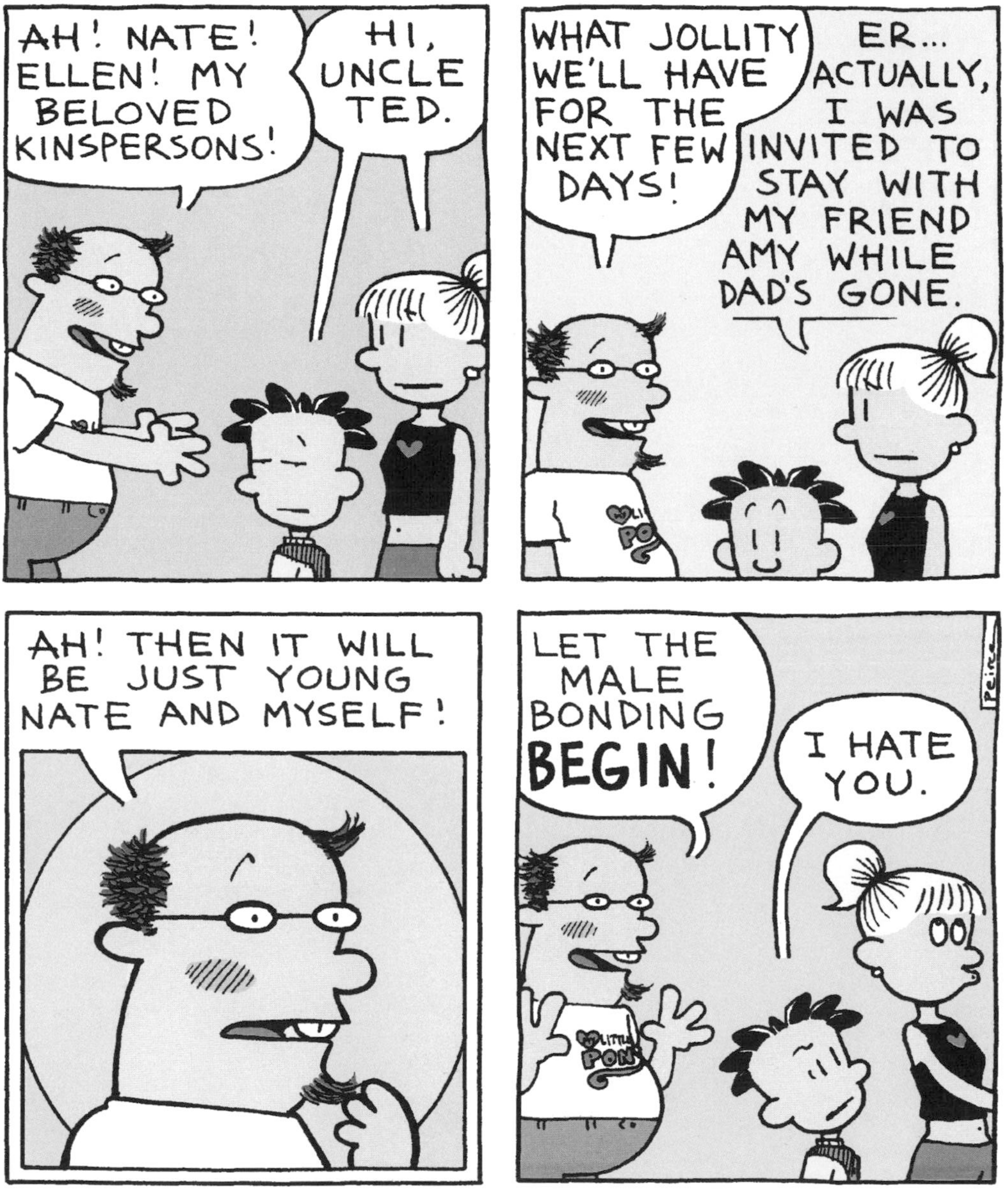
AH! NATE! ELLEN! MY BELOVED KINSPERSONS!
HI, UNCLE TED.
WHAT JOLLITY WE'LL HAVE FOR THE NEXT FEW DAYS!
ER... ACTUALLY, I WAS INVITED TO STAY WITH MY FRIEND AMY WHILE DAD'S GONE.
AH! THEN IT WILL BE JUST YOUNG NATE AND MYSELF!
LET THE MALE BONDING **BEGIN**!
I HATE YOU.
PEIRCE

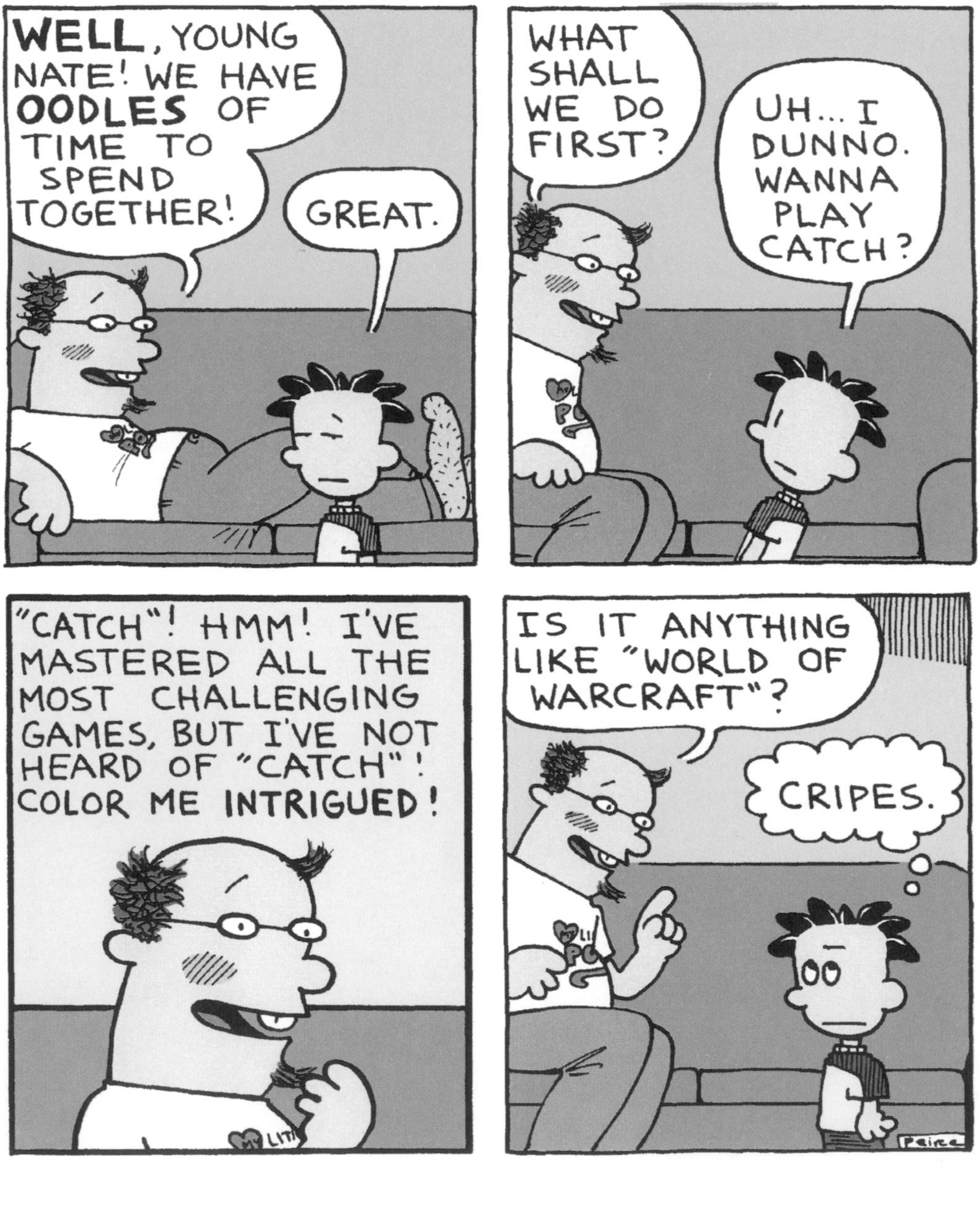
WELL, YOUNG NATE! WE HAVE OODLES OF TIME TO SPEND TOGETHER!
GREAT.
WHAT SHALL WE DO FIRST?
UH... I DUNNO. WANNA PLAY CATCH?
"CATCH"! HMM! I'VE MASTERED ALL THE MOST CHALLENGING GAMES, BUT I'VE NOT HEARD OF "CATCH"! COLOR ME INTRIGUED!
IS IT ANYTHING LIKE "WORLD OF WARCRAFT"?
CRIPES.
Peirce

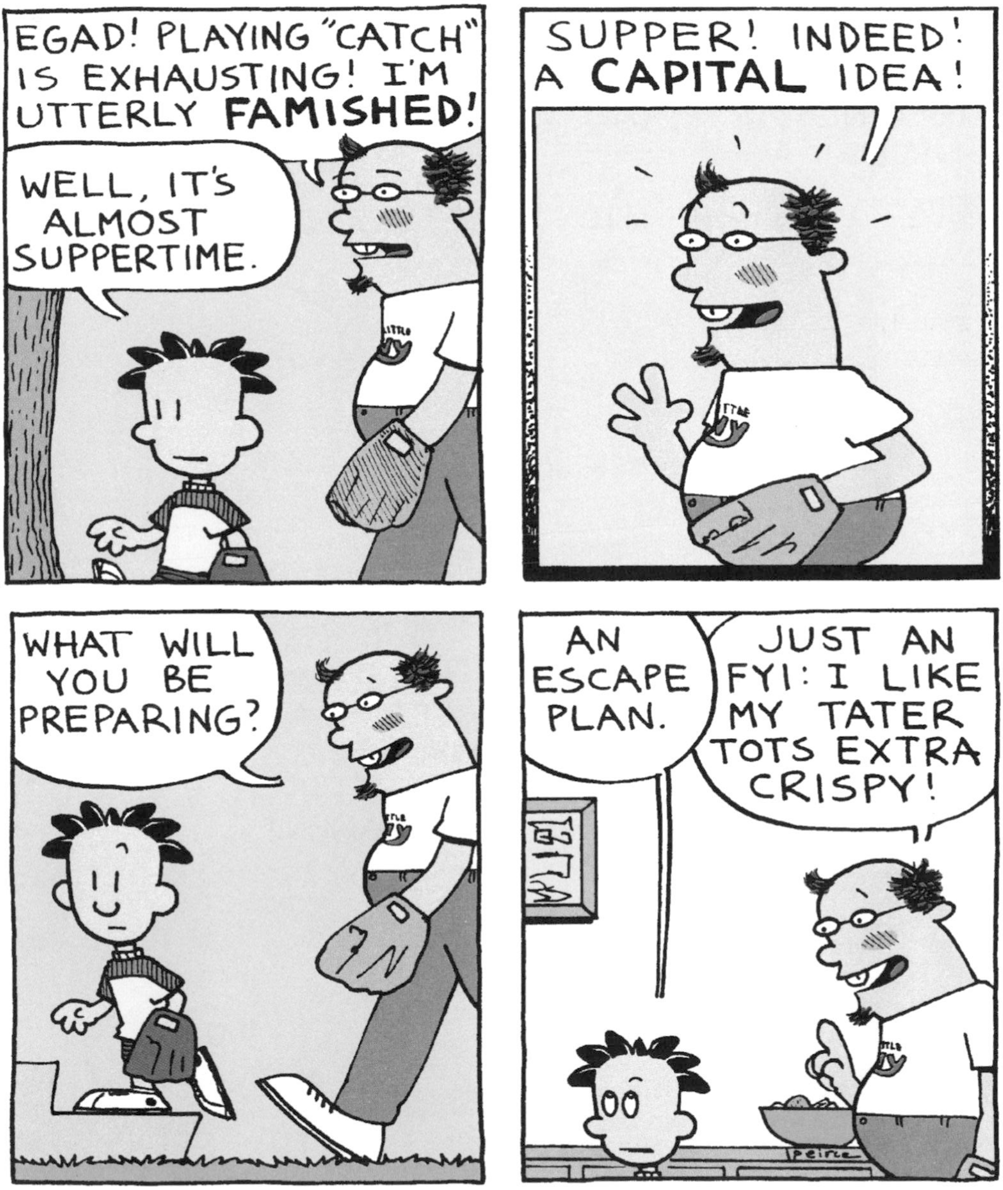
EGAD! PLAYING "CATCH" IS EXHAUSTING! I'M UTTERLY **FAMISHED**!
WELL, IT'S ALMOST SUPPERTIME.
SUPPER! INDEED! A **CAPITAL** IDEA!
WHAT WILL YOU BE PREPARING?
AN ESCAPE PLAN.
JUST AN FYI: I LIKE MY TATER TOTS EXTRA CRISPY!
peirce

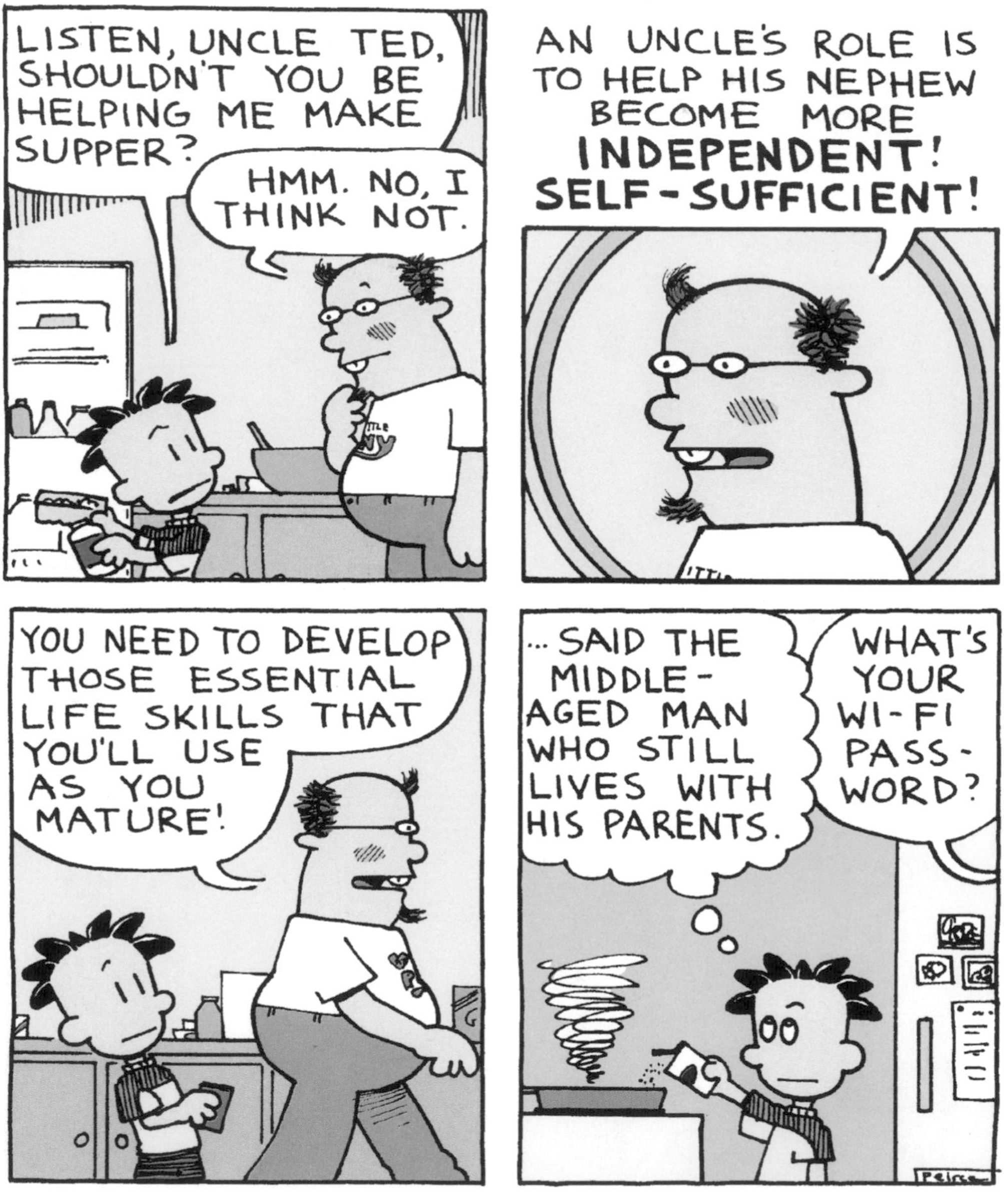
LISTEN, UNCLE TED, SHOULDN'T YOU BE HELPING ME MAKE SUPPER?
HMM. NO, I THINK NOT.
AN UNCLE'S ROLE IS TO HELP HIS NEPHEW BECOME MORE INDEPENDENT! SELF-SUFFICIENT!
YOU NEED TO DEVELOP THOSE ESSENTIAL LIFE SKILLS THAT YOU'LL USE AS YOU MATURE!
...SAID THE MIDDLE-AGED MAN WHO STILL LIVES WITH HIS PARENTS.
WHAT'S YOUR WI-FI PASS-WORD?

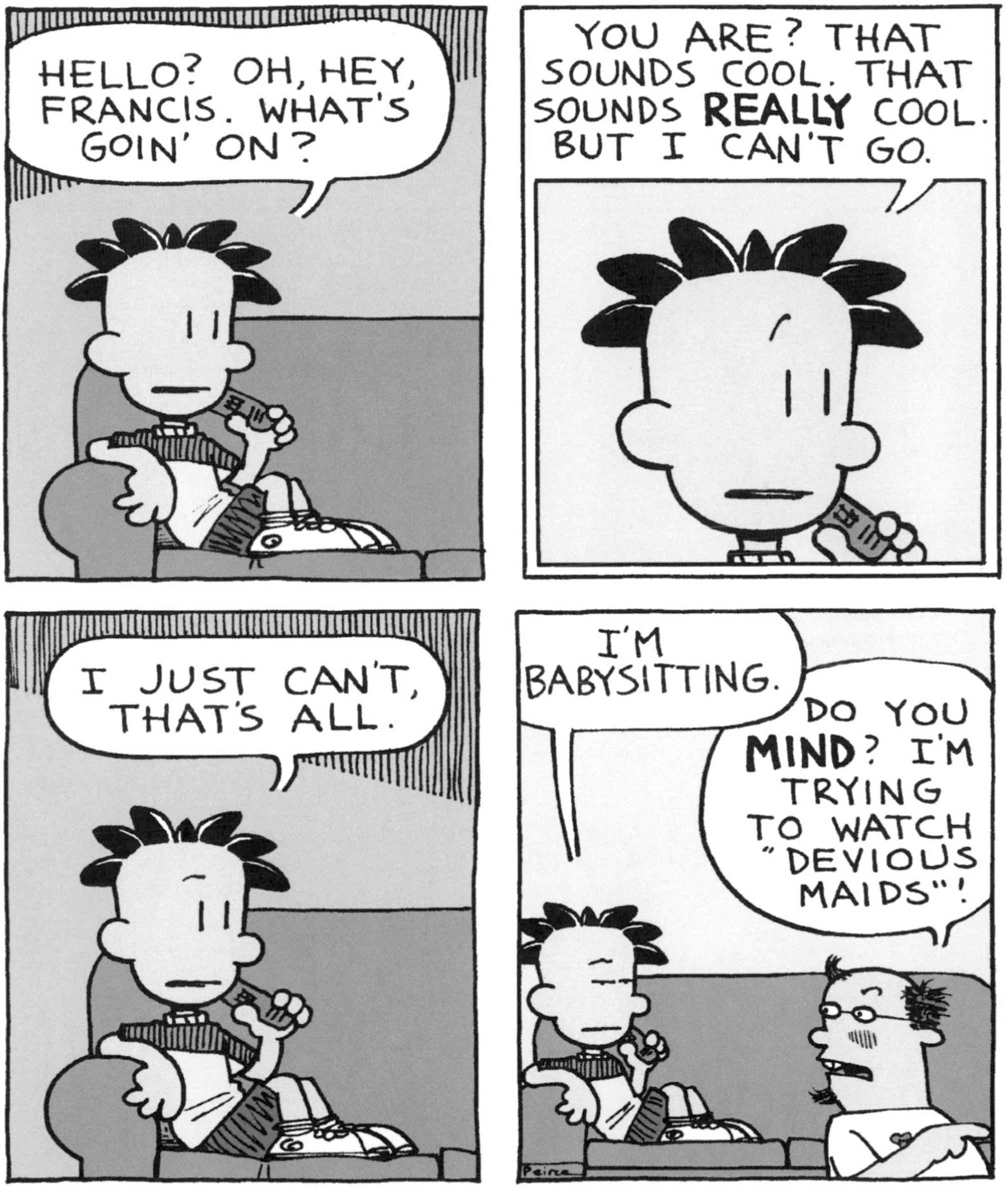
HELLO? OH, HEY, FRANCIS. WHAT'S GOIN' ON?
YOU ARE? THAT SOUNDS COOL. THAT SOUNDS REALLY COOL. BUT I CAN'T GO.
I JUST CAN'T, THAT'S ALL.
I'M BABYSITTING.
DO YOU MIND? I'M TRYING TO WATCH "DEVIOUS MAIDS"!
Peirce

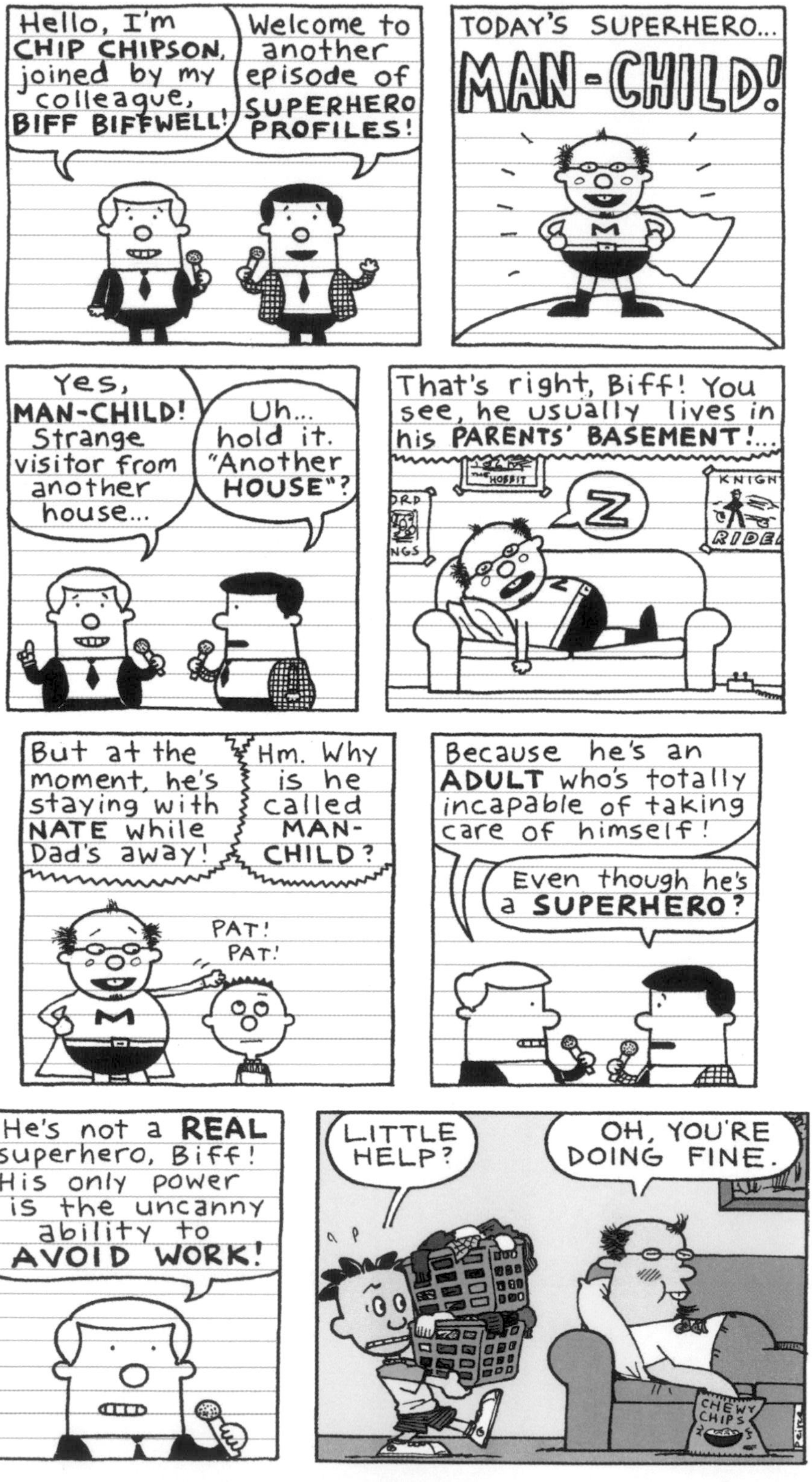
Hello, I'm CHIP CHIPSON, joined by my colleague, BIFF BIFFWELL!
Welcome to another episode of SUPERHERO PROFILES!
TODAY'S SUPERHERO...
MAN-CHILD!
Yes, MAN-CHILD! Strange visitor from another house...
Uh... hold it. "Another HOUSE"?
That's right, Biff! You see, he usually lives in his PARENTS' BASEMENT!...
Z
But at the moment, he's staying with NATE while Dad's away!
Hm. Why is he called MAN-CHILD?
PAT! PAT!
Because he's an ADULT who's totally incapable of taking care of himself!
Even though he's a SUPERHERO?
He's not a REAL superhero, Biff! His only power is the uncanny ability to AVOID WORK!
LITTLE HELP?
OH, YOU'RE DOING FINE.
CHEWY CHIPS

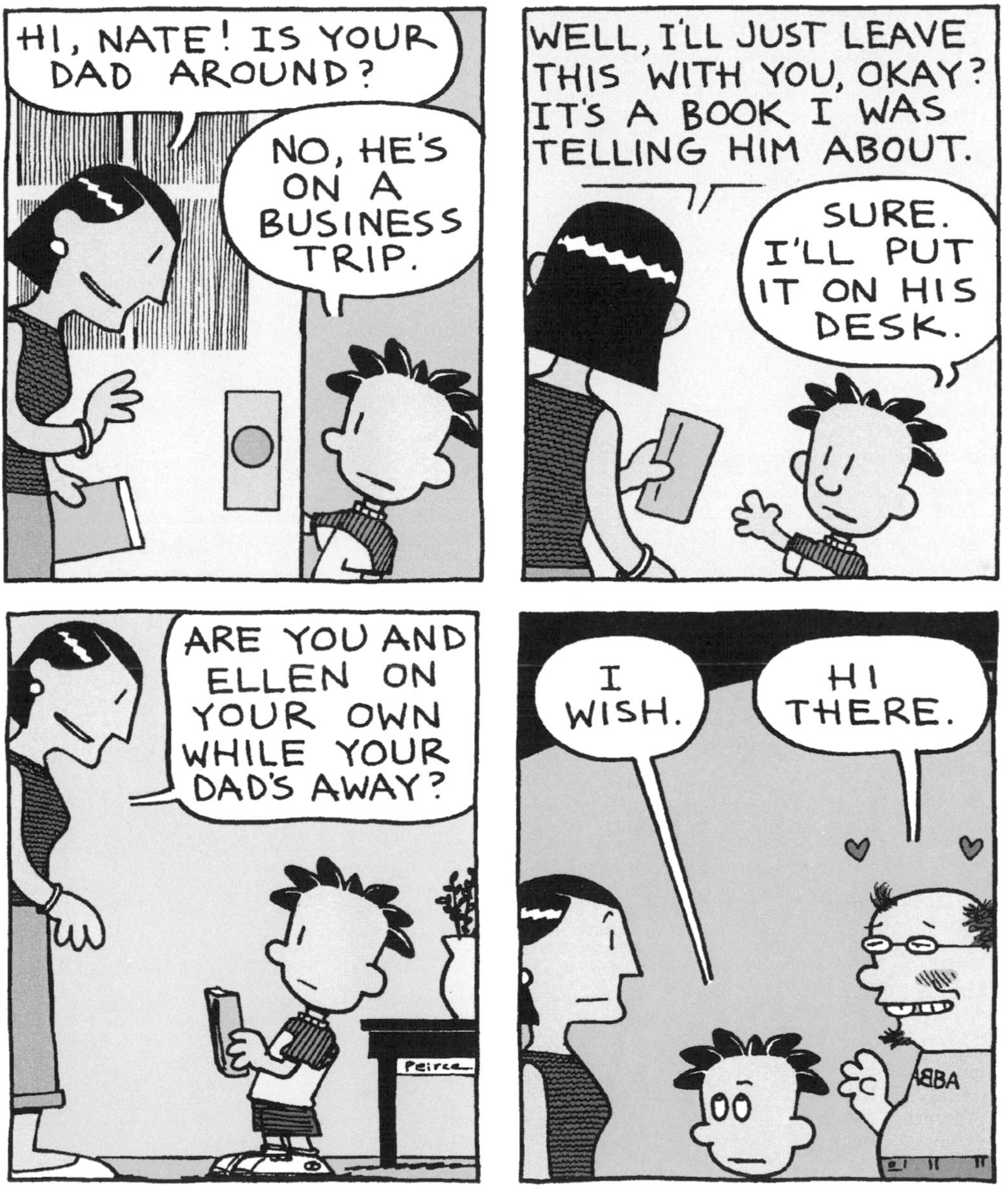
HI, NATE! IS YOUR DAD AROUND?
NO, HE'S ON A BUSINESS TRIP.
WELL, I'LL JUST LEAVE THIS WITH YOU, OKAY? IT'S A BOOK I WAS TELLING HIM ABOUT.
SURE. I'LL PUT IT ON HIS DESK.
ARE YOU AND ELLEN ON YOUR OWN WHILE YOUR DAD'S AWAY?
Peirce
I WISH.
HI THERE.
ABBA

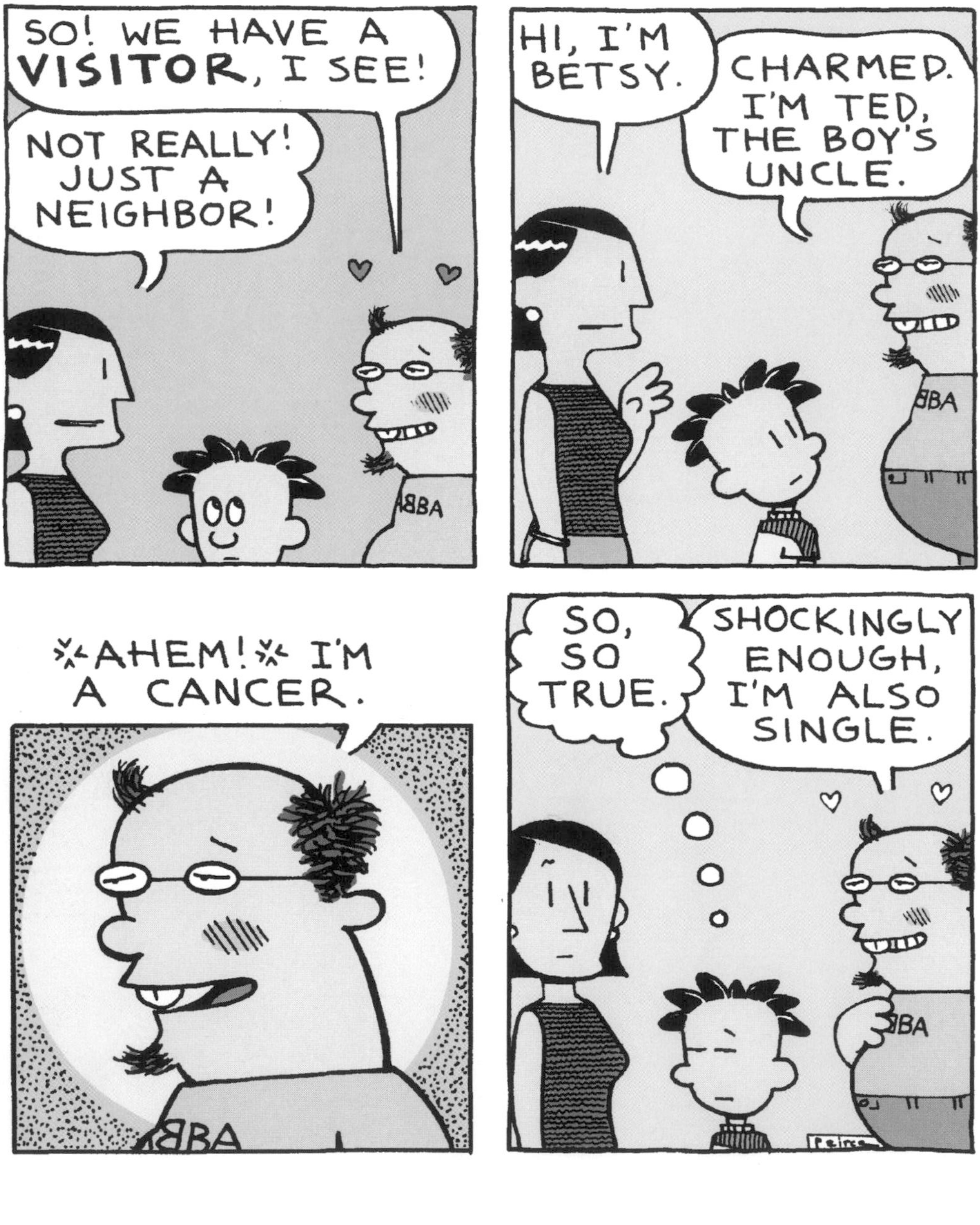
SO! WE HAVE A VISITOR, I SEE!
NOT REALLY! JUST A NEIGHBOR!
ABBA
HI, I'M BETSY.
CHARMED. I'M TED, THE BOY'S UNCLE.
ABBA
AHEM! I'M A CANCER.
ABBA
SO, SO TRUE.
SHOCKINGLY ENOUGH, I'M ALSO SINGLE.
ABBA
Peirce

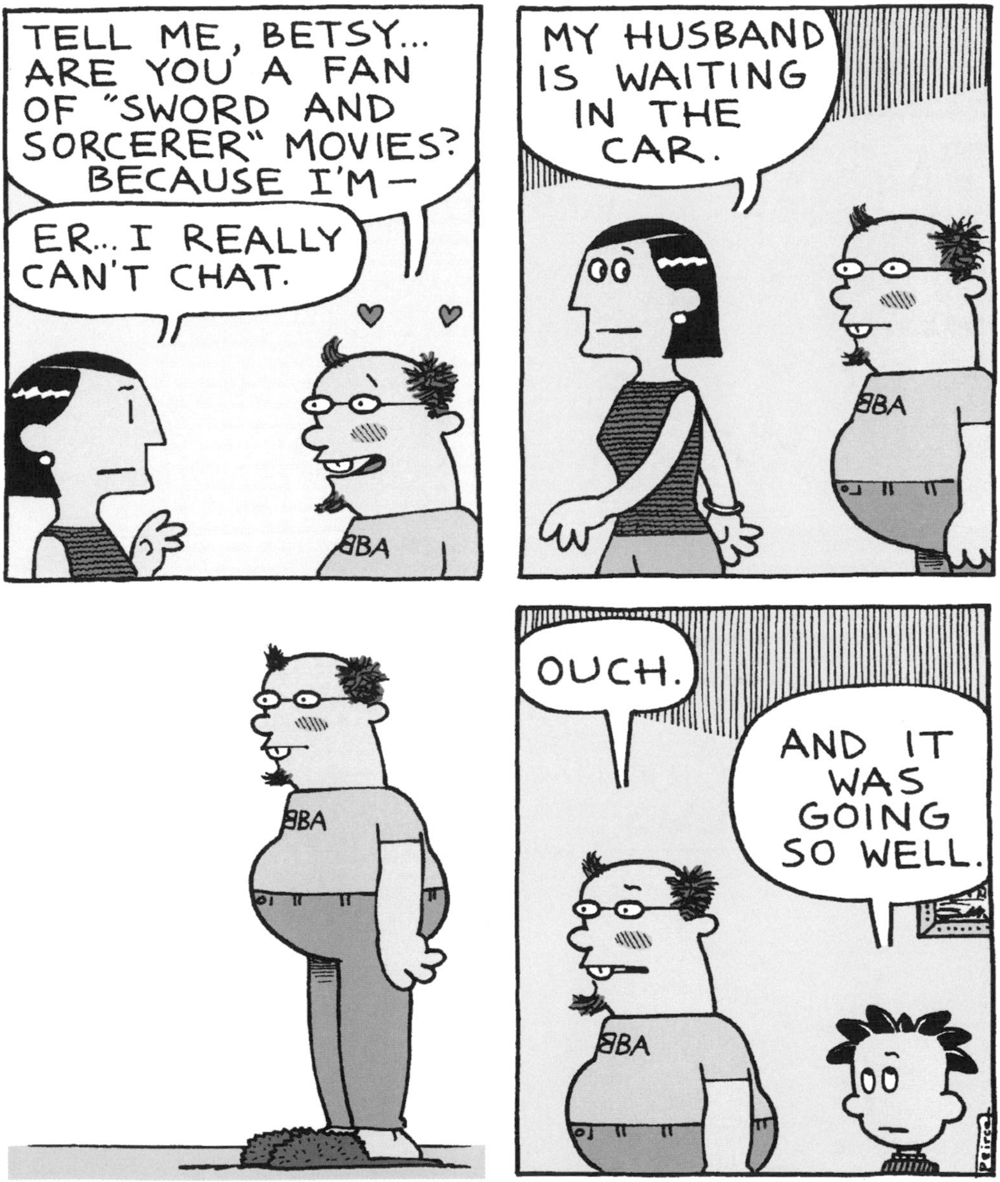
TELL ME, BETSY... ARE YOU A FAN OF "SWORD AND SORCERER" MOVIES? BECAUSE I'M—
ER... I REALLY CAN'T CHAT.
MY HUSBAND IS WAITING IN THE CAR.
OUCH.
AND IT WAS GOING SO WELL.

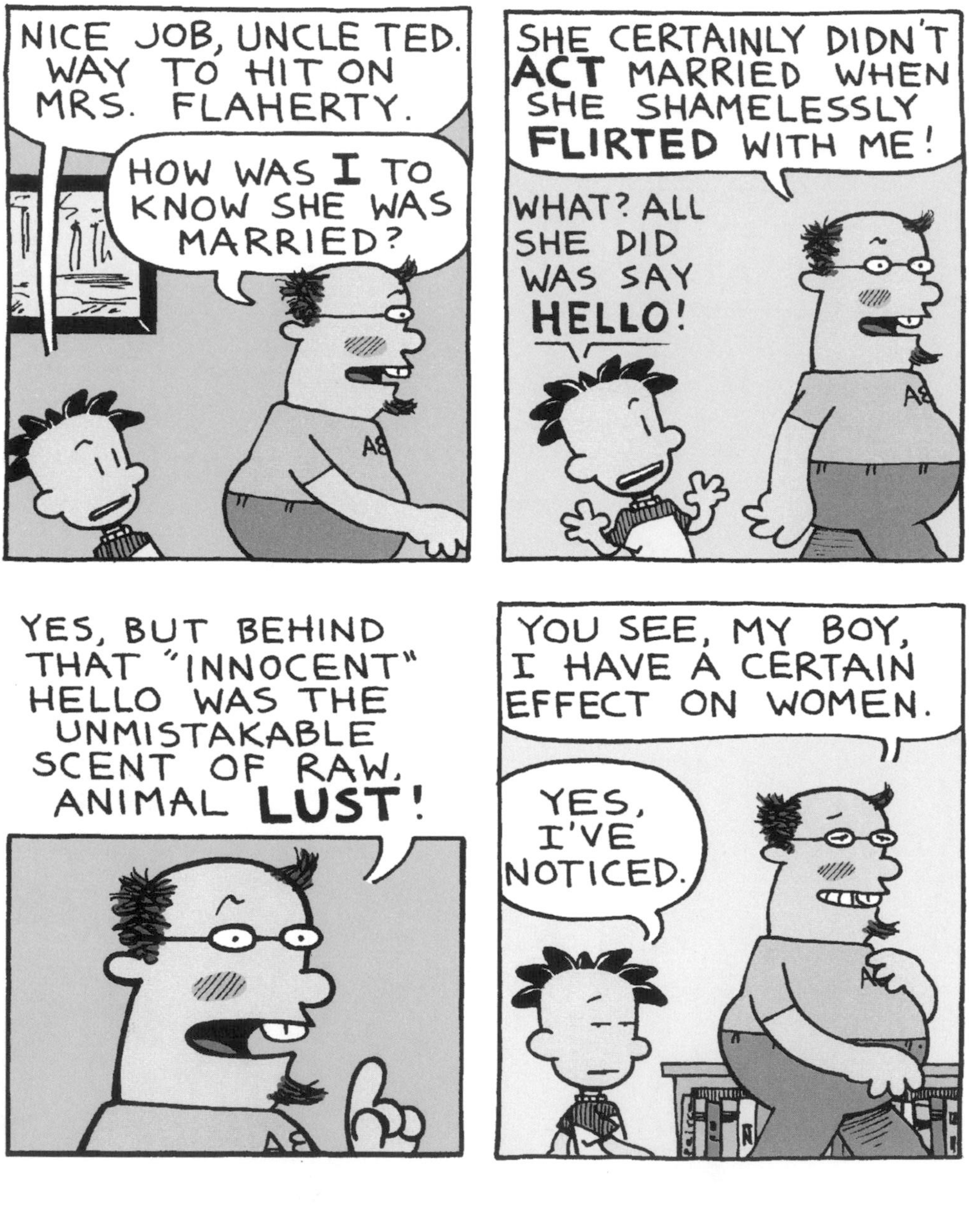
NICE JOB, UNCLE TED. WAY TO HIT ON MRS. FLAHERTY.
HOW WAS I TO KNOW SHE WAS MARRIED?
A8
SHE CERTAINLY DIDN'T ACT MARRIED WHEN SHE SHAMELESSLY FLIRTED WITH ME!
WHAT? ALL SHE DID WAS SAY HELLO!
A8
YES, BUT BEHIND THAT "INNOCENT" HELLO WAS THE UNMISTAKABLE SCENT OF RAW, ANIMAL LUST!
YOU SEE, MY BOY, I HAVE A CERTAIN EFFECT ON WOMEN.
YES, I'VE NOTICED.

HELLOOO! I'M HOME!
DAD!
YOU'RE BACK! OH, MAN, AM I HAPPY TO SEE YOU!
REALLY HAPPY! SO, SO HAPPY!
I MEAN, YOU HAVE NO IDEA HOW HAP-
POINT TAKEN, KID.

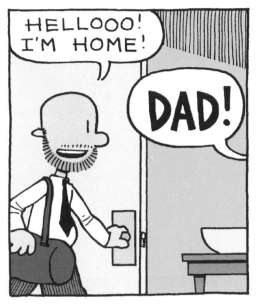

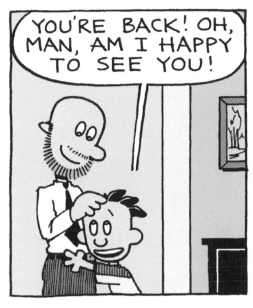

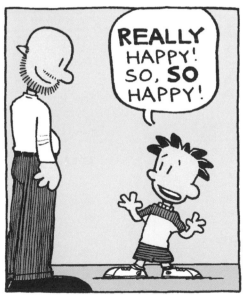

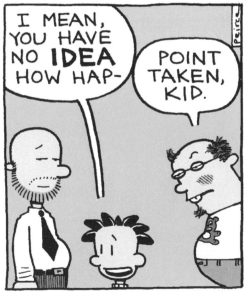

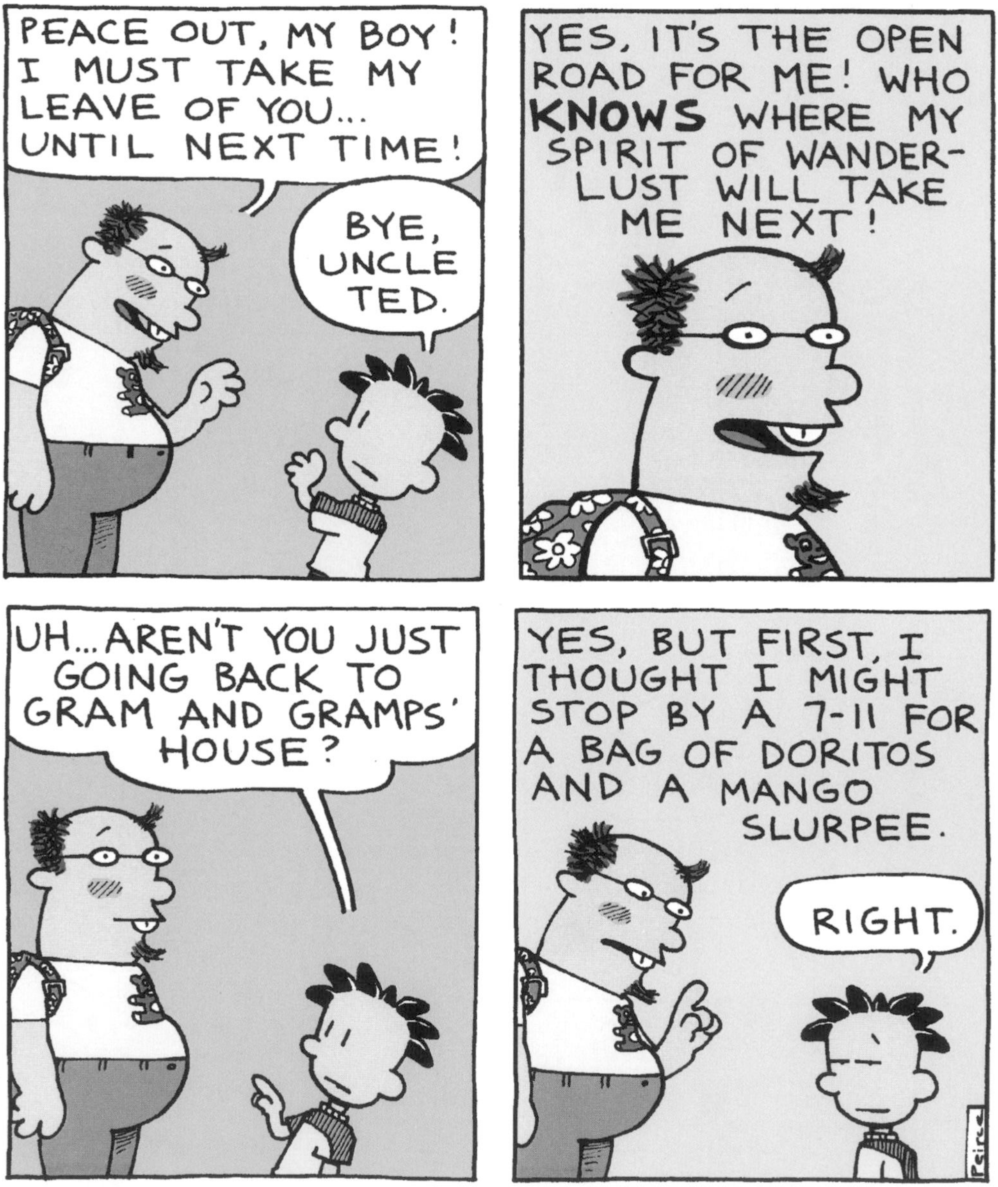
PEACE OUT, MY BOY! I MUST TAKE MY LEAVE OF YOU... UNTIL NEXT TIME!
BYE, UNCLE TED.
YES, IT'S THE OPEN ROAD FOR ME! WHO **KNOWS** WHERE MY SPIRIT OF WANDER-LUST WILL TAKE ME NEXT!
UH... AREN'T YOU JUST GOING BACK TO GRAM AND GRAMPS' HOUSE?
YES, BUT FIRST, I THOUGHT I MIGHT STOP BY A 7-11 FOR A BAG OF DORITOS AND A MANGO SLURPEE.
RIGHT.
Peirce

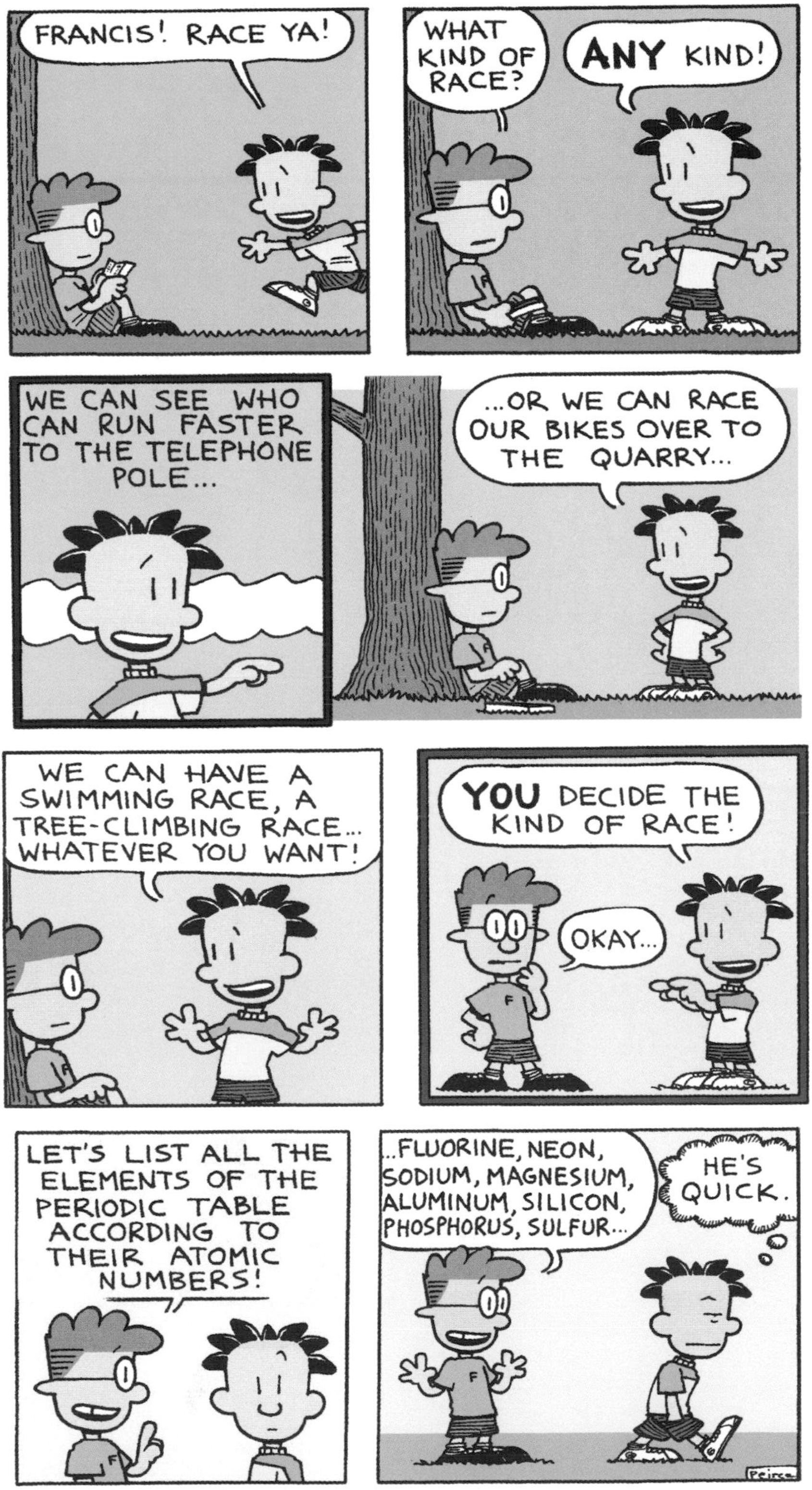

FRANCIS! RACE YA!
WHAT KIND OF RACE?
ANY KIND!
WE CAN SEE WHO CAN RUN FASTER TO THE TELEPHONE POLE...
...OR WE CAN RACE OUR BIKES OVER TO THE QUARRY...
WE CAN HAVE A SWIMMING RACE, A TREE-CLIMBING RACE... WHATEVER YOU WANT!
YOU DECIDE THE KIND OF RACE!
OKAY...
LET'S LIST ALL THE ELEMENTS OF THE PERIODIC TABLE ACCORDING TO THEIR ATOMIC NUMBERS!
...FLUORINE, NEON, SODIUM, MAGNESIUM, ALUMINUM, SILICON, PHOSPHORUS, SULFUR...
HE'S QUICK.
Peirce

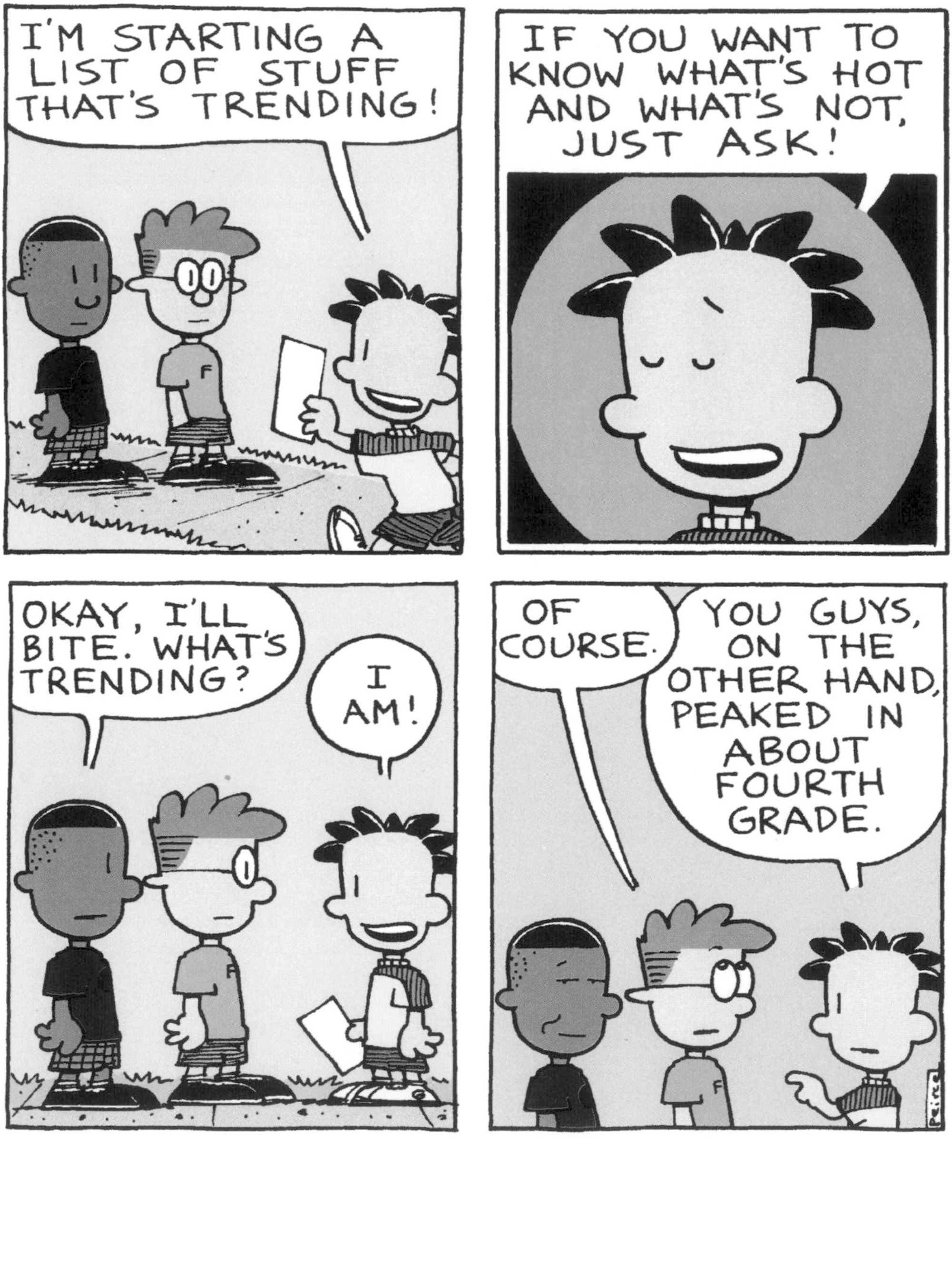
I'M STARTING A LIST OF STUFF THAT'S TRENDING!
IF YOU WANT TO KNOW WHAT'S HOT AND WHAT'S NOT, JUST ASK!
OKAY, I'LL BITE. WHAT'S TRENDING?
I AM!
OF COURSE.
YOU GUYS, ON THE OTHER HAND, PEAKED IN ABOUT FOURTH GRADE.

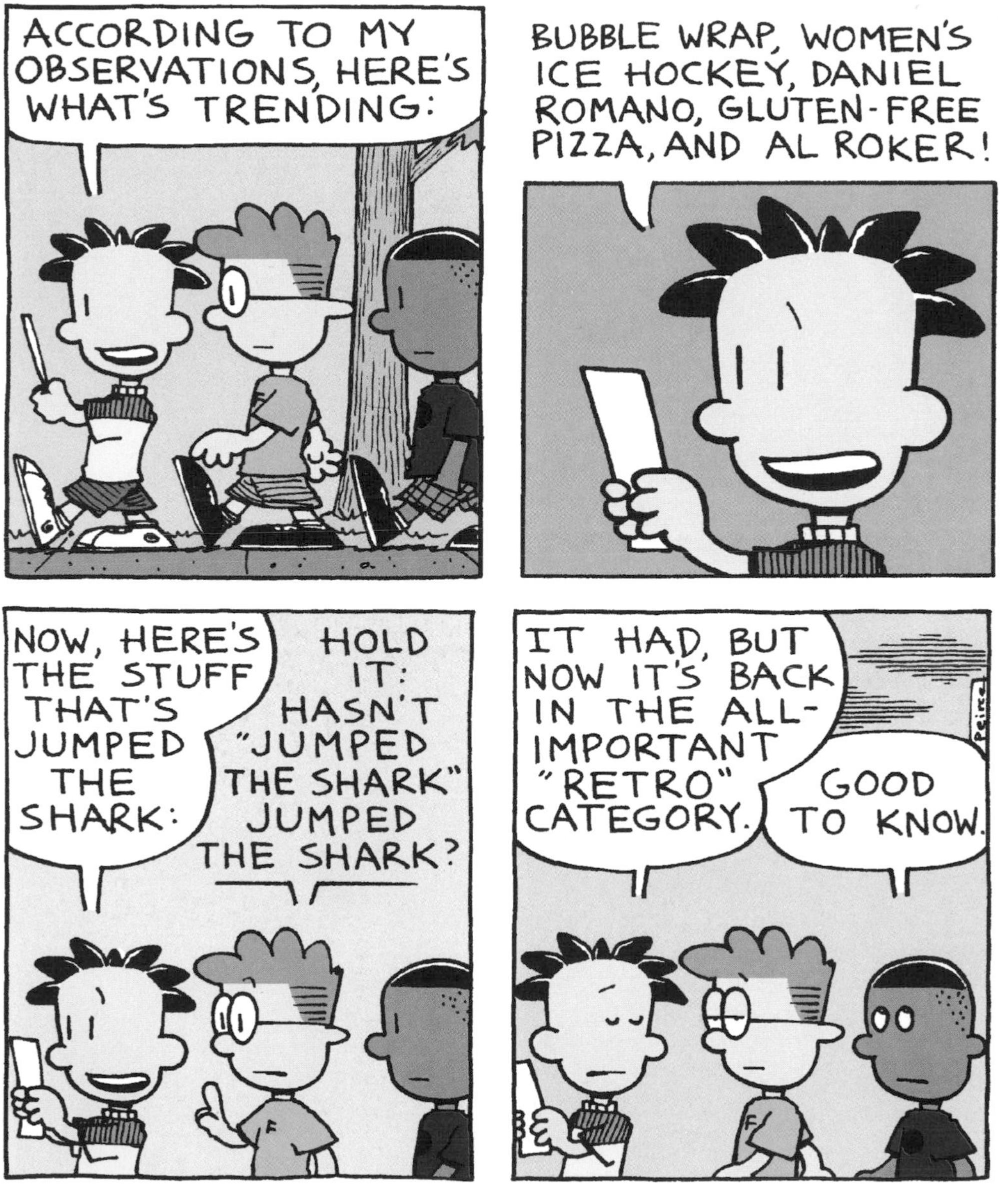
ACCORDING TO MY OBSERVATIONS, HERE'S WHAT'S TRENDING:
BUBBLE WRAP, WOMEN'S ICE HOCKEY, DANIEL ROMANO, GLUTEN-FREE PIZZA, AND AL ROKER!
NOW, HERE'S THE STUFF THAT'S JUMPED THE SHARK:
HOLD IT: HASN'T "JUMPED THE SHARK" JUMPED THE SHARK?
IT HAD, BUT NOW IT'S BACK IN THE ALL-IMPORTANT "RETRO" CATEGORY.
GOOD TO KNOW.
Peirce

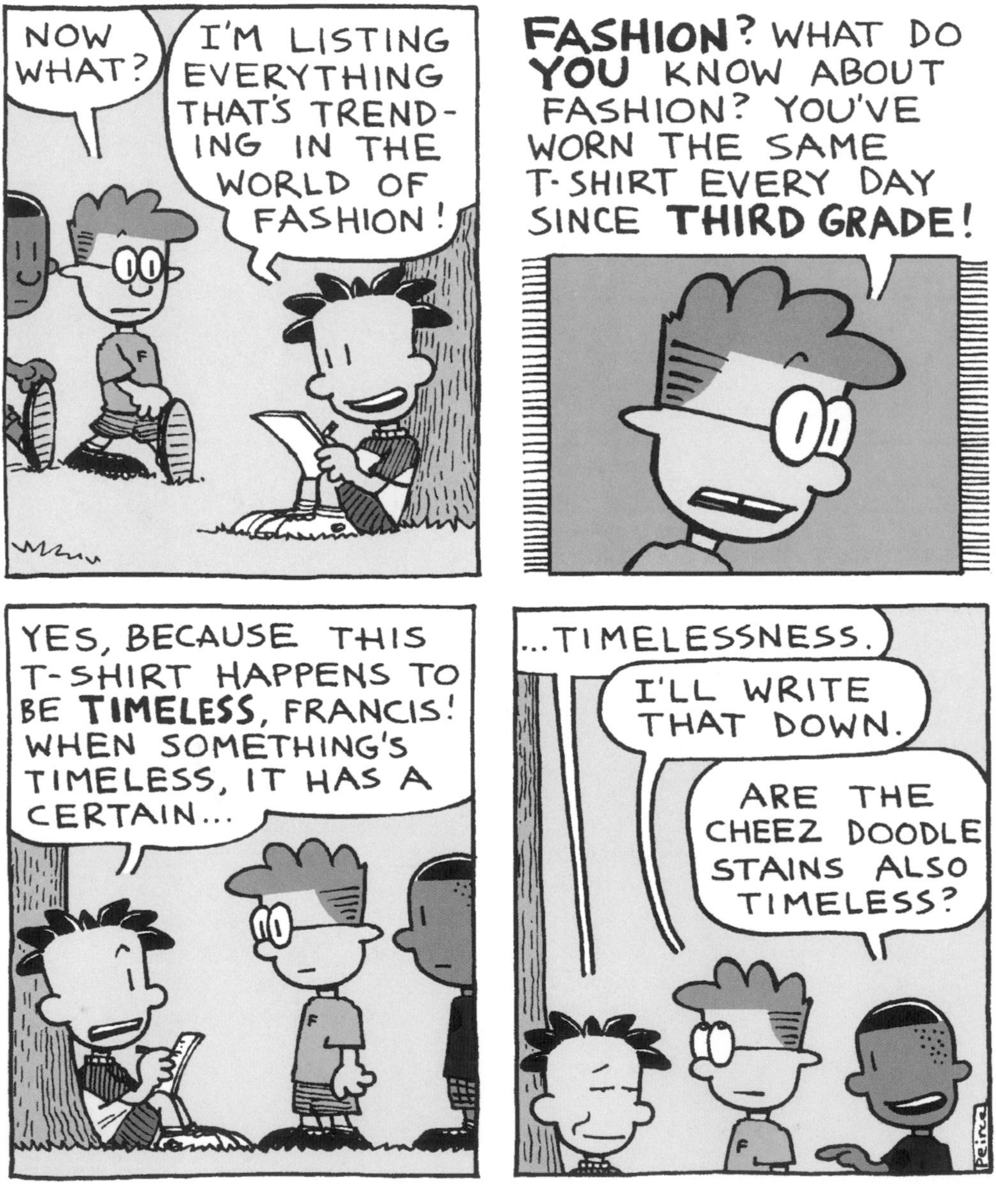
NOW WHAT?
I'M LISTING EVERYTHING THAT'S TREND-ING IN THE WORLD OF FASHION!
FASHION? WHAT DO **YOU** KNOW ABOUT FASHION? YOU'VE WORN THE SAME T-SHIRT EVERY DAY SINCE **THIRD GRADE**!
YES, BECAUSE THIS T-SHIRT HAPPENS TO BE **TIMELESS**, FRANCIS! WHEN SOMETHING'S TIMELESS, IT HAS A CERTAIN...
...TIMELESSNESS.
I'LL WRITE THAT DOWN.
ARE THE CHEEZ DOODLE STAINS ALSO TIMELESS?
Peirce

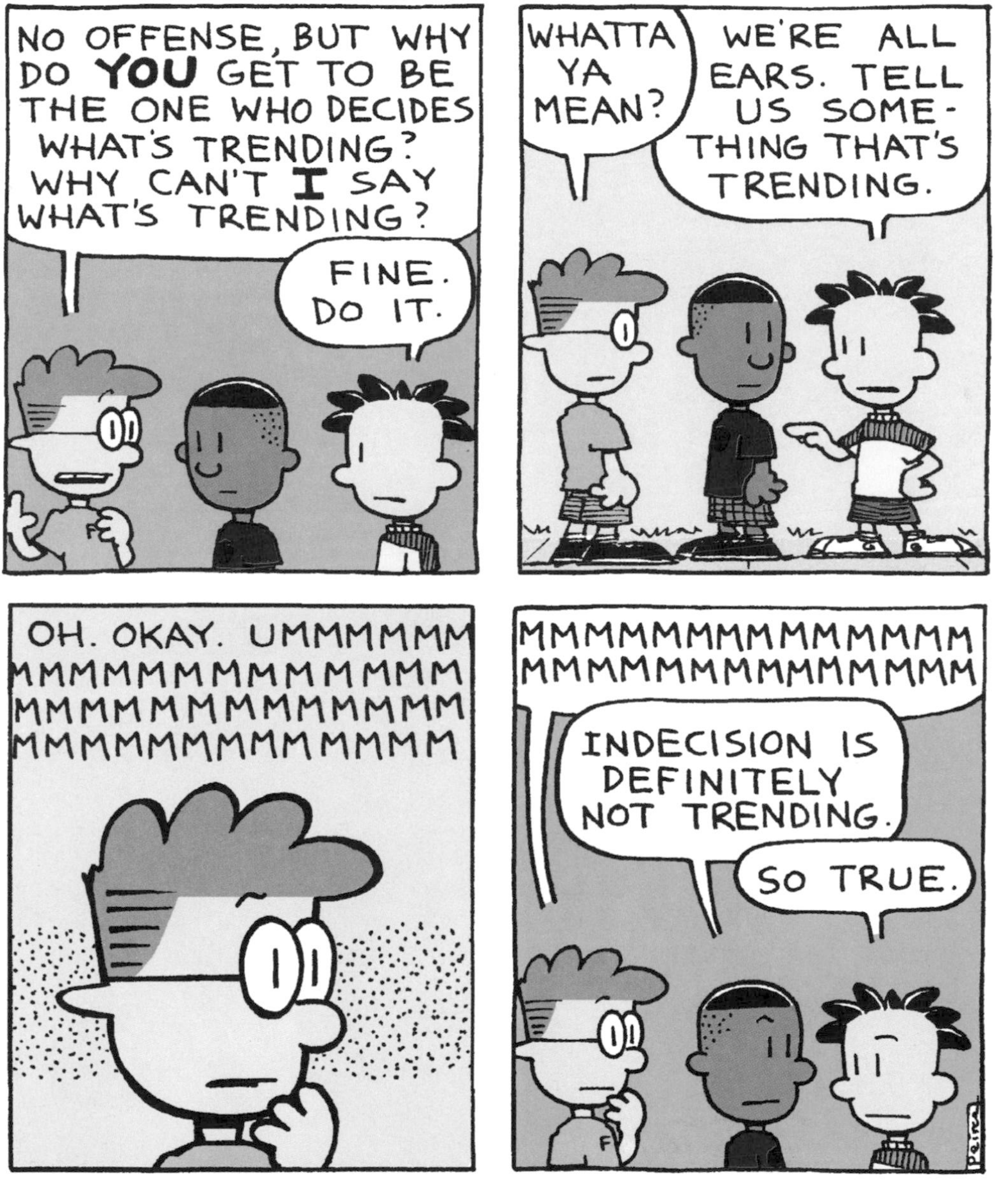
NO OFFENSE, BUT WHY DO **YOU** GET TO BE THE ONE WHO DECIDES WHAT'S TRENDING? WHY CAN'T **I** SAY WHAT'S TRENDING?
FINE. DO IT.
WHATTA YA MEAN?
WE'RE ALL EARS. TELL US SOMETHING THAT'S TRENDING.
OH. OKAY. UMMMMMMMMMMMMMMMMMMMMMMMMMMMMMMMMMMMMMMMMMMMMMMMMMMM
MMMMMMMMMMMMMMMMMMMMMMMMMMMMMMMMMMMM
INDECISION IS DEFINITELY NOT TRENDING.
SO TRUE.
PEIRCE

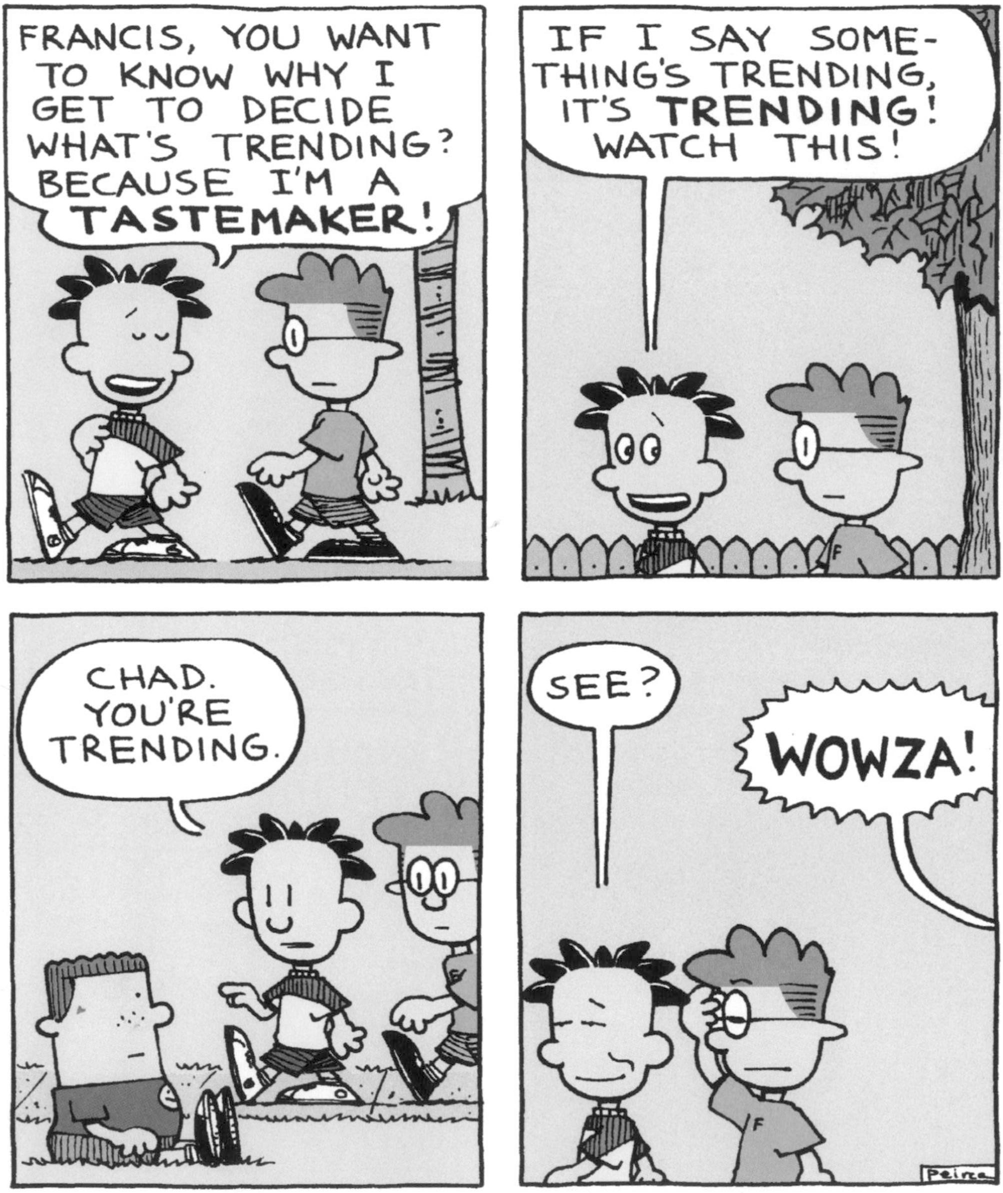
FRANCIS, YOU WANT TO KNOW WHY I GET TO DECIDE WHAT'S TRENDING? BECAUSE I'M A **TASTEMAKER**!
IF I SAY SOME-THING'S TRENDING, IT'S **TRENDING**! WATCH THIS!
CHAD. YOU'RE TRENDING.
SEE?
WOWZA!
Peirce

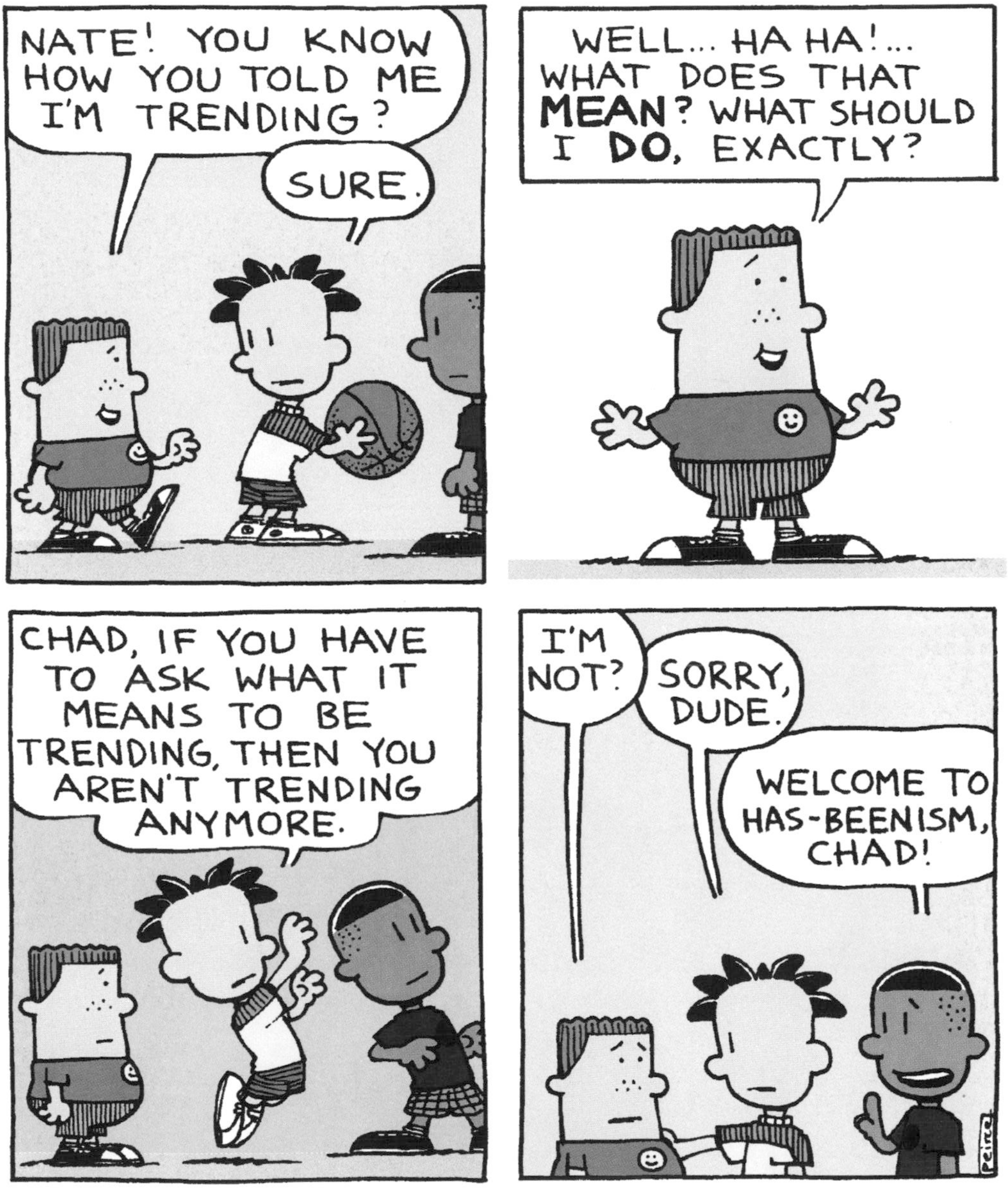
NATE! YOU KNOW HOW YOU TOLD ME I'M TRENDING?
SURE.
WELL... HA HA!... WHAT DOES THAT **MEAN**? WHAT SHOULD I **DO**, EXACTLY?
CHAD, IF YOU HAVE TO ASK WHAT IT MEANS TO BE TRENDING, THEN YOU AREN'T TRENDING ANYMORE.
I'M NOT?
SORRY, DUDE.
WELCOME TO HAS-BEENISM, CHAD!
PEIRCE

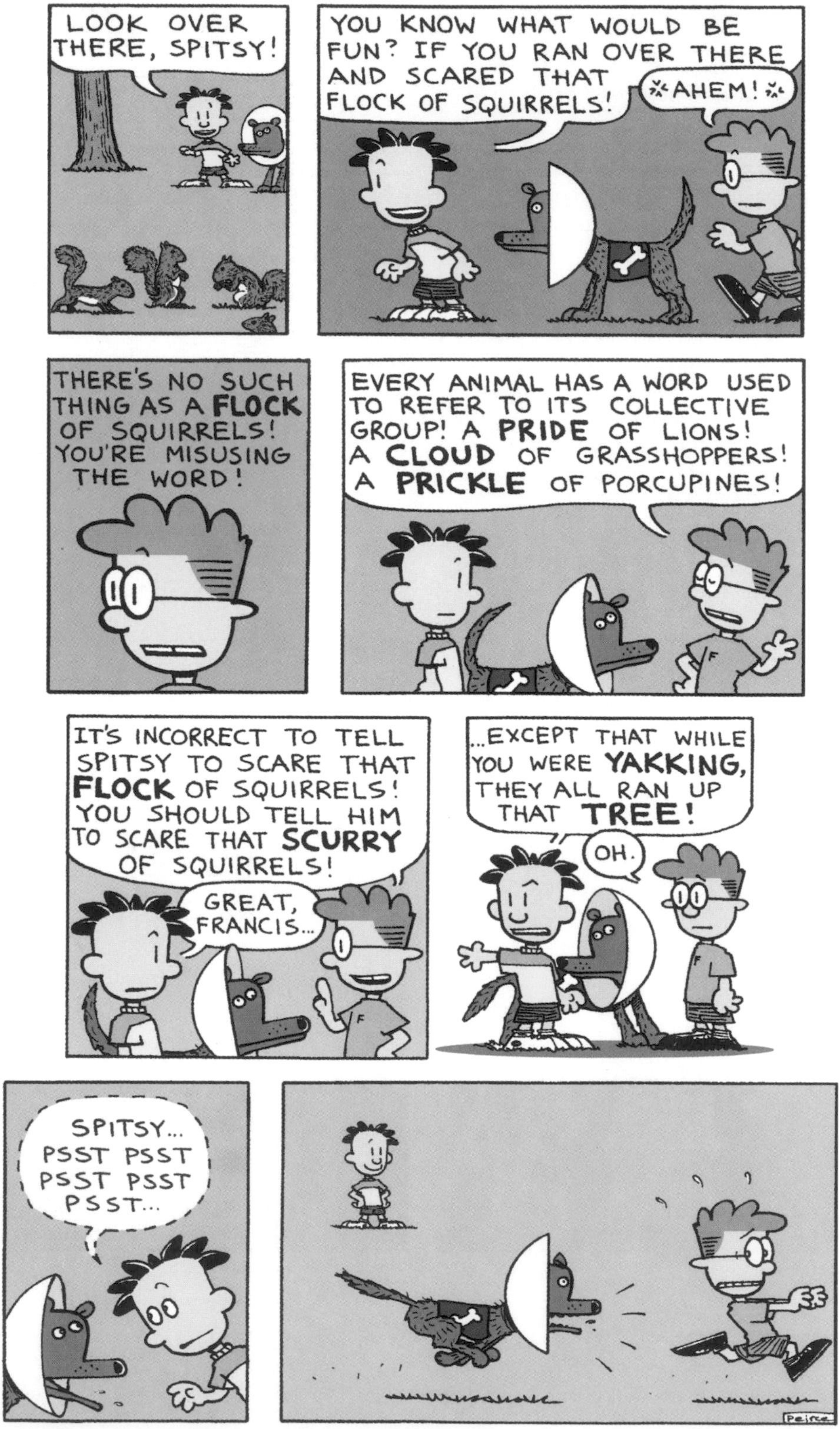
LOOK OVER THERE, SPITSY!
YOU KNOW WHAT WOULD BE FUN? IF YOU RAN OVER THERE AND SCARED THAT FLOCK OF SQUIRRELS!
AHEM!
THERE'S NO SUCH THING AS A FLOCK OF SQUIRRELS! YOU'RE MISUSING THE WORD!
EVERY ANIMAL HAS A WORD USED TO REFER TO ITS COLLECTIVE GROUP! A PRIDE OF LIONS! A CLOUD OF GRASSHOPPERS! A PRICKLE OF PORCUPINES!
IT'S INCORRECT TO TELL SPITSY TO SCARE THAT FLOCK OF SQUIRRELS! YOU SHOULD TELL HIM TO SCARE THAT SCURRY OF SQUIRRELS!
GREAT, FRANCIS...
...EXCEPT THAT WHILE YOU WERE YAKKING, THEY ALL RAN UP THAT TREE!
OH.
SPITSY... PSST PSST PSST PSST PSST...
Peirce

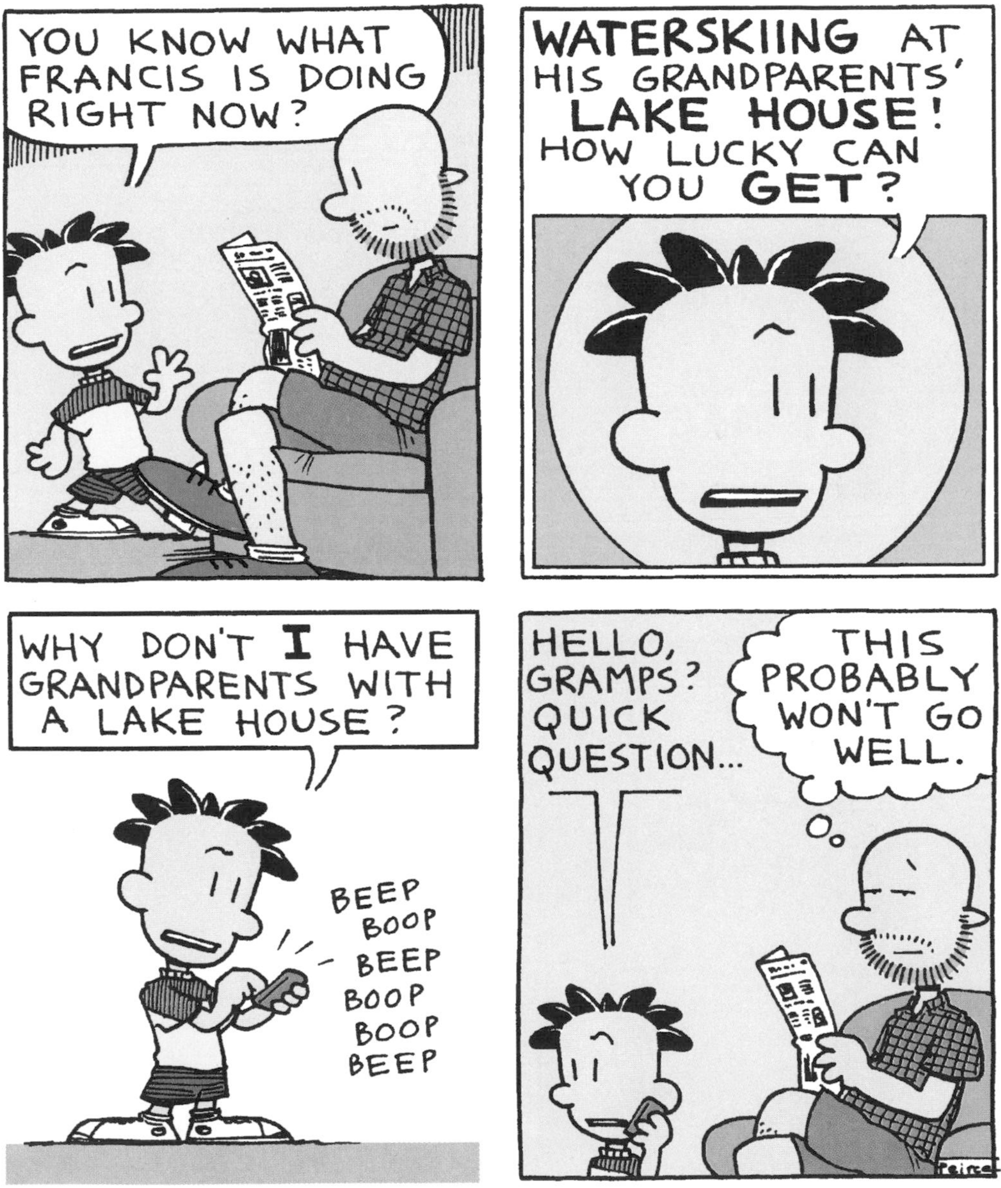
YOU KNOW WHAT FRANCIS IS DOING RIGHT NOW?
WATERSKIING AT HIS GRANDPARENTS' LAKE HOUSE! HOW LUCKY CAN YOU GET?
WHY DON'T I HAVE GRANDPARENTS WITH A LAKE HOUSE?
BEEP BOOP BEEP BOOP BOOP BEEP
HELLO, GRAMPS? QUICK QUESTION...
THIS PROBABLY WON'T GO WELL.
Peirce

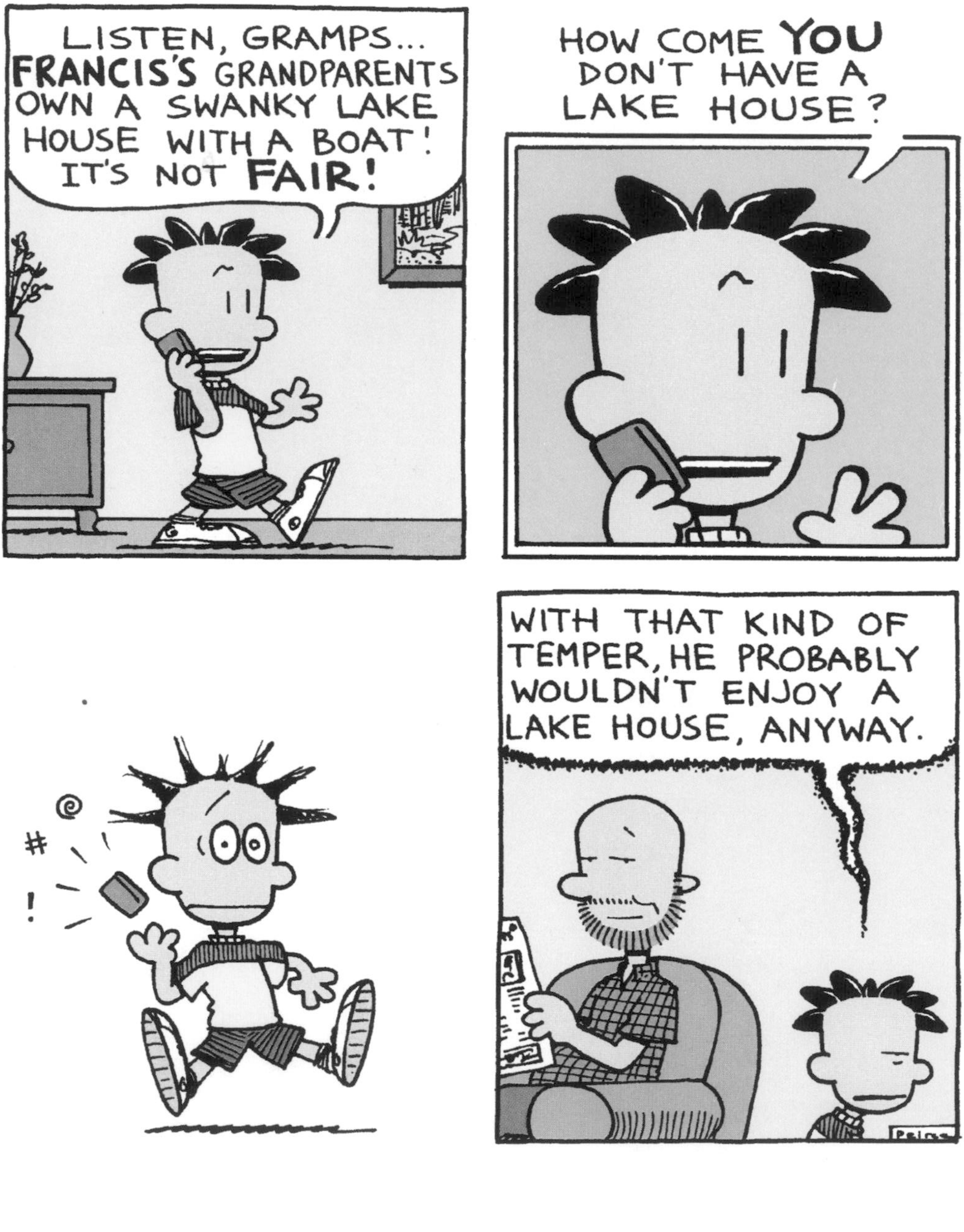
LISTEN, GRAMPS... **FRANCIS'S** GRANDPARENTS OWN A SWANKY LAKE HOUSE WITH A BOAT! IT'S NOT **FAIR**!
HOW COME **YOU** DON'T HAVE A LAKE HOUSE?
#
!
WITH THAT KIND OF TEMPER, HE PROBABLY WOULDN'T ENJOY A LAKE HOUSE, ANYWAY.

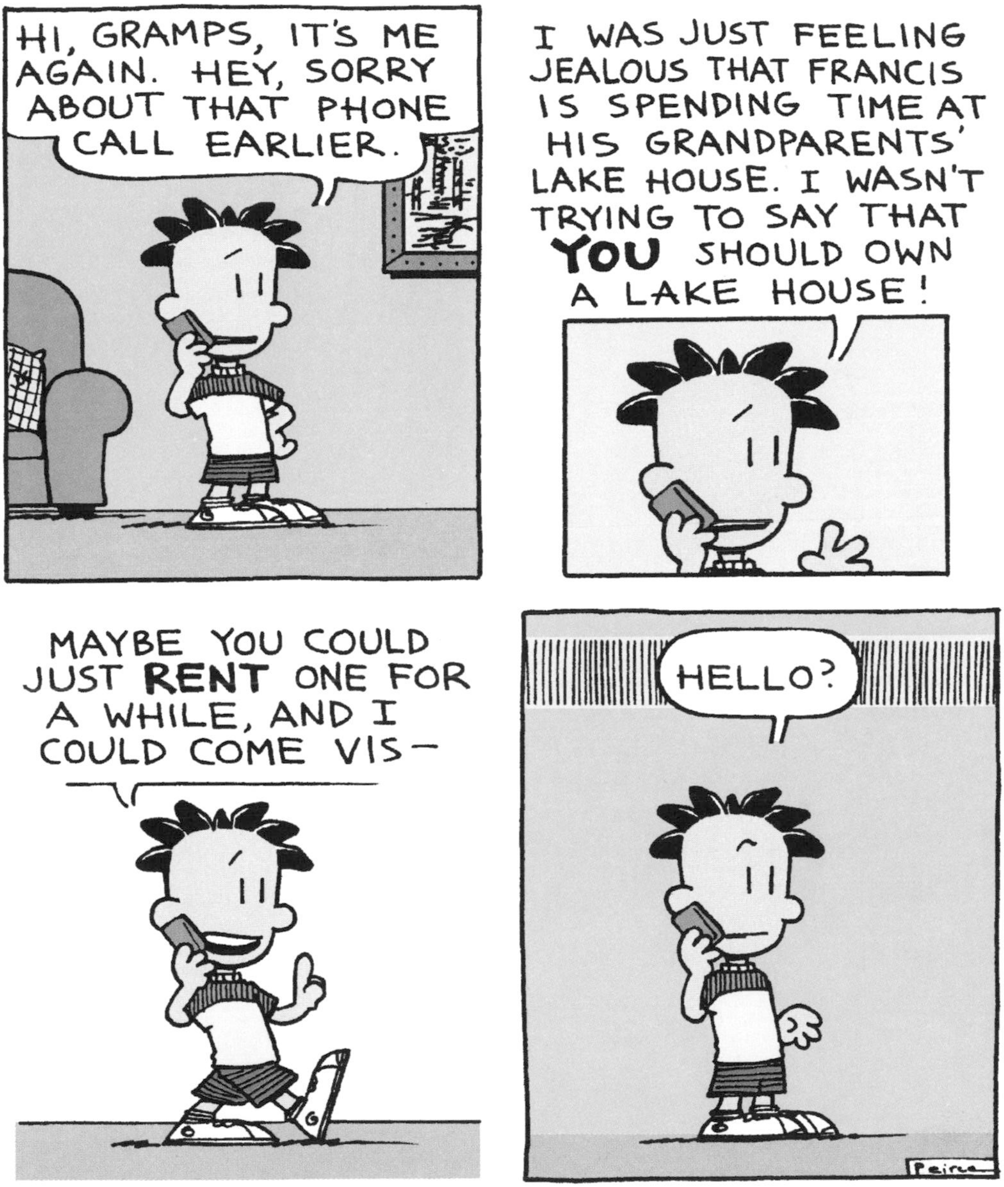
HI, GRAMPS, IT'S ME AGAIN. HEY, SORRY ABOUT THAT PHONE CALL EARLIER.
I WAS JUST FEELING JEALOUS THAT FRANCIS IS SPENDING TIME AT HIS GRANDPARENTS' LAKE HOUSE. I WASN'T TRYING TO SAY THAT YOU SHOULD OWN A LAKE HOUSE!
MAYBE YOU COULD JUST RENT ONE FOR A WHILE, AND I COULD COME VIS—
HELLO?
Peirce

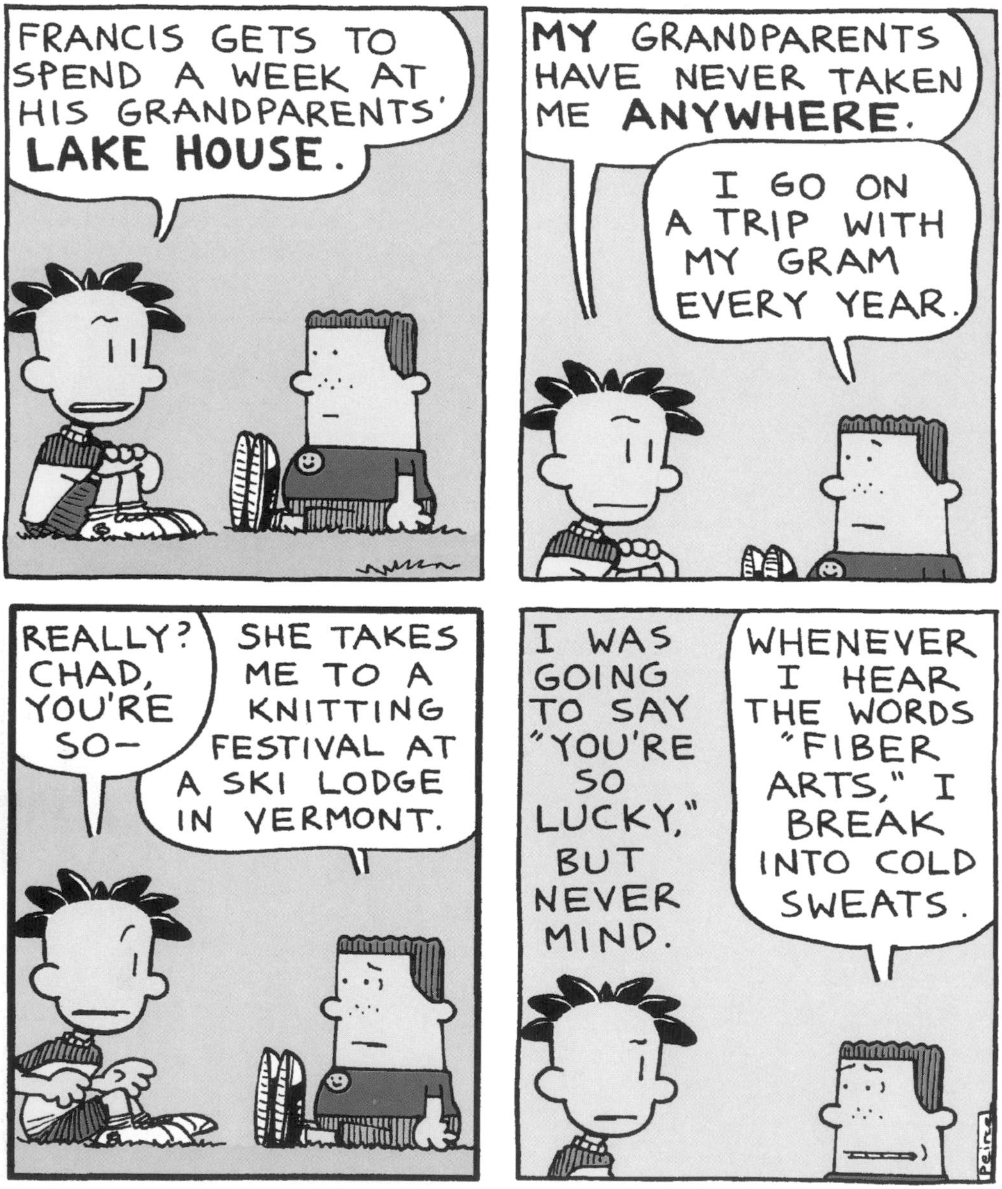
FRANCIS GETS TO SPEND A WEEK AT HIS GRANDPARENTS' **LAKE HOUSE**.
MY GRANDPARENTS HAVE NEVER TAKEN ME **ANYWHERE**.
I GO ON A TRIP WITH MY GRAM EVERY YEAR.
REALLY? CHAD, YOU'RE SO—
SHE TAKES ME TO A KNITTING FESTIVAL AT A SKI LODGE IN VERMONT.
I WAS GOING TO SAY "YOU'RE SO LUCKY," BUT NEVER MIND.
WHENEVER I HEAR THE WORDS "FIBER ARTS," I BREAK INTO COLD SWEATS.
Peirce

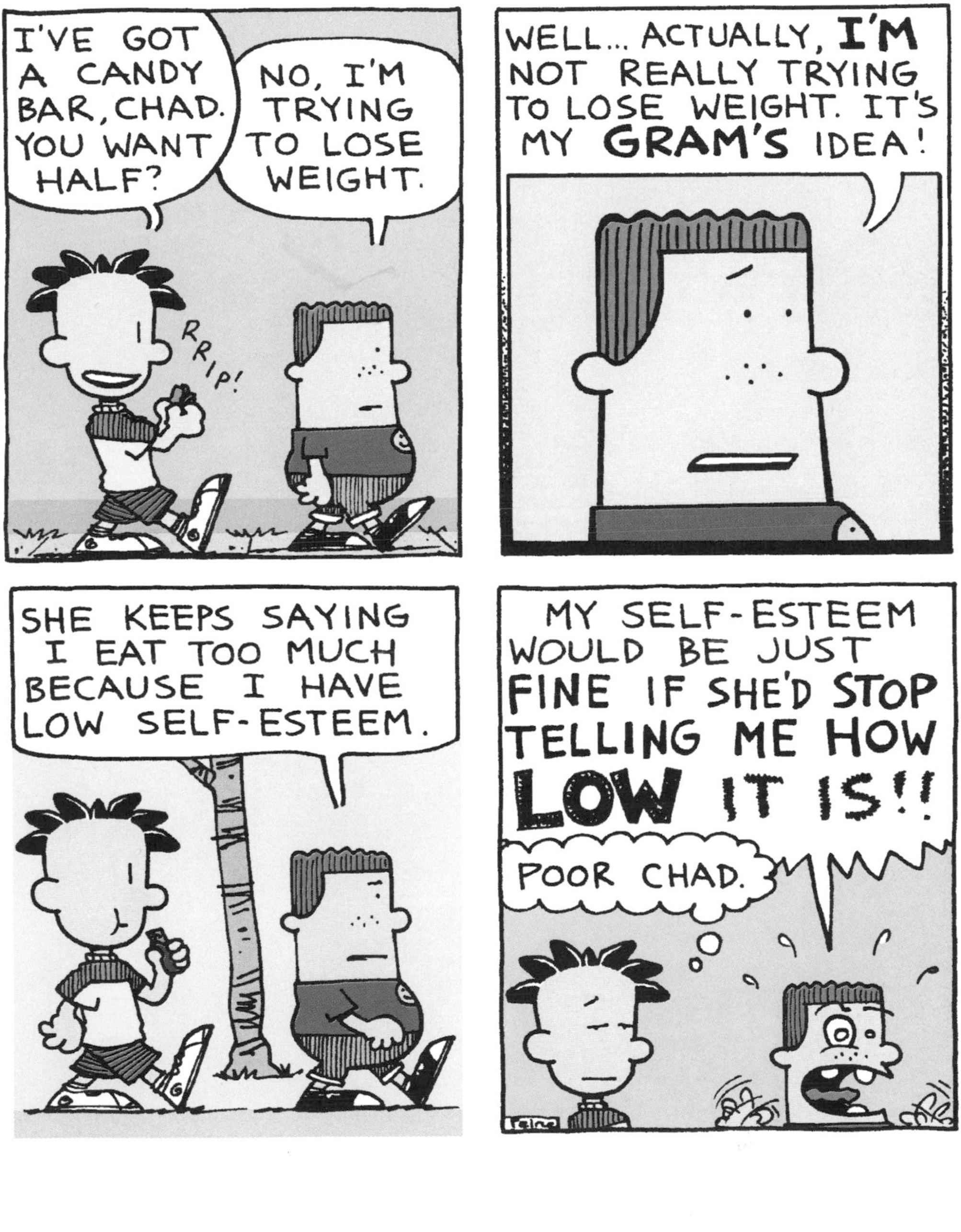
I'VE GOT A CANDY BAR, CHAD. YOU WANT HALF?
NO, I'M TRYING TO LOSE WEIGHT.
RRRIP!
WELL... ACTUALLY, I'M NOT REALLY TRYING TO LOSE WEIGHT. IT'S MY GRAM'S IDEA!
SHE KEEPS SAYING I EAT TOO MUCH BECAUSE I HAVE LOW SELF-ESTEEM.
MY SELF-ESTEEM WOULD BE JUST FINE IF SHE'D STOP TELLING ME HOW LOW IT IS!!
POOR CHAD.

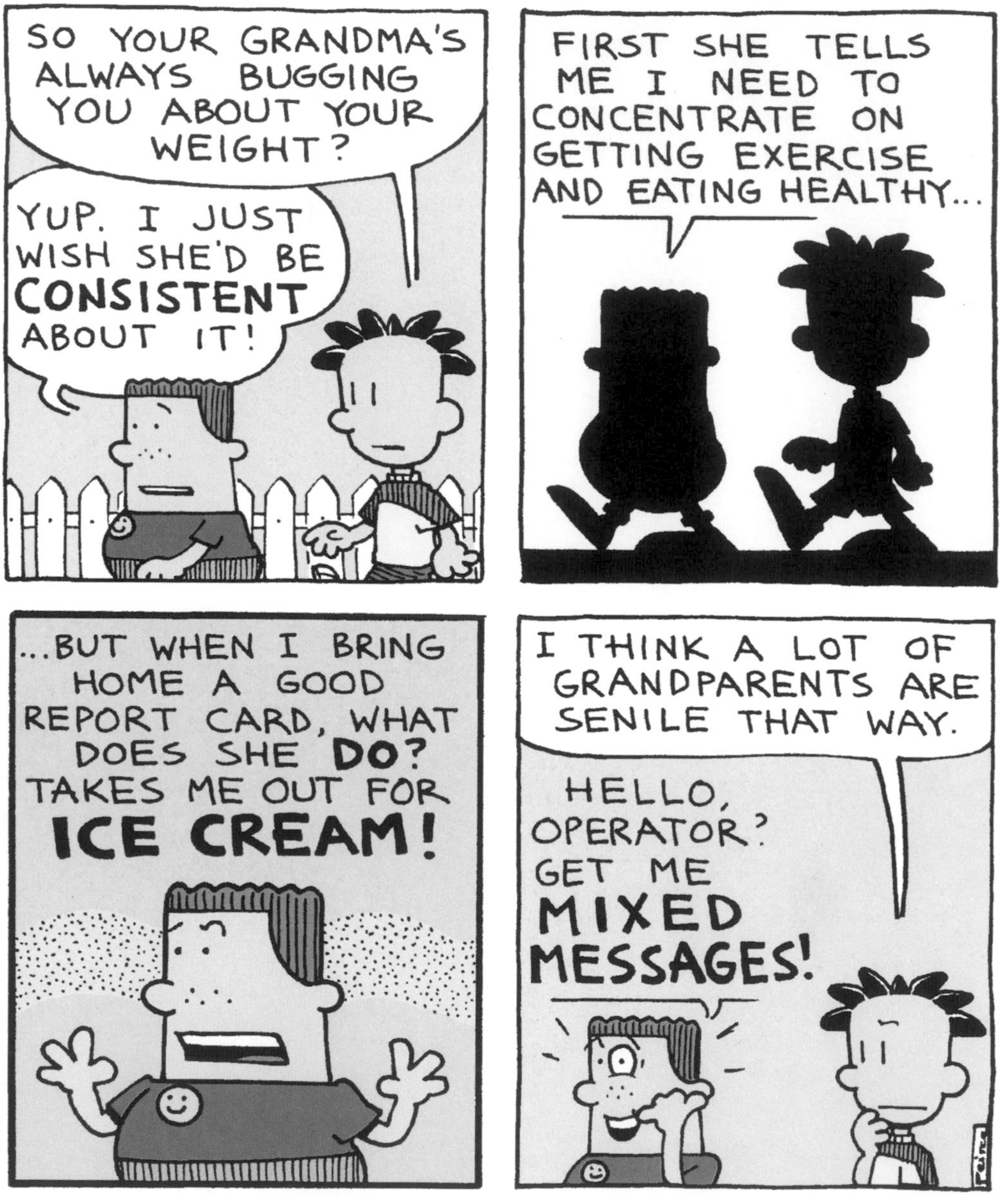
SO YOUR GRANDMA'S ALWAYS BUGGING YOU ABOUT YOUR WEIGHT?
YUP. I JUST WISH SHE'D BE **CONSISTENT** ABOUT IT!
FIRST SHE TELLS ME I NEED TO CONCENTRATE ON GETTING EXERCISE AND EATING HEALTHY...
...BUT WHEN I BRING HOME A GOOD REPORT CARD, WHAT DOES SHE **DO**? TAKES ME OUT FOR **ICE CREAM!**
I THINK A LOT OF GRANDPARENTS ARE SENILE THAT WAY.
HELLO, OPERATOR? GET ME **MIXED MESSAGES!**

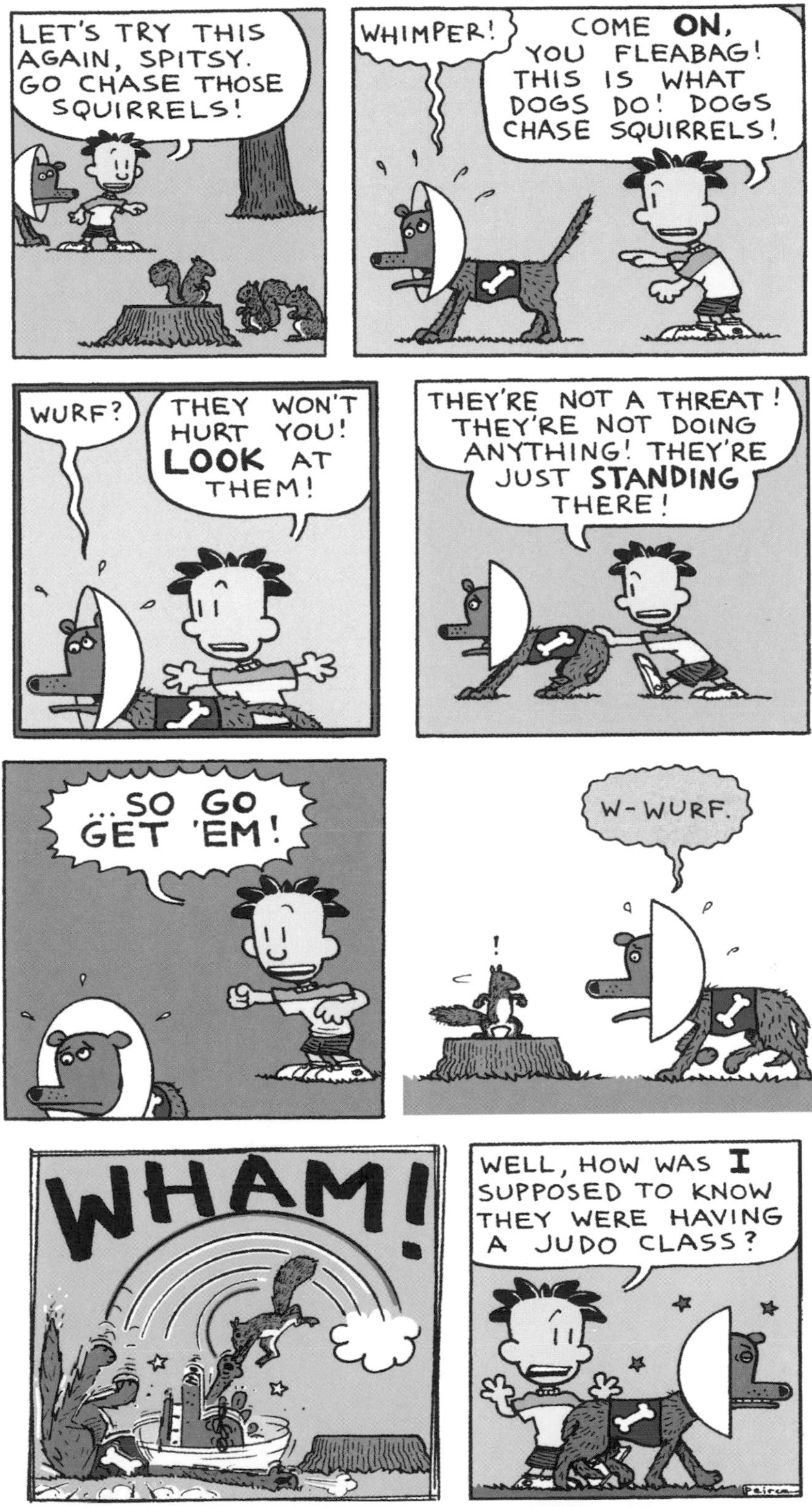
LET'S TRY THIS AGAIN, SPITSY. GO CHASE THOSE SQUIRRELS!
WHIMPER!
COME **ON**, YOU FLEABAG! THIS IS WHAT DOGS DO! DOGS CHASE SQUIRRELS!
WURF?
THEY WON'T HURT YOU! **LOOK** AT THEM!
THEY'RE NOT A THREAT! THEY'RE NOT DOING ANYTHING! THEY'RE JUST **STANDING** THERE!
...SO GO GET 'EM!
W-WURF.
WHAM!
WELL, HOW WAS **I** SUPPOSED TO KNOW THEY WERE HAVING A JUDO CLASS?

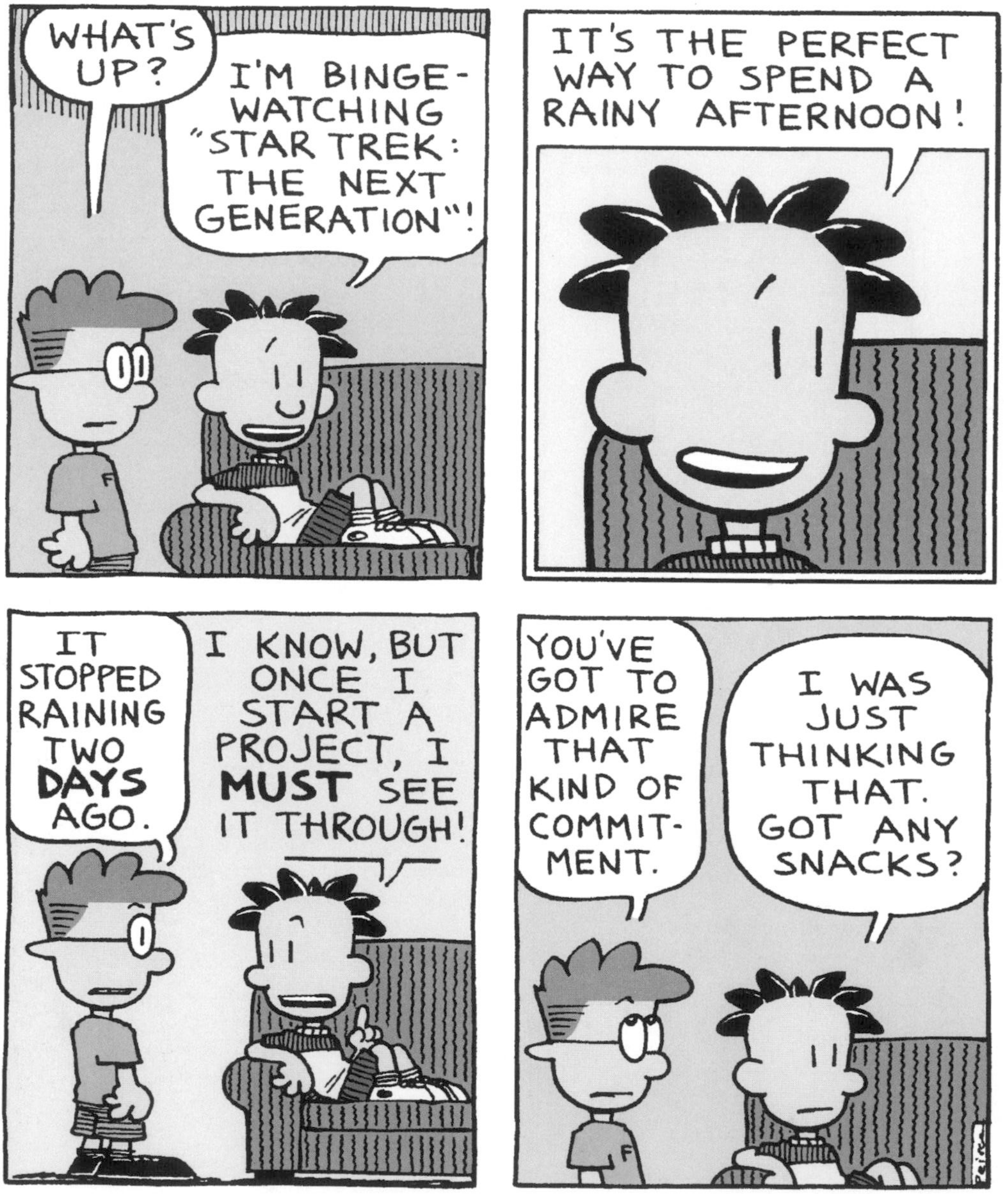
WHAT'S UP?
I'M BINGE-WATCHING "STAR TREK: THE NEXT GENERATION"!
IT'S THE PERFECT WAY TO SPEND A RAINY AFTERNOON!
IT STOPPED RAINING TWO **DAYS** AGO.
I KNOW, BUT ONCE I START A PROJECT, I **MUST** SEE IT THROUGH!
YOU'VE GOT TO ADMIRE THAT KIND OF COMMIT-MENT.
I WAS JUST THINKING THAT. GOT ANY SNACKS?

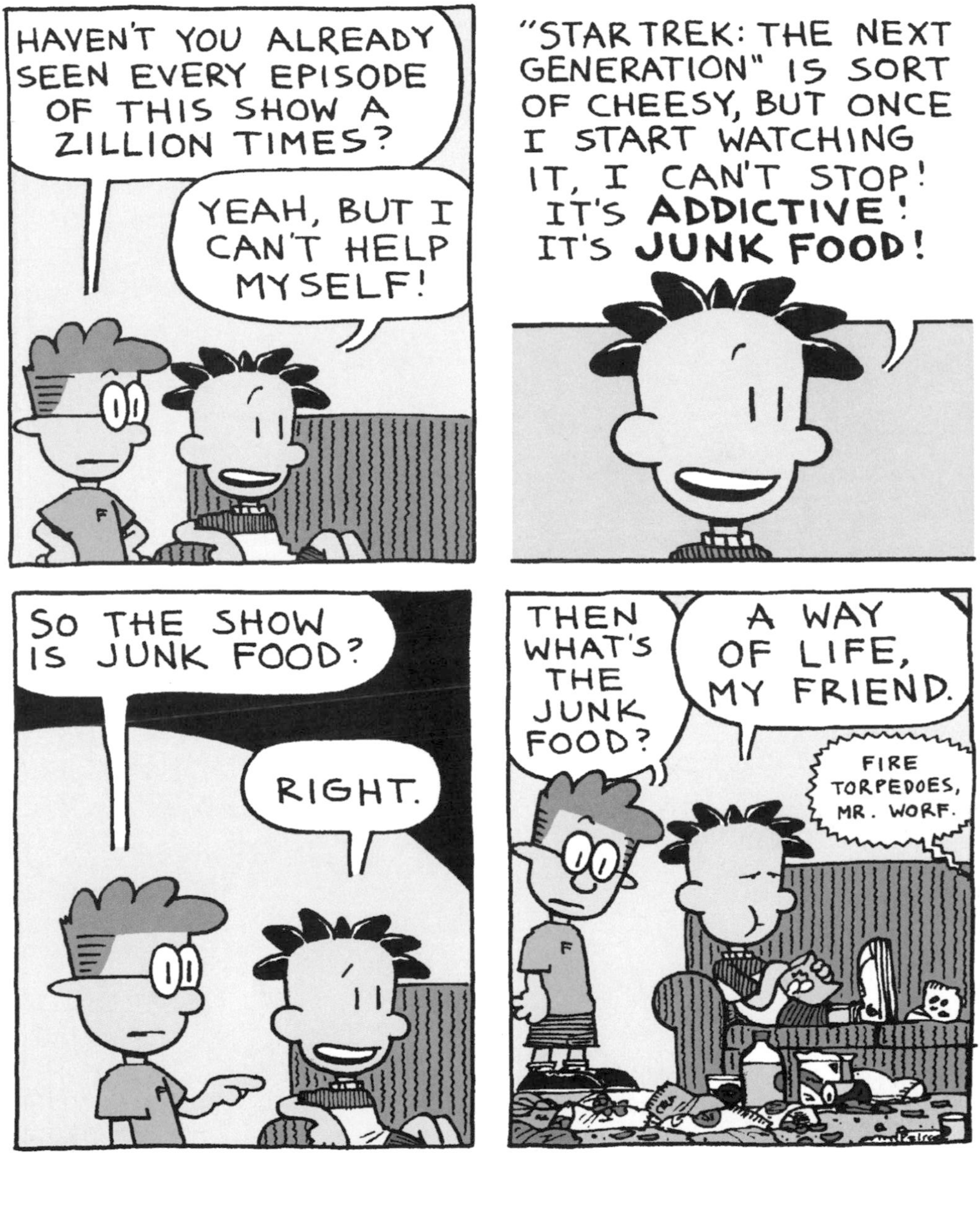
HAVEN'T YOU ALREADY SEEN EVERY EPISODE OF THIS SHOW A ZILLION TIMES?
YEAH, BUT I CAN'T HELP MYSELF!
"STAR TREK: THE NEXT GENERATION" IS SORT OF CHEESY, BUT ONCE I START WATCHING IT, I CAN'T STOP! IT'S **ADDICTIVE**! IT'S **JUNK FOOD**!
SO THE SHOW IS JUNK FOOD?
RIGHT.
THEN WHAT'S THE JUNK FOOD?
A WAY OF LIFE, MY FRIEND.
FIRE TORPEDOES, MR. WORF.

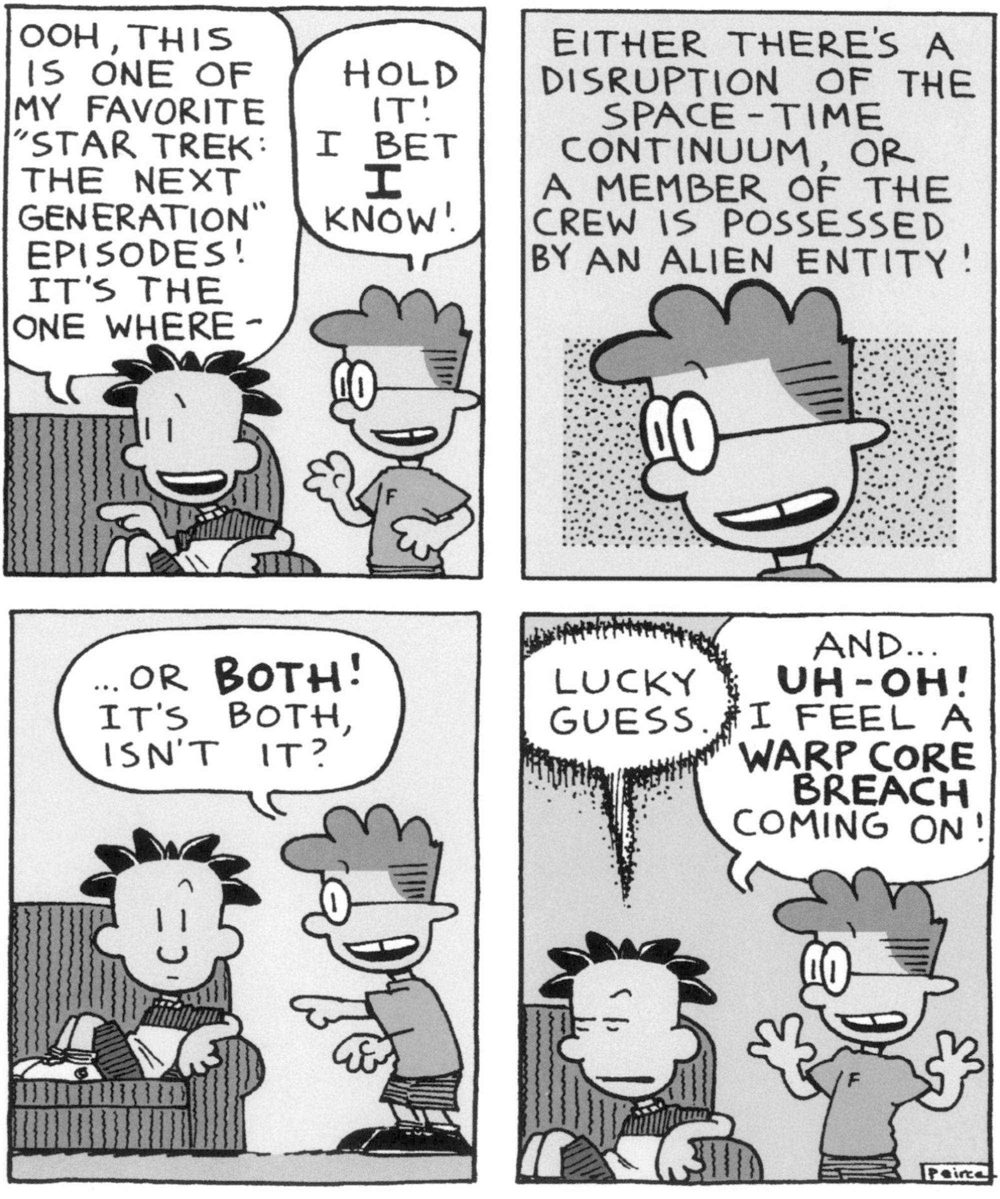
OOH, THIS IS ONE OF MY FAVORITE "STAR TREK: THE NEXT GENERATION" EPISODES! IT'S THE ONE WHERE -
HOLD IT! I BET **I** KNOW!
EITHER THERE'S A DISRUPTION OF THE SPACE-TIME CONTINUUM, OR A MEMBER OF THE CREW IS POSSESSED BY AN ALIEN ENTITY!
...OR **BOTH!** IT'S BOTH, ISN'T IT?
LUCKY GUESS.
AND... **UH-OH!** I FEEL A **WARP CORE BREACH** COMING ON!
Peirce

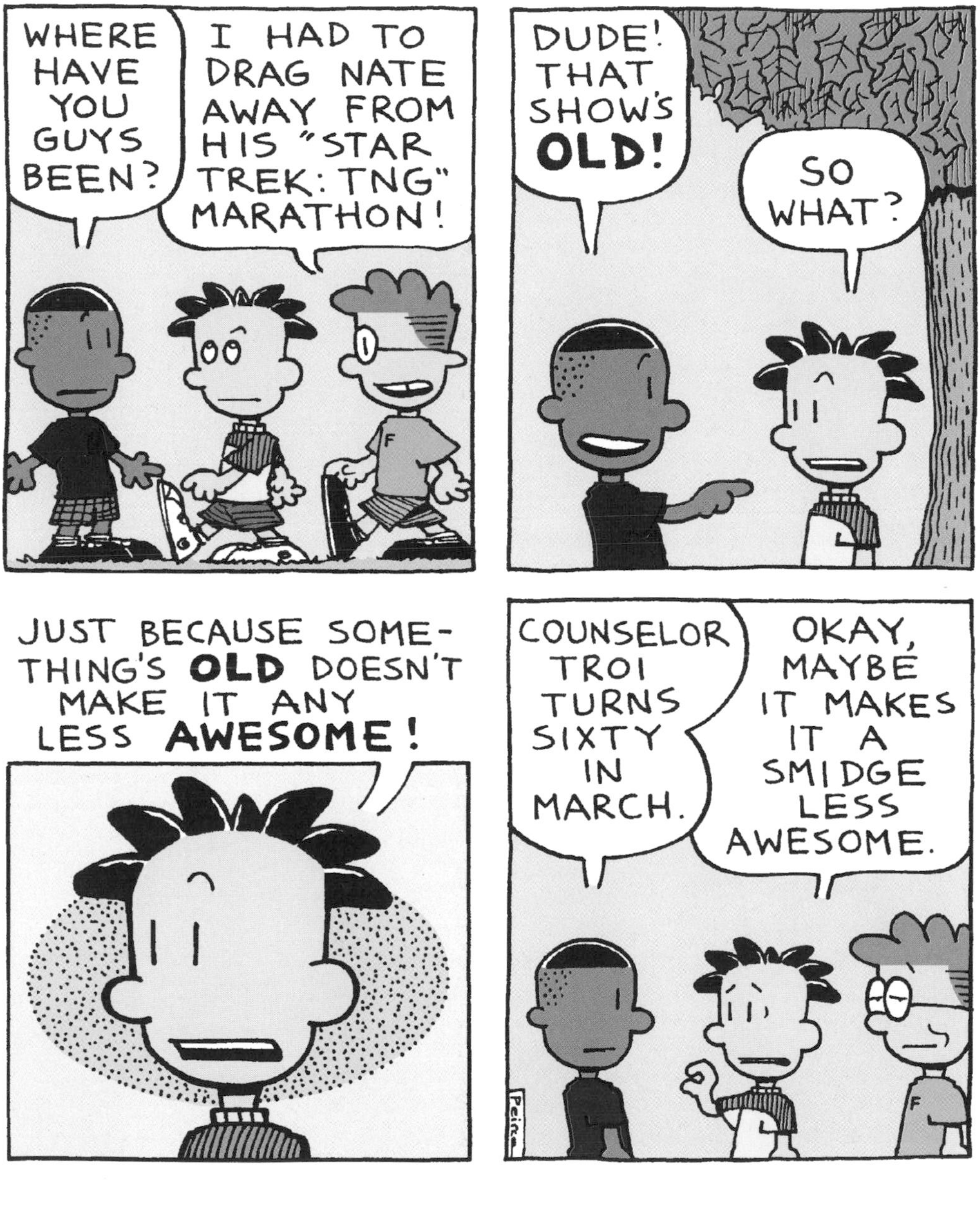
WHERE HAVE YOU GUYS BEEN?
I HAD TO DRAG NATE AWAY FROM HIS "STAR TREK: TNG" MARATHON!
DUDE! THAT SHOW'S **OLD!**
SO WHAT?
JUST BECAUSE SOME-THING'S **OLD** DOESN'T MAKE IT ANY LESS **AWESOME!**
COUNSELOR TROI TURNS SIXTY IN MARCH.
OKAY, MAYBE IT MAKES IT A SMIDGE LESS AWESOME.
Peirce

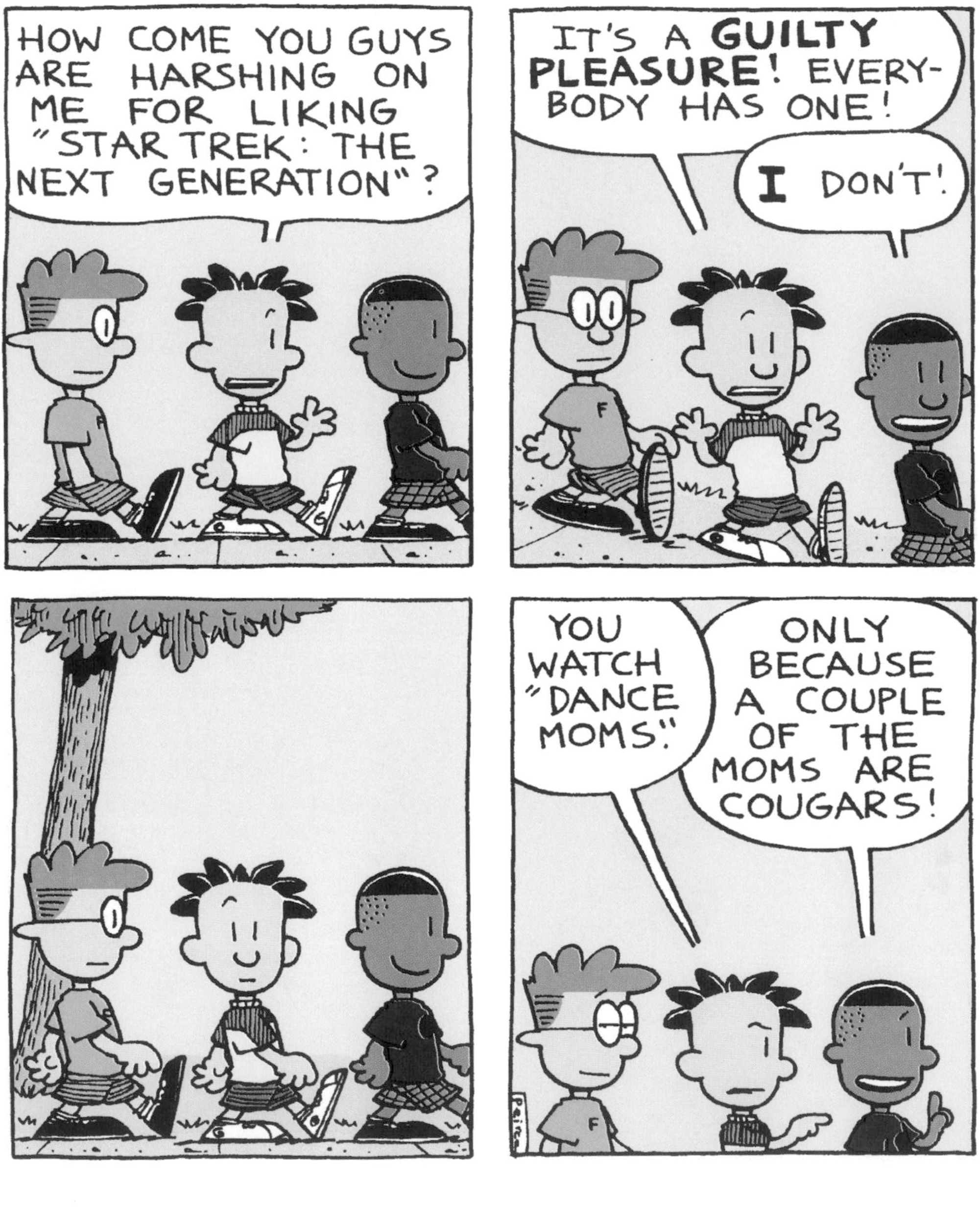
HOW COME YOU GUYS ARE HARSHING ON ME FOR LIKING "STAR TREK: THE NEXT GENERATION"?
IT'S A **GUILTY PLEASURE**! EVERY-BODY HAS ONE!
I DON'T!
YOU WATCH "DANCE MOMS."
ONLY BECAUSE A COUPLE OF THE MOMS ARE COUGARS!

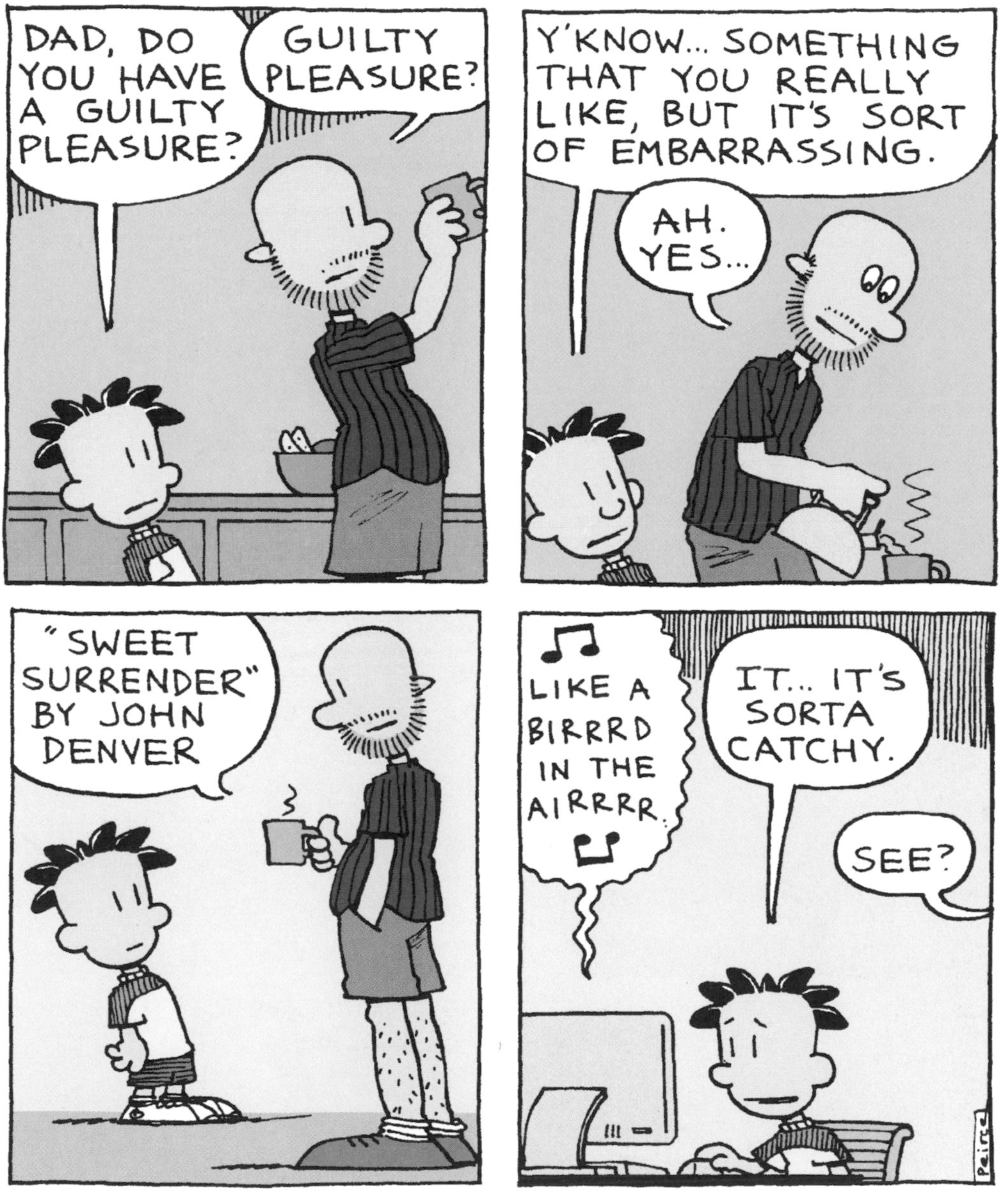
DAD, DO YOU HAVE A GUILTY PLEASURE?
GUILTY PLEASURE?
Y'KNOW... SOMETHING THAT YOU REALLY LIKE, BUT IT'S SORT OF EMBARRASSING.
AH. YES...
"SWEET SURRENDER" BY JOHN DENVER
LIKE A BIRRRD IN THE AIRRRR.
IT... IT'S SORTA CATCHY.
SEE?
Peirce

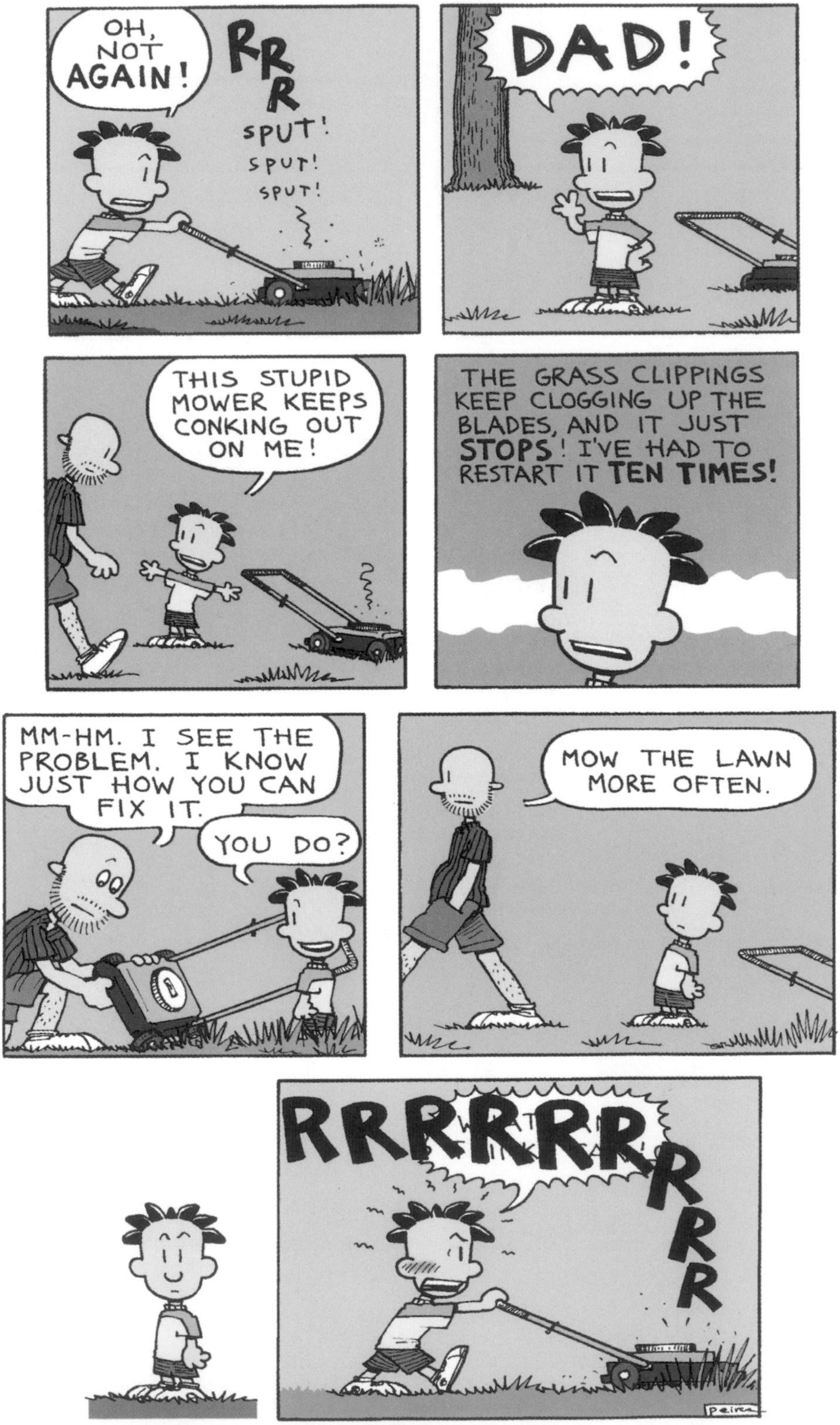
OH, NOT AGAIN!
RRRR
SPUT! SPUT! SPUT!
DAD!
THIS STUPID MOWER KEEPS CONKING OUT ON ME!
THE GRASS CLIPPINGS KEEP CLOGGING UP THE BLADES, AND IT JUST STOPS! I'VE HAD TO RESTART IT TEN TIMES!
MM-HM. I SEE THE PROBLEM. I KNOW JUST HOW YOU CAN FIX IT.
YOU DO?
MOW THE LAWN MORE OFTEN.
RRRRRRRRRR

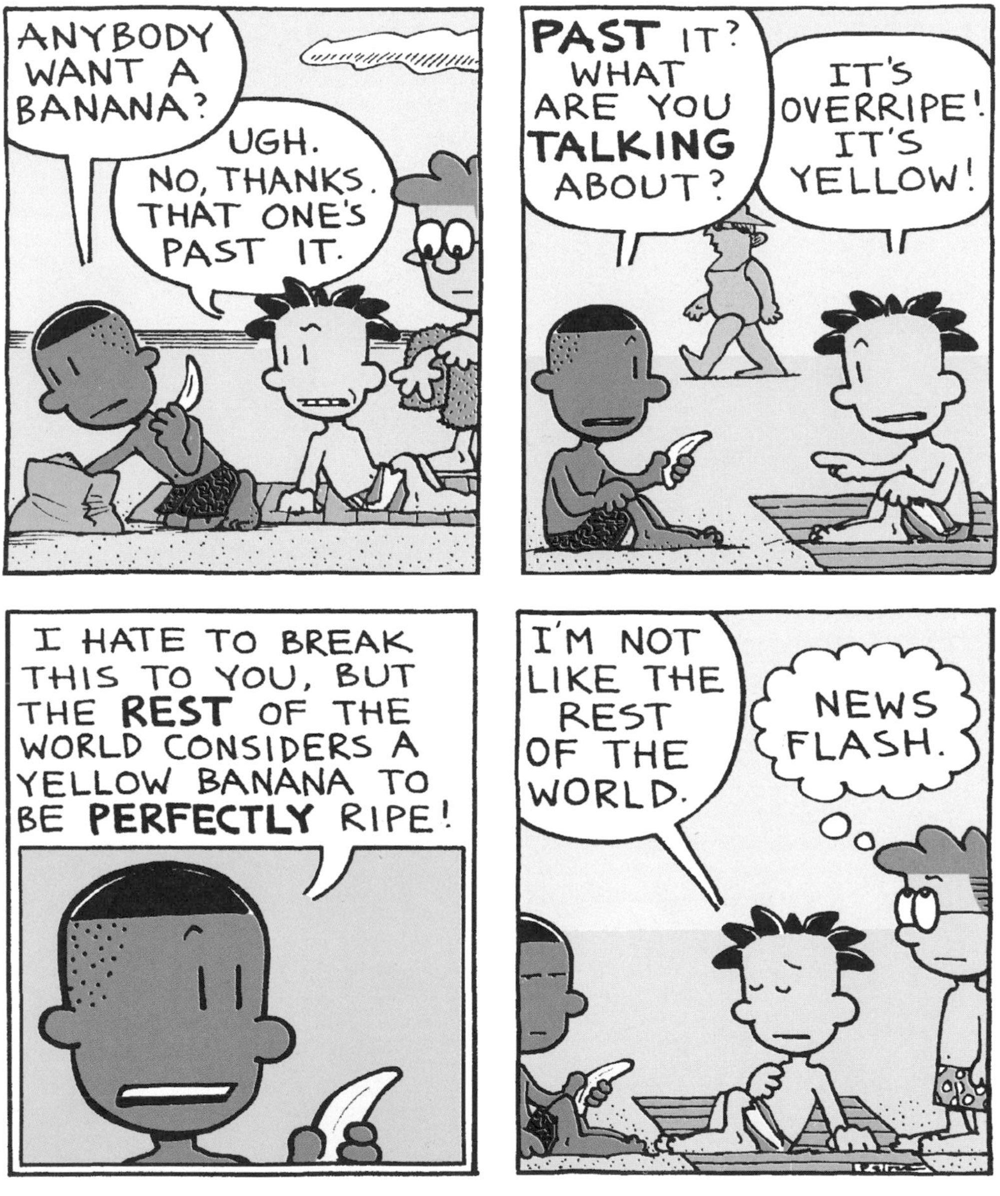
ANYBODY WANT A BANANA?
UGH. NO, THANKS. THAT ONE'S PAST IT.
PAST IT? WHAT ARE YOU **TALKING** ABOUT?
IT'S OVERRIPE! IT'S YELLOW!
I HATE TO BREAK THIS TO YOU, BUT THE **REST** OF THE WORLD CONSIDERS A YELLOW BANANA TO BE **PERFECTLY** RIPE!
I'M NOT LIKE THE REST OF THE WORLD.
NEWS FLASH.

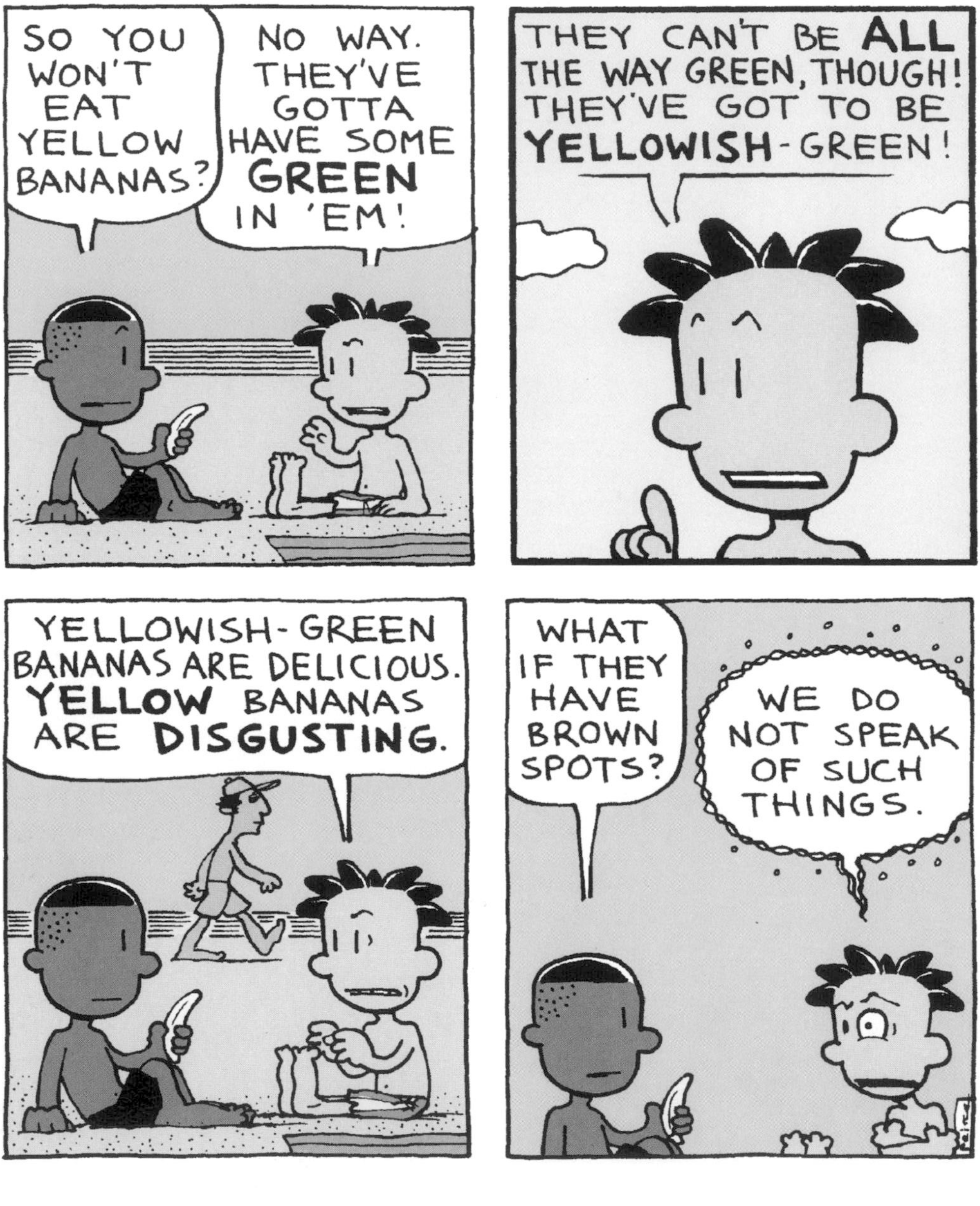
SO YOU WON'T EAT YELLOW BANANAS?
NO WAY. THEY'VE GOTTA HAVE SOME GREEN IN 'EM!
THEY CAN'T BE ALL THE WAY GREEN, THOUGH! THEY'VE GOT TO BE YELLOWISH-GREEN!
YELLOWISH-GREEN BANANAS ARE DELICIOUS. YELLOW BANANAS ARE DISGUSTING.
WHAT IF THEY HAVE BROWN SPOTS?
WE DO NOT SPEAK OF SUCH THINGS.

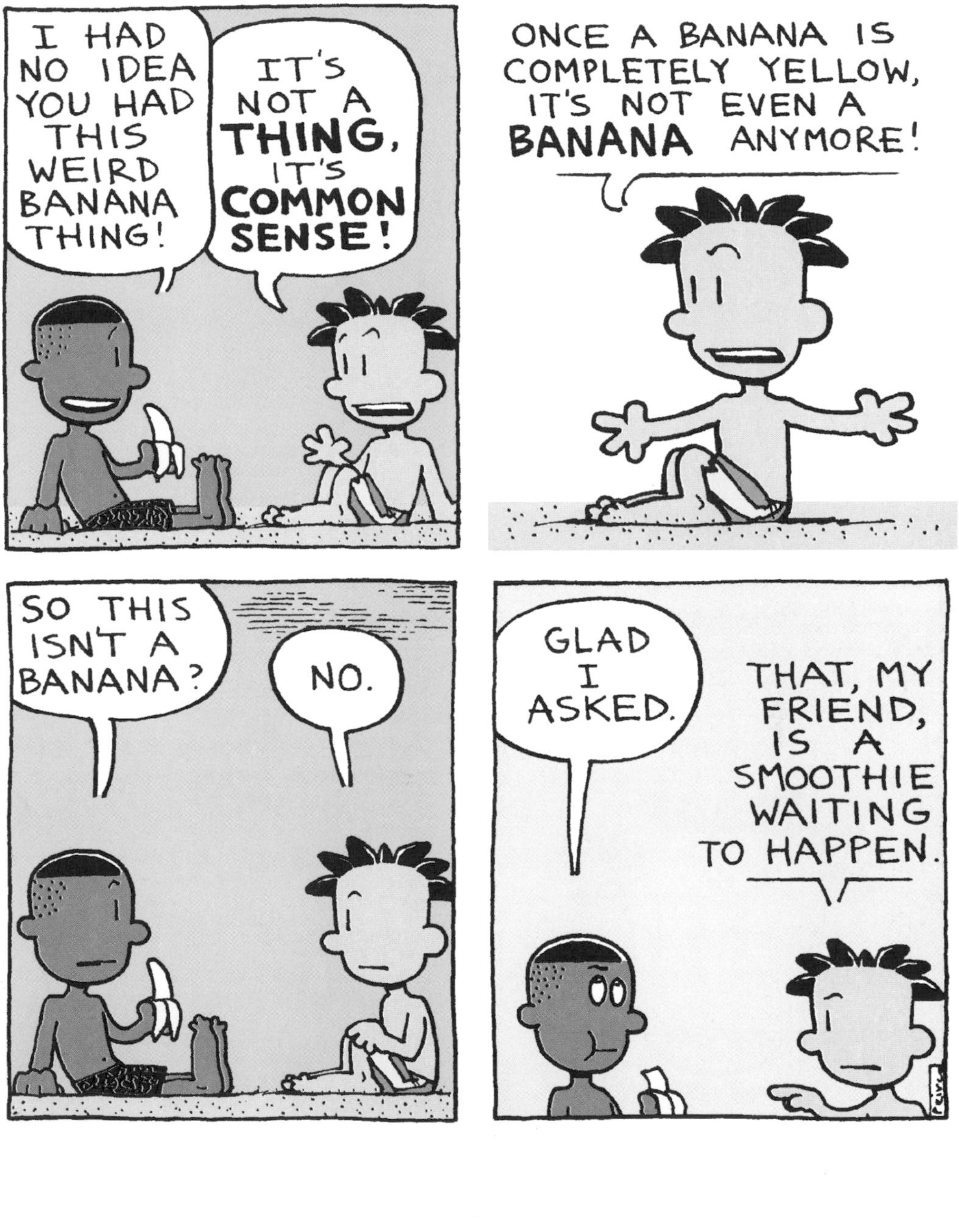
I HAD NO IDEA YOU HAD THIS WEIRD BANANA THING!
IT'S NOT A THING, IT'S COMMON SENSE!
ONCE A BANANA IS COMPLETELY YELLOW, IT'S NOT EVEN A BANANA ANYMORE!
SO THIS ISN'T A BANANA?
NO.
GLAD I ASKED.
THAT, MY FRIEND, IS A SMOOTHIE WAITING TO HAPPEN.

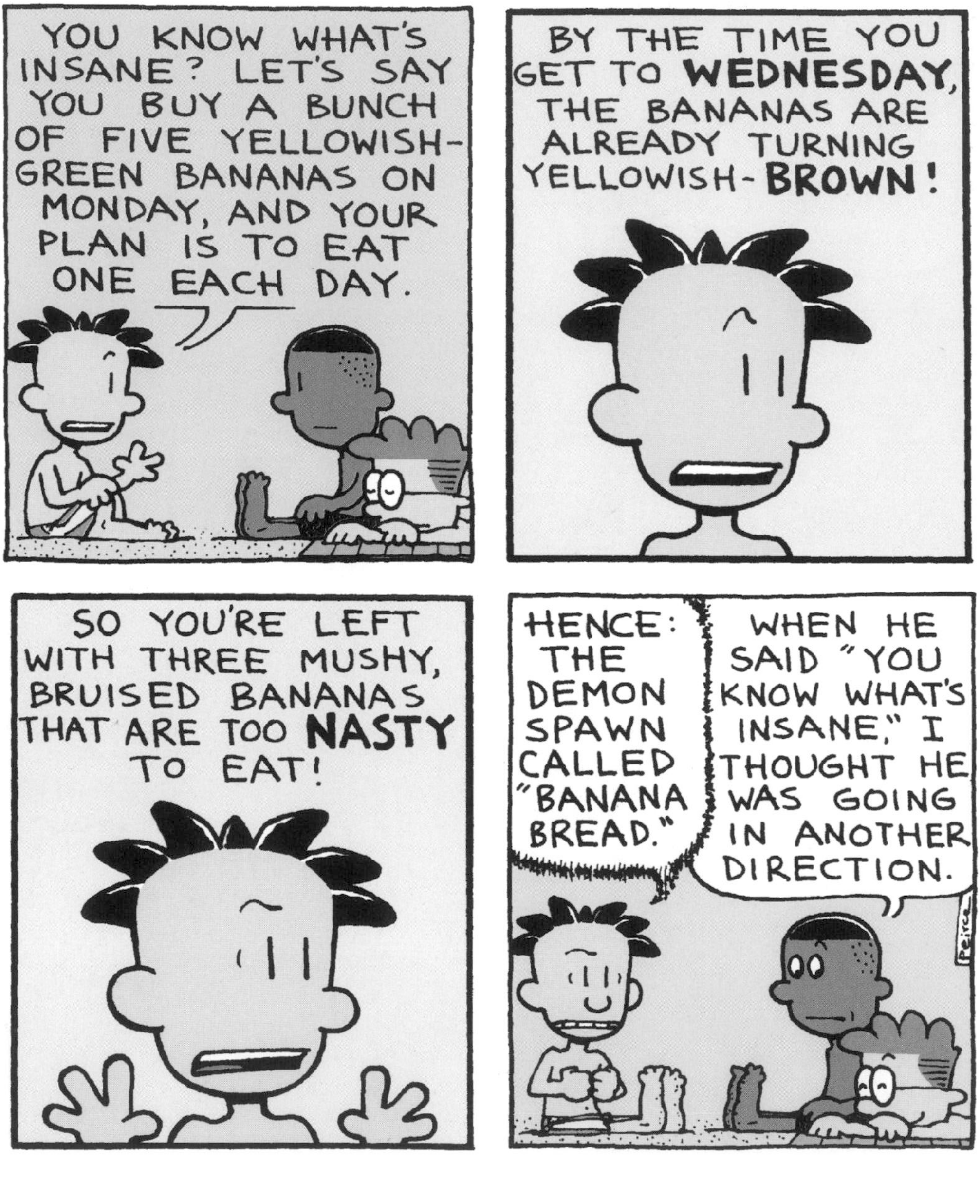
YOU KNOW WHAT'S INSANE? LET'S SAY YOU BUY A BUNCH OF FIVE YELLOWISH-GREEN BANANAS ON MONDAY, AND YOUR PLAN IS TO EAT ONE EACH DAY.
BY THE TIME YOU GET TO WEDNESDAY, THE BANANAS ARE ALREADY TURNING YELLOWISH-BROWN!
SO YOU'RE LEFT WITH THREE MUSHY, BRUISED BANANAS THAT ARE TOO NASTY TO EAT!
HENCE: THE DEMON SPAWN CALLED "BANANA BREAD."
WHEN HE SAID "YOU KNOW WHAT'S INSANE," I THOUGHT HE WAS GOING IN ANOTHER DIRECTION.
Peirce

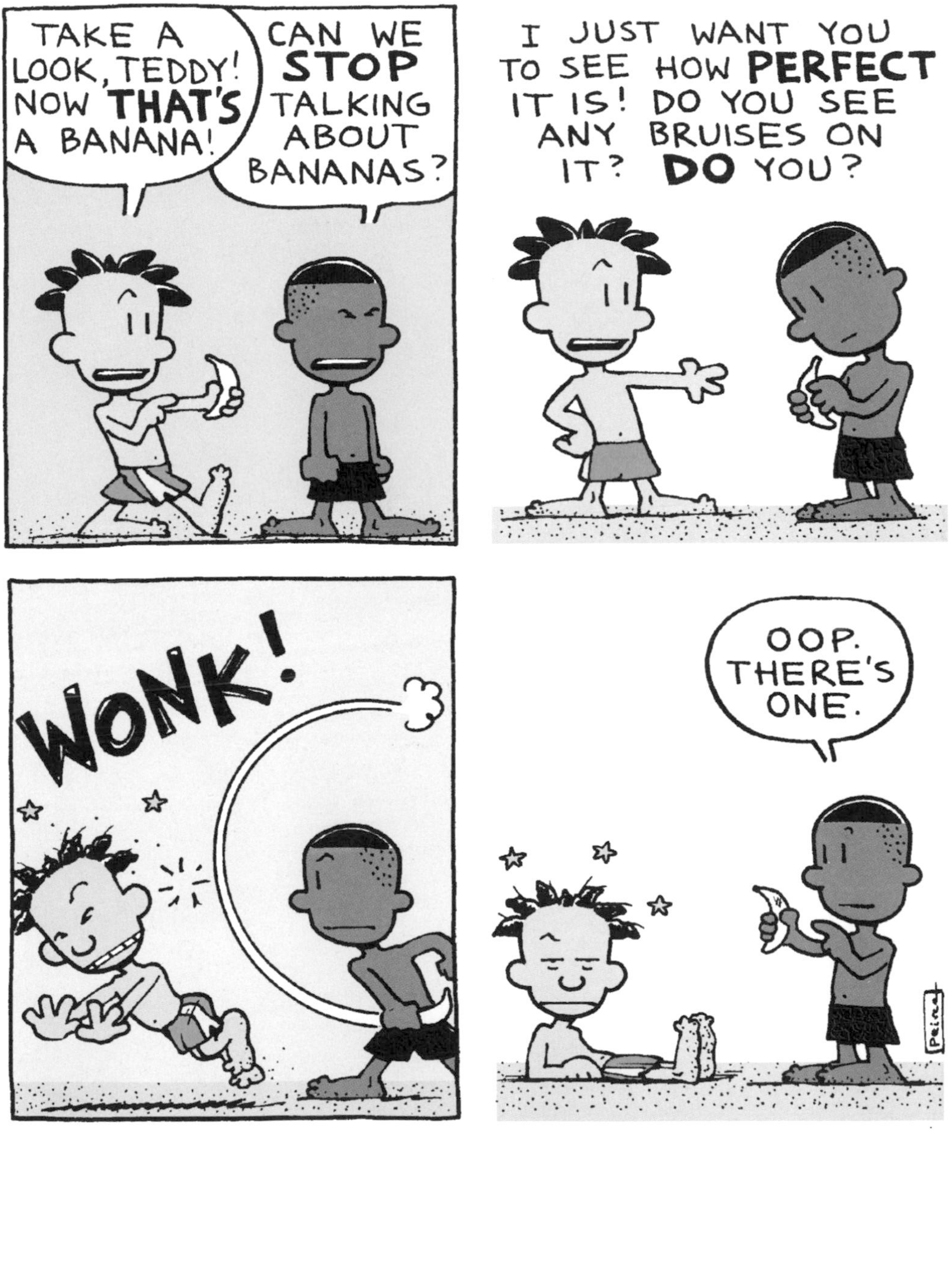
TAKE A LOOK, TEDDY! NOW **THAT'S** A BANANA!
CAN WE **STOP** TALKING ABOUT BANANAS?
I JUST WANT YOU TO SEE HOW **PERFECT** IT IS! DO YOU SEE ANY BRUISES ON IT? **DO** YOU?
WONK!
OOP. THERE'S ONE.

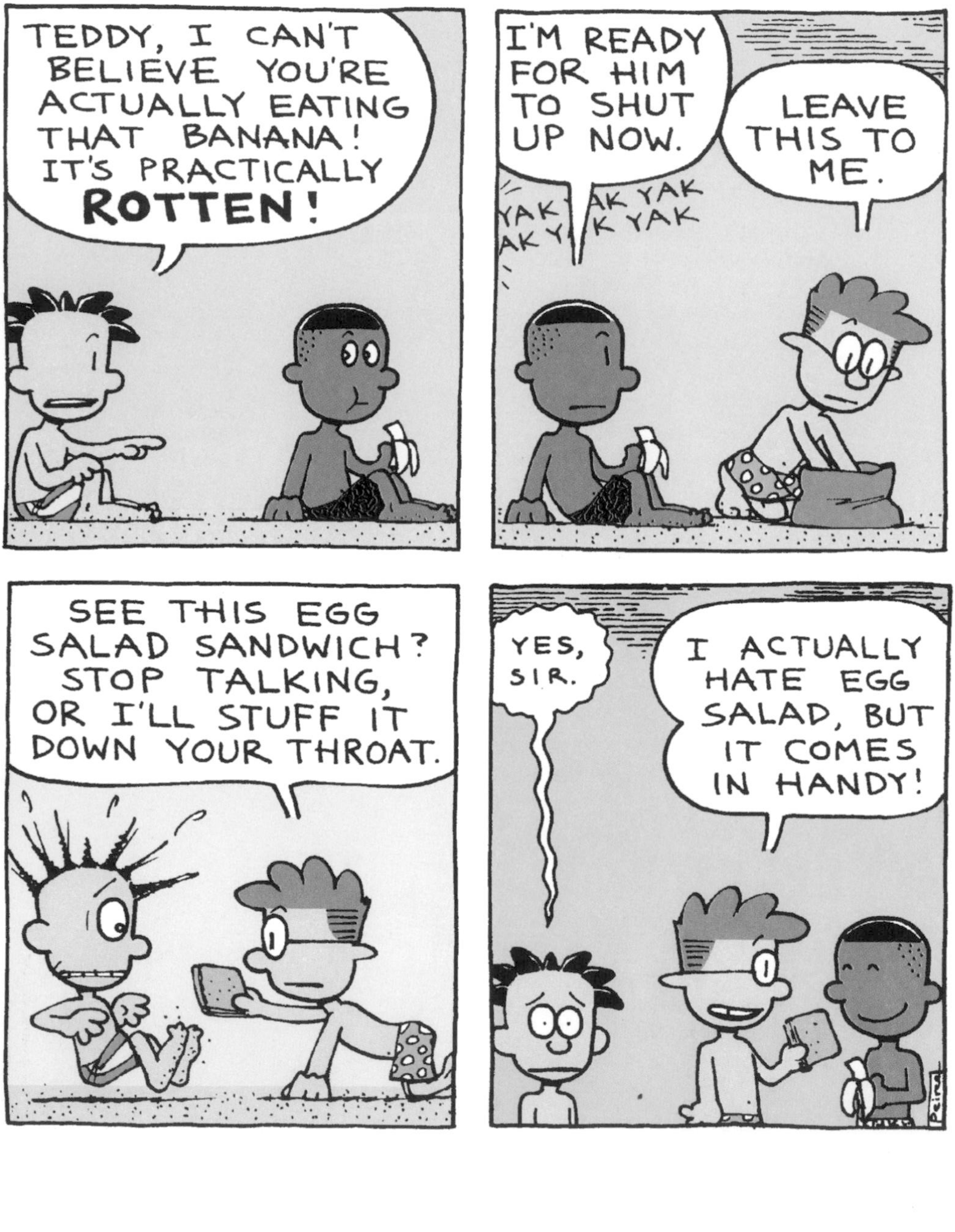
TEDDY, I CAN'T BELIEVE YOU'RE ACTUALLY EATING THAT BANANA! IT'S PRACTICALLY **ROTTEN**!
I'M READY FOR HIM TO SHUT UP NOW.
LEAVE THIS TO ME.
SEE THIS EGG SALAD SANDWICH? STOP TALKING, OR I'LL STUFF IT DOWN YOUR THROAT.
YES, SIR.
I ACTUALLY HATE EGG SALAD, BUT IT COMES IN HANDY!
Peirce

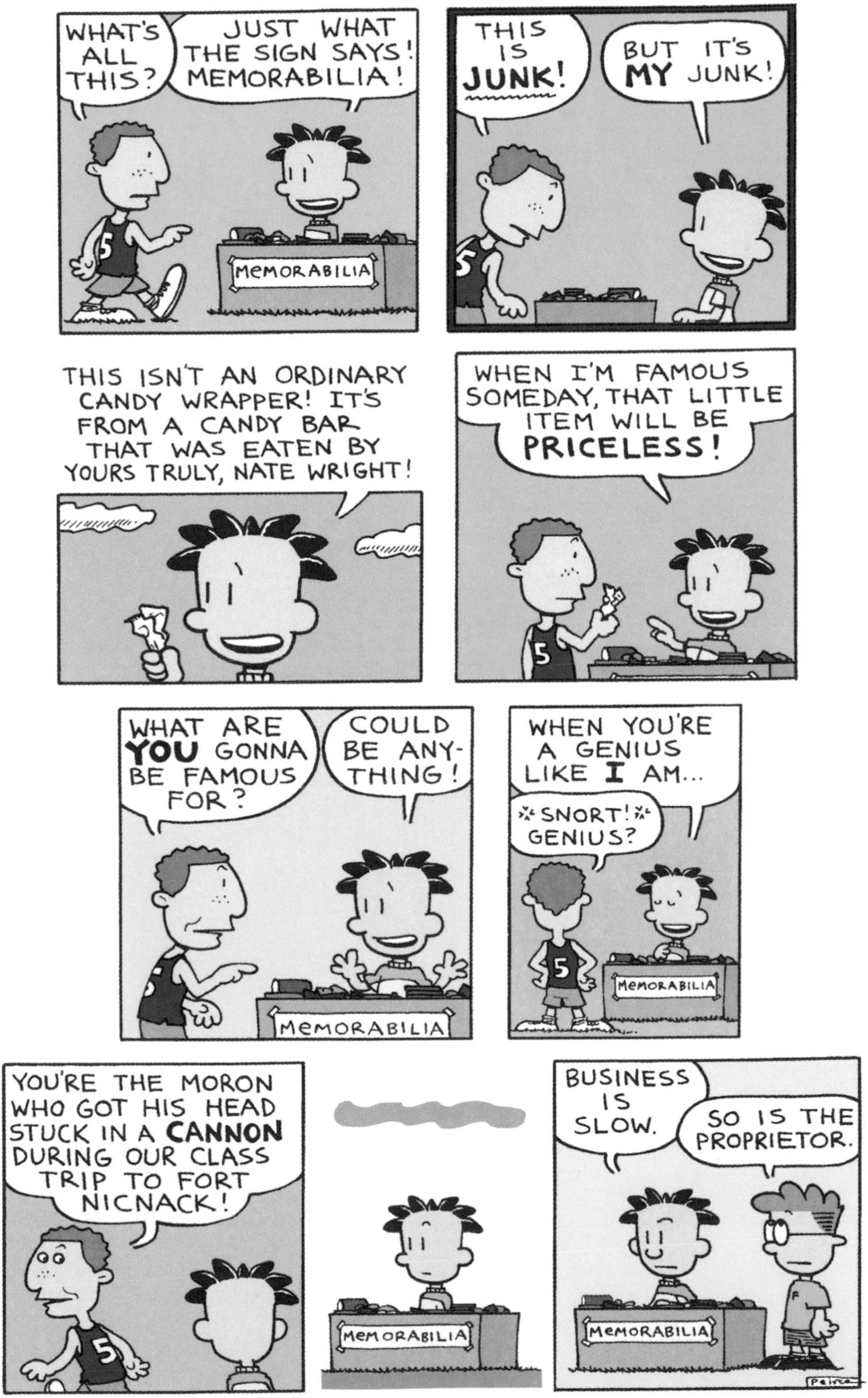
WHAT'S ALL THIS?
JUST WHAT THE SIGN SAYS! MEMORABILIA!
MEMORABILIA
THIS IS JUNK!
BUT IT'S MY JUNK!
THIS ISN'T AN ORDINARY CANDY WRAPPER! IT'S FROM A CANDY BAR THAT WAS EATEN BY YOURS TRULY, NATE WRIGHT!
WHEN I'M FAMOUS SOMEDAY, THAT LITTLE ITEM WILL BE PRICELESS!
WHAT ARE YOU GONNA BE FAMOUS FOR?
COULD BE ANY-THING!
MEMORABILIA
WHEN YOU'RE A GENIUS LIKE I AM...
SNORT! GENIUS?
MEMORABILIA
YOU'RE THE MORON WHO GOT HIS HEAD STUCK IN A CANNON DURING OUR CLASS TRIP TO FORT NICNACK!
MEMORABILIA
BUSINESS IS SLOW.
SO IS THE PROPRIETOR.
MEMORABILIA

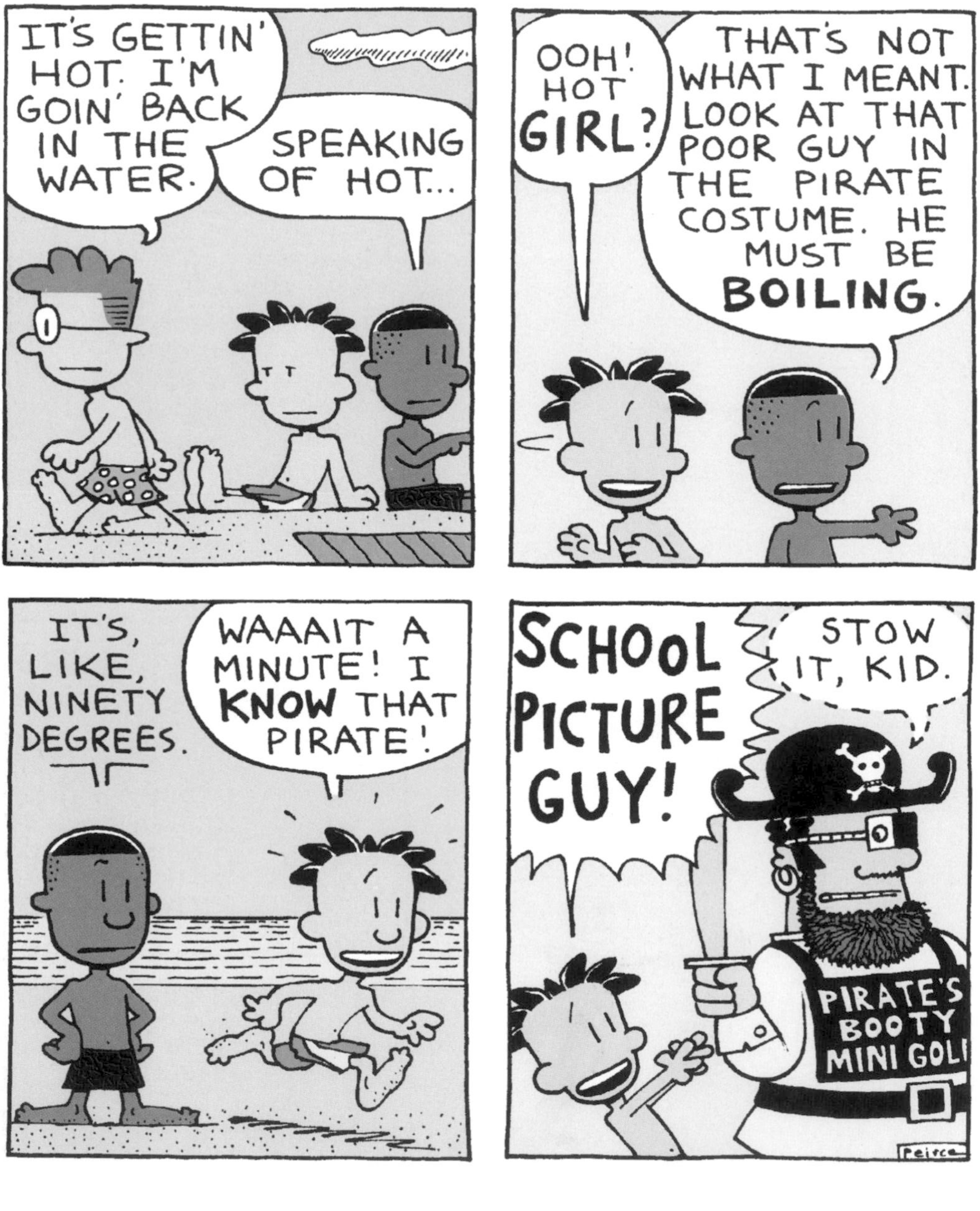
IT'S GETTIN' HOT. I'M GOIN' BACK IN THE WATER.
SPEAKING OF HOT...
OOH! HOT GIRL?
THAT'S NOT WHAT I MEANT. LOOK AT THAT POOR GUY IN THE PIRATE COSTUME. HE MUST BE BOILING.
IT'S, LIKE, NINETY DEGREES.
WAAAIT A MINUTE! I KNOW THAT PIRATE!
SCHOOL PICTURE GUY!
STOW IT, KID.
PIRATE'S BOOTY MINI GOL
Peirce

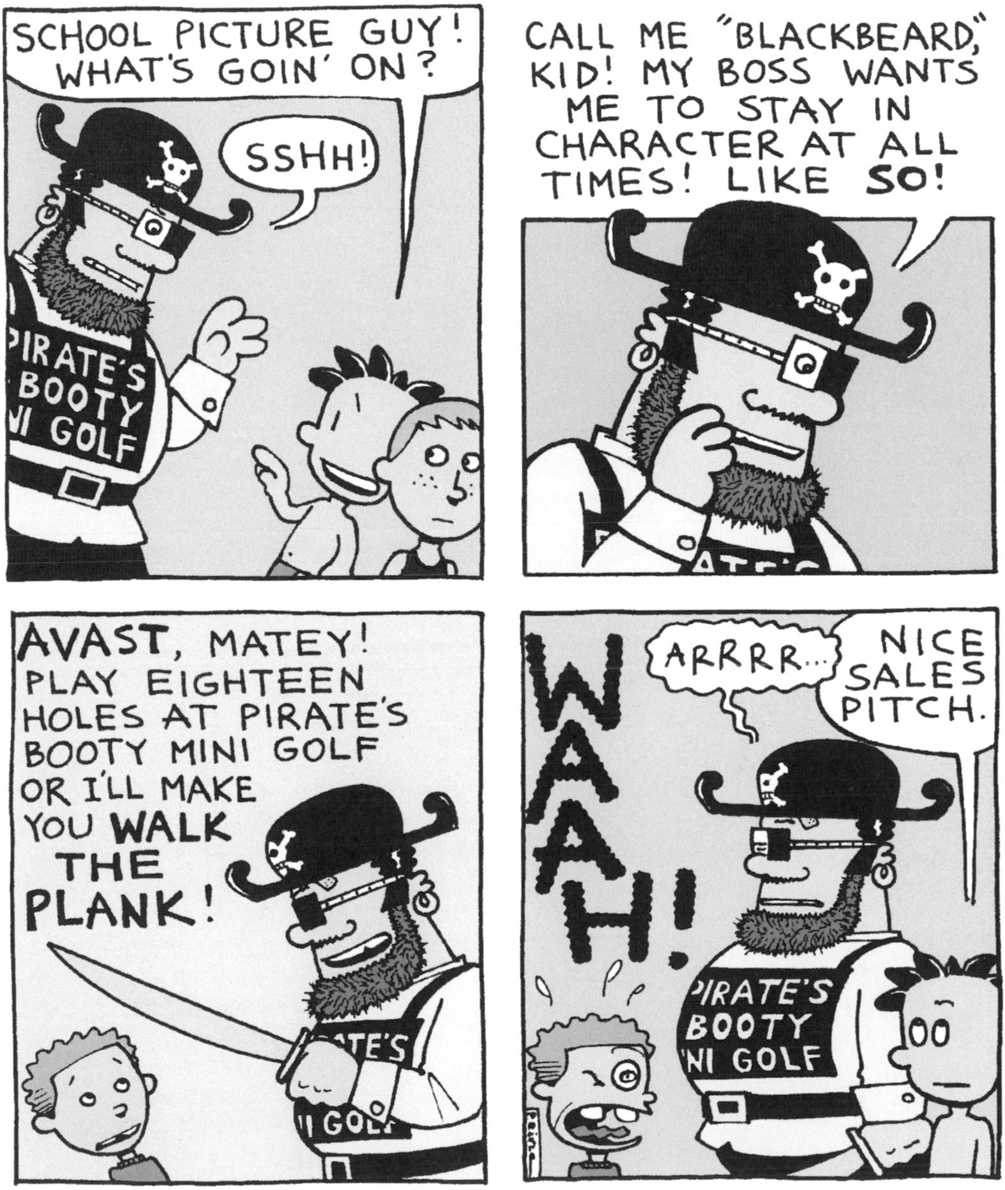
SCHOOL PICTURE GUY! WHAT'S GOIN' ON?
SSHH!
PIRATE'S BOOTY NI GOLF
CALL ME "BLACKBEARD," KID! MY BOSS WANTS ME TO STAY IN CHARACTER AT ALL TIMES! LIKE SO!
AVAST, MATEY! PLAY EIGHTEEN HOLES AT PIRATE'S BOOTY MINI GOLF OR I'LL MAKE YOU WALK THE PLANK!
WAAH!
ARRRR...
NICE SALES PITCH.
PIRATE'S BOOTY NI GOLF

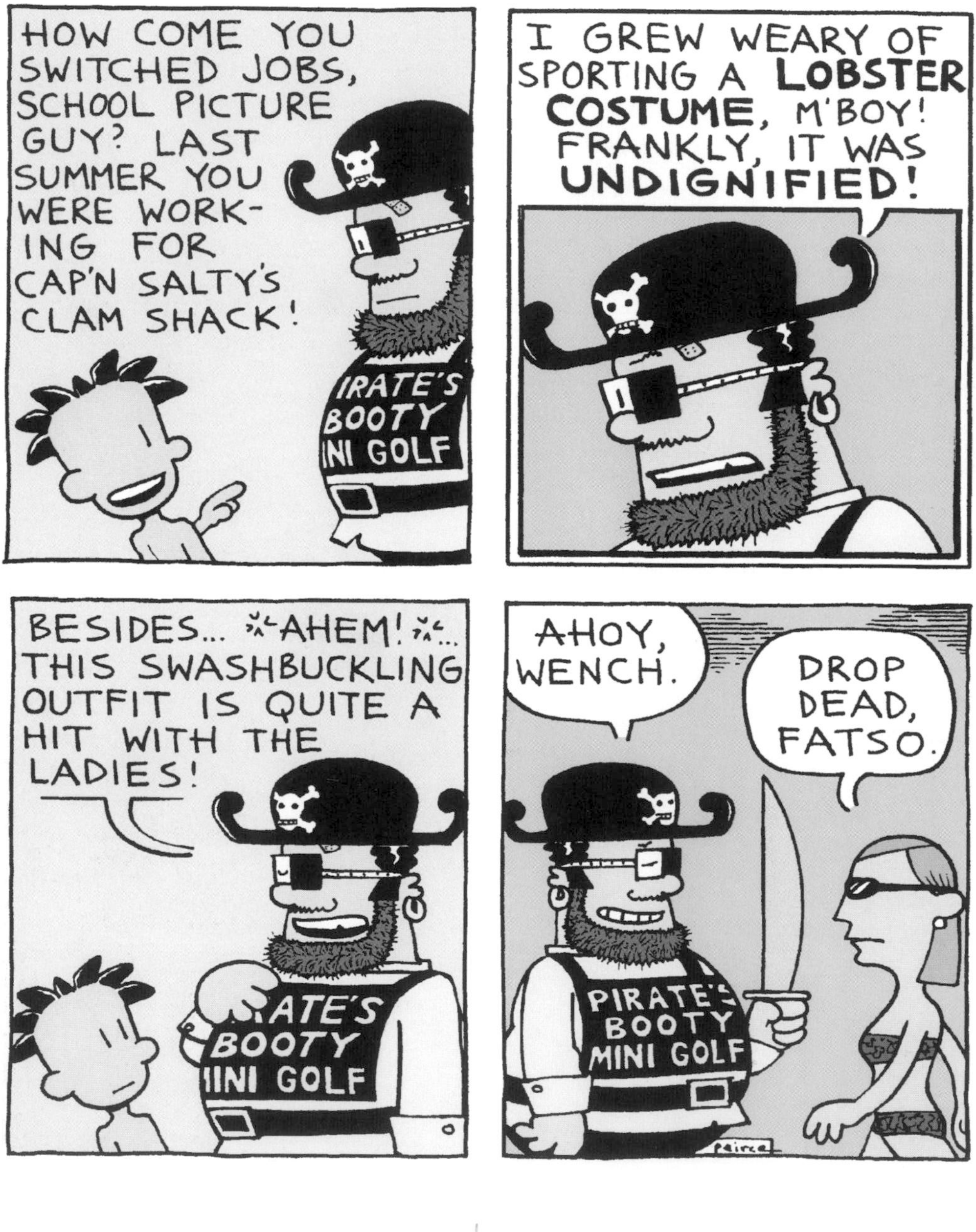
HOW COME YOU SWITCHED JOBS, SCHOOL PICTURE GUY? LAST SUMMER YOU WERE WORKING FOR CAP'N SALTY'S CLAM SHACK!
IRATE'S BOOTY INI GOLF
I GREW WEARY OF SPORTING A LOBSTER COSTUME, M'BOY! FRANKLY, IT WAS UNDIGNIFIED!
BESIDES... *AHEM!*... THIS SWASHBUCKLING OUTFIT IS QUITE A HIT WITH THE LADIES!
ATE'S BOOTY INI GOLF
AHOY, WENCH.
DROP DEAD, FATSO.
PIRATE'S BOOTY MINI GOLF
peirce

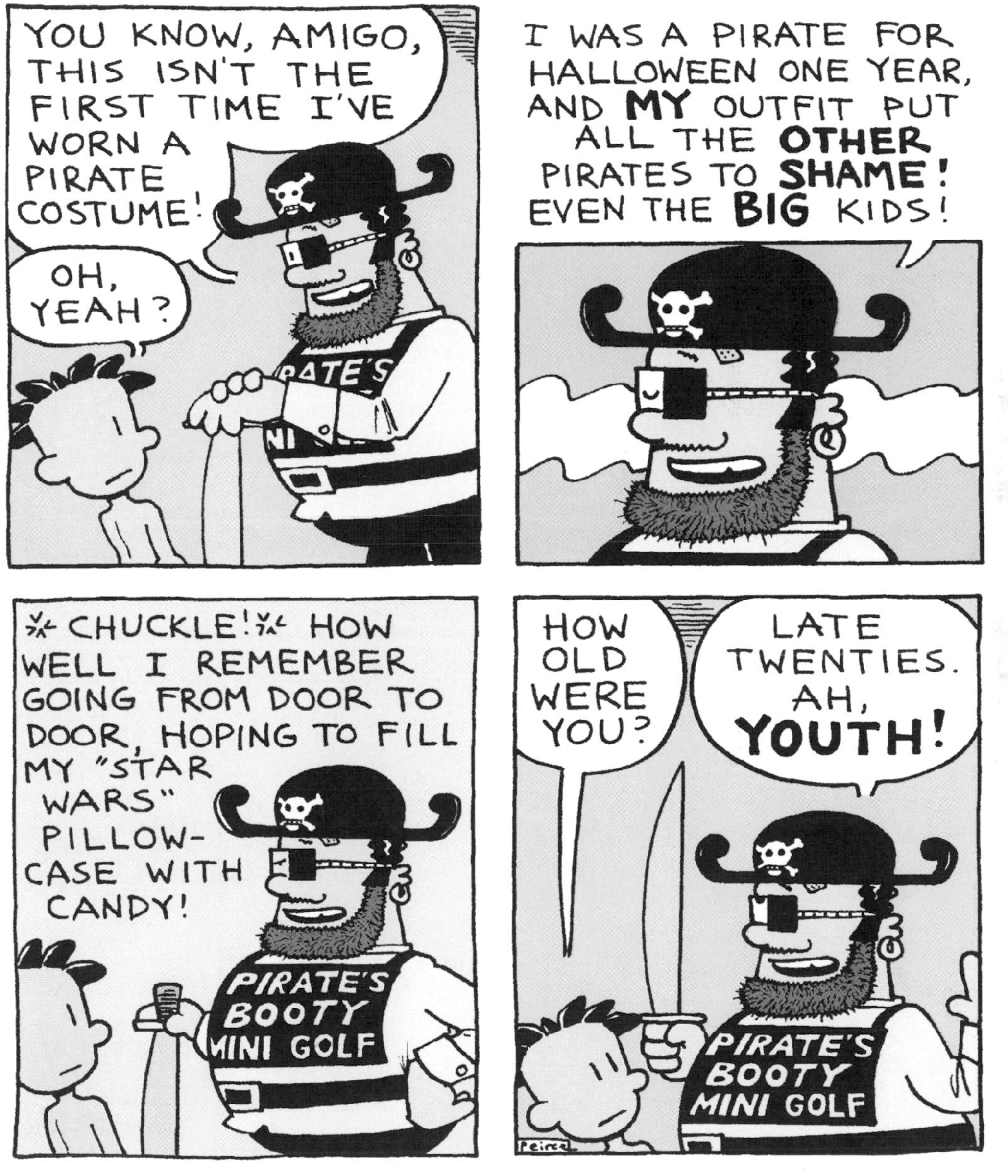
YOU KNOW, AMIGO, THIS ISN'T THE FIRST TIME I'VE WORN A PIRATE COSTUME!
OH, YEAH?
I WAS A PIRATE FOR HALLOWEEN ONE YEAR, AND **MY** OUTFIT PUT ALL THE **OTHER** PIRATES TO **SHAME**! EVEN THE **BIG** KIDS!
CHUCKLE! HOW WELL I REMEMBER GOING FROM DOOR TO DOOR, HOPING TO FILL MY "STAR WARS" PILLOW-CASE WITH CANDY!
PIRATE'S BOOTY MINI GOLF
HOW OLD WERE YOU?
LATE TWENTIES. AH, **YOUTH**!
PIRATE'S BOOTY MINI GOLF
Peirce

HERE YOU GO, FOLKS! THIS COUPON IS GOOD FOR A 20 PERCENT DISCOUNT AT PIRATE'S BOOTY MINI GOLF!
PLEASE EXCUSE. WE ARE FROM FINLAND. WHAT IS IT, THIS "MINI GOLF"?
PUTT LIKE A PRO
IT'S A LEISURE SPORT WHEREIN ONE USES A MALLET TO PROPEL A WOODEN BALL THROUGH A SERIES OF STRATEGICALLY PLACED WIRE WICKETS.
DUDE, THAT'S CROQUET.
FOR EIGHT BUCKS AN HOUR, KID, IT'S WHATEVER I SAY IT IS.
PIRATE' BOOTY MINI GOLF

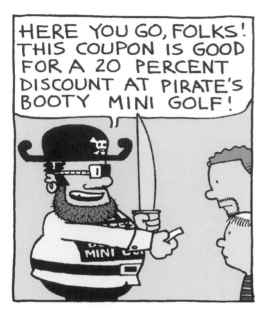

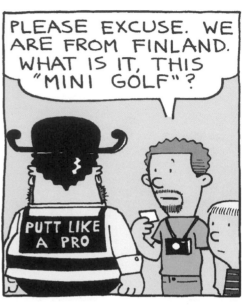

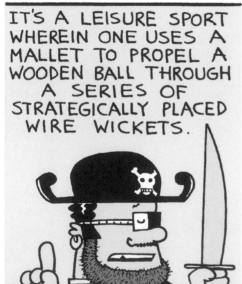

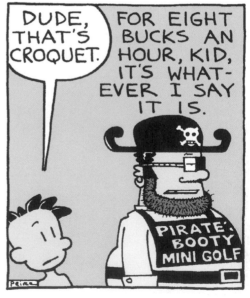

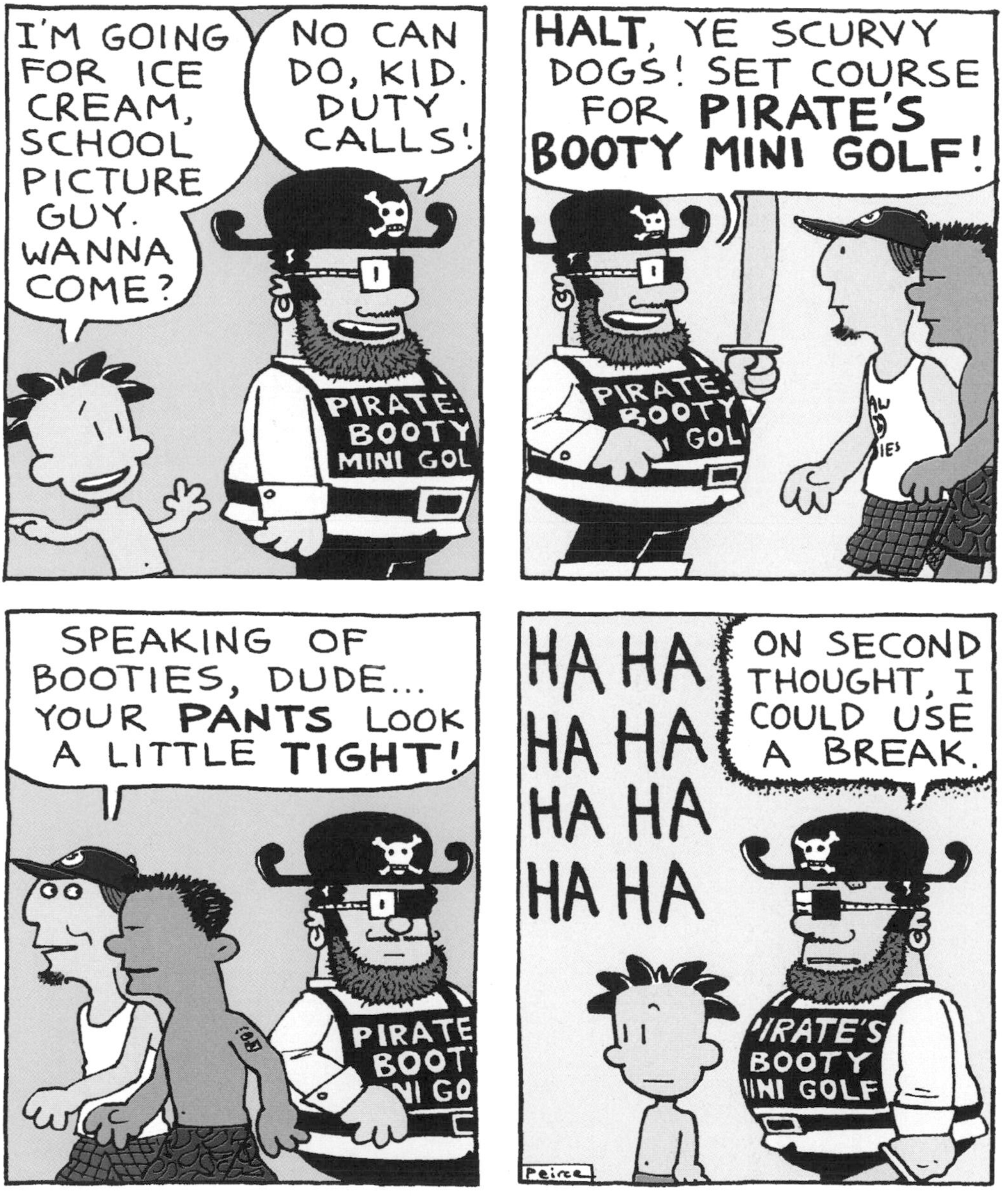
I'M GOING FOR ICE CREAM, SCHOOL PICTURE GUY. WANNA COME?
NO CAN DO, KID. DUTY CALLS!
PIRATE: BOOTY MINI GOL
HALT, YE SCURVY DOGS! SET COURSE FOR PIRATE'S BOOTY MINI GOLF!
SPEAKING OF BOOTIES, DUDE... YOUR PANTS LOOK A LITTLE TIGHT!
HA HA HA HA HA HA HA HA
ON SECOND THOUGHT, I COULD USE A BREAK.
IRATE'S BOOTY INI GOLF
Peirce

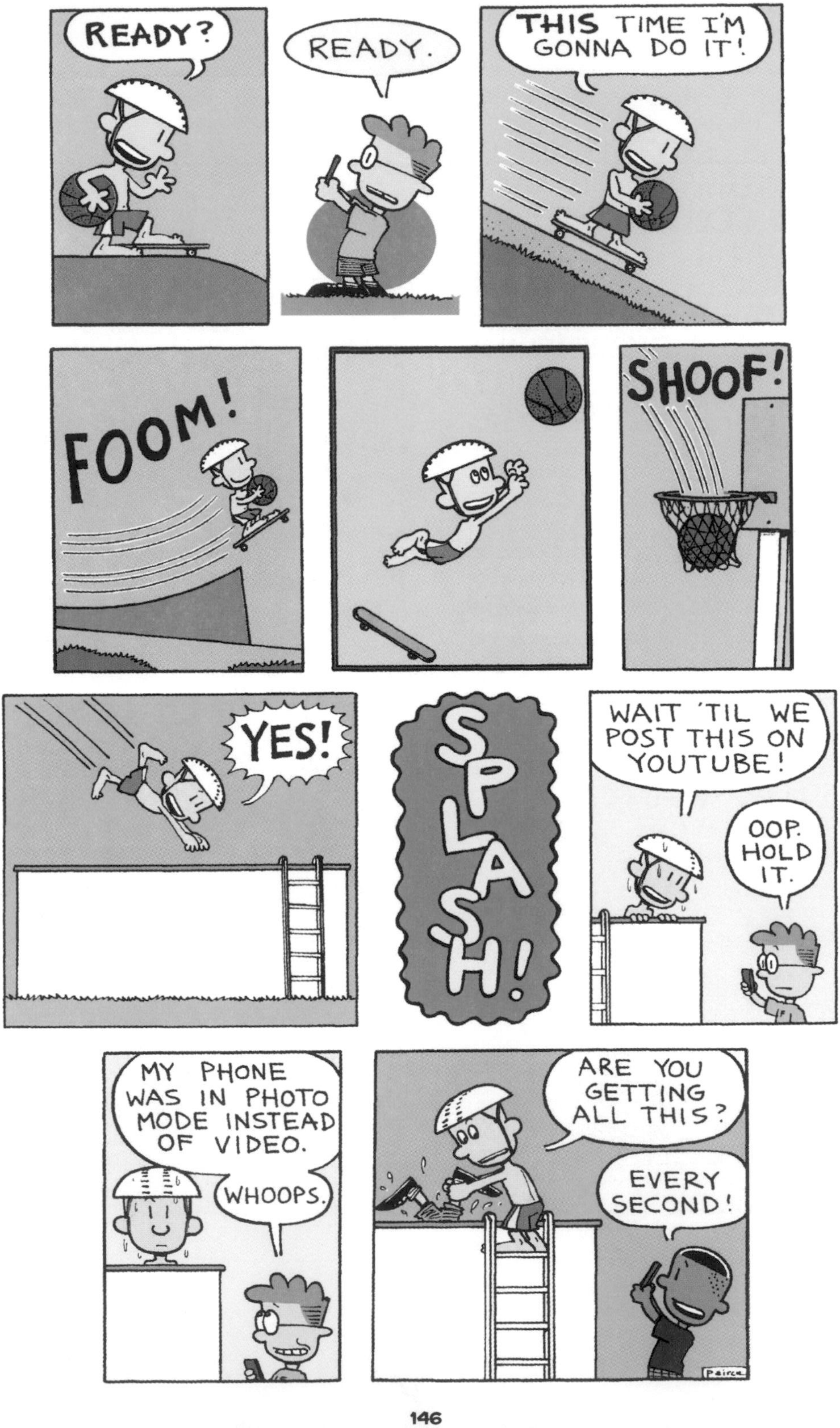
READY?
READY.
THIS TIME I'M GONNA DO IT!
FOOM!
SHOOF!
YES!
SPLASH!
WAIT 'TIL WE POST THIS ON YOUTUBE!
OOP. HOLD IT.
MY PHONE WAS IN PHOTO MODE INSTEAD OF VIDEO.
WHOOPS.
ARE YOU GETTING ALL THIS?
EVERY SECOND!
Peirce

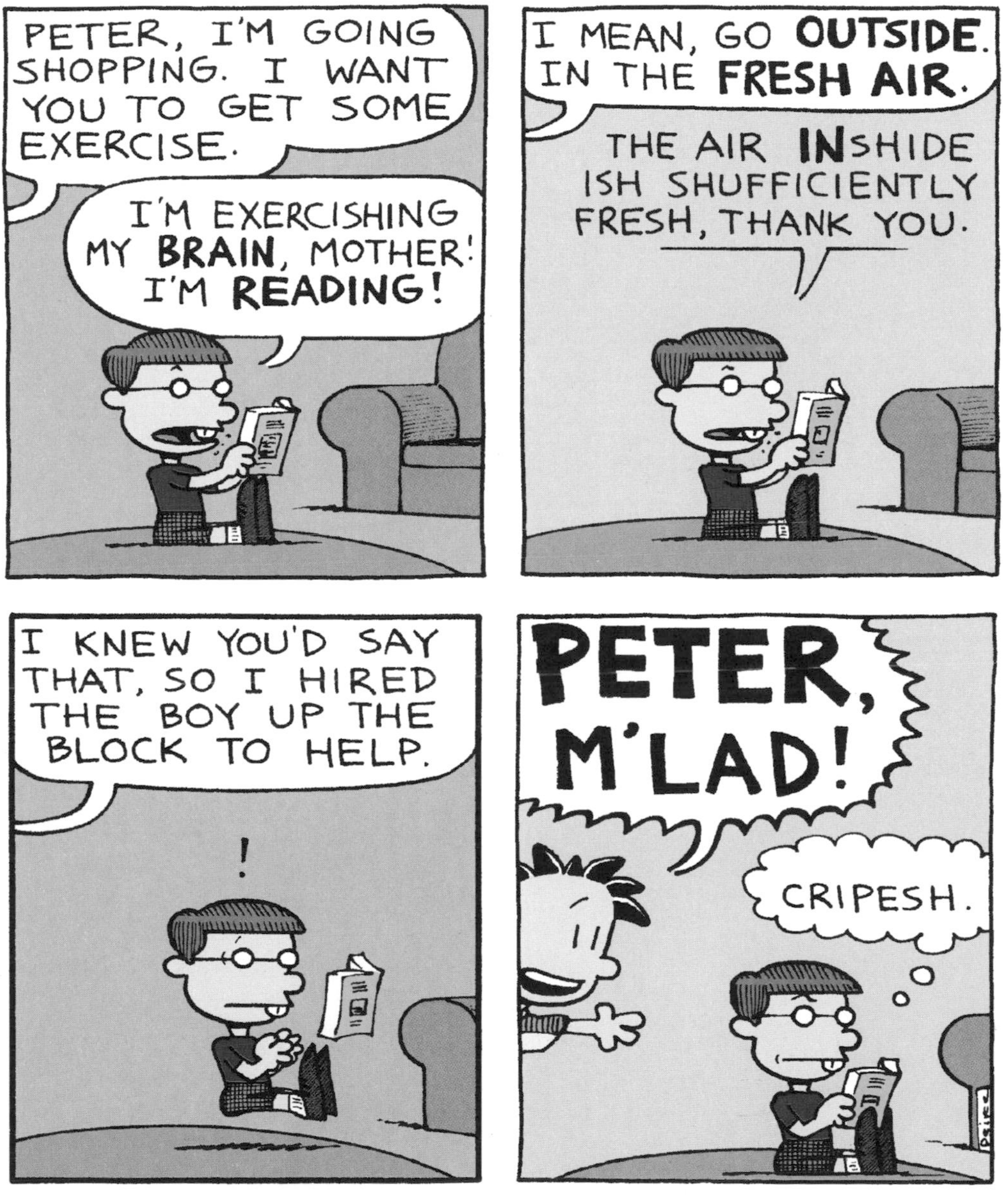
PETER, I'M GOING SHOPPING. I WANT YOU TO GET SOME EXERCISE.
I'M EXERCISHING MY BRAIN, MOTHER! I'M READING!
I MEAN, GO OUTSIDE. IN THE FRESH AIR.
THE AIR INSHIDE ISH SHUFFICIENTLY FRESH, THANK YOU.
I KNEW YOU'D SAY THAT, SO I HIRED THE BOY UP THE BLOCK TO HELP.
!
PETER, M'LAD!
CRIPESH.

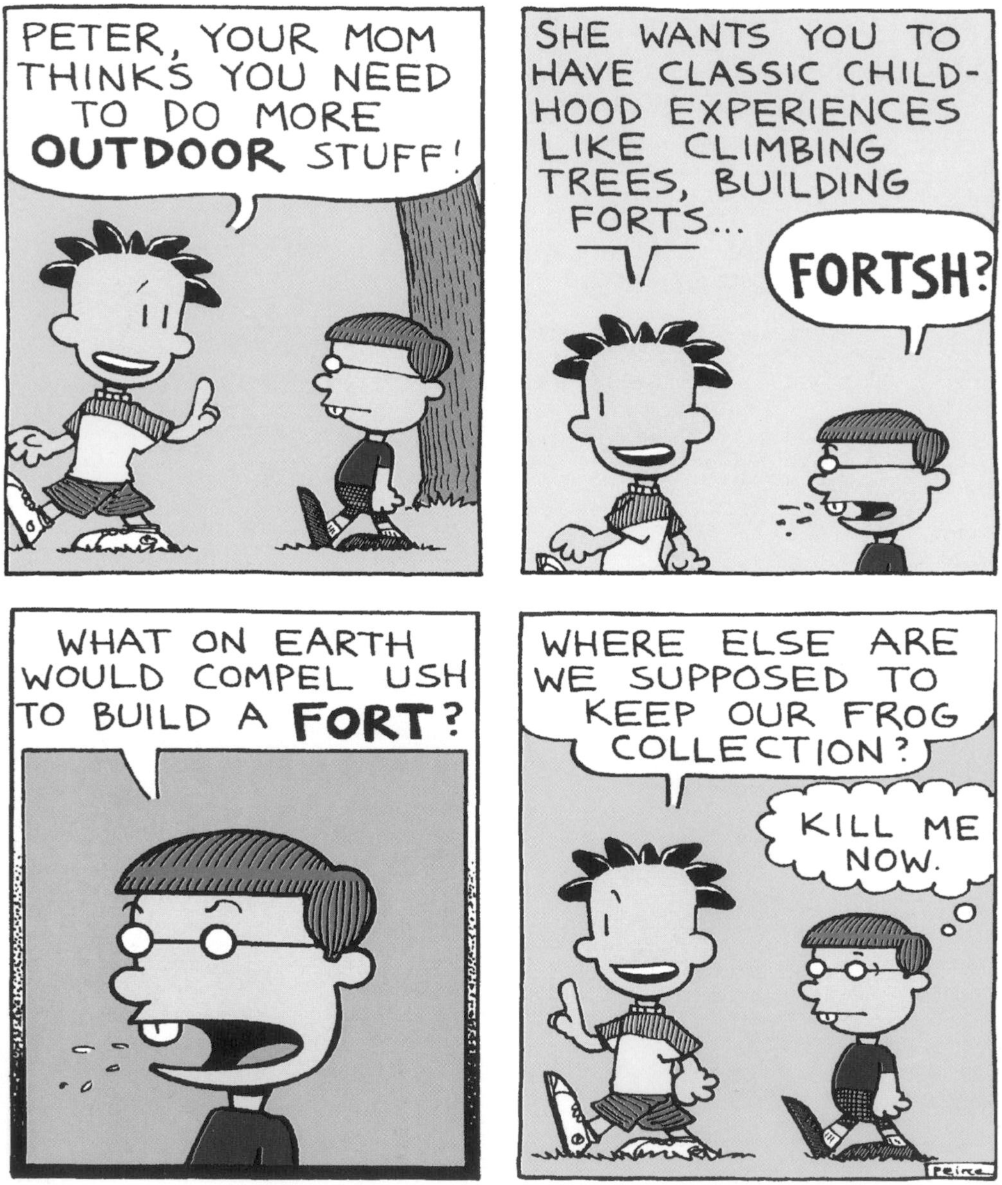
PETER, YOUR MOM THINKS YOU NEED TO DO MORE **OUTDOOR** STUFF!
SHE WANTS YOU TO HAVE CLASSIC CHILD-HOOD EXPERIENCES LIKE CLIMBING TREES, BUILDING FORTS...
FORTSH?
WHAT ON EARTH WOULD COMPEL USH TO BUILD A **FORT**?
WHERE ELSE ARE WE SUPPOSED TO KEEP OUR FROG COLLECTION?
KILL ME NOW.
PEIRCE

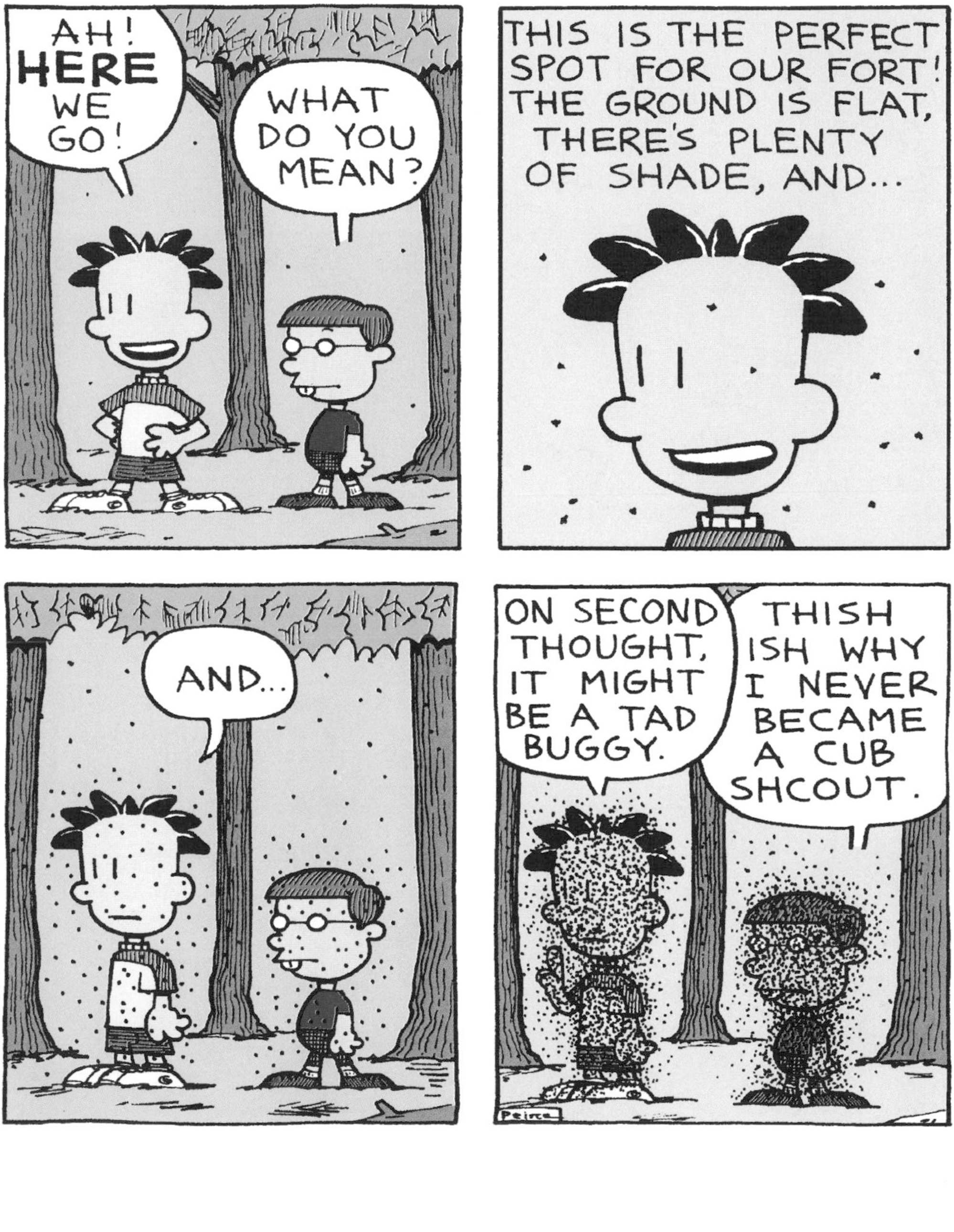
AH! HERE WE GO!
WHAT DO YOU MEAN?
THIS IS THE PERFECT SPOT FOR OUR FORT! THE GROUND IS FLAT, THERE'S PLENTY OF SHADE, AND...
AND...
ON SECOND THOUGHT, IT MIGHT BE A TAD BUGGY.
THISH ISH WHY I NEVER BECAME A CUB SHCOUT.
Peirce

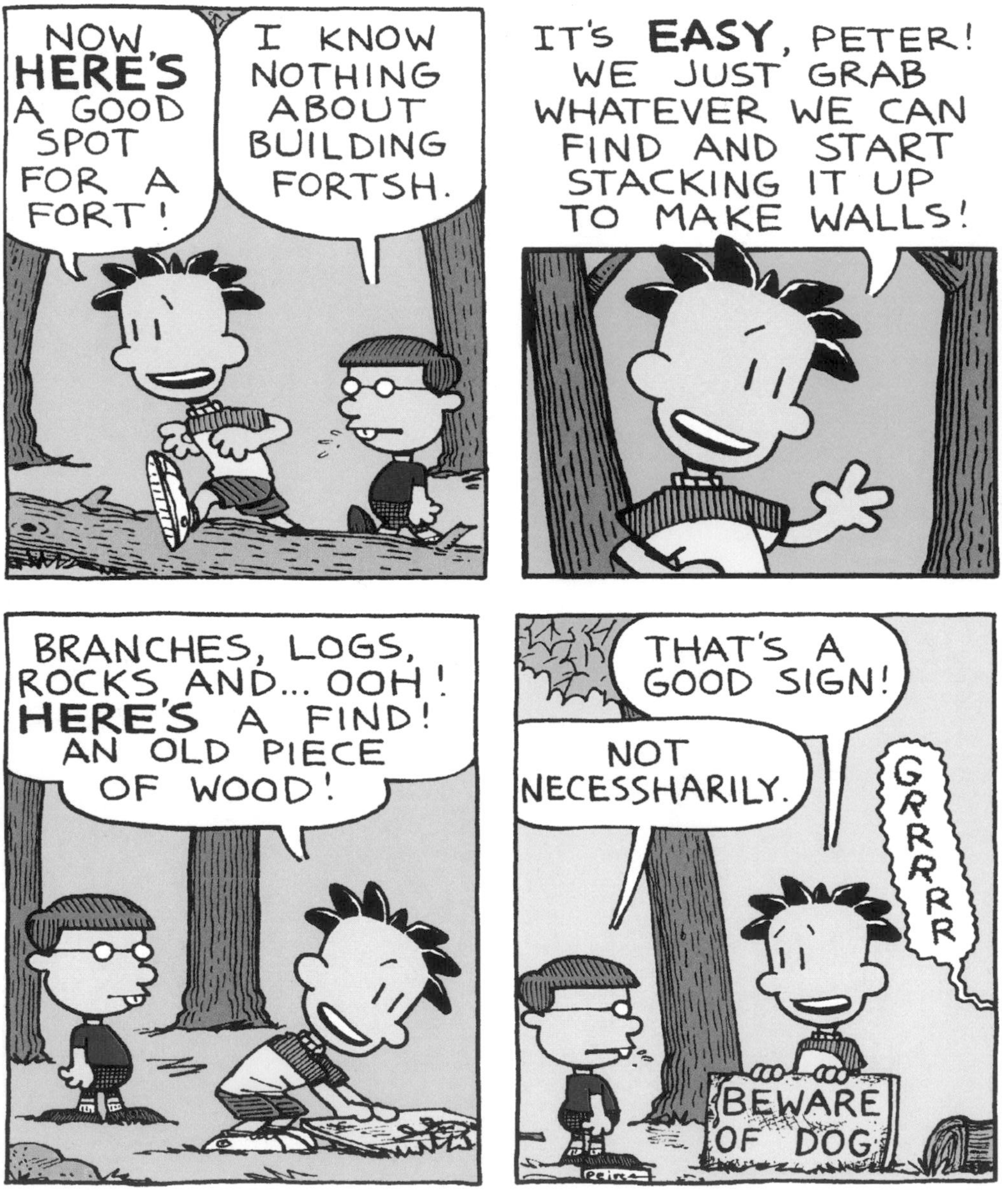
NOW, HERE'S A GOOD SPOT FOR A FORT!
I KNOW NOTHING ABOUT BUILDING FORTSH.
IT'S EASY, PETER! WE JUST GRAB WHATEVER WE CAN FIND AND START STACKING IT UP TO MAKE WALLS!
BRANCHES, LOGS, ROCKS AND... OOH! HERE'S A FIND! AN OLD PIECE OF WOOD!
THAT'S A GOOD SIGN!
NOT NECESSHARILY.
GRRRRR
BEWARE OF DOG

ISN'T THIS GREAT, PETER? DOESN'T IT GIVE YOU A SENSE OF ACCOMPLISHMENT?

OH, SHURE.

EARLIER TODAY, I WAS FRITTERING AWAY MY TIME READING **MOBY DICK** BY HERMAN MELVILLE!

BUT **NOW** I'M SHPENDING THE AFTERNOON MAKING A WALL OF **DEAD BRANCHESH** AND CALLING IT A **FORT!**

YESH, WHAT A **SHTAGGERING** ACCOMPLISHMENT!

PETER, YOUR ATTITUDE KIND OF BLOWS.

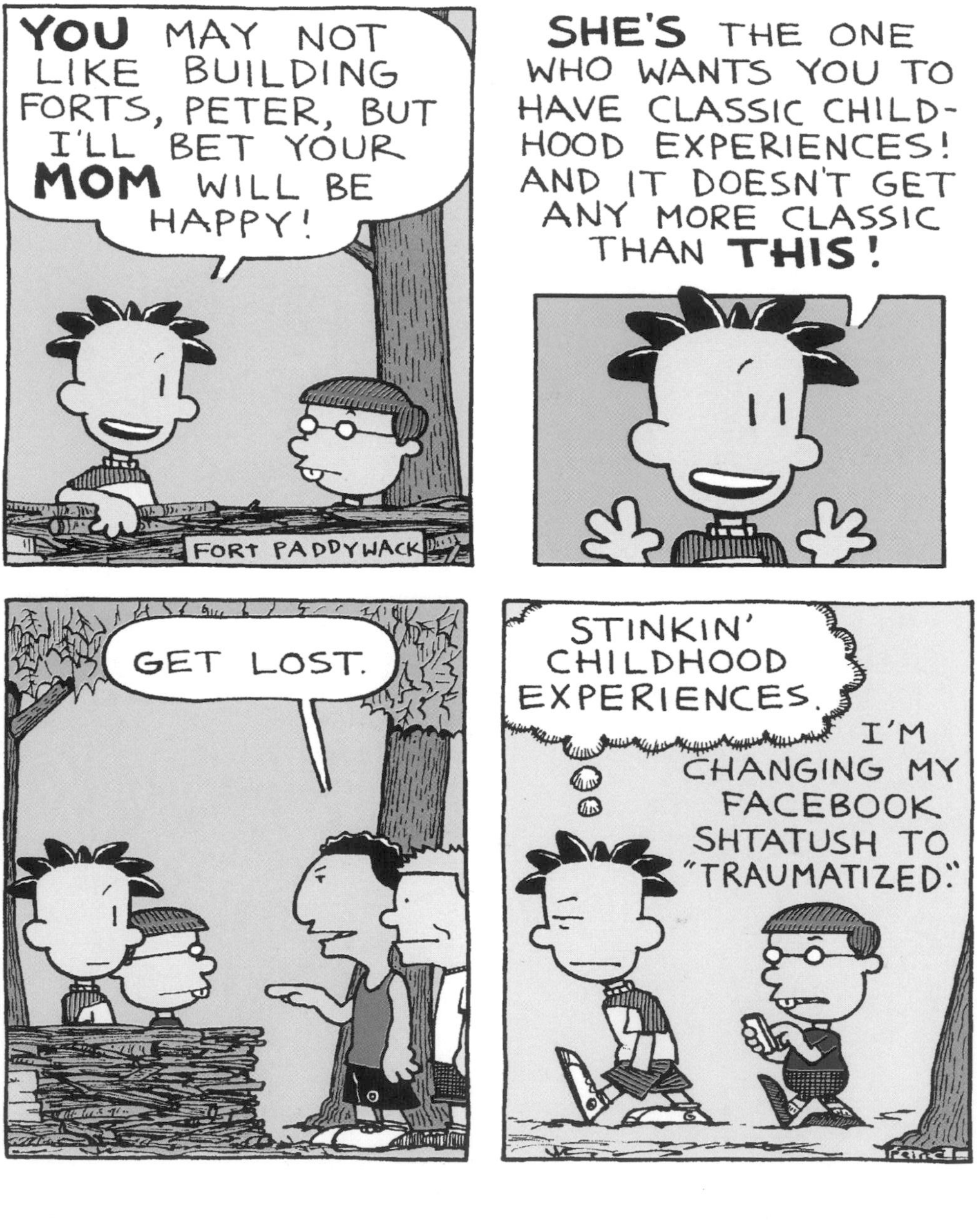
YOU MAY NOT LIKE BUILDING FORTS, PETER, BUT I'LL BET YOUR MOM WILL BE HAPPY!
FORT PADDYWACK
SHE'S THE ONE WHO WANTS YOU TO HAVE CLASSIC CHILDHOOD EXPERIENCES! AND IT DOESN'T GET ANY MORE CLASSIC THAN THIS!
GET LOST.
STINKIN' CHILDHOOD EXPERIENCES.
I'M CHANGING MY FACEBOOK SHTATUSH TO "TRAUMATIZED."

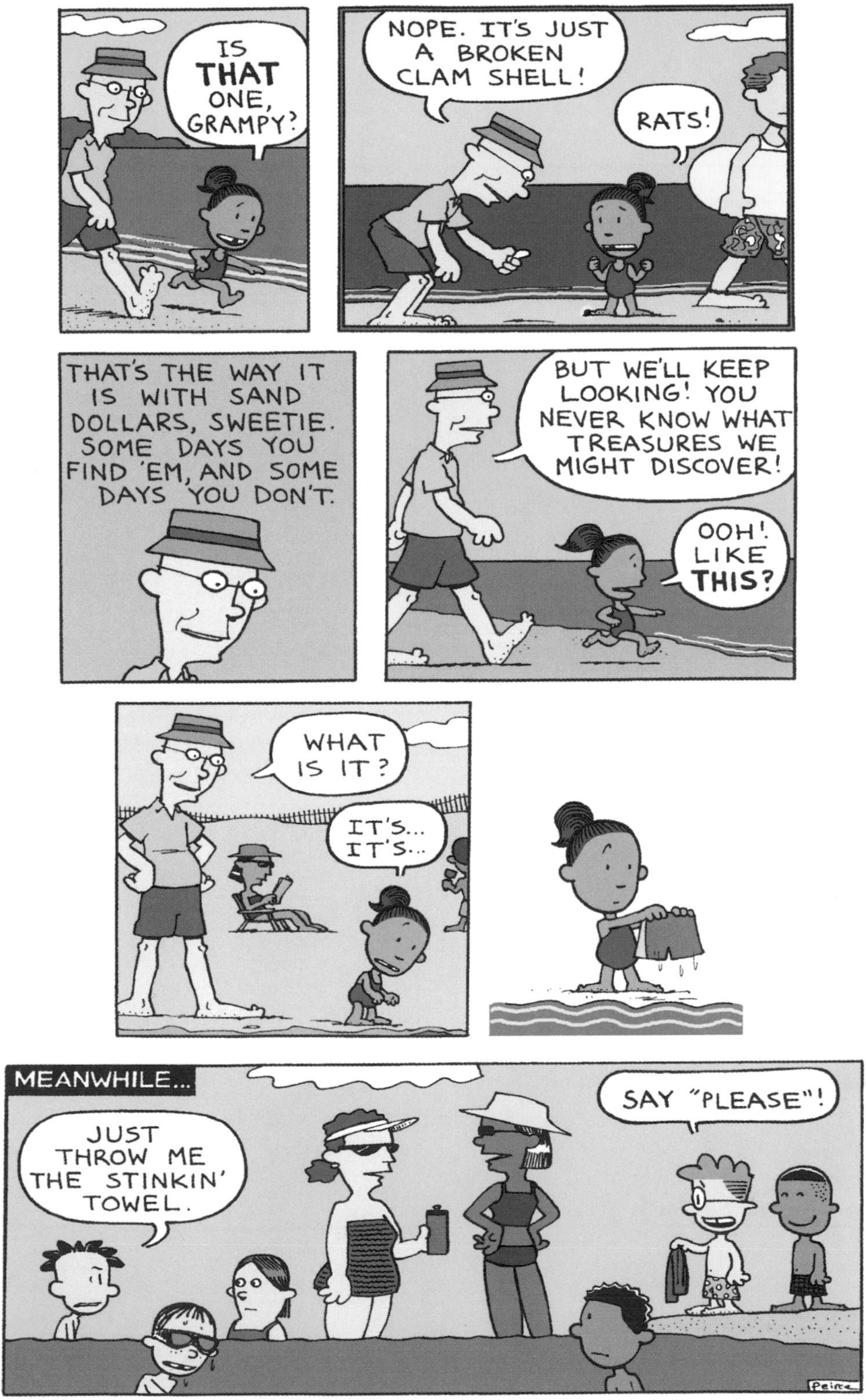
IS THAT ONE, GRAMPY?
NOPE. IT'S JUST A BROKEN CLAM SHELL!
RATS!
THAT'S THE WAY IT IS WITH SAND DOLLARS, SWEETIE. SOME DAYS YOU FIND 'EM, AND SOME DAYS YOU DON'T.
BUT WE'LL KEEP LOOKING! YOU NEVER KNOW WHAT TREASURES WE MIGHT DISCOVER!
OOH! LIKE THIS?
WHAT IS IT?
IT'S... IT'S...
MEANWHILE...
JUST THROW ME THE STINKIN' TOWEL.
SAY "PLEASE"!
Peirce

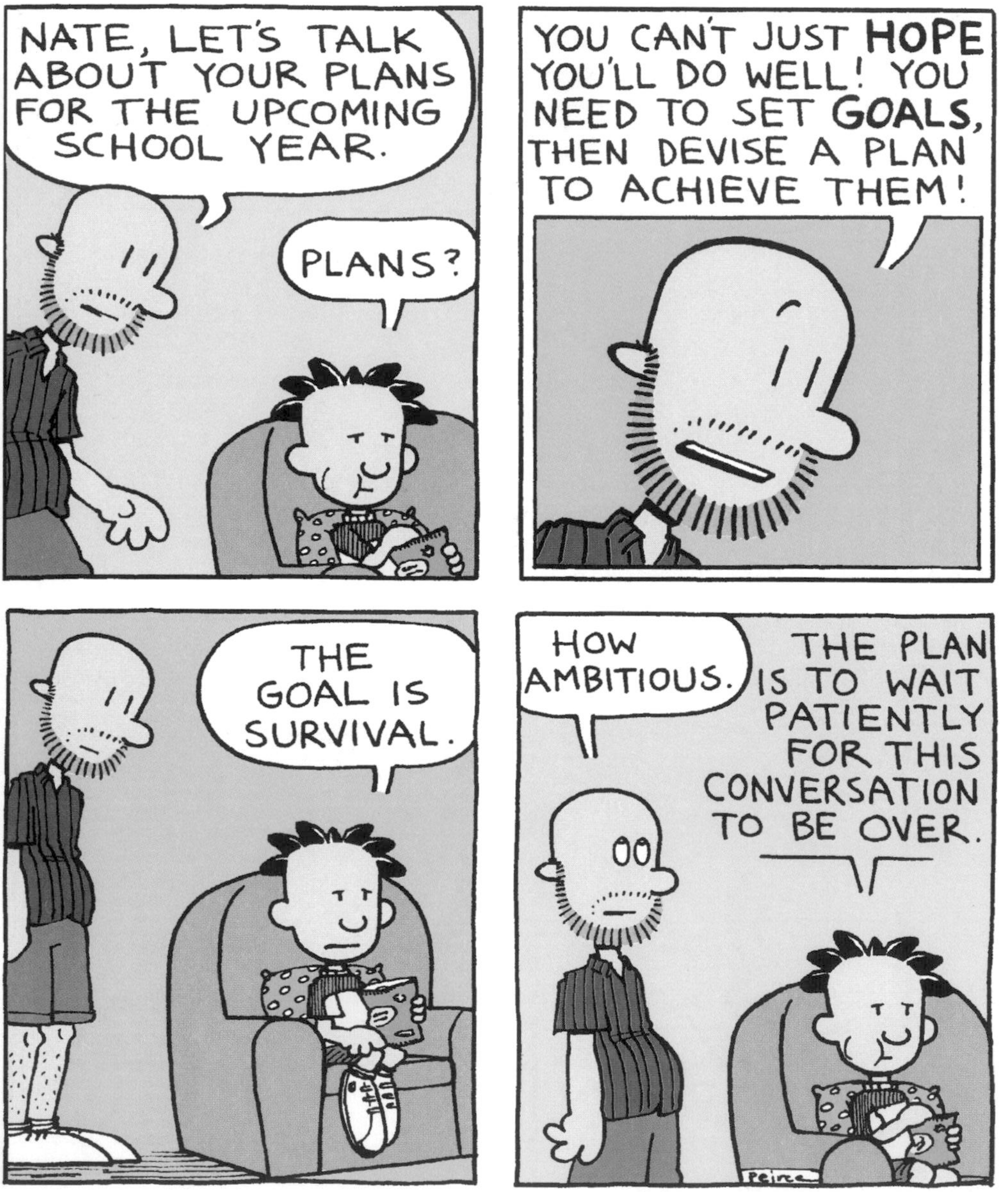
NATE, LET'S TALK ABOUT YOUR PLANS FOR THE UPCOMING SCHOOL YEAR.
PLANS?
YOU CAN'T JUST HOPE YOU'LL DO WELL! YOU NEED TO SET GOALS, THEN DEVISE A PLAN TO ACHIEVE THEM!
THE GOAL IS SURVIVAL.
THE PLAN IS TO WAIT PATIENTLY FOR THIS CONVERSATION TO BE OVER.
HOW AMBITIOUS.
PEIRCE

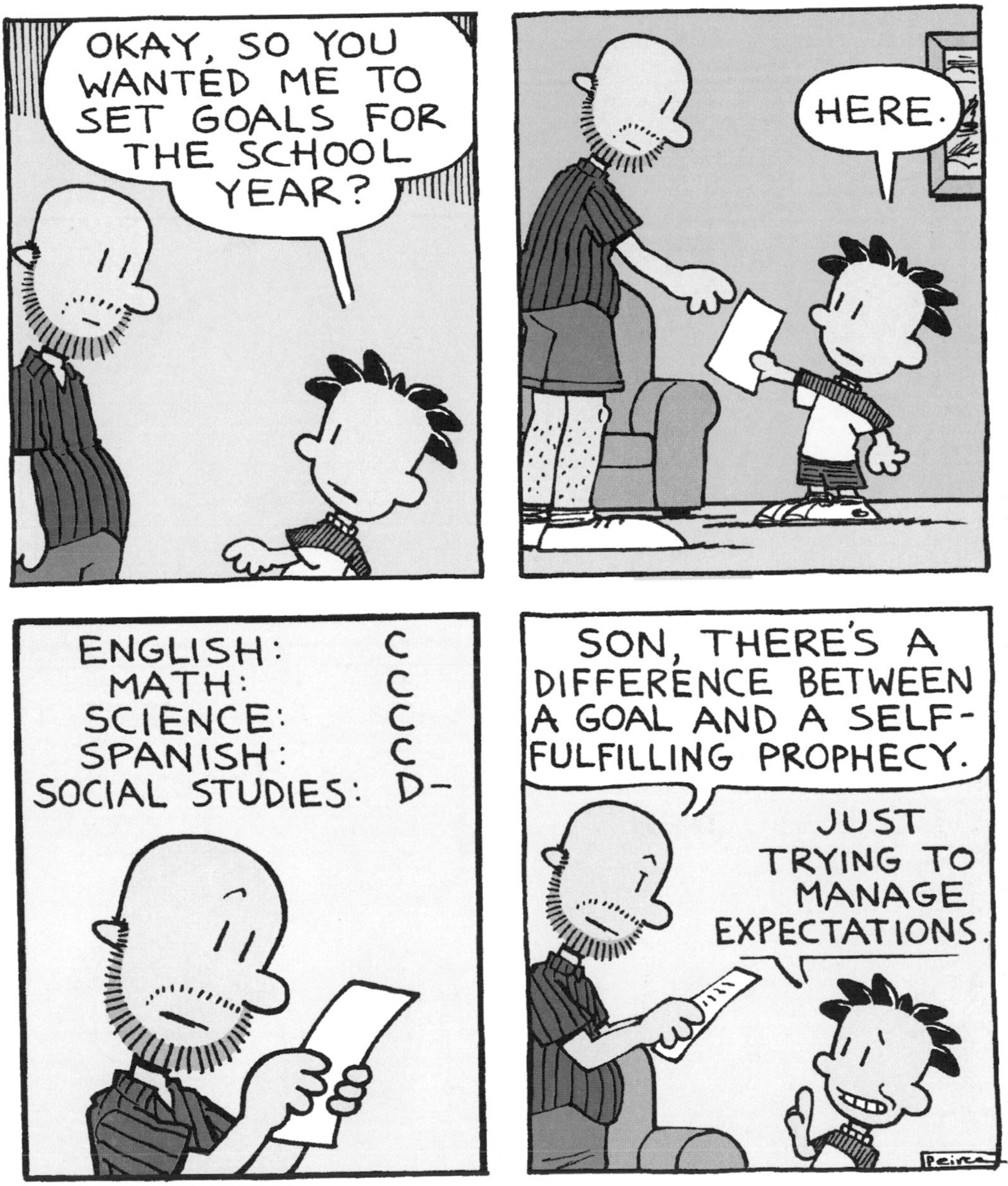
OKAY, SO YOU WANTED ME TO SET GOALS FOR THE SCHOOL YEAR?
HERE.
ENGLISH: C
MATH: C
SCIENCE: C
SPANISH: C
SOCIAL STUDIES: D-
SON, THERE'S A DIFFERENCE BETWEEN A GOAL AND A SELF-FULFILLING PROPHECY.
JUST TRYING TO MANAGE EXPECTATIONS.
Peirce

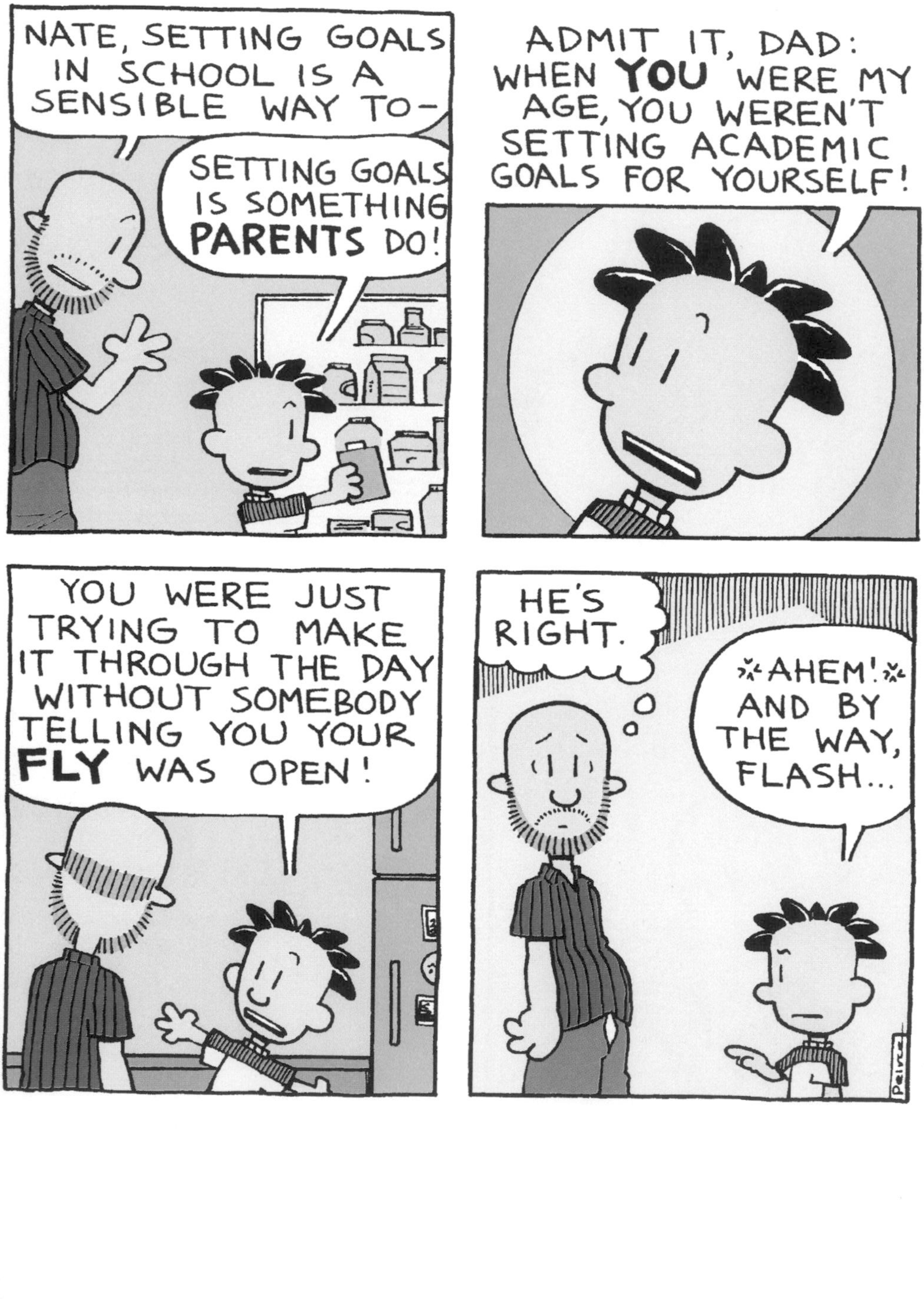
NATE, SETTING GOALS IN SCHOOL IS A SENSIBLE WAY TO–
SETTING GOALS IS SOMETHING PARENTS DO!
ADMIT IT, DAD: WHEN YOU WERE MY AGE, YOU WEREN'T SETTING ACADEMIC GOALS FOR YOURSELF!
YOU WERE JUST TRYING TO MAKE IT THROUGH THE DAY WITHOUT SOMEBODY TELLING YOU YOUR FLY WAS OPEN!
HE'S RIGHT.
AHEM! AND BY THE WAY, FLASH...
Peirce

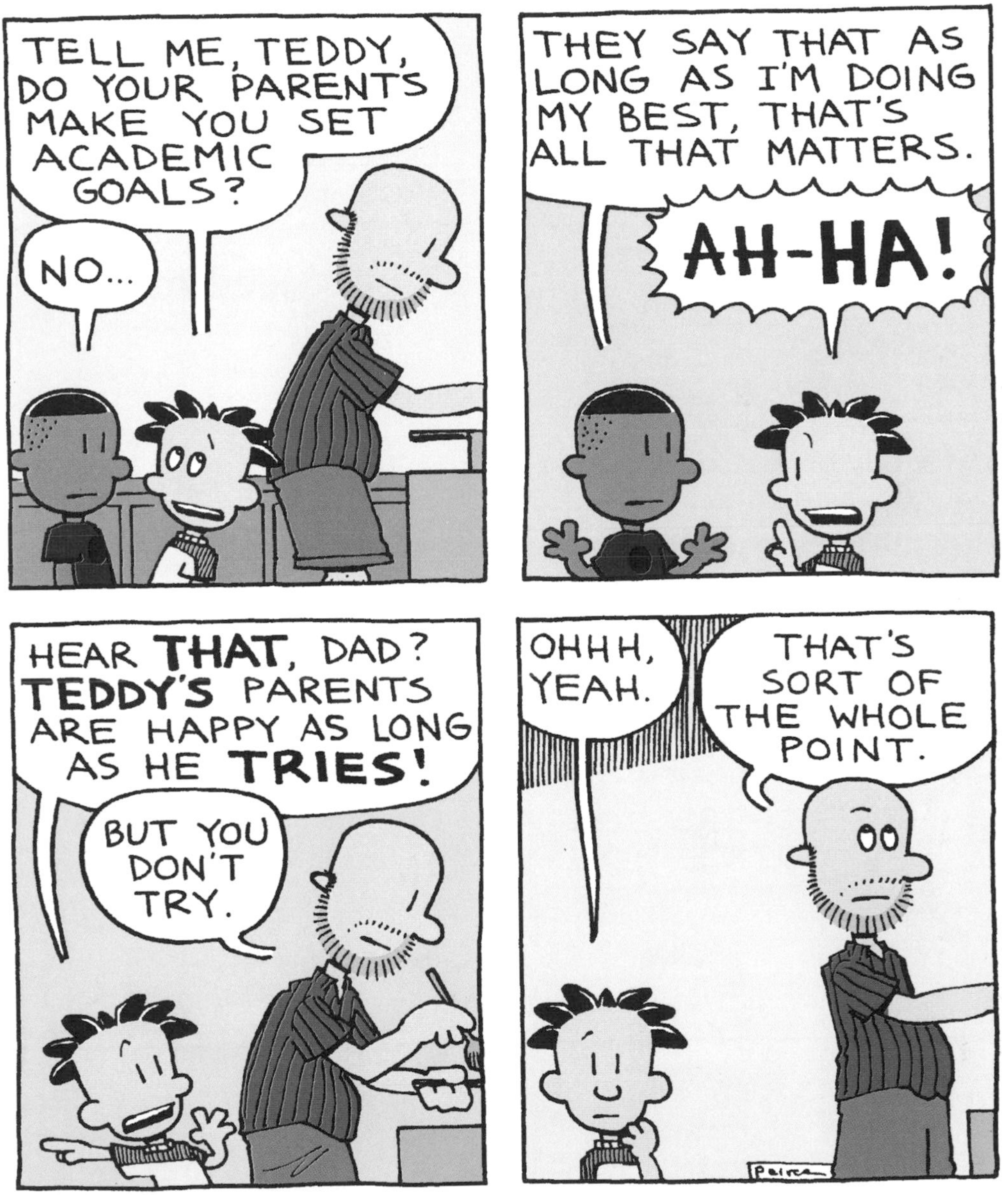
TELL ME, TEDDY, DO YOUR PARENTS MAKE YOU SET ACADEMIC GOALS?
NO...
THEY SAY THAT AS LONG AS I'M DOING MY BEST, THAT'S ALL THAT MATTERS.
AH-HA!
HEAR THAT, DAD? TEDDY'S PARENTS ARE HAPPY AS LONG AS HE TRIES!
BUT YOU DON'T TRY.
OHHH, YEAH.
THAT'S SORT OF THE WHOLE POINT.
Peirce

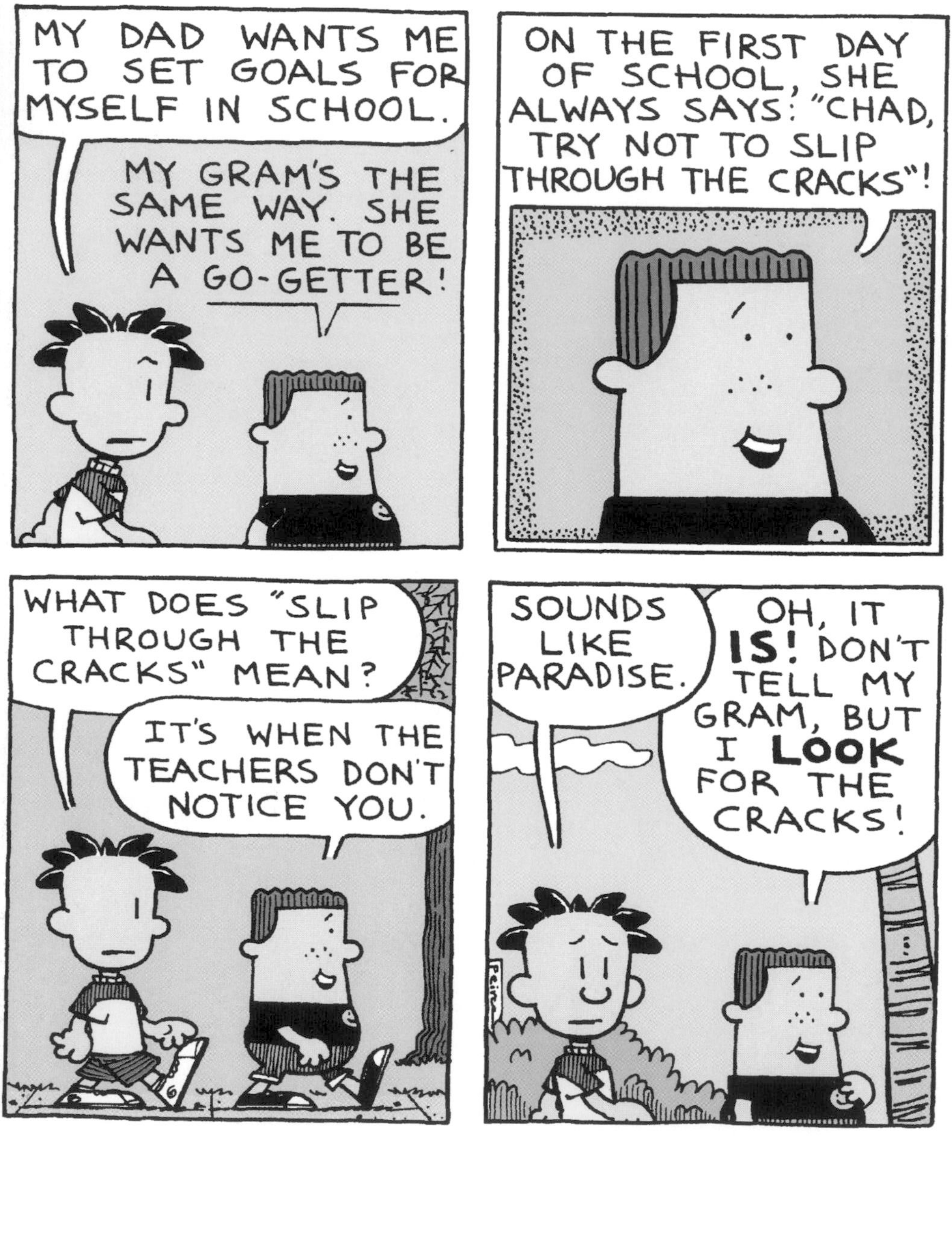
MY DAD WANTS ME TO SET GOALS FOR MYSELF IN SCHOOL.
MY GRAM'S THE SAME WAY. SHE WANTS ME TO BE A GO-GETTER!
ON THE FIRST DAY OF SCHOOL, SHE ALWAYS SAYS: "CHAD, TRY NOT TO SLIP THROUGH THE CRACKS"!
WHAT DOES "SLIP THROUGH THE CRACKS" MEAN?
IT'S WHEN THE TEACHERS DON'T NOTICE YOU.
SOUNDS LIKE PARADISE.
OH, IT **IS**! DON'T TELL MY GRAM, BUT I **LOOK** FOR THE CRACKS!
Peirce

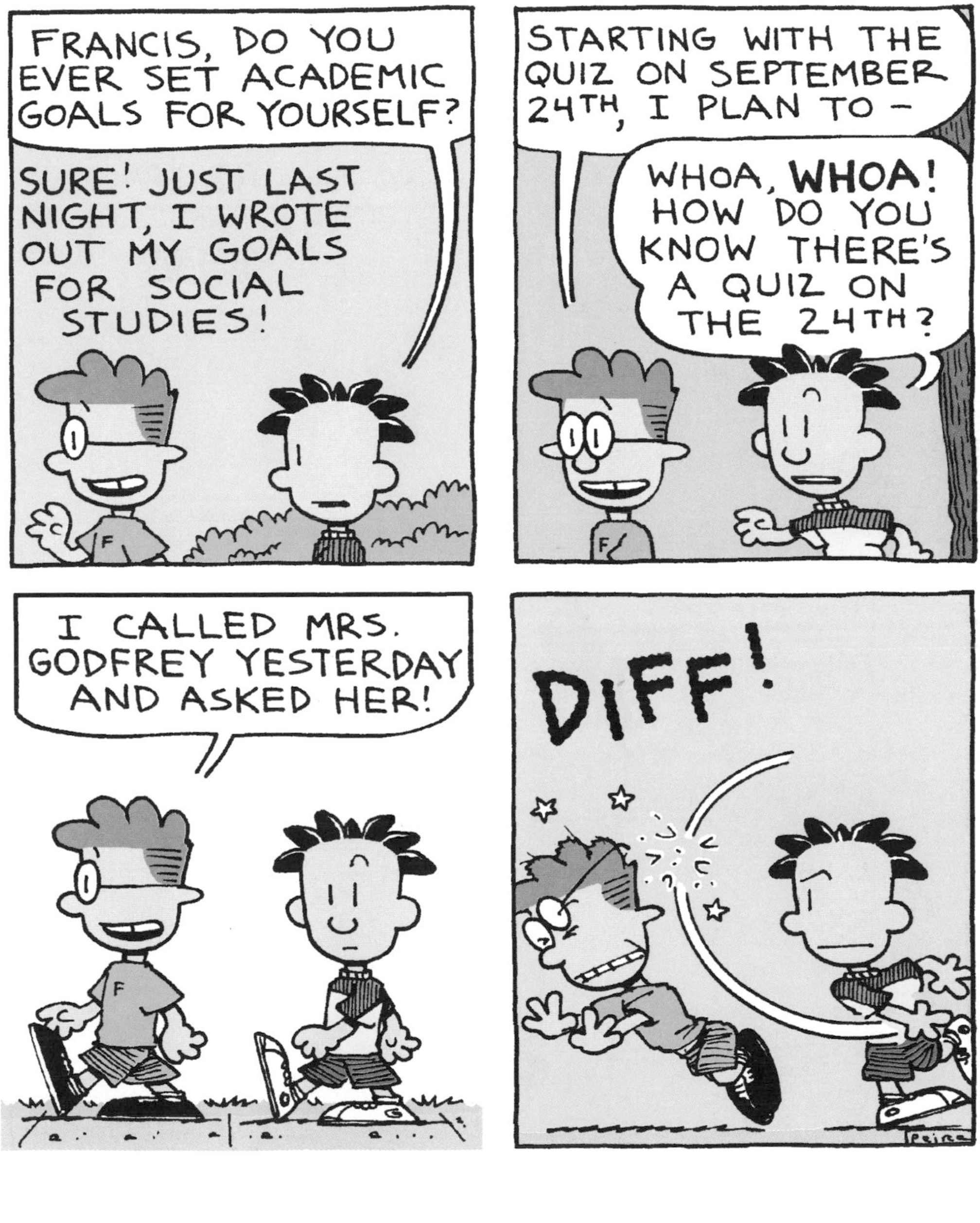
FRANCIS, DO YOU EVER SET ACADEMIC GOALS FOR YOURSELF?
SURE! JUST LAST NIGHT, I WROTE OUT MY GOALS FOR SOCIAL STUDIES!
STARTING WITH THE QUIZ ON SEPTEMBER 24TH, I PLAN TO –
WHOA, **WHOA**! HOW DO YOU KNOW THERE'S A QUIZ ON THE 24TH?
I CALLED MRS. GODFREY YESTERDAY AND ASKED HER!
DIFF!

HELLO, BOYS! CAN I HELP YOU?

I NEED A NOTEBOOK.

THESE ARE VERY POPULAR!

NO, THAT HAS A PLASTIC COVER. I CAN'T DRAW ON PLASTIC.

AH! SO YOU WANT A SKETCH-BOOK!

NO, A NOTEBOOK. WITH LINED PAPER.

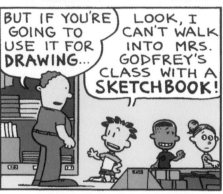

BUT IF YOU'RE GOING TO USE IT FOR DRAWING...

LOOK, I CAN'T WALK INTO MRS. GODFREY'S CLASS WITH A SKETCHBOOK!

UH... YOU CAN'T?

NO! SHE EXPECTS ME TO TAKE NOTES!

I NEED A NOTEBOOK THAT SHE THINKS I'M USING AS A NOTEBOOK, BUT WHICH I'M ACTUALLY USING TO DRAW COMICS!

OH. WELL, I...

NEVER MIND. I'LL FIND IT MYSELF.

MUST BE HIS FIRST DAY ON THE JOB.

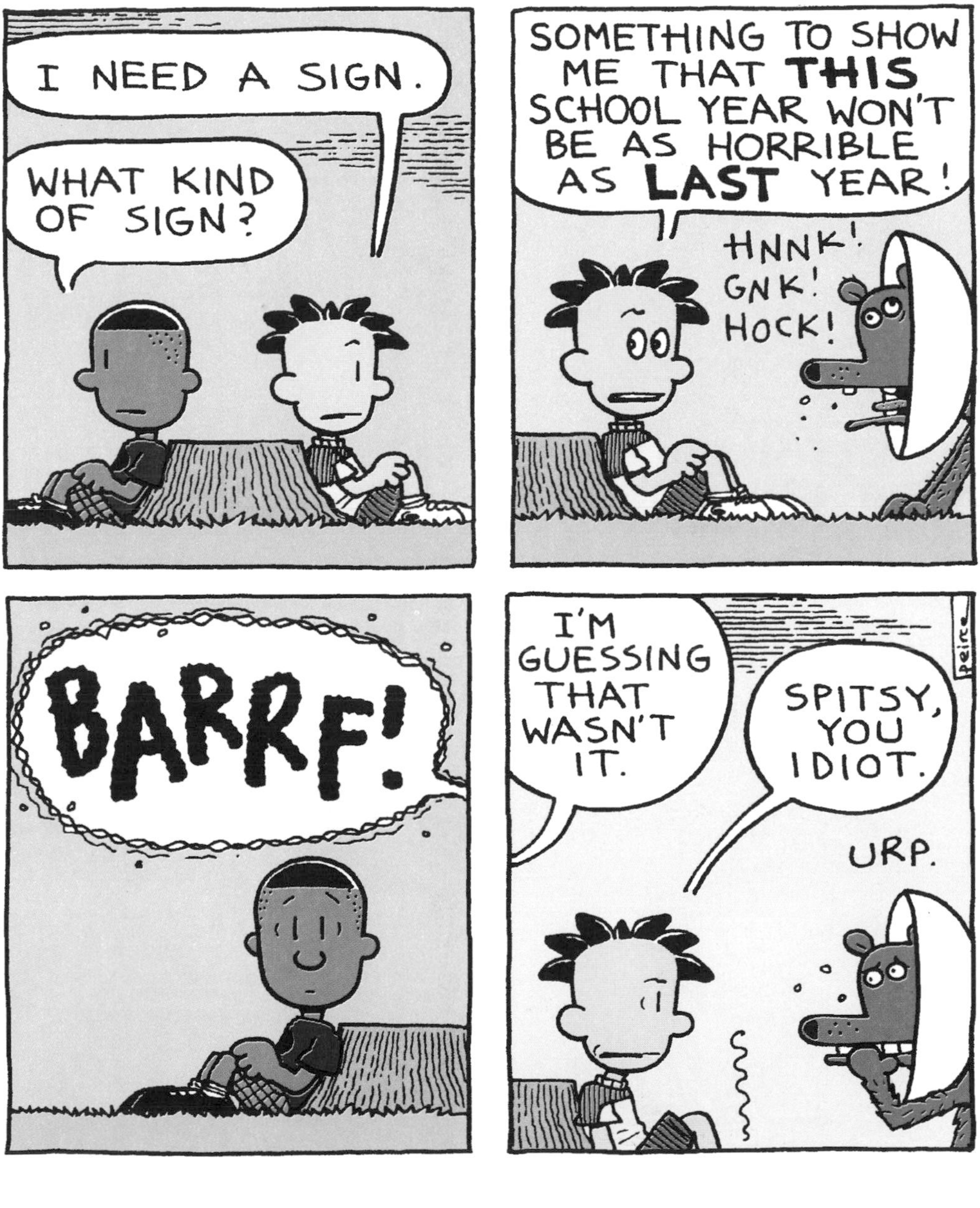
I NEED A SIGN.
WHAT KIND OF SIGN?
SOMETHING TO SHOW ME THAT **THIS** SCHOOL YEAR WON'T BE AS HORRIBLE AS **LAST** YEAR!
HNNK! GNK! HOCK!
BARRF!
I'M GUESSING THAT WASN'T IT.
SPITSY, YOU IDIOT.
URP.
peirce

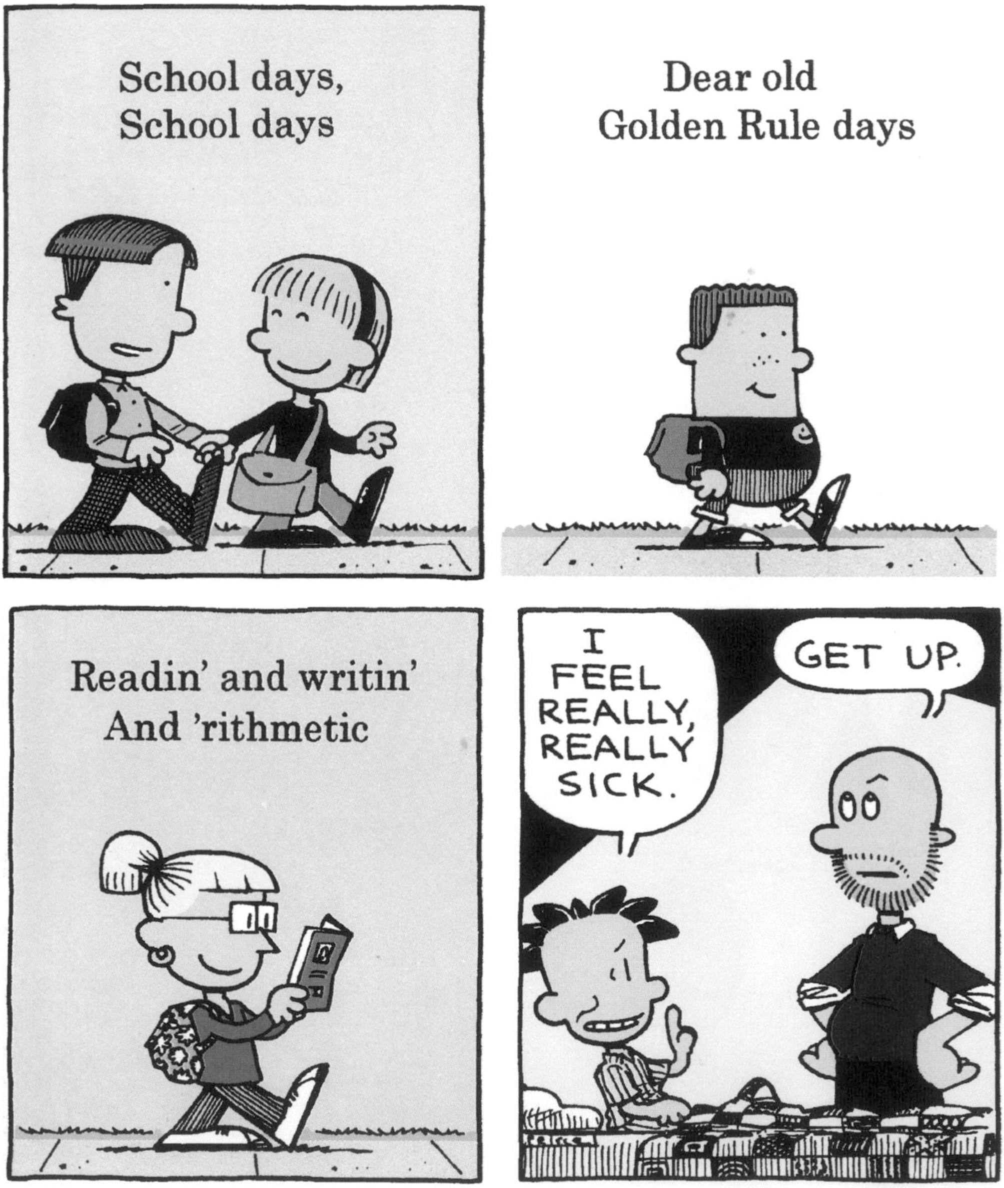
School days,
School days
Dear old
Golden Rule days
Readin' and writin'
And 'rithmetic
I FEEL REALLY, REALLY SICK.
GET UP.

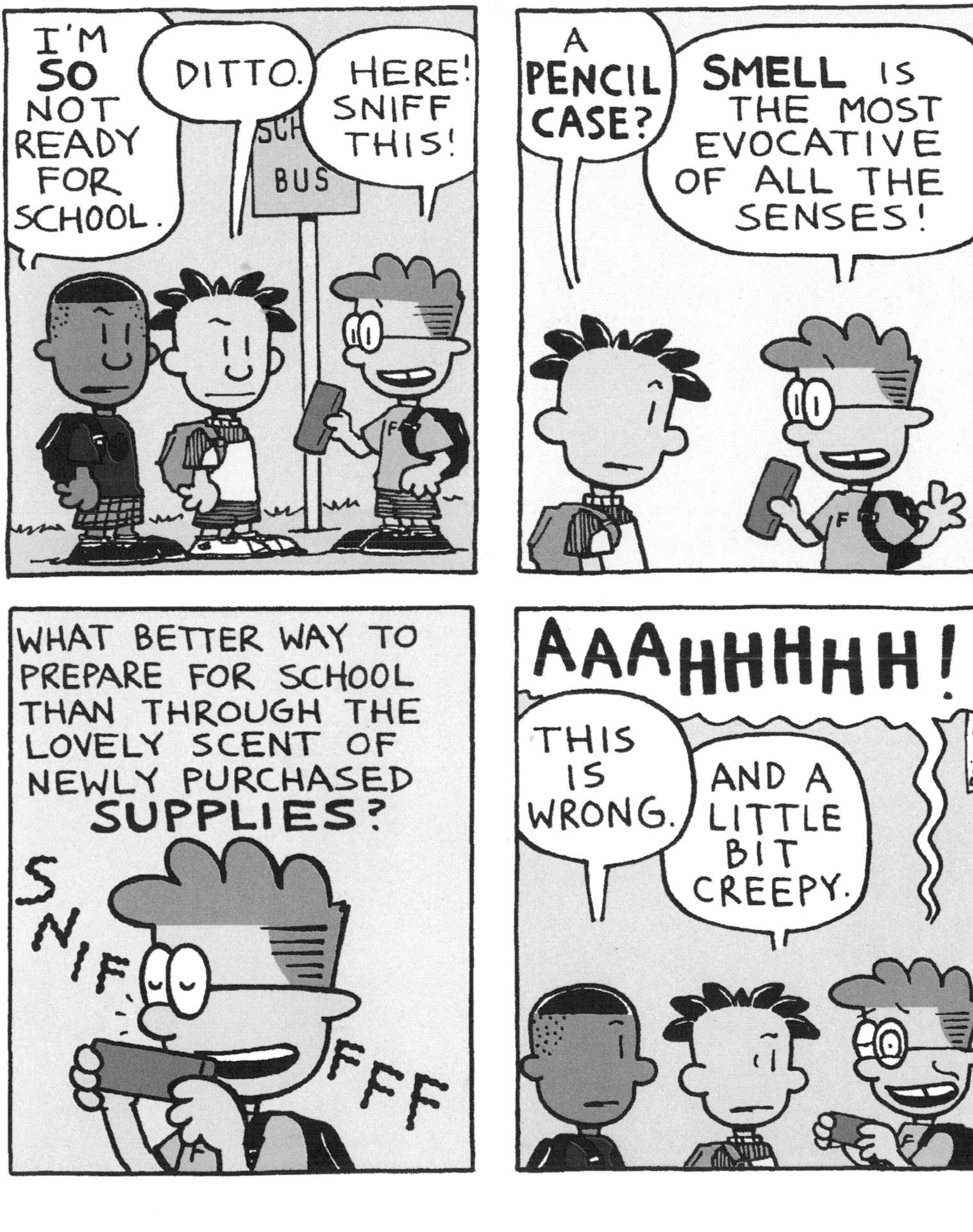
I'M SO NOT READY FOR SCHOOL.
DITTO.
HERE! SNIFF THIS!
SCH BUS
A PENCIL CASE?
SMELL IS THE MOST EVOCATIVE OF ALL THE SENSES!
WHAT BETTER WAY TO PREPARE FOR SCHOOL THAN THROUGH THE LOVELY SCENT OF NEWLY PURCHASED SUPPLIES?
SNIFFFF
AAAHHHHH!
THIS IS WRONG.
AND A LITTLE BIT CREEPY.
Peirce

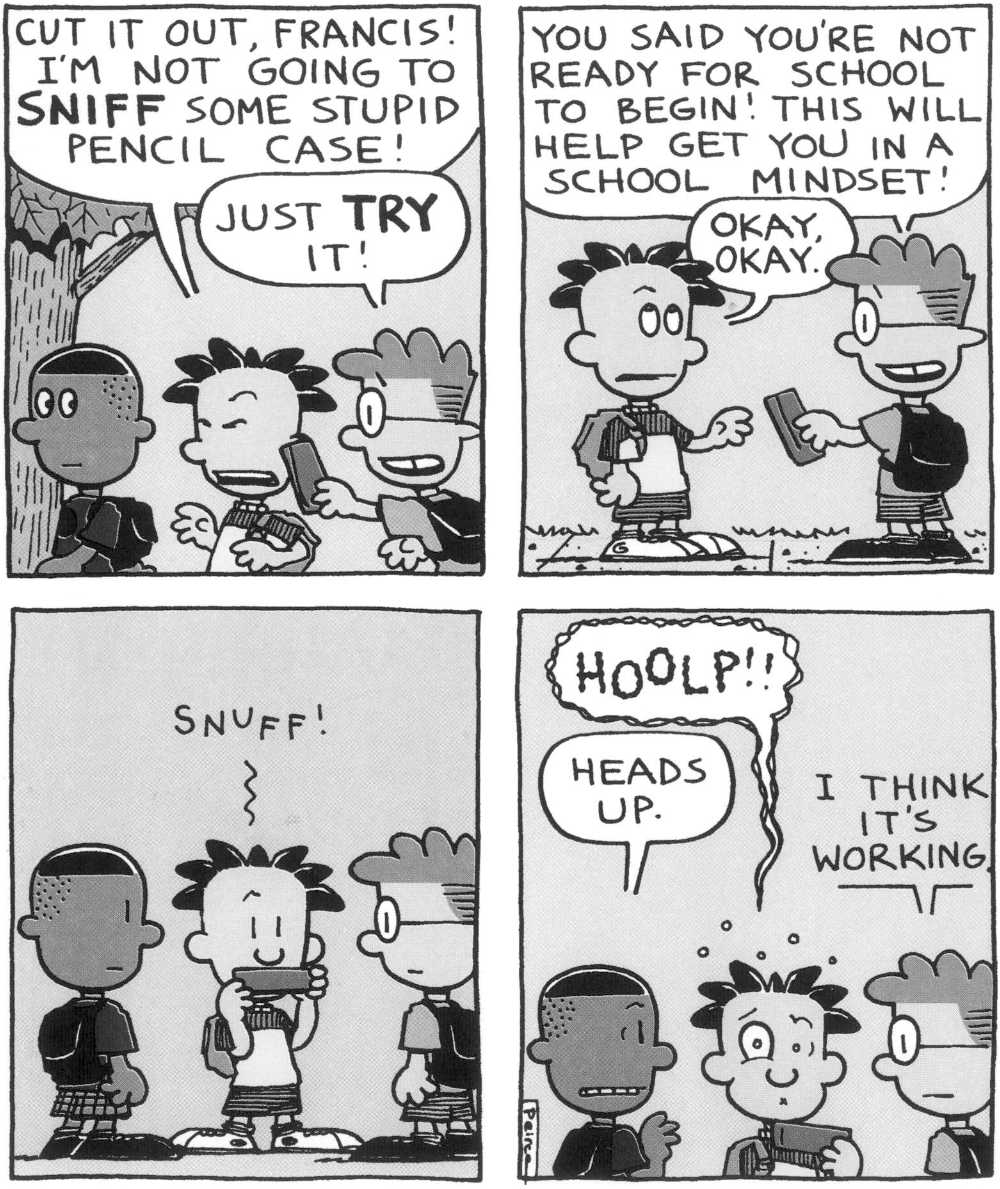
CUT IT OUT, FRANCIS! I'M NOT GOING TO **SNIFF** SOME STUPID PENCIL CASE!
JUST **TRY** IT!
YOU SAID YOU'RE NOT READY FOR SCHOOL TO BEGIN! THIS WILL HELP GET YOU IN A SCHOOL MINDSET!
OKAY, OKAY.
SNUFF!
HOOLP!!
HEADS UP.
I THINK IT'S WORKING.

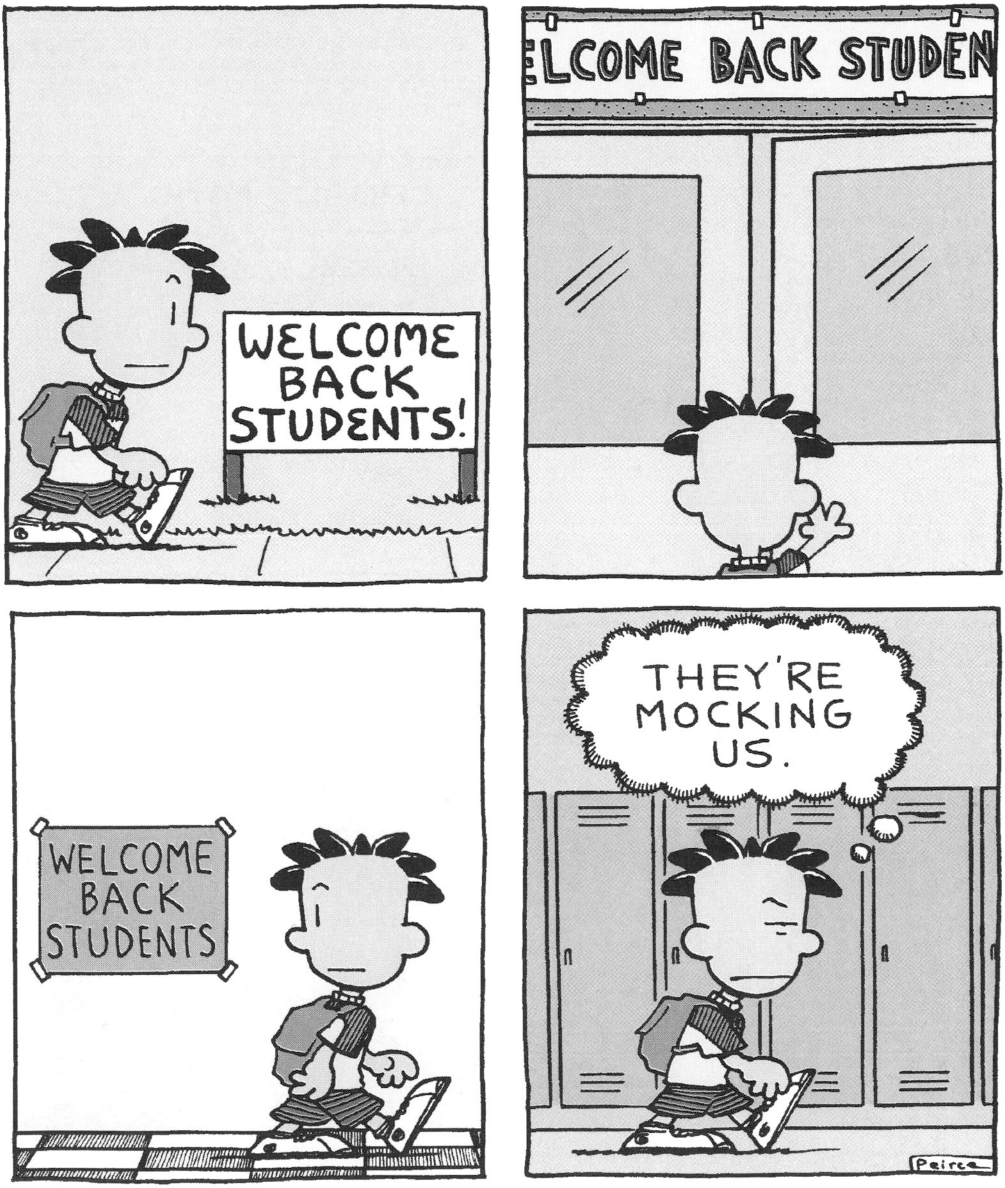
WELCOME BACK STUDENTS!
ELCOME BACK STUDEN
WELCOME BACK STUDENTS
THEY'RE MOCKING US.
Peirce

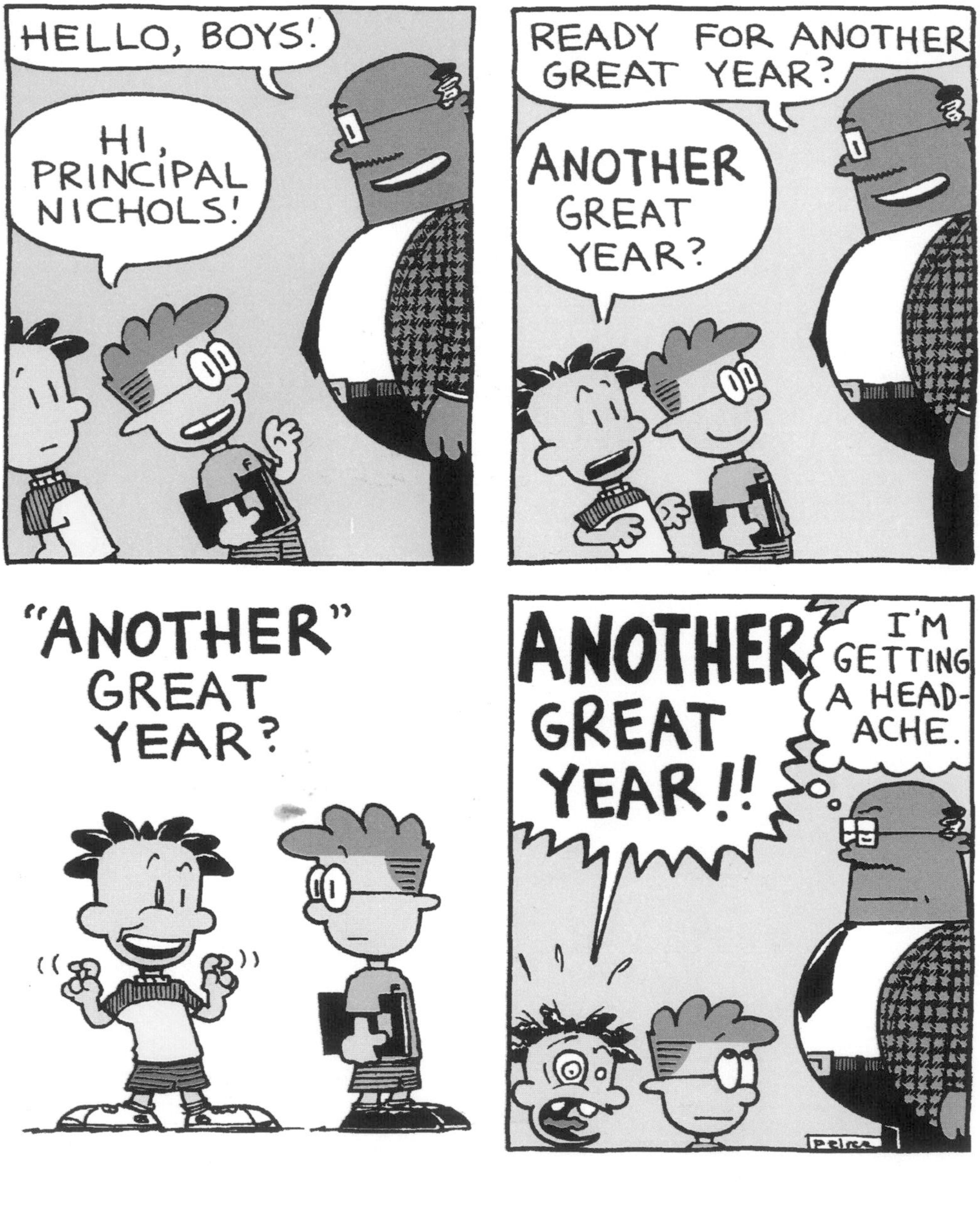
HELLO, BOYS!
HI, PRINCIPAL NICHOLS!
READY FOR ANOTHER GREAT YEAR?
ANOTHER GREAT YEAR?
"ANOTHER" GREAT YEAR?
ANOTHER GREAT YEAR!!
I'M GETTING A HEAD-ACHE.

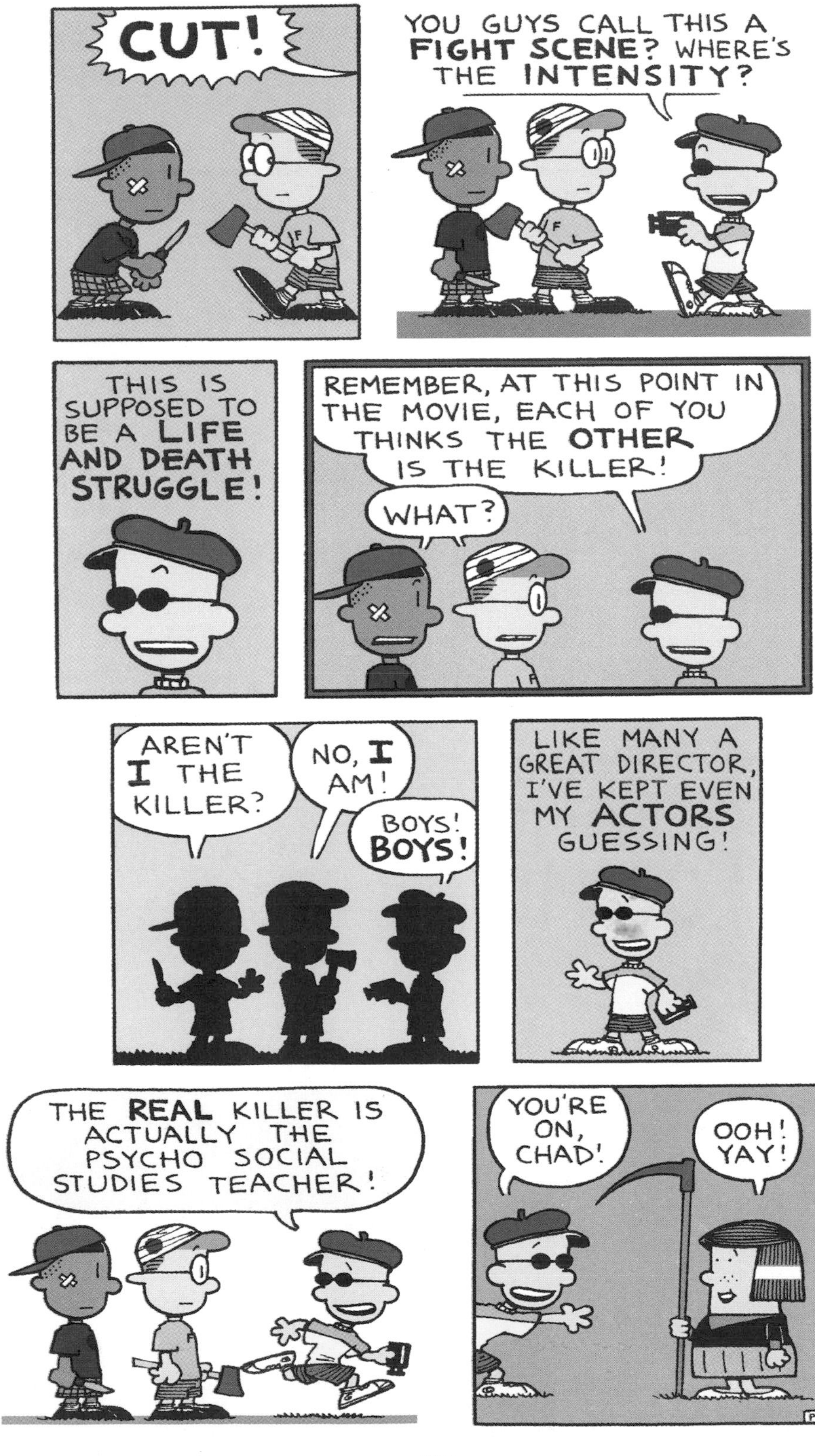
CUT!
YOU GUYS CALL THIS A FIGHT SCENE? WHERE'S THE INTENSITY?
THIS IS SUPPOSED TO BE A LIFE AND DEATH STRUGGLE!
REMEMBER, AT THIS POINT IN THE MOVIE, EACH OF YOU THINKS THE OTHER IS THE KILLER!
WHAT?
AREN'T I THE KILLER?
NO, I AM!
BOYS! BOYS!
LIKE MANY A GREAT DIRECTOR, I'VE KEPT EVEN MY ACTORS GUESSING!
THE REAL KILLER IS ACTUALLY THE PSYCHO SOCIAL STUDIES TEACHER!
YOU'RE ON, CHAD!
OOH! YAY!
Peirce

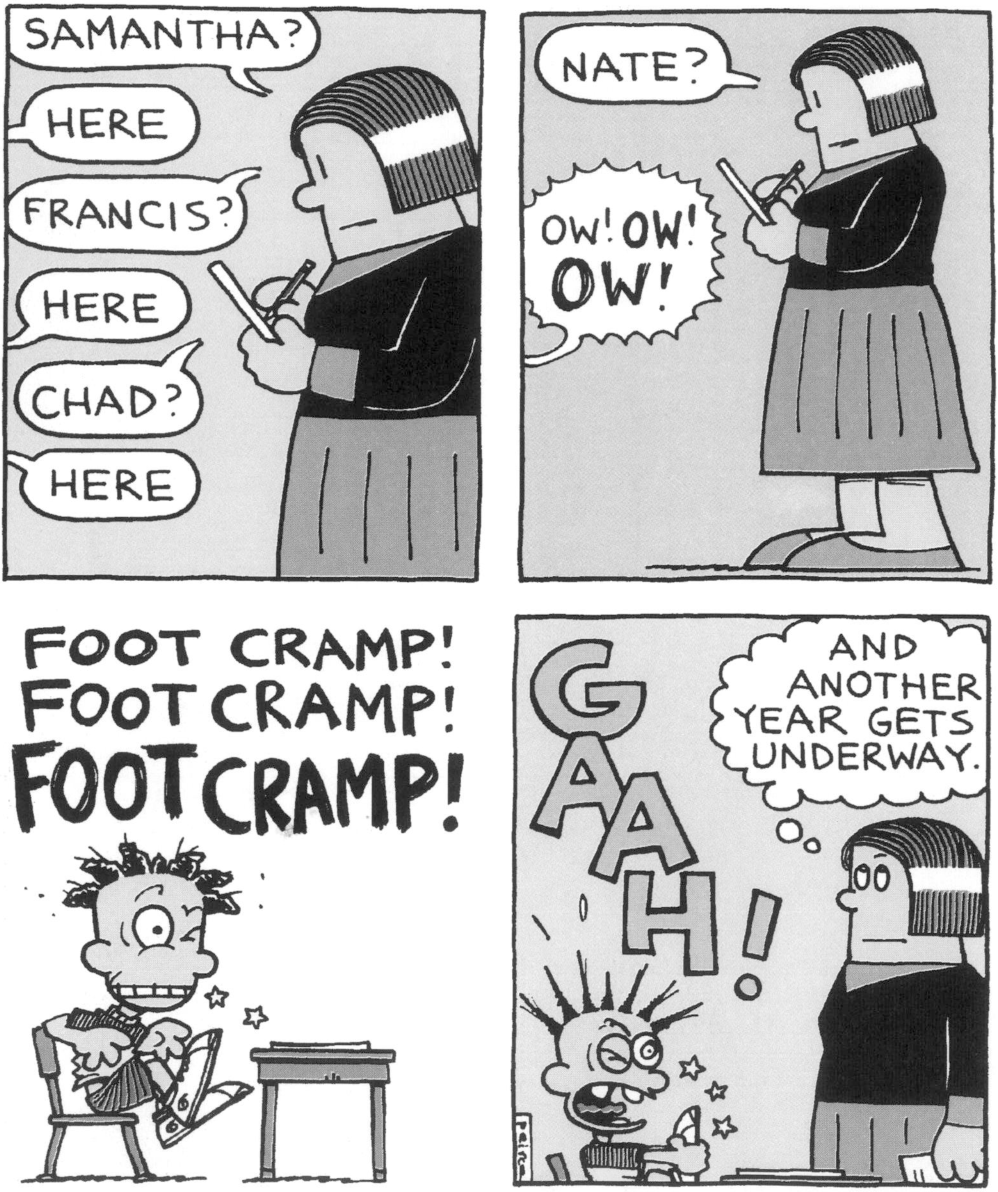
SAMANTHA?
HERE
FRANCIS?
HERE
CHAD?
HERE
NATE?
OW! OW! OW!
FOOT CRAMP!
FOOT CRAMP!
FOOT CRAMP!
GAAH!
AND ANOTHER YEAR GETS UNDERWAY.

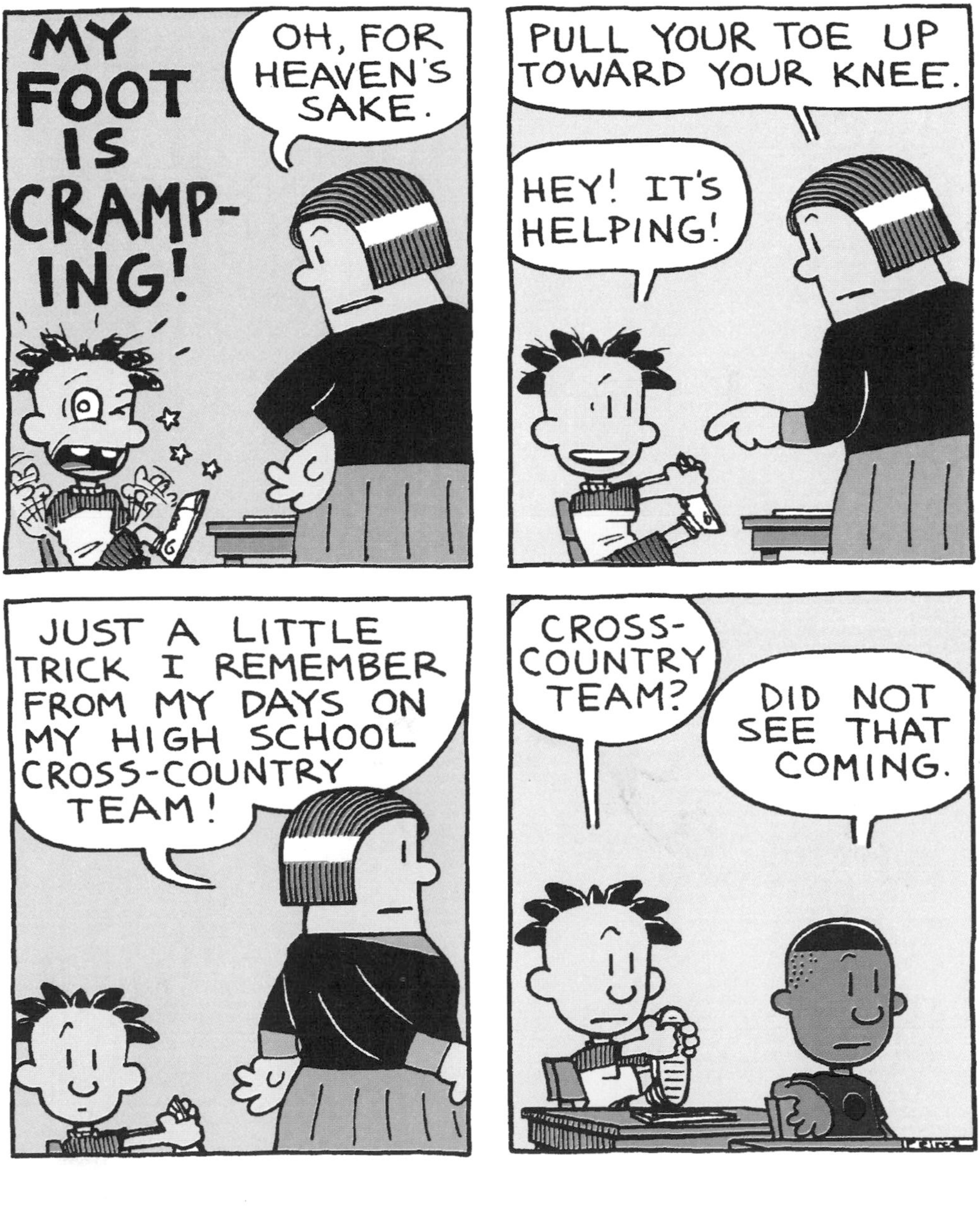
MY FOOT IS CRAMP-ING!
OH, FOR HEAVEN'S SAKE.
PULL YOUR TOE UP TOWARD YOUR KNEE.
HEY! IT'S HELPING!
JUST A LITTLE TRICK I REMEMBER FROM MY DAYS ON MY HIGH SCHOOL CROSS-COUNTRY TEAM!
CROSS-COUNTRY TEAM?
DID NOT SEE THAT COMING.

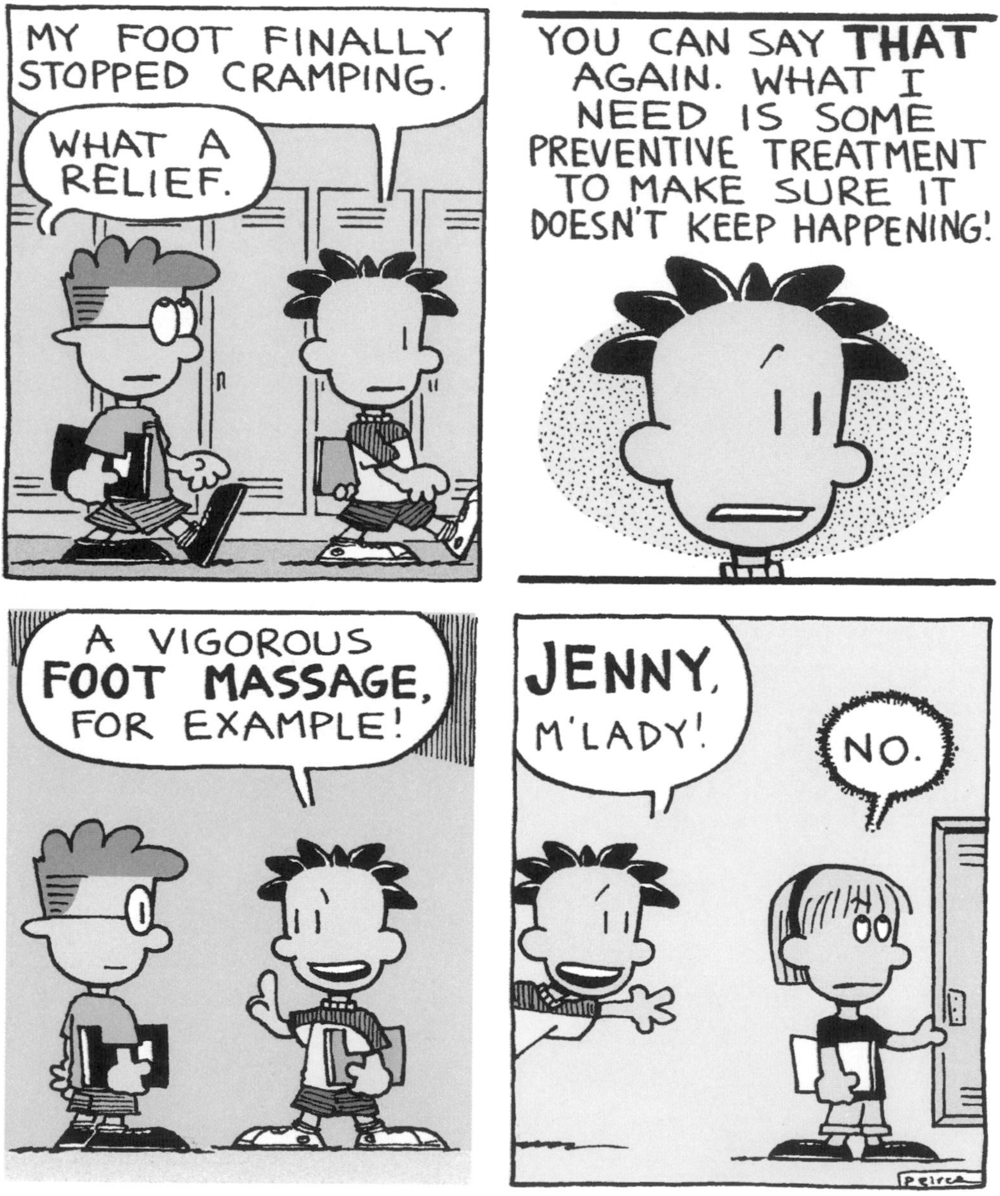
MY FOOT FINALLY STOPPED CRAMPING.
WHAT A RELIEF.
YOU CAN SAY **THAT** AGAIN. WHAT I NEED IS SOME PREVENTIVE TREATMENT TO MAKE SURE IT DOESN'T KEEP HAPPENING!
A VIGOROUS **FOOT MASSAGE**, FOR EXAMPLE!
JENNY, M'LADY!
NO.
PEIRCE

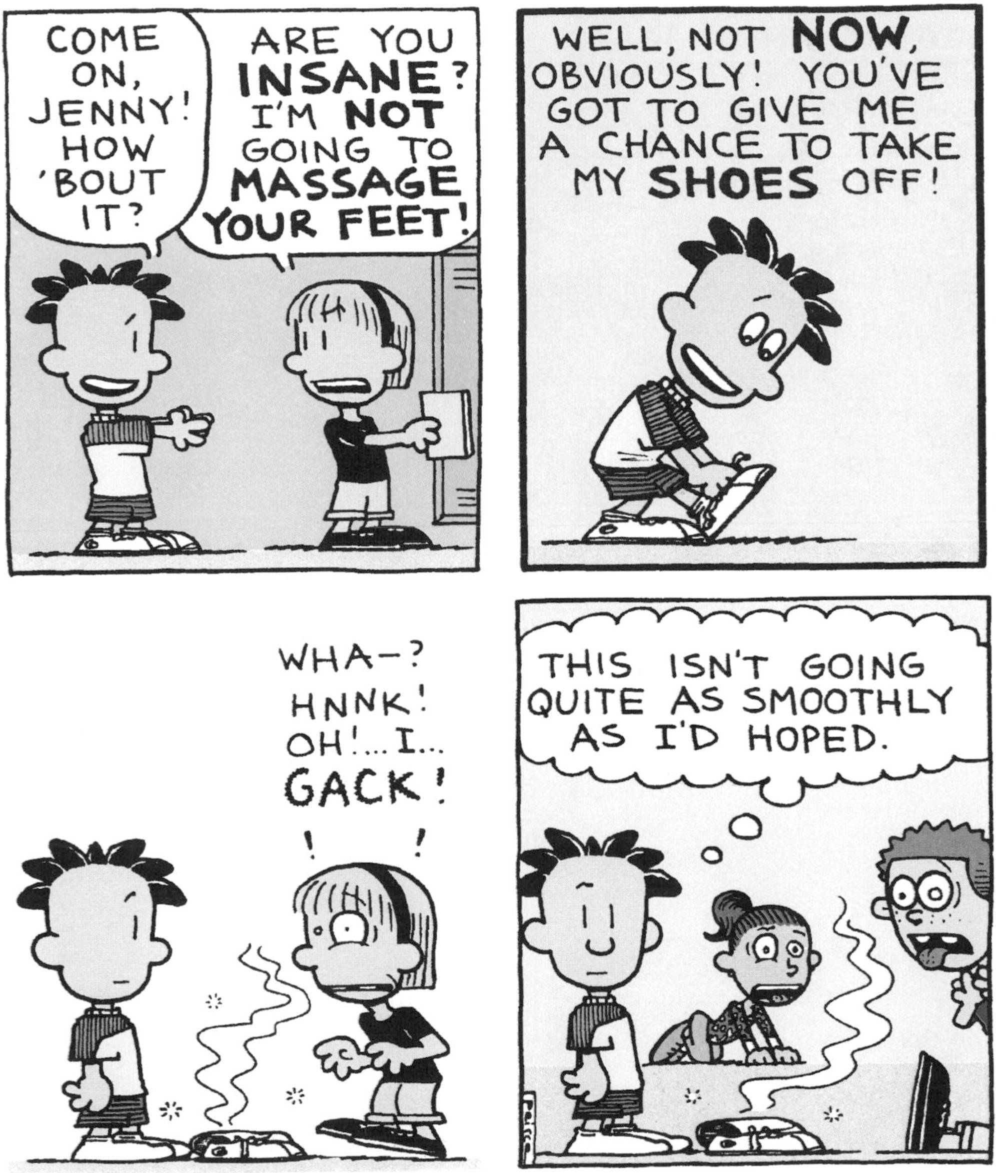
COME ON, JENNY! HOW 'BOUT IT?
ARE YOU INSANE? I'M NOT GOING TO MASSAGE YOUR FEET!
WELL, NOT NOW, OBVIOUSLY! YOU'VE GOT TO GIVE ME A CHANCE TO TAKE MY SHOES OFF!
WHA-? HNNK! OH!... I... GACK!
! !
THIS ISN'T GOING QUITE AS SMOOTHLY AS I'D HOPED.
Peirce

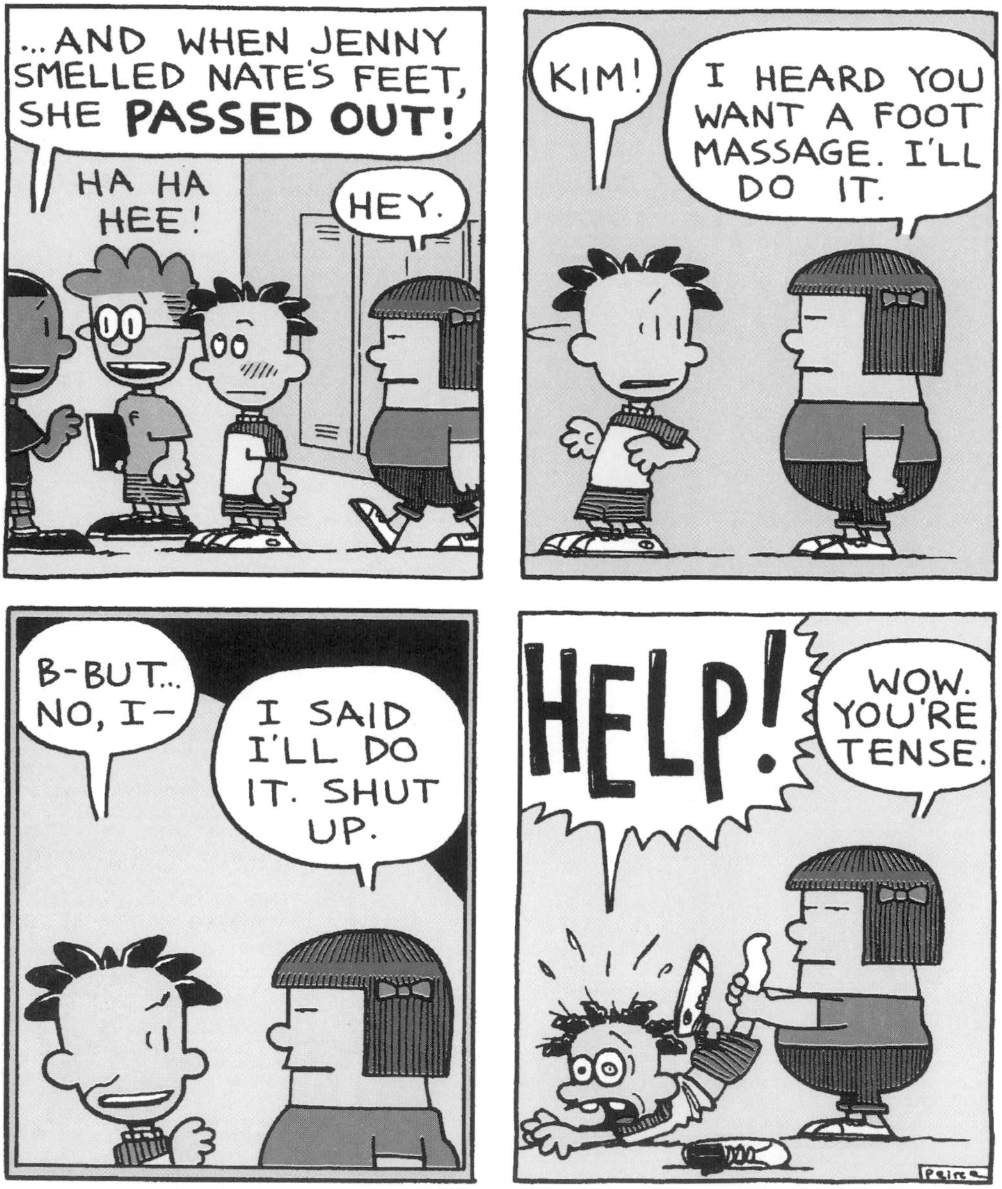
...AND WHEN JENNY SMELLED NATE'S FEET, SHE **PASSED OUT**!
HA HA HEE!
HEY.
KIM!
I HEARD YOU WANT A FOOT MASSAGE. I'LL DO IT.
B-BUT... NO, I–
I SAID I'LL DO IT. SHUT UP.
HELP!
WOW. YOU'RE TENSE.
PEIRCE

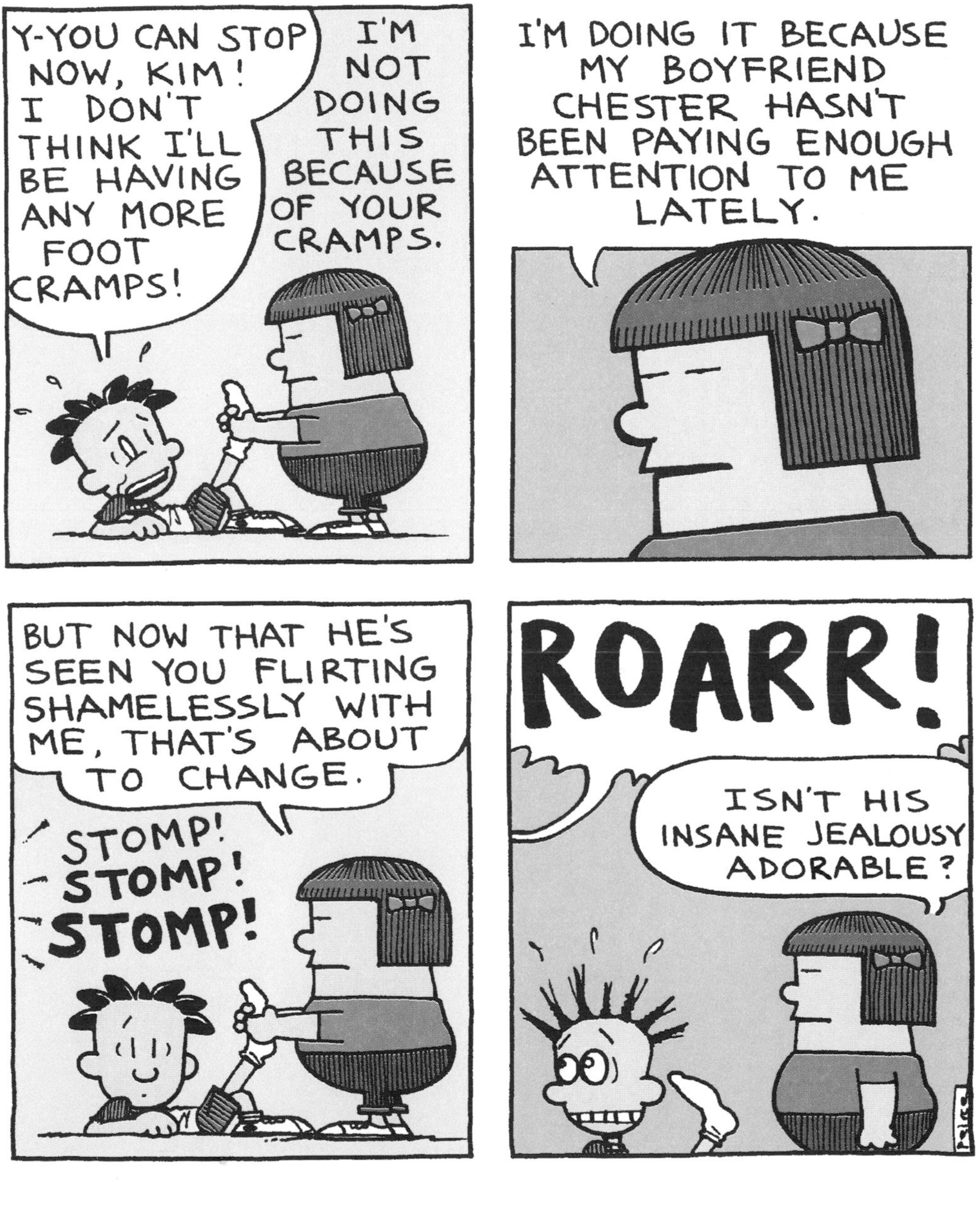
Y-YOU CAN STOP NOW, KIM! I DON'T THINK I'LL BE HAVING ANY MORE FOOT CRAMPS!
I'M NOT DOING THIS BECAUSE OF YOUR CRAMPS.
I'M DOING IT BECAUSE MY BOYFRIEND CHESTER HASN'T BEEN PAYING ENOUGH ATTENTION TO ME LATELY.
BUT NOW THAT HE'S SEEN YOU FLIRTING SHAMELESSLY WITH ME, THAT'S ABOUT TO CHANGE.
STOMP! STOMP! STOMP!
ROARR!
ISN'T HIS INSANE JEALOUSY ADORABLE?

Andrews McMeel Publishing
a division of Andrews McMeel Universal
1130 Walnut Street, Kansas City, Missouri 64106

www.andrewsmcmeel.com

18 19 20 21 22 SDB 10 9 8 7 6 5 4 3 2 1

ISBN: 978-1-4494-8995-3

Library of Congress Control Number: 2018932793

Made by:
Shenzhen Donnelley Printing Company Ltd.
Address and location of manufacturer:
No. 47, Wuhe Nan Road, Bantian Ind. Zone,
Shenzhen China, 518129
1st Printing—6/25/18

These strips appeared in newspapers from March 30, 2014, through September 13, 2014.

Big Nate can be viewed on the Internet at
www.gocomics.com/big_nate

ATTENTION: SCHOOLS AND BUSINESSES

Andrews McMeel books are available at quantity discounts with bulk purchase for educational, business, or sales promotional use. For information, please e-mail the Andrews McMeel Publishing Special Sales Department:
specialsales@amuniversal.com.

Check out these and other books from Andrews McMeel Publishing

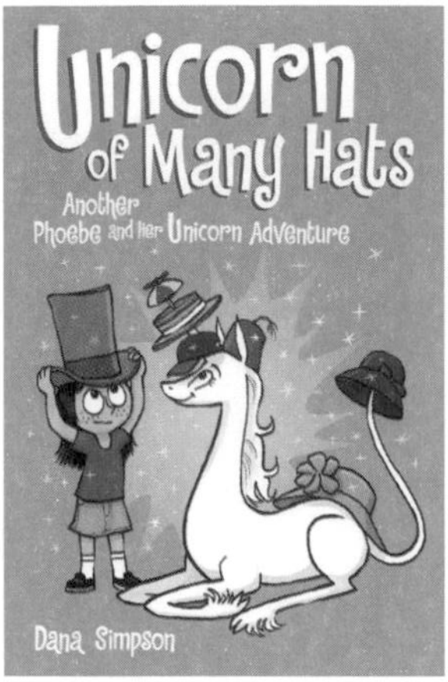
Unicorn of Many Hats
Another Phoebe and her Unicorn Adventure
Dana Simpson

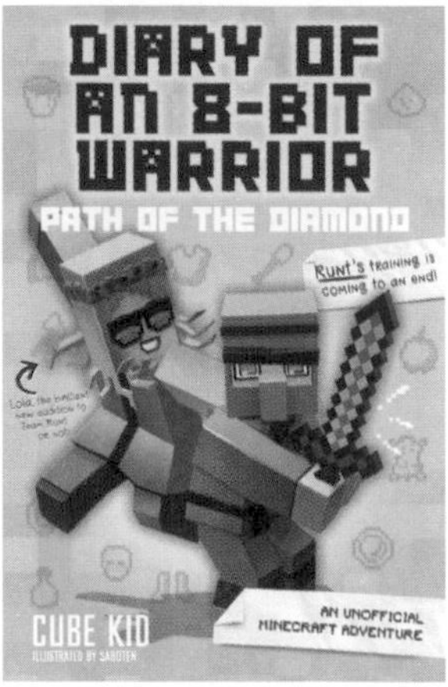
DIARY OF AN 8-BIT WARRIOR
PATH OF THE DIAMOND
Runt's training is coming to an end!
AN UNOFFICIAL MINECRAFT ADVENTURE
CUBE KID

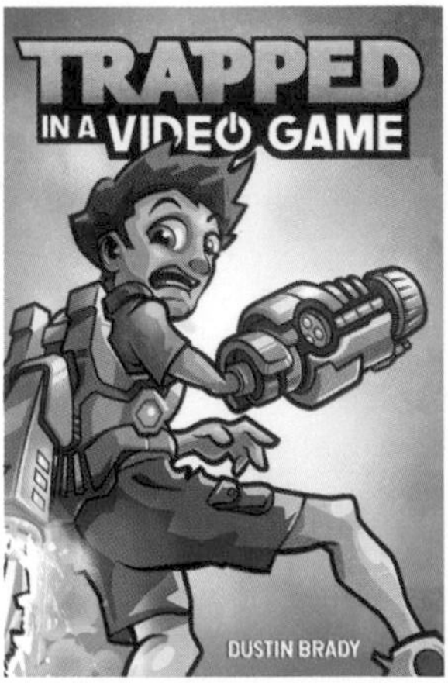
TRAPPED IN A VIDEO GAME
DUSTIN BRADY

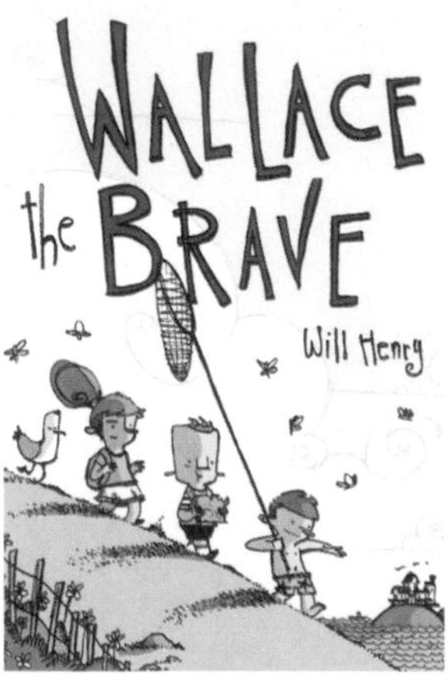
WALLACE the BRAVE
Will Henry

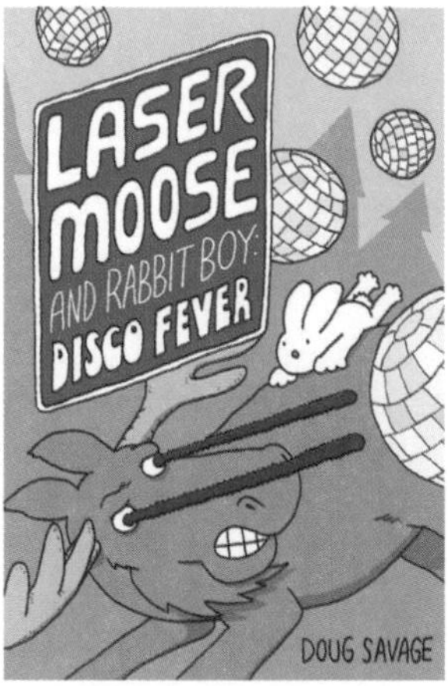
LASER MOOSE AND RABBIT BOY: DISCO FEVER
DOUG SAVAGE

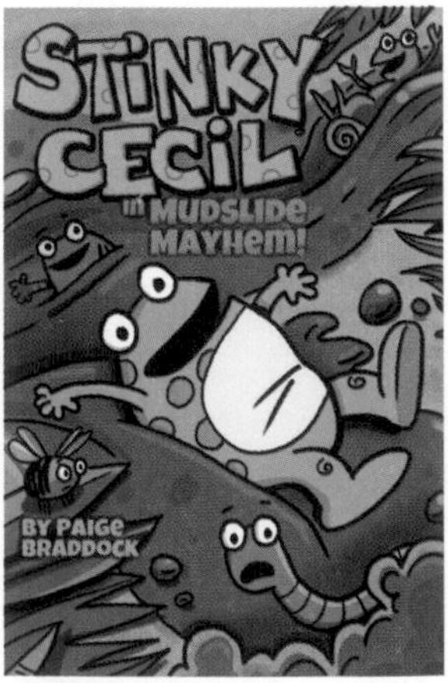
STINKY CECIL in MUDSLIDE MAYHEM!
BY PAIGE BRADDOCK

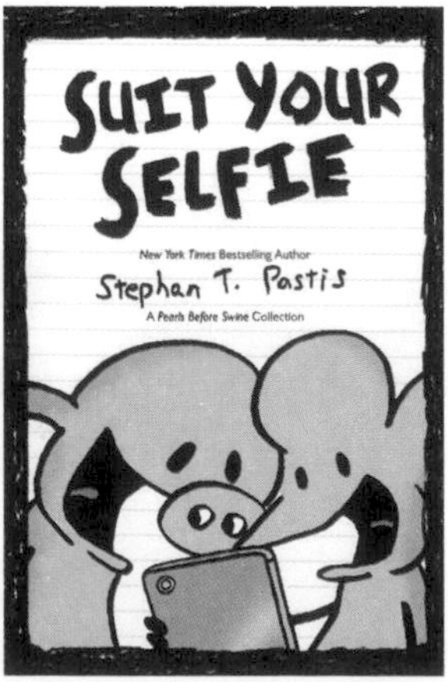
SUIT YOUR SELFIE
New York Times Bestselling Author
Stephan T. Pastis
A Pearls Before Swine Collection

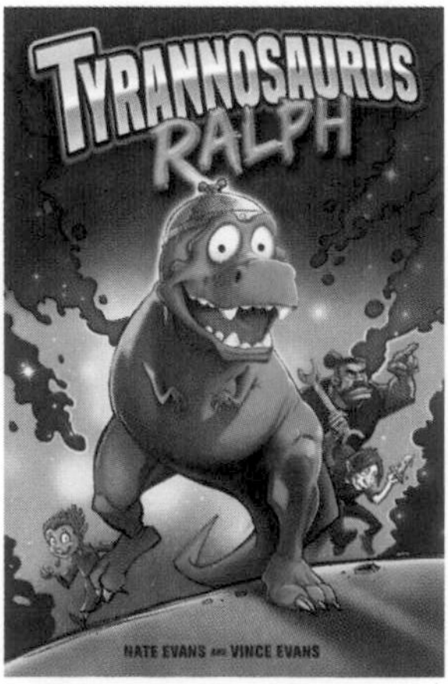
TYRANNOSAURUS RALPH
NATE EVANS AND VINCE EVANS

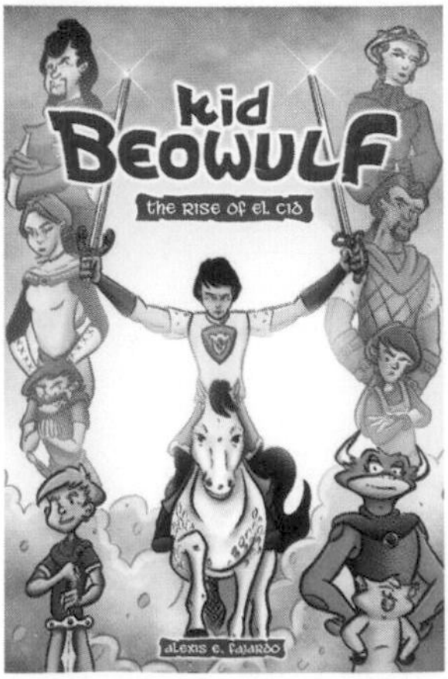
kid BEOWULF
the RISE of EL CID
alexis e. fajardo

EL PICAFLOR

David M. Schwartz, galardonado autor de libros infantiles, ha escrito libros sobre diversas materias que han deleitado a niños de todo el mundo. El amplio conocimiento de las ciencias y el sentido artístico de Dwight Kuhn se combinan para producir fotografías que captan las maravillas de la naturaleza.

David M. Schwartz is an award-winning author of children's books, on a wide variety of topics, loved by children around the world. Dwight Kuhn's scientific expertise and artful eye work together with the camera to capture the awesome wonder of the natural world.

Please visit our web site at: www.garethstevens.com
For a free color catalog describing Gareth Stevens Publishing's list of high-quality books and multimedia programs, call 1-800-542-2595 (USA) or 1-800-461-9120 (Canada). Gareth Stevens Publishing's Fax: (414) 332-3567.

Library of Congress Cataloging-in-Publication Data

Schwartz, David M.
    [Hummingbird. Spanish]
    El picaflor / David M. Schwartz; fotografías de Dwight Kuhn; [Spanish translation, Guillermo Gutiérrez and Tatiana Acosta]. — North American ed.
        p. cm. — (Ciclos de vida)
    Includes bibliographical references and index.
    Summary: Describes the physical characteristics, behavior, and habitat of the hummingbird.
    ISBN 0-8368-2999-9 (lib. bdg.)
    1. Hummingbirds—Juvenile literature. [1. Hummingbirds. 2. Spanish language materials.] I. Kuhn, Dwight, ill. II. Title.
QL696.A558S3818   2001
598.7'64—dc21   2001042674

This North American edition first published in 2001 by
Gareth Stevens Publishing
A World Almanac Education Group Company
330 West Olive Street, Suite 100
Milwaukee, WI 53212 USA

Also published as *Hummingbird* in 2001 by Gareth Stevens, Inc.
First published in the United States in 1999 by Creative Teaching Press, Inc., P.O. Box 2723, Huntington Beach, CA 92647-0723.
Text © 1999 by David M. Schwartz; photographs © 1999 by Dwight Kuhn. Additional end matter © 2001 by Gareth Stevens, Inc.

Gareth Stevens editor: Mary Dykstra
Gareth Stevens graphic design: Scott Krall and Tammy Gruenewald
Translators: Tatiana Acosta and Guillermo Gutiérrez
Additional end matter: Belén García-Alvarado

Printed in the United States of America

1 2 3 4 5 6 7 8 9 05 04 03 02 01

EL PICAFLOR

David M. Schwartz
fotografías de Dwight Kuhn

TRAMPOLÍN A LA
CIENCIA

Gareth Stevens Publishing
A WORLD ALMANAC EDUCATION GROUP COMPANY

Con un ruidoso zumbido y un destello verdoso, un diminuto pájaro vuela ligero de una flor a otra. Sus alas son una sombra borrosa. Se detiene en pleno vuelo y queda suspendido en el aire. Su brillante plumaje parece cambiar de color bajo el sol. Es un picaflor, el ave más pequeña del mundo.

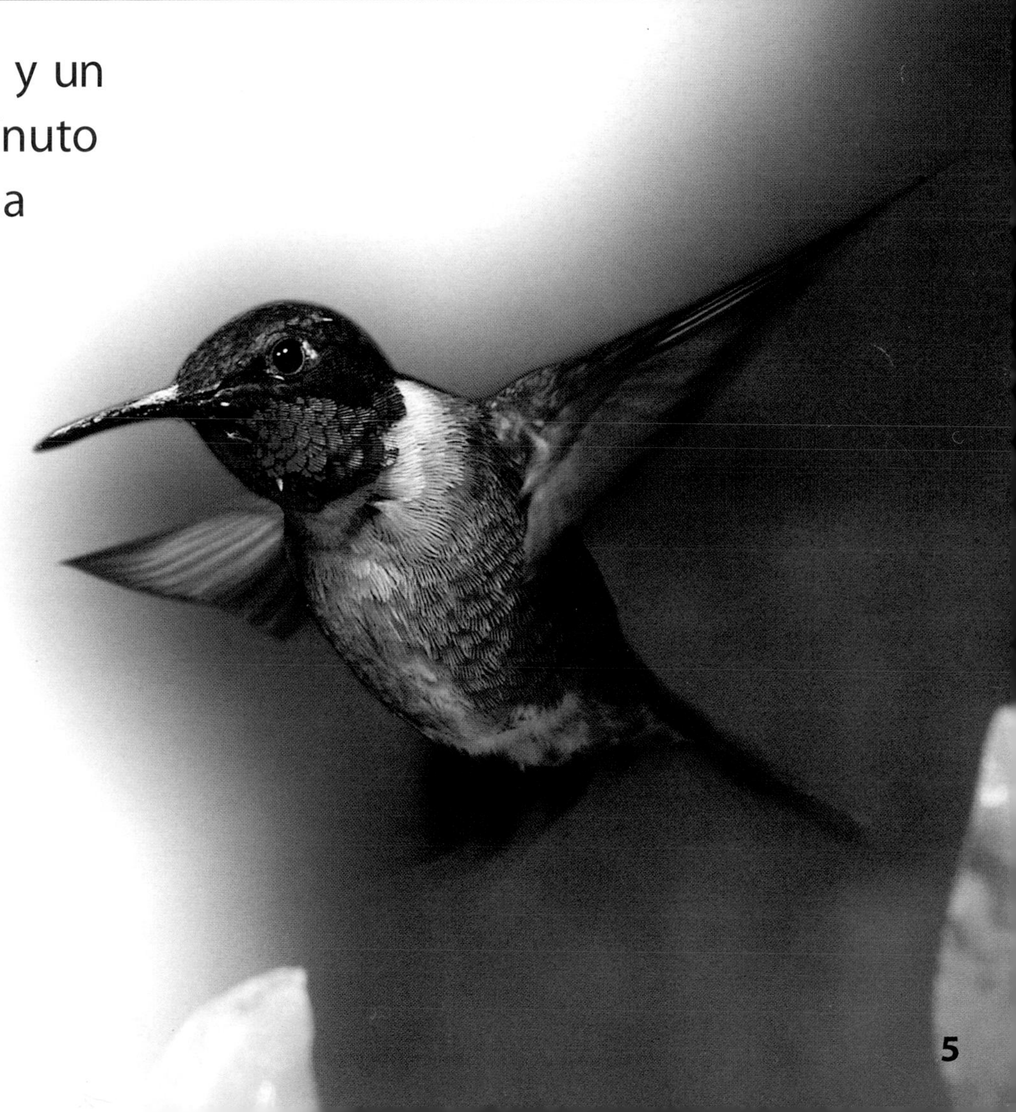

El nido de un picaflor es un pequeño cuenco del tamaño de una cáscara de nuez. ¡Dentro no cabe nada más grande que un centavo! La hembra construye el nido sin ayuda, usando telarañas y trocitos de plantas.

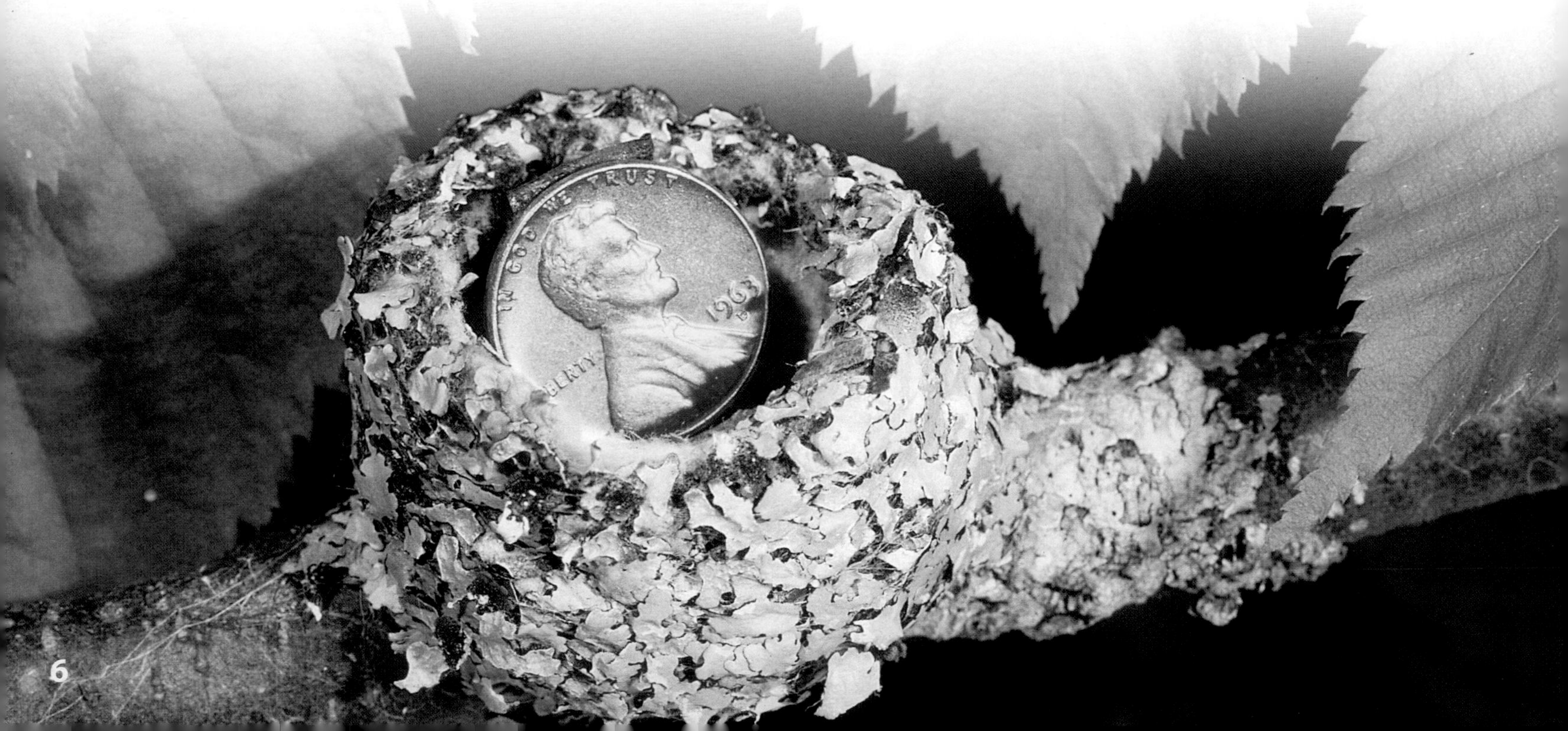
IN GOD WE TRUST
1963

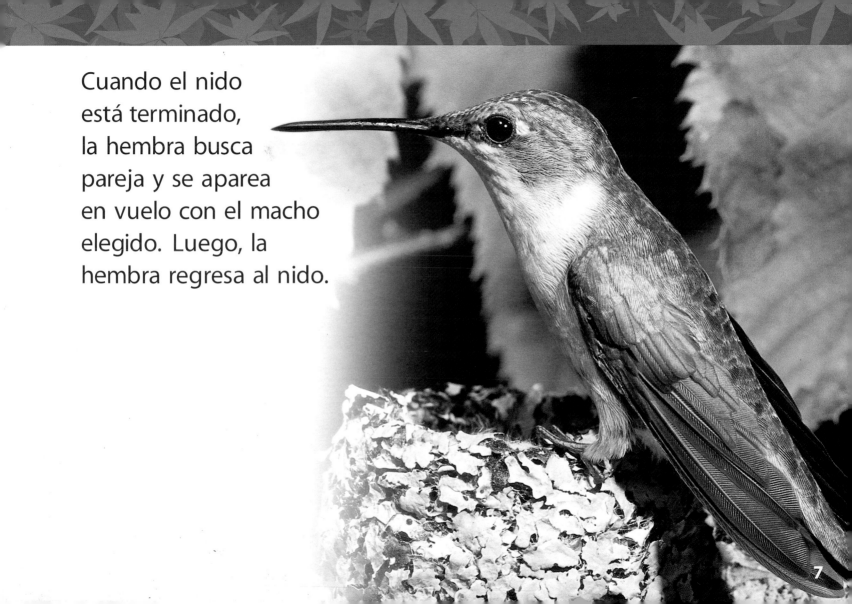

Cuando el nido
está terminado,
la hembra busca
pareja y se aparea
en vuelo con el macho
elegido. Luego, la
hembra regresa al nido.

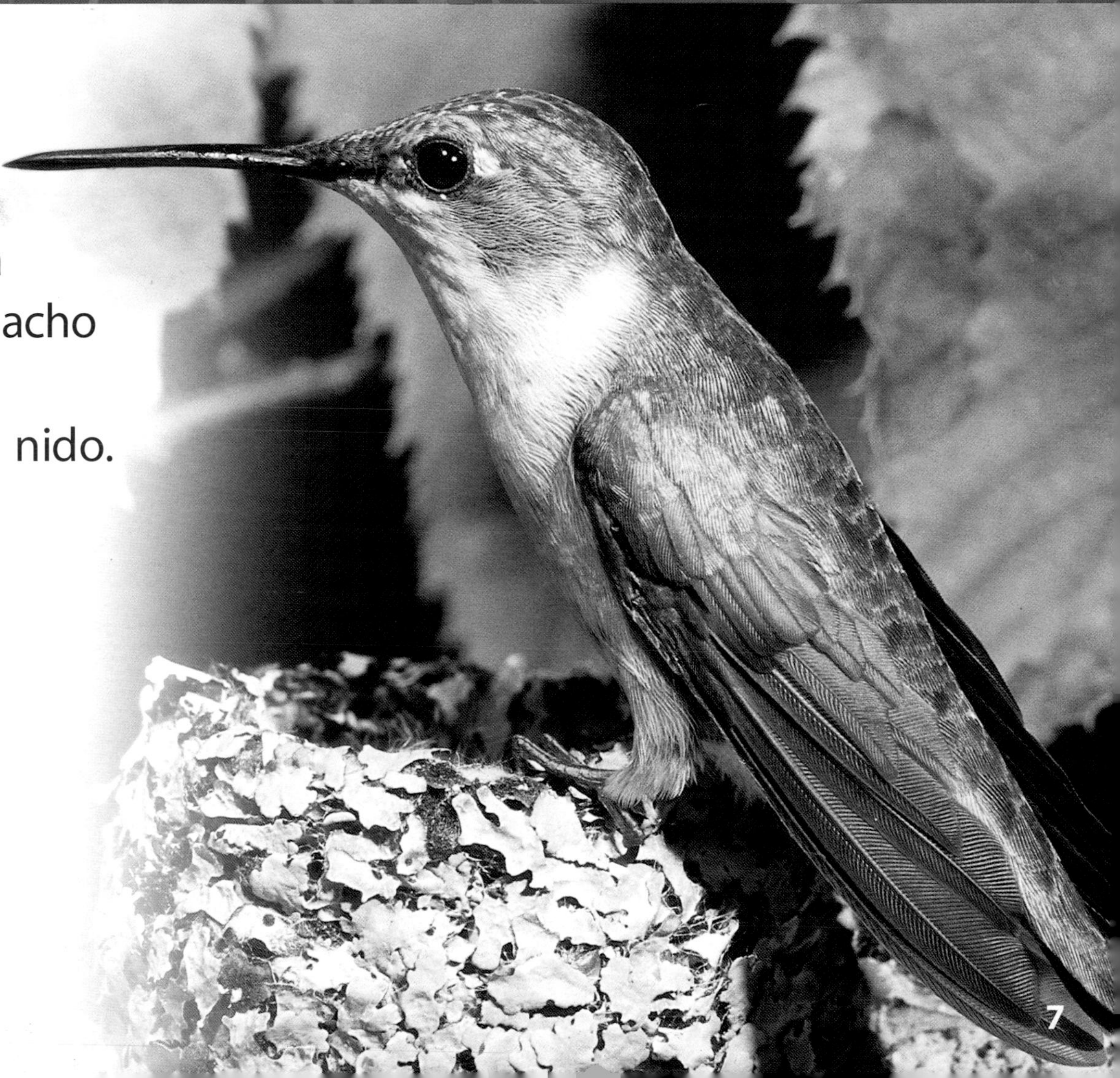

La hembra pondrá uno o dos huevos diminutos, del tamaño de una pasa. Los huevos de picaflor son los más pequeños del mundo. ¡En comparación, un huevo de gallina es gigantesco!

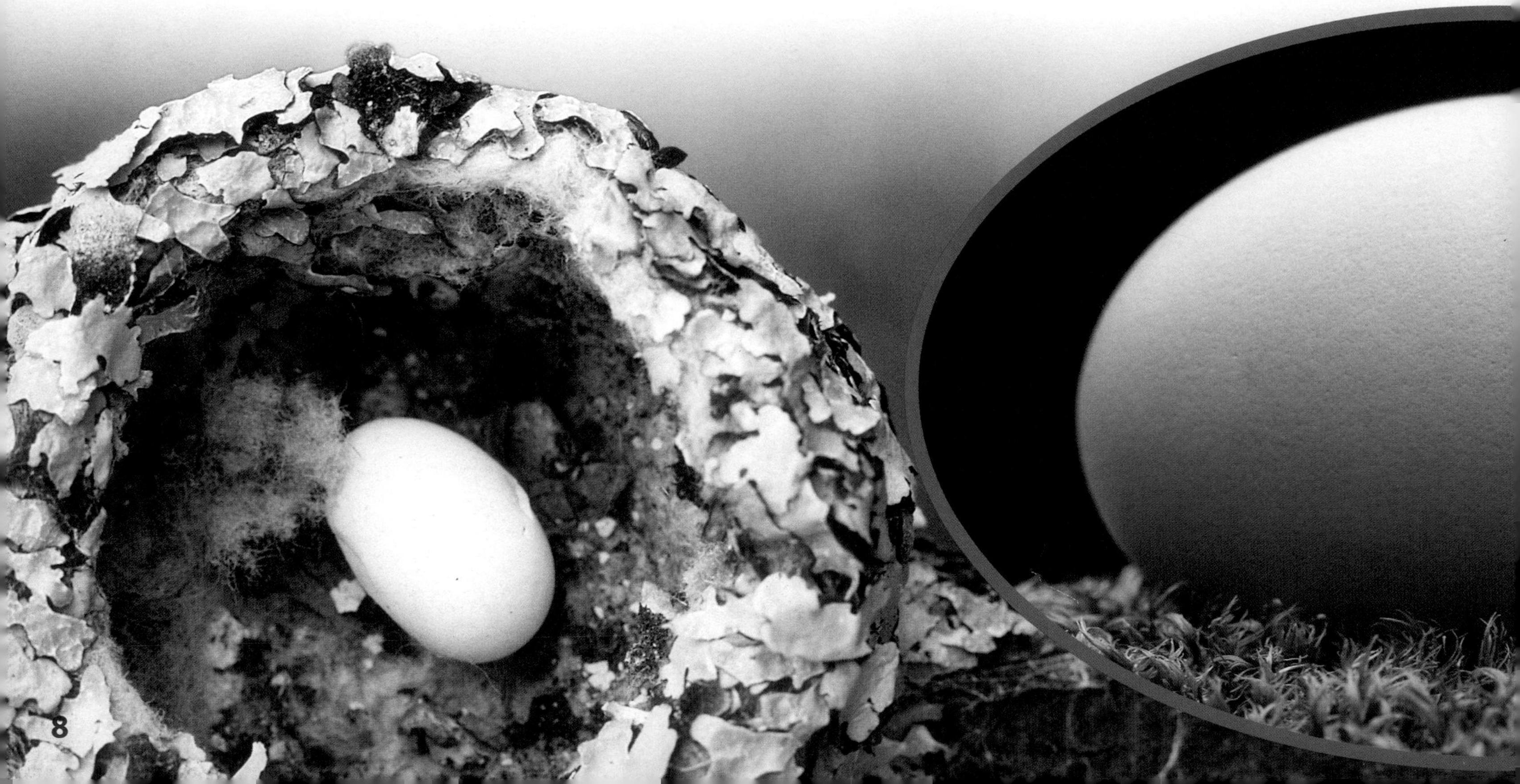

La madre empolla los huevos sentándose sobre ellos entre dos y tres semanas. Luego, los huevos se abren.

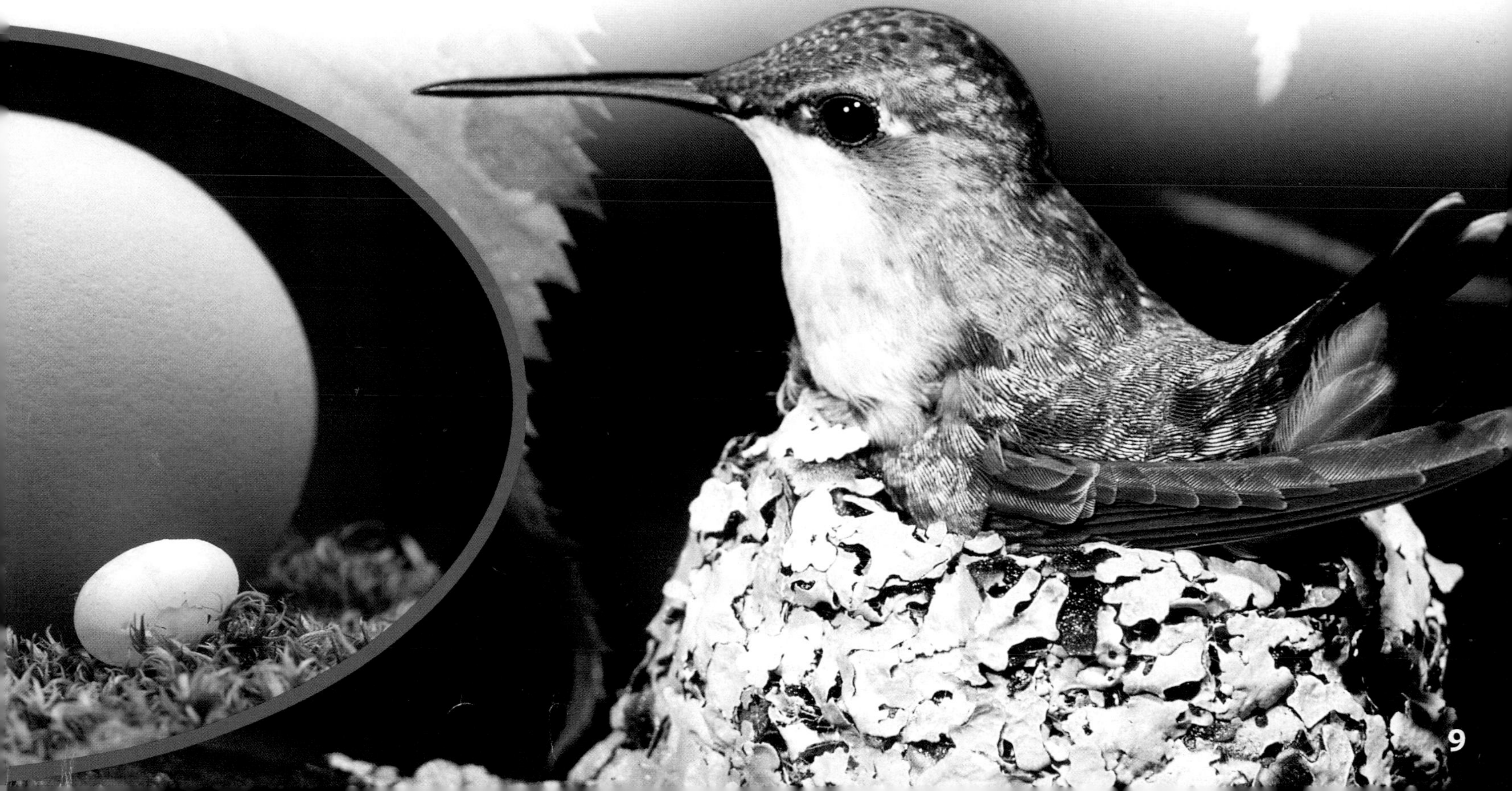

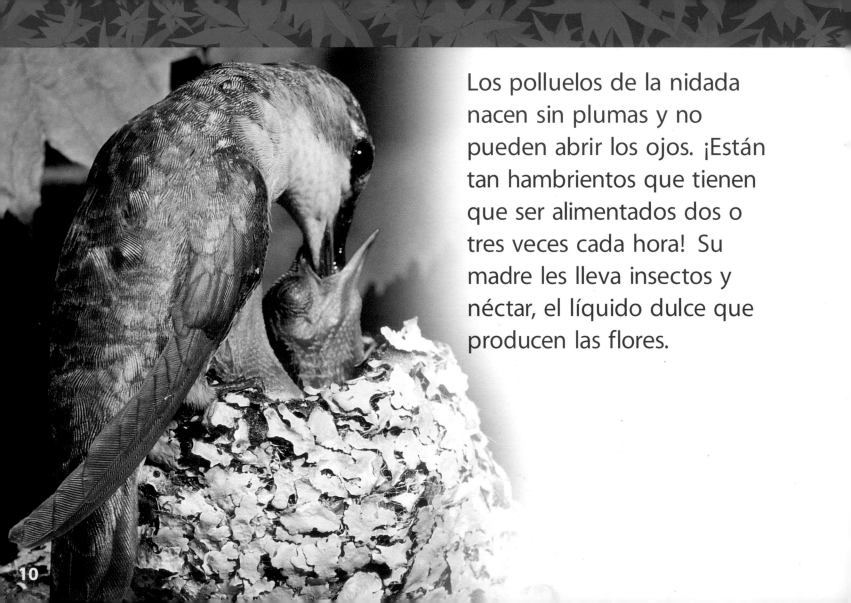

Los polluelos de la nidada nacen sin plumas y no pueden abrir los ojos. ¡Están tan hambrientos que tienen que ser alimentados dos o tres veces cada hora! Su madre les lleva insectos y néctar, el líquido dulce que producen las flores.

Las crías permanecen en el nido unas tres semanas. En ese tiempo, abren los ojos y les comienzan a crecer las plumas.

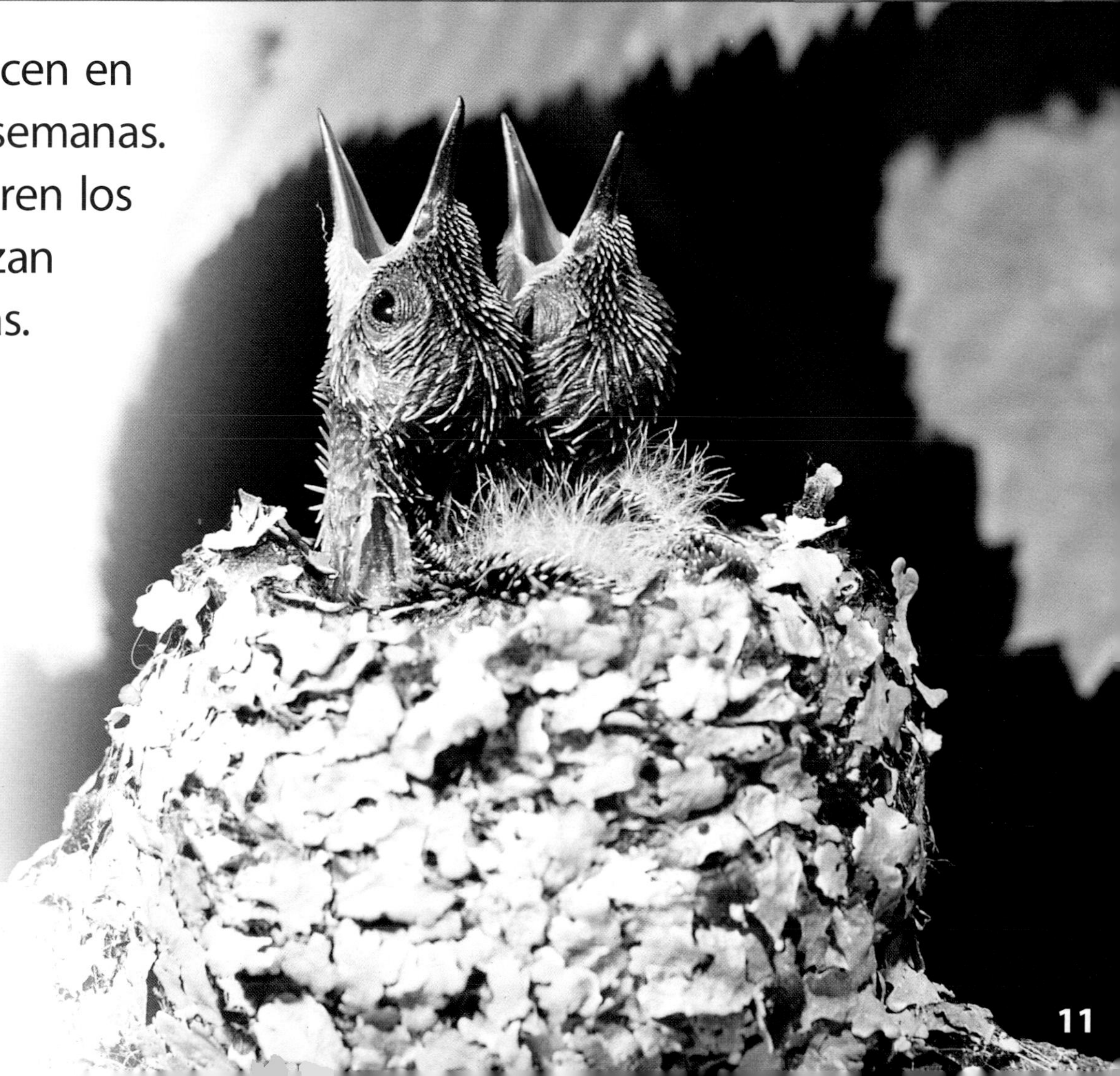

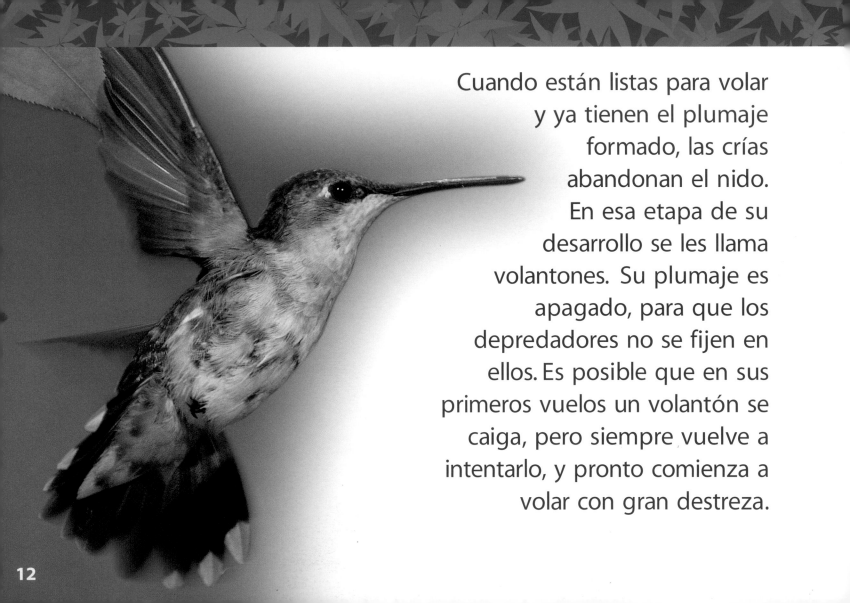

Cuando están listas para volar y ya tienen el plumaje formado, las crías abandonan el nido. En esa etapa de su desarrollo se les llama volantones. Su plumaje es apagado, para que los depredadores no se fijen en ellos. Es posible que en sus primeros vuelos un volantón se caiga, pero siempre vuelve a intentarlo, y pronto comienza a volar con gran destreza.

Un picaflor puede volar hacia adelante, hacia atrás y de lado, y es capaz de mantenerse suspendido en el aire como un helicóptero. ¡Este diminuto pájaro consigue mover las alas hasta 80 veces por segundo!

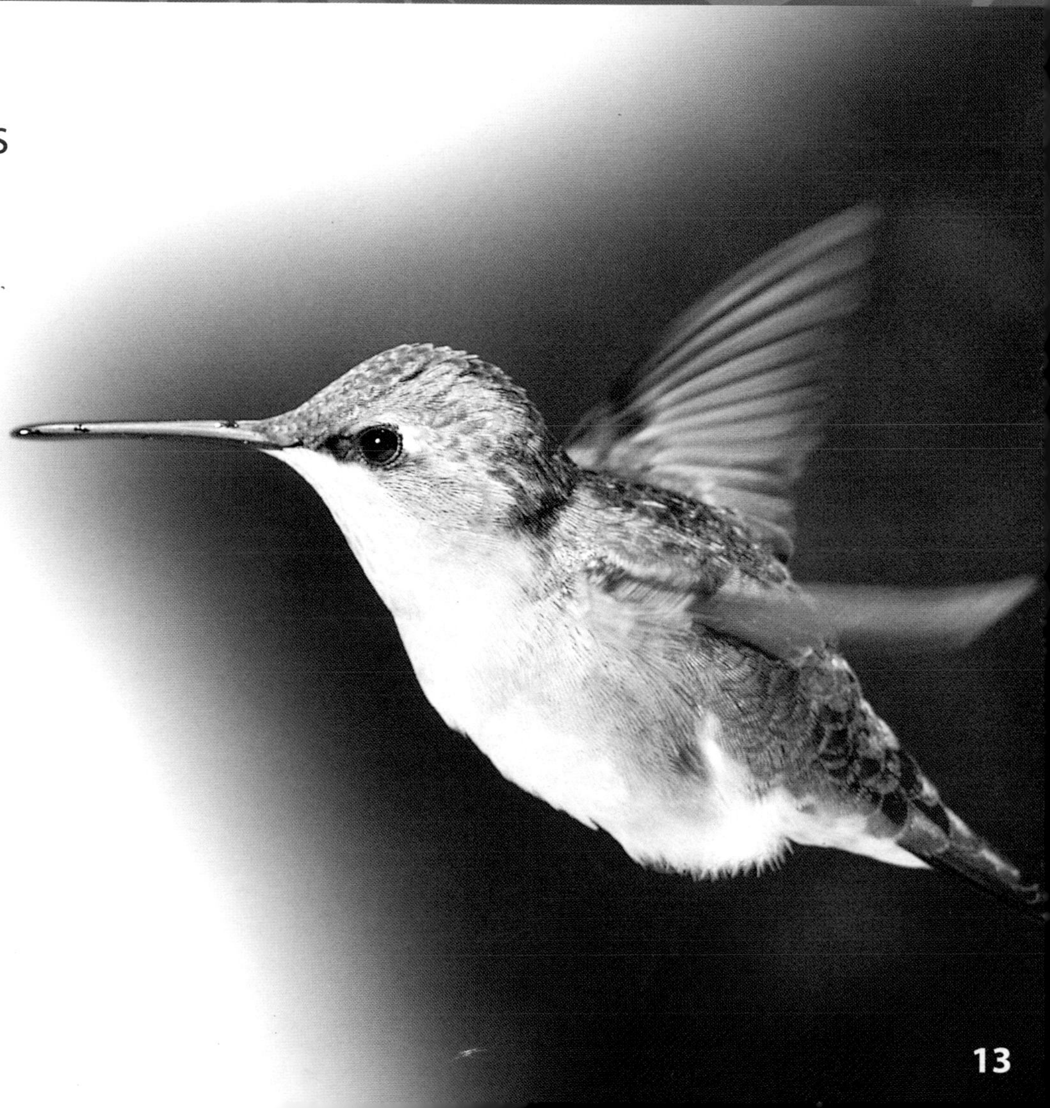

Para los picaflores, una flor es como una tienda de golosinas. La golosina es el dulce néctar, que da mucha energía. Para obtenerlo, un picaflor mete su largo y fino pico dentro de la flor. Luego, mueve su larga lengua y se toma el néctar como si fuera un gatito bebiendo leche. ¡Mientras bebe el néctar, un picaflor puede dar 13 lengüetadas en un segundo! El picaflor recibe su nombre por su costumbre de ir de flor en flor tomando néctar.

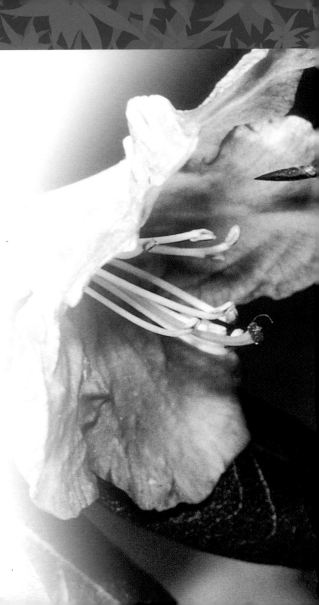

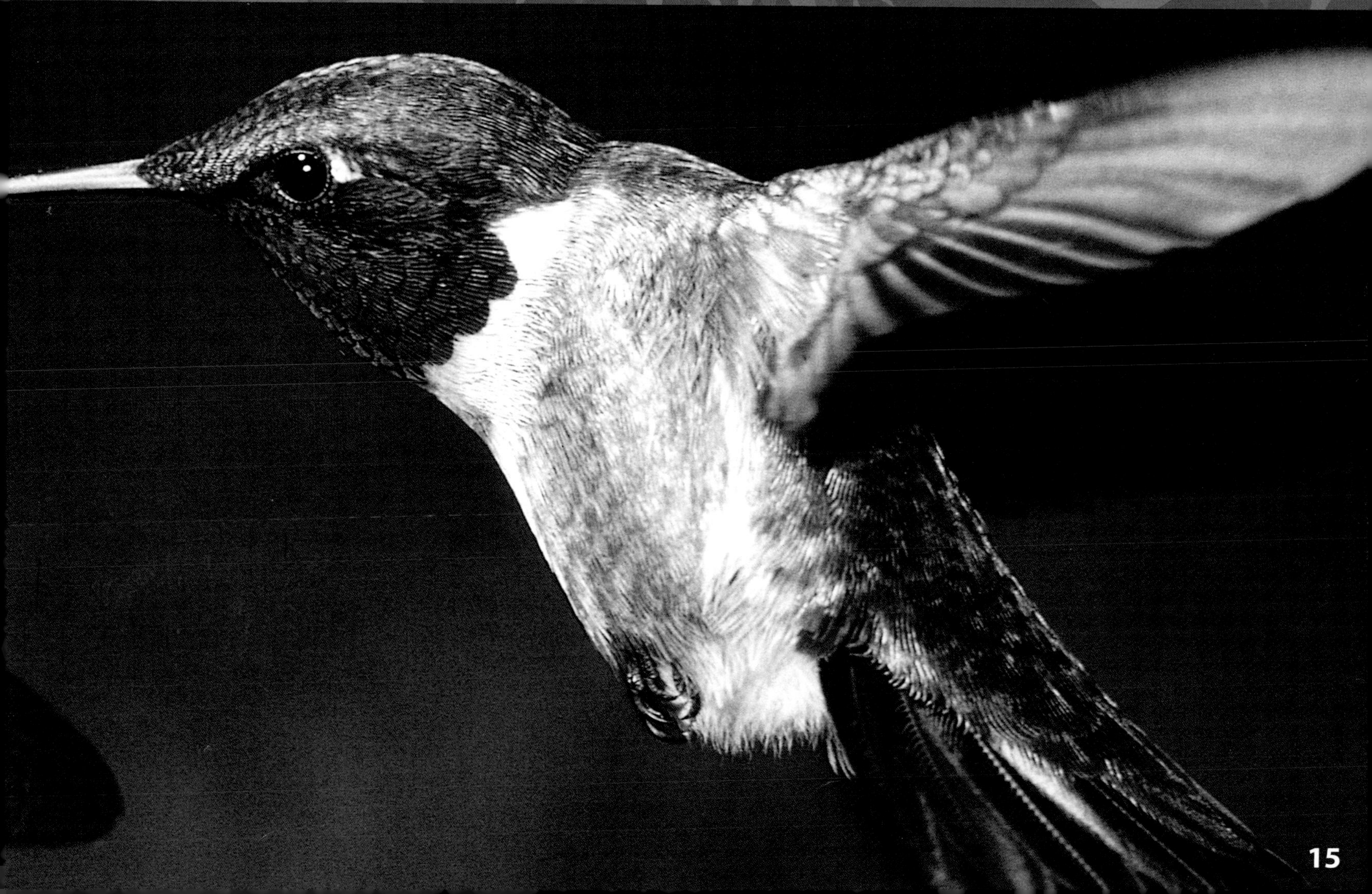

Los picaflores beben también agua azucarada que la gente pone en comederos. Los comederos para picaflores suelen ser rojos, porque éste es el color de muchas flores de abundante néctar.

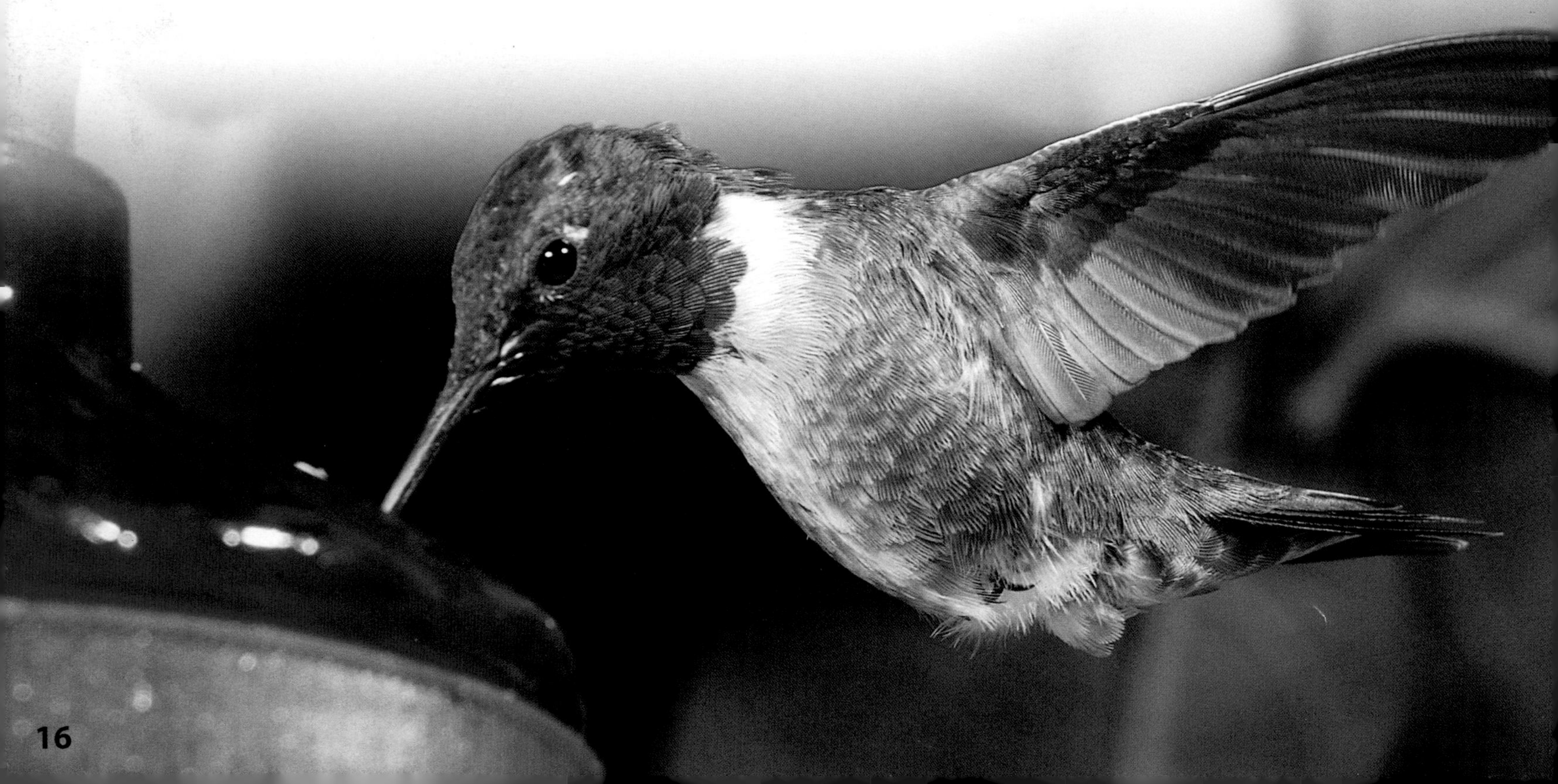

Este picaflor macho se ha posado a descansar en una rama, pero no estará ahí por mucho tiempo. Quizás volará en busca de pareja, y nacerá así una nueva generación de diminutos picaflores.

¿Puedes poner en orden las siguientes
etapas del ciclo de vida de un picaflor?

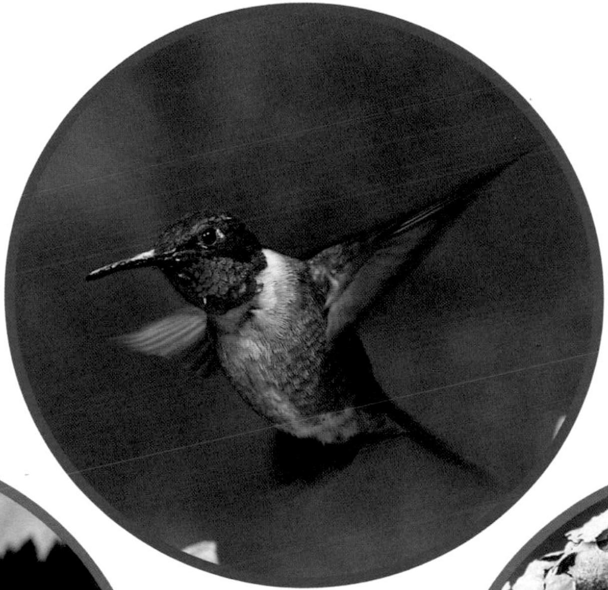

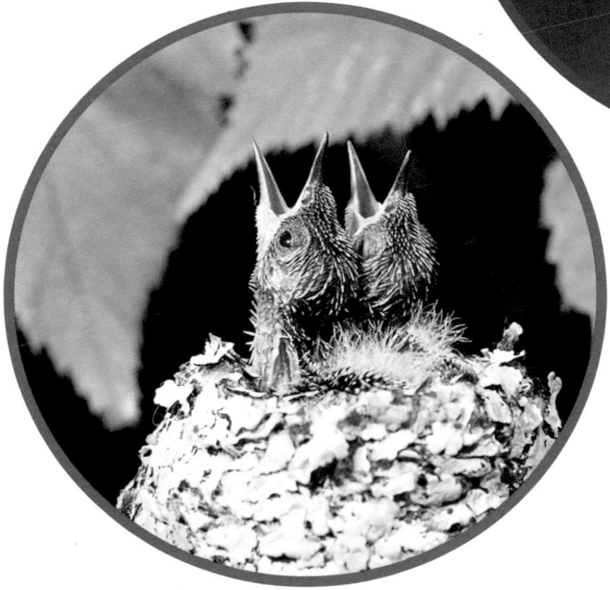

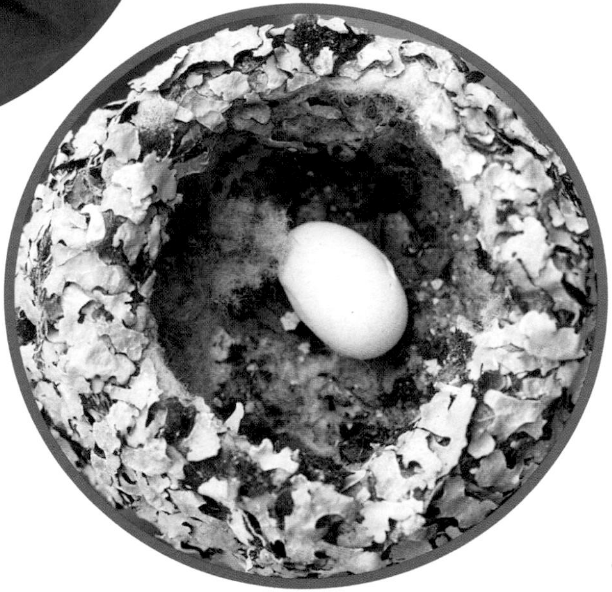

Respuesta

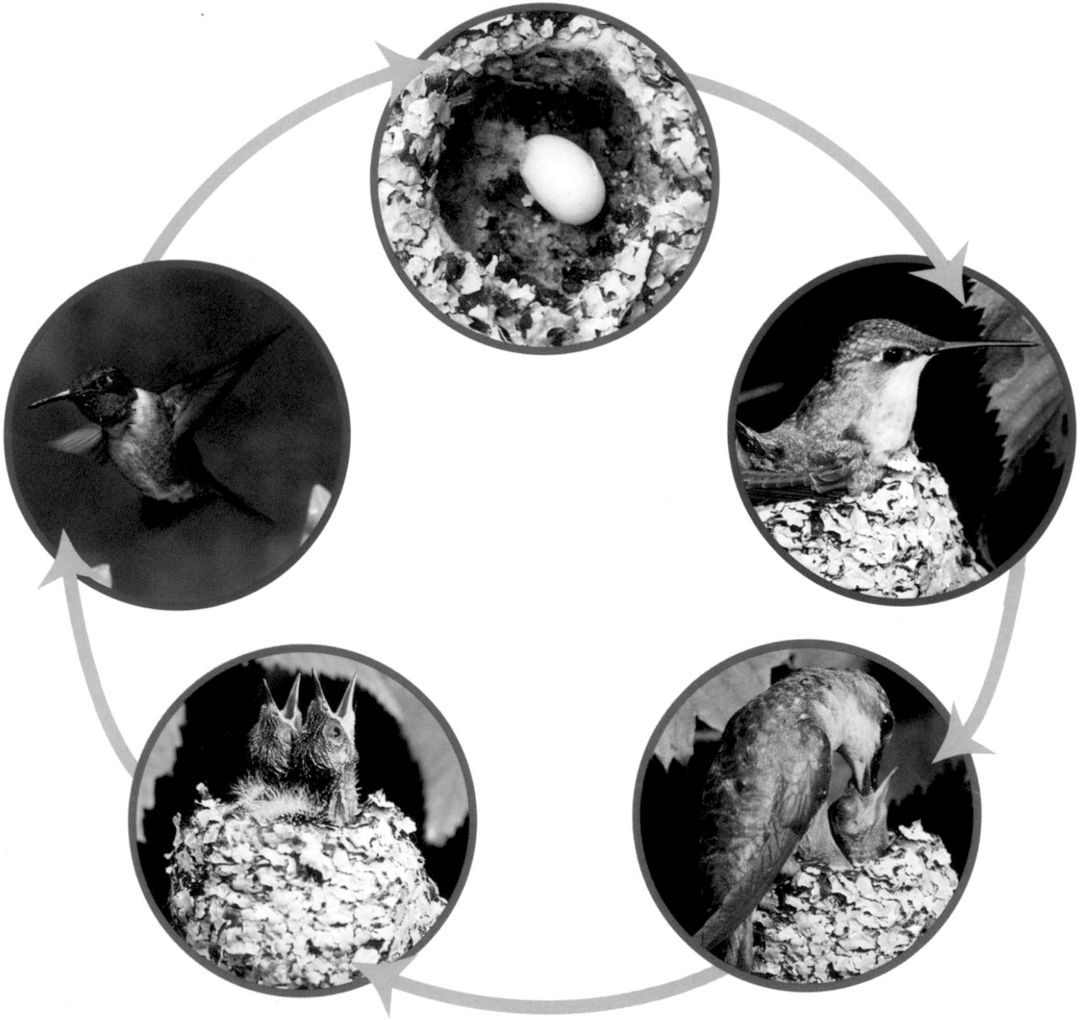

aparearse: unirse a otro animal para tener crías.

borroso: difícil de ver.

depredador: animal que se alimenta de otros animales.

destello: brillo de corta duración.

destreza: capacidad para hacer bien una determinada tarea.

empollar: sentarse un ave sobre los huevos para calentarlos hasta que los polluelos están.

generación: grupo de personas o animales nacidos en un mismo periodo de tiempo.

lengüetada: movimiento hecho con la lengua para lamer o tragar.

néctar: líquido dulce que hay en las flores y que les gusta a muchos insectos y pájaros.

nidada: grupo de polluelos de un nido.

pareja: compañero con fines de reproducción en una especie animal.

suspendido: colgado en el aire, sin cambiar de dirección.

telaraña: red que fabrican las arañas.

volantón: pájaro que está listo para aprender a volar o que vuela por primera vez.

ACTIVITADES

Hogar, dulce hogar

Los nidos de los pájaros pueden ser de muchos tamaños y formas, desde los diminutos de los picaflores hasta los gigantescos de los halcones y las águilas. Da un paseo por un bosque o un parque, o visita un jardín botánico, y busca nidos. Intenta averiguar qué pájaros hicieron esos nidos. En una biblioteca podrás encontrar libros con ilustraciones de nidos y con descripciones de los materiales utilizados por las aves para construirlos.

Igual, pero distinto

Observa con atención las fotografías de este libro. ¿Son iguales todos los picaflores? Consulta libros en la biblioteca, o en Internet, para buscar información sobre diferentes especies, o tipos, de picaflores. ¿Cuántas variedades puedes encontrar? ¿En qué se diferencian las especies? ¿Qué tienen todas en común?

Deliciosa golosina

Prepara un poco de "néctar" en tu propia cocina. Mezcla 1 taza (200 gramos) de azúcar y 4 tazas (1 litro) de agua. Pídele a un adulto que hierva el líquido en la cocina o en el microondas, y después métalo en el refrigerador. Cuando tu "néctar" se haya enfriado, llena con cuidado un comedero para picaflores y cuélgalo en tu jardín. Luego, observa cómo los sedientos picaflores se acercan a probar tu golosina.

¿Para qué sirve ese pico?

A veces basta con mirar el tamaño y la forma del pico de un pájaro para saber lo que éste come. El pico largo y fino del picaflor es perfecto para beber néctar de las flores, pero no serviría para abrir semillas. Observa las ilustraciones de un libro de aves y trata de adivinar qué come cada una fijándote en las características del pico.

Más libros para leer

Aves. Lynn M. Stone (Rourke Corporation)
Asombrosas aves. Jerry Young, fotógrafo (Lectorum Publications, Inc.)
Descubre las aves. Scott Weidensaul, Pablo M. O'Neill, Lorie Robare
   (Forest House Publishing Company, Inc.)
El pájaro. (Lectorum Publications, Inc.)
Las aves. Colección "I Can Read About" (Troll Publishing)
El rey colibrí: Leyenda guatemalteca. Argentina Palacios (Troll Communications)

Páginas Web

http://sssp.fws.gov/puerto/lasaves.htm
http://www.conabio.gob.mx/biodiversitas/maripos.htm
http://www.eltercertiempo.net/leyendas/leyen-05.htm

Algunas páginas Web no son permanentes. Puedes buscar otras páginas Web usando un buen buscador para localizar los siguientes temas: *picaflor, colibrí, pájaros, aves, comederos, nidos, migraciones* y *bosques.*

ÍNDICE